QUIZZLEBOON

JOHN OLIVER HODGES

PMMP

Perpetual Motion Machine Publishing
Cibolo, Texas

Quizzleboon

Copyright © John Oliver Hodges 2017

All Rights Reserved

ISBN:978-1-943720-10-1

www.PerpetualPublishing.com

Cover Art by Matthew Revert
www.matthewrevert.com

For Brady and Sarah

1.

DIRT WAS CLEAN, they said, and soap was banned, as were tampons and aspirins. Their pants were dirty if they wore them, and Leon saw dirt down in their ear holes even. Were lotions banned? Yes, and cleaning products, razors and meat. Was it weird making love to smelly women with dirty feet? There was dirt in the sweat of their neck creases, and the hairy pits and legs to drip through afternoon. After Sparrow Leon lingered with a lady of a Pinocchio nose down there, Butterfly by name, and Lichen. Leon double-dogged Junebug, and the Windstorm. There was Mary, and a Soil, but Leon fell in love with Beacon. If not for that dirty monkey Leon might still be in the good life.

Damn girl put him back on the coke is why, what he swore off at Muskegon Correctional where he did two years for busting out a cop's front teeth—two years! Leon may well have killed the pig had the eye stayed in his head like it was supposed to. Thing bounced across the lot to slide under somebody's truck. Leon picked it out of the goo, but more goons arrived. Leon was polishing it with his shirt hem, getting ready to stick it in his face when the guns flopped out. He was thirty-six now, and very much in love.

So he chomped into Beacon's boob, ripped off a mouthful and chewed it up good and swallowed it down—so delicious! In the El Camino he snaked her to Asheville for eight ball fun. They'd check into The Aardvark and party 'til Monday. In the bed there, Uncle L, as the dirt people called Leon, informed Beacon of the *ping pong ping*, or *pang*, which is more like it.

The pangs to attack Leon's heart Mr. Quizzleboon knew not the likes of. The reward for info leading to Leon's arrest was twenty grand. Did Leon tell Beacon that? Why yes, Mr. Quizzleboon saw it all, straight through Leon's own eyeball, through tar and timber, there she is on the double bed pumping Leon silly while high on cocaine, the Grateful Dead crooning through boombox speakers. Boy could the girl go to it, her fine young tits swinging back and forth like sacks of sugar to beat somebody over the head with. Beacon sucked his jizzle up deep into her soul and fell down limp upon his muscular-ass torso. He held her tight with his tatted arms, fingers to vertebrae as if playing the flute, and told her of the robberies, Mr. Big Man, full of pride, trying to impress the ladies.

Leon trusted Beacon that spring, but come a night at the dirt farm, in the kitchen with Sparrow and Two-Stone, and this dude whose name was Castle, Leon said, "Let's fuck dinner for the skrunk tonight." Beacon said, "I think we ought to eat, Leon. All I had today was a cantaloupe and string beans." That was the first hint. Nobody lipped off on Leon, the man with money, the Kahooey Bigtime Monster Bash Man. Hadn't Leon forked a fortune out for these dumbass dirt scrounger motherfuckers? Hadn't Leon paid off their mortgage? He bought them a new roof. He bought them a Massey Ferguson tractor, and mopeds, and enough wine to drown a hippopotamus in. If Leon said jump your ass into that lake, Dirt Monkey, you'd best hop to it lickety-split. Leon was not so goddamn foolish as to look the other way when Danger was at hand. The eyeball amiss from his head, what he'd told the Dirties he gave to Mr. Quizzleboon from the moon, watched out for him, was to warn him should Danger lurk in the tip of the toe in the tulips, in the crunch of leaf in the bushes and shit. Should Leon say I won't listen, his bad brain only was to blame.

His bitch was up to some-ass thing or other, so while the Dirties worked another masterpiece—pesto this time, peeling leaves off heaps of basil branches—Leon coaxed her to the junk shed. Amidst the broke mowers and bike parts he talked it out of her, yanked her hair, shook her and slapped her a good one. Finally this country girl from Kickback, Alabama, with tears and much apology puked it up. Leon left her in the dirt with her dress yanked down to the waist, a rubber bike pedal shoved in her mouth.

2.

LEON CLEARED OUT, shot down to Asheville for boilermakers at Wolf's Lair. He drank 'til Chintzy came in breathing hard to say the farm was raided by the FBI. We talking a helicopter and trucks and cars and a gazillian dudes in jackets running over the place looking for clues on Leon Hicks. Leon toasted his great fortune then drove south, Mr. Quizzleboon watching all the while. The Quiz was proud of Leon. Damn boy split the farm with dignity intact. What's more, Leon had twenty grand left from the New York banks, *ding dong ding*, three in a row. Dang if that wasn't bringing in the sheaves. In the same week! The downside was Beacon, that sweet package of rubber bands, was to twist his heart up like some rag of nast, hold it with both fists and twist it and twist, can you hear it go drip?

Everybody knows strong men drive south to escape the claws of the courts. Did that mean Leon ought drive north? Seemed the smart thing, only his sister's ex-husband lived in Florida, and was a contact he could try. The man had been attorney to some bigtime dudes in Miami in 1978, all during the Cuban-Columbian drug wars. He was Edward Rooks, and the boy had connections. Leon's sister said Edward was blind now, but he still practiced law on the side. Edward moved to Tallahassee after his partner's throat was slit in their office by a client who'd expected his payments to sway the opinions of every judge in the Miami-Dade Circuit Court. Kids were cut up back then, their heads put in boxes delivered to their parents' doorsteps. Open it up, check out your kid's head in the box. That's the stuff Edward Rooks and his partner dealt with daily.

Leon pulled up to the split-level ranch house in Indianhead Acres, where a car was on fire in the yard. Leon walked by it and knocked and Edward, just a dude in a Hawaiian shirt, answered. The dude wore khaki shorts and Birkenstock sandals, the pale toes down there hairy, their color matching the man's hoary fly-backs. A clean shave on Edward Rooks. Guy wore funky green-framed shades, each lens shaped like a Playboy bunny emblem. Leon's hefty snort for the meeting was in full-blossom. Edward looked like *the man*.

"Who dat?" Edward asked.

"Leon."

"Once upon a time I married your piece-a-shit sister."

"She gave me your address."

"Yes, yes, glad you made it."

"Something I gotta tell you."

"What is it?"

"There's a car on fire in your yard."

"What kind of car is it, Leon?"

"Looks to me like one them overdrive sonsofbitch Fords."

"Will it explode?"

"I couldn't tell you that."

"What should we do? Should I call the fire department?"

"You got a hose?"

"I do. Can you put it out?"

Leon slipped through the crawlway of the overgrown holly bushes. He unloosed the spigot turnscrew, hauled the hose out there, and sprayed water through the windows where the seats were burning up—so much for that fire.

Edward was delighted. He harbored Leon under the condition that he cook for him. Edward's last cook—the owner of the flaming Ford, it so turned out—was picked up by the cops in the middle of Frenchtown wearing a sock and thong, only a sock and thong! The cook was gone, buddy, and blind men needed cooks, goddamnit, so "Oh, sure," Leon said, "I can cook." Leon scrambled Edward eggs in the afternoons, and roasted hams or potatoes come night. People always were coming over, crack whores and lower sorts upon whose ears news arrived of a blind man housing wayward bums and addicts in Indianhead. The bums wanted to cook for Edward, for he was a generous man, a sharing man. They did what they could to be on his good side, on the in of his unmatched drug world connections. We're talking hydrocodone pills and Xanax and debs. Edward always had some of those, and he could get crystal meth and morphine and methadone and pretty much whatever you wanted. Roofies? No problemo. How about some Kryptonic? Ever try Afghanica or Chem Dog? What about these here frogs that if you licked one's back you saw God? Edward bragged he knew where to get those frogs.

Leon crashed in the basement, what the druggies

called the boiler room. Had its own door to the outside, which was nice, but the lowlifes upstairs took advantage on Edward. They stunk up the rooms with crack smoke and body odor and used Edward's phone and left toenail clippings on the floor. They raided his fridge. High school girls dropped in while skipping class, girls who, like so many others, for a high, for a skrunk, to get skrunked out, were willing to disrobe for the blind man, let him touch them, and they gave him blumpkins on occasion. Some stunk him, or let Edward skunk them, their grunts and screams in the open for all. Edward liked when they said "hit me," that was his thing, so "hit me," they begged in soft voices to creep along the walls. One time Leon heard one say "hit me harder," which caused the blind attorney to cry out, "No, no, not harder, just hit me, Jesus, is that too much to ask? I swear to God, sometimes you gotta explain everything to people." Leon's new environment. It was so depressing.

3.

EDWARD WAS KNOWN by the smalltime criminals of the area as Kind Edward. The kind one discovered Leon's lack in the cook department quick. In this way Leon's role was redefined as do-shit-for-me bodyguard. Early on, Edward had felt Leon's face, while it still had the beard, and said, "Good Lord," and felt Leon's arms, sizing them up such as he did the girls to come over from Lincoln High School. Edward told the girls apart, he said, by reading the "braille" of their nipples. His other special talent was tying tampon strings into knots with his tongue.

In exchange for Leon's services, which included package deliveries and kicking folks out of the house when they got too rowdy, Edward provided for Leon a good American passport that matched a new driver's license, social security number, and certificate of live birth. Thus Leon Hicks became Cliff Highnote, but he didn't like the name Cliff. In the joint there'd been a Cliff, a meth addict. Whenever another methhead came in Cliff licked the sores of the guy, and sucked them and chewed the scabs to get high, right there in the damn cafeteria and shit. Damn dude got his ass kicked, and finally leaned over the railing of his tier, brought his legs up behind him and slipped down head first to crack his skull open and squash his brain—good job. As a result of that particular Cliff, Leon introduced himself as Highnote, only Highnote. His hot El Camino he sold to a westward-traveling druggy, and purchased a 1970 Camaro Z28, matte black with some dents on both sides to give it character. Though Highnote hated to give up the blue El Camino with its cherry-red pinstripe running over the hood, the Camaro looked tolerable sweet. More important was Highnote now had a legitimate pink slip. His first job as muscle to Kind Edward was to collect eight hundred bucks from a Joe Brown.

Highnote sniffed a shitload then drove out to Brown's, way out in the boonies, Brown's. Highnote knocked on Brown's door. The door opened. A very small woman in furry slippers and a white nightie stood there, a white girl with bleached hair, couldn't've been but four foot ten. Her fat lips shone wet with some kind of oil, and her eyes emitted tiny blue sparks. "Get Joe," Highnote said.

"What you want Joe fur?"

"I'm here for Kind Edward. Get Joe."

"Tell Kind Edward check's in the mail." The little girl tried to close the door, but Highnote stuck his arm in. When the door didn't close, the girl pulled it wide, then slammed it. Cliff Highnote cried out. Sounded so sissyish, like he was a pup whose back got broke under some fool dude's boot. That he screamed in front of her angered him more than the pain, so he pushed the door and the bitch fell. Reminded him of the junk shed incident, when he knocked poor Beacon into the dirt and stuffed the bike pedal in her mouth, the crank still on it and the greasy chain hanging down against her chest. Seeing Beacon that way had made Highnote—*no, he was not no Highnote back then, he was Leon*—want to kick the shit out of her, which is exactly what he did do. Leon was not proud of that sad moment in his life, so Highnote, who hoped to be a better man than Leon ever was, strove to avoid such incidents. In a calm voice Highnote said, "Where the fuck's Joe?"

Little girl stood up haughty like to straighten her nightie. Had Highnote come to get it on with some strange?

"I ain't after no ass, baby. Just get me Joe."

"Didn't I say check's in the mail?"

"We both know it ain't."

"Kind Edward can suck his daddy's dick."

Highnote scanned the living room then grabbed a doorknob, what stood to reveal a bedroom with a Joe in it. He slung it wide, but Blondie jumped on his back. She scratched his face, a nail grazing his good eye. Highnote yanked his head away while at the same time bringing up a hand to hold in the prosthesis. Highnote had had enough of running after his damn eye. If not for his eye, Highnote would have backhanded her, to hell with his resolve on being kind to women. Such resolve opened doors to bad stuff, such as Blondie right now biting into his neck. Once more Highnote yelped like a broke-back dog. He'd felt the girl's teeth sink in, piercing nerve endings and flesh. A screaming passion in the girl promised more of same. Highnote threw her off and ducked out of the house and made to his car as if he'd just delivered a pizza, nothing peculiar going on here, no sir. He backed down Brown's drive gentlemanly, and drove away clutching his neck.

QUIZZLEBOON

Again Kind Edward felt Highnote's muscles, ran pale fingers over Highnote's bulldog face, felt the scratches, divined the bite mark on the neck. With a look of genuine disgust, the blind attorney said, "She gotcha good, Highnote," and stepped away, and said, looking into space as if the idea forming in his mind was, actually, quite delicious, "Why didn't you clock her?" Kind Edward's voice normally was scratchy and sucky, breathy, but now it was higher-pitched. "I mean, are you a Galahad?"

"I ain't no gotdern Galahad."

"You believe in honor and chivalry?"

"I believe in a few things."

"Did she have the power of Diana in her bosom?"

"I don't know what you're talking about."

"Maybe I should've made that passport say *Low*note."

Cliff Highnote laughed with Kind Edward. Had Highnote not been derailed in his purpose by a goddamn midget in a see-through nightie? Cliff remembered her slippers flying off as she jumped onto his back, and thought *Low*note, sure, and that night shot the last of the eight. The afternoon of the next day Cliff bought two newbies, and drove through South Tallahassee of Aerosmith fame, to Brother's Bar, where he the big dog, none of that Skynard backstep shit with him, bloodied a face in the lot. For two weeks Cliff ran pipe into some fine-looking redneck women but always told them, upfront, that he was took by a woman "in the North country," name of Beacon. "She's my beacon," he said, and imagined her face while rolling the dice—there was a Renee, a Jane, a Kimberly—their faces became *her* face—there in his car, in a stall, and by the fire. All of it he saw through the eye on the moon, what he cut from his head for the Moon Man. Through the eye that was his each good got noted, each bad, each flickering lid to tell of deception.

It was the story Cliff Highnote, back when he was Leon Hicks, made up for the dirt kids one night by the bonfire at the farm. Watching the flames in their big wet eyes, he'd said:

"Mr. Quizzleboon come down from the moon one night while I drunk a beer by the fire. The moon man said, Son, I been watching your ass. Of the folks I seen from up on the moon, you got the best aim. Look at that eight-point buck yonder. You must've been two hundred yards off, yet you shot that sonofabitch right square in the eye. I seen you shoot turkeys out trees with your bows and arrows. I seen you at the whiskey bars throw darts and shit, and the bullseyes always got hit smack to the middle. You was the best dirt clod fighter when you was little, and you played a mean ball. I can't tell you how many times I seen you swish it from half-court.

"Mr. Quizzleboon had all kind of great things to say on me, but I cut him off. I said, What the hell's your business, mister? You want my eight-point buck yonder? Go ahead, take it, it's yours. That's too much meat for me. Take it to the moon with you and feed the damn moon people.

"Mr. Quizzleboon wasn't interested in my buck. He said, Leon, I traveled all the way from the moon to collect your eyeball, buddy. Don't you think that deserves a little respect?

"I said, What the hell you talking, Mr. Quizzleboon? You ain't takin my goddamn eyeball.

"That's when Mr. Quizzleboon said he needed it more than me.

QUIZZLEBOON

"I said, You'd best get your ass back to the moon, bitch.

"Mr. Quizzleboon stood there smelling his fingers like he had some serious business on his mind. He said, If I don't feed your eyeball into my machine up yonder, I won't be able to keep track of everybody because the eyeball we got now has done growed old, partner. Sometimes we mistake one man for another, give out the wrong word. People go to jail who ain't supposed to. People die in electric chairs ain't supposed to. Men go marry the wrong woman, and sometimes a child takes a wrong step for a nail that's stuck up from a board to go all the way through his foot. Who knows all what kind of bad things'll happen if we don't get this eyeball sitchiation under control. You might could even save the world, Leon.

"Save the world? I said.

"You heard me, old buddy, Mr. Quizzleboon said. He said without a good eye like mine, evil was bound to run rampant. Don't you wanna save the world, Leon?

"I said, Well, since you put it that way.

"Mr. Quizzleboon smiled, and I just, you know, pulled out this knife right here. I unfolded it just like this and cut my eyeball out and hund it over. Mr. Quizzleboon thunk me kindly. He give me this plastic eye, then climbed into his flying saucer."

The children were quiet, but a dorky little blond girl in a antique dress, name of Ambrosia, said, "Whiskey Bars got rooves, Uncle L."

Leon said yes, indeed, whiskey bars do got rooves, and scratched her head, good girl, smart for knowing the Quiz could not see him throw darts in no whiskey bar. Some things was plain mysterious in the world, he told her. That machine Mr. Quizzleboon talked on, what he fed the eyeball to, must hold the secret to how a man can watch another throw darts through timber and tar.

These Tallahassee redneck women were Leon's reward for what he sacrificed. By popping them up with some fine loads he was goddamn sure as hell doing the world a favor. Twenty grand ain't shit when you're in a greasified groove of the snort, though. All that shooting, all that highfalutin pride-walk and -talk and be. Not much time at all went by, a mere four months at Kind Edward's, yet Cliff Highnote once more was a noteless lowdown clown with a frown from out of town.

"I gotta get some cash from you soon," Kind Edward said.

"I'm doing your bodyguard business."

"I loved your sister once upon a time, but we called it quits. More like she dumped me. Glinda turned out to be a piece of shit. Now I've got you."

So Highnote looked for opportunities to prove his muscle. One night Kind Edward spat lasagna onto the coffee table. Had too much oregano in it, and some of the pasta strips weren't cooked all the way through. Too chewy. That's not to mention the black pepper overkill. Kind Edward's new cook grew offended, grabbed the attorney's arm and ripped a button off his Hawaiian shirt. Highnote busted the dude's face, broke his nose. The good deed did Highnote no good. Kind Edward felt indebted to the cook now. Was that the kind of thing a kindly king might need? Hell naw! Edward commented on Lownote causing trouble. "You and your sister both will be eviscerated in hell," the attorney said. Though Highnote had never heard that word, "eviscerated," and could not discern what it meant, he considered telling Edward what Blondie said, that Edward should go suck his daddy's dick right this instant, but let it slide, and that night considered the changes taking place inside his body. Leon would not have had the wherewithal, Highnote thought, to stand for this crap. As Highnote, Leon was a bit more mature a man.

Desperate for cash, Highnote tried getting back in with the ping pong pang of yore, and broke into a wrinkle-neck fellow's house up the way, a tall-facer to walk his lapdog wrinkle-neckedly daily—and oldly—some kind of shrunken down Doberman pinscher, the dog. Highnote hoped to run off with Mr. Wrinkle's TV and other goodies. Near three in the morning, he sliced through the living room window mesh, popped the screen off and climbed through. Highnote heard the guy in the other room snoring, and loaded his TV into the Camaro. When he returned for the microwave, the old man hit him over the head with a picture frame. Leon's eye popped out, but he caught it with his right hand as he dropped to the floor. The old man continued to slam Leon in the dark, and the tiny dog did bite and bark. The man's Magnavox Highnote pawned for twenty, but Kind Edward wanted two hundred for August, putting the idea of banks once more in the mind of *The L.* Back then, yes, he was Leon. He'd done three banks in upstate New York, the first in Schenectady—*bing!*—then he hit Amsterdam—*bong!*—hello Buffalo—*bang!* Could he do it again?

Bling, blong, blang!

Could he do it?

Highnote just missed, so bad, his life in Asheville where he'd been king, his life in the hills sugar fluff,

Turkish rugs upon which nekid young ladies stood, their feet honest and bare. He missed Beacon. With a fresh two hundred grand, would she be his again? He'd buy her the eight balls, and buy the silence of the others, just stuff the farm up with new guitars and shit, new amps and whatever their dusty hearts desired. New suits for harvesting their honey? Why not? The reason Beacon opened her fat mouth was for the money, the twenty thou, poor girl. With a fresh two hundred gees at her filthy feet, what reason could she have? In dreams he saw her so high, his girl who loved the needle. In Highnote's dreams he gave it, recording his give through the eye that was his. His eye watched everybody on the earth. It sucked their doings, what they did, inside for safekeeping.

"That old geezer's in his late seventies," Kind Edward said, and laughed in Leon's face.

"He's old, I'll give you that."

"Old?"

"Old."

"People tell me he's got a bad leg."

"He limps, I've seen him limp."

"Limp?"

"Limp."

"And that girl."

"She was a brute."

"A brute?"

"A brute."

"What would you do if you were me? Everybody's talking about how you were beat up by a little girl and this here that some old man with a bad leg busted your balls."

"I'll get your money," Highnote said, and Mr. Quizzleboon gave Leon—*no, he was Cliff Highnote*—a wink.

QUIZZLEBOON

Cliff Highnote bought a .38 Special from a dude at Brother's Bar, a nickel-plated oldie-but-goodie with a flap-hammer. He bought some face glue and pancake makeup, cotton balls and Play-Doh, and screwed with his face, his nose in particular, made himself look like what he thought Mr. Quizzleboon looked like, rounded in feature with a crater mid-forehead—*ha!*—the scar the Quiz took one night during a meteor shower. The burning rock piece screamed down from the sky and slammed his ass into the moon dirt. Highnote chuckled, thinking of his good buddy reaching into his forehead to dislodge the burning splinters—shit had to be painful. Highnote cut the fangs off the vampire teeth he bought at The Party Palace. He stuck them in his mouth and drove over to Southern Trust on Monroe Street.

Bulletproof glass was dumb. As a child it had irked him whenever he'd gone in with his mother to cash her measly weekly hundred dollar checks in Virginia Beach. The checks were made out by one Mr. Quigley, a thin-lipped slob in a yellow suit who, if Leon's two good eyes could be trusted, delighted in the watch of his mother's cleaning of toilets. Quigley stood about telling her do this, do that, calling her "Superscrub" and "Fuckwad" and "Faggotass," depending on his mood. This money she earned making Quigley's beds, washing sheets, and scrubbing out the toilets and such at the White Lady Motel where they lived. Leon's mother, Sandra by name, got money other ways, too, but what waste, that thick-ass glass! Tellers walked in and walked out of the area all day long. Sometimes a door locked them behind the glass, but more often than not the door was ajar. The dumbest were the half-doors you could jump to raid the cutie-pie greenback palace.

Now Mr. Quizzleboon entered the Southern Trust bank. He jumped the half-door, and pulled his gun, zero snag, a clean slipper of pockety pull. He backed the tellers to the corner, handed the dumpy blond a trash sack, and said in a near whisper, "Sixty seconds, bitch." The girl hopped to it, filled the sack, and gave it to Mr. Quizzleboon with fifteen seconds to spare. The whole thing was hush-hush—Quizzleboon could as well've been the man to come check the computers—but as he left, a black woman in high heels, one of those financial advisors for the poor, catching onto something, said, "Sir?" Mr. Quizzleboon didn't have time for this, so he clocked her. She dropped to the tiles like a feed sack. Quizzleboon passed through the doors of glass to a Brinks truck pulling to the curb. Mr. Quizzleboon could rob it too, but no. He crossed Paul Russell Road to Winn Dixie, where the Camaro waited under a flowering dogwood.

Mr. Quizzleboon set out for Asheville. He stopped at a rest area, peeled off his face and threw it in the garbage, then back in the car gave his day's work a once-over. A great whopping thirteen thousand motherfucking dollars and something. It was a ping, forget the pong, forget the pang and the bing and the bong. With this he could buy some coke or cane sugar, take your pick, enough to fill a hat to the brim, and Leon felt like Leon now, not no damn Highnote. He was Leon as Leon was Leon, but he marveled over the strangeness he'd felt come over him as he'd entered the bank. It was like he really was the man from the moon. Something right strange had happened there.

That night Leon checked into the Clermont Hotel on Ponce de Leon Avenue in Atlanta, drank Pabst

QUIZZLEBOON

Blue Ribbon while watching the strippers down in the lounge, skanks for the most part, too skinny to fuck without being self-conscious on it, and them speaking in some weird language too. Leon heard somebody say they were Polish. Poor things were white like somebody threw powder on them, just nothing compared to Beacon of the cool skin you could look at just to look at. He just loved Beacon's long brown hair—sorrel, she called it—and the funny fact of her missing pinky finger.

"That one had a leg broke one time or other," the guy beside Leon said. "You can tell on the kink below the knee. That one leg bows inward, you see it? I think she had surgery, do you see the scar?"

"Don't talk to me."

"A doctor went in there and messed around inside her leg, but I don't go to doctors. You couldn't pay me to see a doctor."

Leon thought of the first time he made love to Beacon of the oily-ass forehead. They were still connected, man to woman. Leon was growing soft inside her, and he asked her, because he'd always been curious, how she got her name. She said, "It's for the light of hope I give out, Uncle L. I'm a proverb." Leon didn't ask for more, and he still didn't know what a proverb was, but he liked the sound of the word.

"Hang on, wait a second, did you see that?" the fellow said. "I mean, did you see that? When she squatted something dropped out. I wonder if I was the only one who saw that? What was it is what I'd like to know. I mean, what exactly was it that dropped out?"

Beacon's skin was no color to name.

"Pussy crust," the man said.

It was a sort of pink-white-olive to slide over muscle as she moved, when she stretched arms over her head, or brought legs up while propped on a bed ledge. To see her muscles ripple below the skin delighted Leon, the strings of muscle in her calves abristle with a promise of temporary annihilation, what all men craved but none deserved. Leon just loved the sex with her. He loved all the positions they did, though sometimes, he had to admit, he felt awkward when she was on top. At first he'd thought it might could be the relinquish of power in it, but no, it wasn't that. What it was, he discovered, was her goddamn neck and the bottom of her jaw, when took together when she was on top, looked exactly like a ginormous wanger.

"Are you even listening to me?" the man said, and said, "just think if you was some tiny little dude down there and that piece of pussy crust fell on top of your head. Maaan, that shit would knock you flat on your ass! You ever been to New York City? Ever seen them air conditioners up there? It'd be like if one were to fall out and land on you."

Leon walked away from the guy, in the morning ate a burger with extra pickles and mustard up the hill at the Majestic Grill, tipped the young waitress ten bucks, and drove north for Asheville, north for the dirt people, the dirty people who lived on the mountain, the men interesting in their histories, and those women who stuffed orange dirt into their vaginas before sex, apparently correct in their belief that it was an effective form of birth control. For their monthlies they did what? Used green leaves and crushed up cardamom seeds and various kinds of herbs like mint and rosemary and they did this thing to where it soaked up the blood while at the same time "rejuvenated their labs," which Leon had heard Soil say of the process to involve mysterious things Leon cared not to ponder. In this ignorance he was happy, but he knew most of the women saw it as too much trouble. The most of them, during that time of month, walked about with bleedy streaks to their thighs that run down to their feet. The women were proud of their bleedy stripes, but Leon couldn't care for it. He'd never been one much for blood. For as long as he could remember, the sight of it, even if it was just watered-down cow blood in a package of ground beef, gave him shivers.

If the dirt people welcomed Leon warmly, upon what would be based this homecoming? The lust dirty people feel for money? No, they were *anticaps*, which had nothing to do with if you did or did not like to wear baseball caps—it was short for anticapitalists. They called themselves Commies, talked of community, said Anarcho-syndicalism was the hope of us. Didn't Jesus do this and didn't Jesus do that? Let's follow the lead of Jesus, and Ben Franklin, and Socrates, and Iggy Pop. Small communities needed to practice law in their own special ways, they said, and they said that they had "really good" reasons for "succeeding from the Union." Of course Leon wanted to help them succeed, as he had helped them before, but first he needed to fuck that little traitor Beacon, get it out of the way so he could think straight. For four months she'd broke into his thoughts uninvited, even while he'd pumped the ladies of the Florida Panhandle, which seemed really unfair to the ladies of the Florida Panhandle, but what could be done for it? When drunk or skrunked silly off coke it was agony. He'd wish ill upon Beacon, that she'd turn quick into the skank-breath ho of her future, that a flaw would develop upon her body, a horrible sore he could picture spreading, something to hold against her, but she was in the machine, it was all recorded, her perfection, straight down to her missing pinky finger that made her so damn special. It'd all been took in by Leon's eyeball, what he lost while a child for eternity. After robbing the banks in upstate New York—*zinga, zonga, zanga!*—Leon should'a drove south, like the song says, not to no Carolina bullshit, but to El Paso, Guatemala, say, or Are-The-Fuck-Gen-Tina.

4.

LEON DROVE NORTH. In Asheville he drank a dry martini at the Wolf's Lair. He met with his old connection, bought five eight balls and a hundred-count pack of disposable darts. Driving up into the pumpkin-sweet hills, wheeling his black Camaro through sand and tall grass to the dirty place where the dirty people lived, Leon's nerves tingled—he was nervous, his nostalgia centered in the loves he'd left, and the cukes and maters and squash of the wonderful thriving community of anarchism and togetherness. When Leon stepped out of his car in the new rattlesnake skin boots he bought on Peachtree Street in Atlanta, slamming the door the way he liked to slam it to let people know somebody important, a real man, had arrived, "Uncle L!" he heard, a small voice like what the children might cry out in *Little House on the Prairie*, a show Leon had watched long ago with his mother, oh, little girls in summery dresses hopping through tall grass. The theme song came back to him in an instant, the melody playing as Ambrosia bounced runningly his way from the Great House, barefoot in a dirty white smock worn over her bathed-in-the-lake-water self. Pure was Ambrosia, unmuddied by the dictates of the "outside world," what would pollute her without conscience or consent. The child's mother of the Pinocchio nose down there—*Butterfly*—didn't let her daughter watch the boobs of the tubes. The child was free of the poison, and Leon squatted in the grass, held out his arms and Ambrosia ran into them and he lifted her off the ground and swung her in circles. "Uncle L," she kept singing, and clung to him with her messed-up twigs-for-legs and weird long toes. She said, "I missed you, Uncle L."

"I missed you, too." Leon set her down. Ambrosia grabbed Leon's hand—yessiree, he was Leon now, not no damn Cliff—and tried tugging him all yippee ki-yay to the gravesite of a cat whose ninth life ended in the jowls of a visiting anarcho-syndicalist's Rottweiler. Leon wanted to oblige her, but felt the need to tend to grown-up matters, let the folks know he was here before he went on fieldtrips into the bushes, which he was glad to do, he told the child, just not right this second.

Ambrosia was upset that Leon would privilege adults, but she pursed her mouth. "Is Mr. Quizzleboon still watching us?"

"He watches everything we do."

"Everthang?"

"Ever tiny little thang, yes dear, why?"

"It don't matter." Ambrosia dragged Leon up to the Great House where, in the kitchen, who should he see but Sparrow and Beacon, their mouths ajar. After the shock Sparrow ran up to Leon and hugged him good, and Leon hugged Sparrow good back, but he was looking over her shoulder at Beacon, who stood against the sink in her favorite combination, a messy short black skirt and black tee with ripped-off arms.

"Baby!" Sparrow kept saying. Sparrow had been Leon's girlfriend back in the day, when they'd grown up in Virginia Beach. It was through Sparrow that he came to know the Dirties not long after his release from prison.

"Good to see you," Leon said.

"I'm so glad you're not busted, baby," Sparrow said.

"I'd've been here all this time if not for her."

"Her? What do you mean, her?" Sparrow pushed Leon away from her so that she could see his face.

"Beacon." Leon didn't want to betray Beacon this way, but fuck it, he was only answering Sparrow's question. He'd never seen Beacon looking so damn hot, neither. In her shame, blushing all over and beginning to sweat, his *proverb* was more perfect than ever before.

"Bitch turned me in," Leon said.

"Huh?"

"Twenty grand. She called the FBI on me, but the Quiz let me know. That's why I hauled ass to get the fuck out, you understand?"

Sparrow looked at Beacon. Beacon looked into the sink.

"Bitch sold me down to the F mother B of I."

"Huh?"

"Tell her, Beacon." Leon felt weak in the knees, gee wiz, and so awful mean. She don't deserve this shit, he thought, and sorta wished he could beat himself up here at the moment to protect her dignity.

But she spoke. She said yes, she'd contacted the F mother B of I after Leon revealed the secret on how he came to have so much money. At that moment, Ambrosia, bless her goddamn heart, picked an organic carrot off the huge table in the middle of the room. That table was once a platform down in Asheville in the slavery days, what the merchandise had stood upon during the auctions. The table was later used in a butcher's shop—that's what the dirty people said—*the Dirties*, Leon thought of them as. They weren't hippies. They weren't reformed skinheads. They weren't misfits and punkers or dipshits from Yonkers. They were Dirties. Ambrosia whipped Beacon with her organic carrot's weedy protuberances, *whip whip*.

Windstorm came into the room, nekid, she the one with purple inverted nipples, and there was a massive tornado tattooed to her back, a detail Leon had liked during their double-doggage, all but for the fact of it emerging from her anus. "Uncle L," she said lovingly, and hugged him.

Tinbuck came in, nekid to the bone, and said, "Uncle L!" and opened his arms while walking Leon's way, as if he might like a hug.

"No." Leon held his hand up in a halting gesture and said, "I'm not here to hug nobody," and forked greenbacks out for a dozen gallons of red wine. A bonfire blazed in the field that night. The children gathered around Leon in the firelight. They begged him to please, please, tell them extra stuff on Mr. Quizzleboon who lived on the moon.

Leon said, "He watches y'all, that's all y'all need to know, ever little thing you do, it's recorded," and for dramatic effect Leon pulled out his eyeball. "This here is the replacement Mr. Quizzleboon give me," he said, holding it between his thumb and index finger. "I don't think you guys can imagine how much pain I suffered when I cut my real eyeball out."

QUIZZLEBOON

The kids, and everybody else gathered by the fire, grimaced and oohed. "The most painful thing I ever done," Leon admitted, and was quiet in the memory of his mother—Leon looked like he was in a trance—how she came into the room from scrubbing toilets, and saw him on the couch, Mr. Quigley kicked back in the cozy chair smoking a BlackStone cigar. Mr. Quigley's face had smoke all around it, and when Leon's mother, seeing her little boy that way, his eyeball dangling from the hole, attached by a string of guts, she turned and shut the door soft to go back to her scrubbing duties—*yeah, scrub out the toilet, bitch!* It was Mr. Quigley who carried Leon into the parking lot and set him on the back seat of his Cadillac convertible.

Or was this Mr. Quizzleboon's fancy business, Mr. Q adding info into the machine to fill in the blank spots? Something is better than nothing, right? Leon was little then with his terrible pain. How could he know? Best thing to think on it was say fuck it to hell. He'd done pressed the eject button, and told the children, said, "When I give Mr. Quizzleboon my precious eyeball, I knew everything I remembered from now on could not be made up. How could I be fooled by my own eye? If it was my eye to see it, could I be fooled? Hell naw, so I give it over, and in this way guaranteed the safety of all the childs of the earth."

The childs by the fire were nine by number, wore loose dresses, rags, or were nekid white slabs of pork fat in the beginning stages of drip, faces worrisome or greasy in the firelight, despondent in the smoke. Seeing them this way Leon laughed too loud and abrupt for them to think it a happy laugh, as laughs are supposed to be. Leon saw fright in their brows, their chins, and smoothed it over, saying, "By my eye I see the good you do. You might think you done bad, but it could be good. You do something people think is bad, it might could be good."

Relieved by their uncle's wisdom, the kids ran off to play amongst the fireflies and bats and skeeters, leaving Leon with a few main "elders" of the dirty farm. These men, each nekid by the fire, mostly to rub Leon wrong. Leon preferred nekid women, all out with their titties hanging in the fresh air and shit, but where were they? Had somebody told them to leave the fire to the important business of the men? How irksome. Leon was irked. He felt a bit ridiculous sitting with a buncha goddamn nekid men.

"It's tragic, it's despicable, it sickens me to think that one of our own . . . I mean, what was she thinking? I mean . . . what should we do about this?" That was Potato spouting off, him another of the young studs to plow a field like a mule could plow a field, just with a hoe instead of whatever mules plow fields with.

"It's tragic," Tinbuck said.

"Pure tragic," the fellow sporting the involuntary hard-on said.

"I think we should banish her," Potato said.

"But she works awesomely," Tinbuck said. "She's one of the best workers, she's always worked, she's always done her part. What should we do, Uncle L?"

Mr. Quizzleboon gave Leon a wink, and Leon said, to the nekid men, "This is a anarchist community I hear you guys say all the time."

"Damn straight," Potato said. The others voiced agreement.

"Beacon broke the shit in two," Leon said.

QUIZZLEBOON

"The witch had her own agenda," Potato said, Potato one of the main dudes of the farm. Potato was not named Potato over his head looking like a potato, which is what most people thought was why he was called Potato, but for his love of the eat of the spud. Potato always fried them up in the kitchen, all with butter, and like to did stuff with spice on them, and seasalts and cheese. Potato said the potato was the best veggie on the planet. Potatoes were eighty percent water, Potato said, so if you were stranded in a desert somewhere, and had a potato in your pocket, you could suck it to save your life by. Potato said potatoes were grown in space, did you know that? Right now this minute satellite tater farms cruised earth's curvature, in orbit. NASA started the project for the reason that we humans at some point must and will inhabit other planets. What better food to have your back than the potato?

"What I heard on witches," Leon said, "was they could be punished into reformed states where they wouldn't do nothing bad no more. Stuff like to dunk em in cold water."

"Sounds sound to me," Potato said, and said, "Banishment is another option. I don't think she'd fare too well out in the world. That's just plain cruel."

"Bring her to the fire. Let's see if she gives a shit," Leon said.

Tinbuck and Chintzy left the fire. Some ten minutes later they returned, each holding one of Beacon's arms. They held her steady as the elders by the fire said they were alarmed over what they'd heard. "Did you really do that?" She nodded yes, and they said they were concerned and just so horrified and plain downright disgusted, if you really wanted to know the truth. "You are the reason our home was raided by the FBI," Potato said. "Several of us were arrested on weed charges. *You* did this to us? Really? For a stupid reward? The farm could have been confiscated, and not only that, but look at all the cool shit Leon did for us. You had to go slap him in the face and try and ruin things for everybody, didn't you?"

"I'm deeply sorry."

"She wants to blames drugs, look at her," the guy with an involuntary hard-on said, and stood up like he was really pissed off.

"Drugs," Potato said.

"What should we do?" Jericho said, and everybody looked to Leon for the answer.

Leon said, "I will consult Mr. Quizzleboon tonight. As for now, Beacon says she's sorry, so I say let her stay. Let Beacon work the fields. Let her cook some delicious meals. I love her Eggs Benedict and what she does with asparagus."

"I just hate people like her," the involuntary hard-on guy said.

"Her body is filled with worms," Leon said. "Sometimes worms live in people. They get in there and start fucking and having babies and before long you got a problem. I don't doubt that Beacon wishes they weren't in there. She needs help getting them out is what I reckon, so who's to blame is hard to say, see what I'm saying? They were in her, yet we didn't see jack. We were too dumb. On this I'm'a have to ask the Quiz."

5.

LEON SLEPT IN the old bed that night, on the second floor of the Great House, alone. He didn't want to become entangled with a woman yet, especially Sparrow who struck him more and more as a sorry suckup ass-kisser. He remembered her all right, back from their high school days in Virginia Beach—together they'd partied a ton—but even now Leon thought of her as Lisa, just Lisa, normal Lisa who everybody behind her back called Dog Girl over the chin to recede and how slutty she was. Anybody could fuck Lisa was the word, the practice she practiced and, not to look negative on a woman for being generous with her body or nothing like that but, in some ways she disgusted Leon, she just did not have that fire Beacon had—nor the magic missing finger!—and Leon wanted to stay pure for what he saw as God's finest work of art. He fell asleep nice enough that night, but his dream was too nasty for comfort. In his dream had Mr. Quizzleboon done gave the word on what to do on Beacon?

Leon did not remember, exactly, where the dream began, but at some point he and Beacon were "high on cocaine," as the Grateful Dead like to sing. They had shot up in the junk shed, but Leon was afraid to fuck her with no rubber, so they left the shed to search one out. The cabinets of the Great House they opened. They checked under the library couch, pulled up cushions to see was one there, and even opened the refrigerator. The feeling Leon had was of extreme care for Beacon, of looking out for her while at the same time wanting like crazy to dornkt her. These dream-feelings conflicted, yet harmonized to produce a sensation of well-being that went on for hours. Leon would've been happy, now that he was awake, to have gone on this way for the remainder of the dream, but Ambrosia danced downwardly through the tall grass. As Leon and Beacon ransacked the interior of Leon's Camaro, searching out the elusive rubber, Ambrosia skipped up to say, "I know what y'all're doing. Come along with me. I'll show you where it's at." Leon and Beacon followed her through the trees and they crossed a creek and went up a hill to a clearing where the guy with the involuntary hard-on was on his knees, digging at the earth with bare hands. Leon's first thought was, *you son of a bitch*, because he did not like to see a nekid man with a hard-on, involuntary or otherwise, in the proximity of a child. Leon balled his fists and was going to mess up the man's world, but when the man turned his face Leon's way, his two hands deep in the earth, it was Kind Edward's face. Blood seeped from both corners of his mouth. "Fancy seeing you here, Highnote," the attorney said, and sneezed, and laughed then super-loudly in the ridiculous bleating manner that was classic Rooks.

Highnote checked his pocket, he needed to pay Rooks what he owed, but it was empty but for the trusted Buck. "You know what I want," Kind Edward said, pulling from the ground a thing covered in dirt. The thing started wiggling. A cat. "He's alive!" Ambrosia shrieked. The cat darted off through the woods. Ambrosia chased it. Kind Edward stood, his hands black with soil, and then he leaped up high into the air and landed behind Beacon, grabbed her arms. Cliff Highnote unfolded his knife. Kind Edward was licking her ear now, laughing, and he nibbled her lobe as Cliff—*or was it Leon?*—cut out Beacon's eyeball, she struggling and screaming and bleeding from the eye. Cliff—*or was it Leon?*—carved and prodded. Using the blade as lever, he turned his head back and forth from the trees to make sure Ambrosia could not see what he was doing. When Beacon's eye was in his palm, he pulled out his prosthesis. He stuffed his plastic eye into Beacon's head and stuffed Beacon's real eye into his own head. Now he saw through both eyes, but the blind attorney was gone, he'd disappeared, and the next thing Leon saw, with his improved sight, really disturbed him. Just Beacon, flat on the earth beside the hole the cat sprung from, skirt up and legs took apart, blood all over her face, said, "You can fuck me now, Leon. Come on, baby, it's okay now, you can do it. I want you to fuck me. Do you hear me?"

Leon smelled the good cooking. It rose from the kitchen below, cumin flowers and peppermint crystals to blossom in the room, but the dream, Jesus. It would set any man off his vittles. It was all out yucky in the last part. Gave Leon shivers to think of Beacon that way, and for the first time since he could not remember, he felt a bit some afraid. What was Mr. Quizzleboon trying to say to him? Leon tried to forget it, but it came back, so he ripped free the needle pack to prep a syringe.

Whenever Leon ran coke the red swirls was the sorry part. Leon preferred the snort, but the snort, too, after he'd done enough, led to blood. The stuff was like cherry syrup in your body, and if you weren't careful it could spill out to leave you a crumpled chunk of nothing special on the sidewalk or wherever it was you lost your blood. His mother had bled from the nose. She'd thrown her used tampons into the wastebasket beside the commode in their room at the White Lady. His mom, because she was a maid and cleaned the rooms of others, did not clean her own. The tampons with blood on them in the waste basket would begin to reek, the smell scurrilously alive, tangy in the nose. The blood smelled of rotted meat, of metal and garbage and dead rats.

Leon popped himself a quarter gram and fell wayward into the sheets, lost in bliss for a minute, his heartbeat maxing out then calming as *the mystical drug bells* ceased their reverberations, and his tunneled monovision gave way to a remembrance party of last night's dreamamoly. What a bigtime shame here over the fact of the morning so beautiful out there and all, with chirping birds, a owl sounding off. It had rained during the night. Fresh breezes puffed through the window screens, and they felt wonderful against his face. It was going to waste. Leon could not enjoy it. He saw himself cutting out Beacon's eyeball, putting it in his own face and then suddenly seeing in stereo, a miracle, but so horrible, she on the ground, the pink wiggle of her pussy matching the blood-ripped flaps of her mutilated socket.

Leon rose, and slipped the tight jeans up. His clean yellow tee read: IF YOU CAN'T PISS WITH

QUIZZLEBOON

THE BIG DOGS STAY OFF THE PORCH—had a cartoon print of a small dog, something like a little dumbass dog with his wiener out, trying to squeeze in with the big dogs who were pissing off the porch. In his rattlesnake skin boots Leon stomped loud down the stairs for whoever was down there to know that the big dog was on his way—*prepare your goddamn selves!*

At the bottom Leon grabbed the stairwell knob and turned it, and stepped into the people-packed kitchen, the people rising up with, "WE LOVE YOU UNCLE L!" all these people, shit, it was the dirt people gathered. Amongst the sea of faces Leon saw Junebug and Windstorm, Vertigo and Butterfly, Lichen, Lilly, Lolly, Pinecone—all good people—and Gretchen, Hulda, Baby Bear and Monica—those were the women whose company Leon had greatly enjoyed, he putting himself into them as they themselves were wrapped all around him—he recognized them as a piece—and Sparrow, of course, smiling, not in the least bit ashamed of her rotted teeth. They shouted again, in unison, "WE LOVE YOU UNCLE L!" and kept on with it, "Uncle L, we love you," but it was tangled now, a hodgepodge sound of laughter and merriment, and streamers were festooned along the walls, and a banner in pastel colors read: WELCOME HOME LEON.

Was this part of the dream? The kids ran up to hug him and everybody cheered, and on the table plates stacked high with pancakes steamed. Casserole bowls ran amok with egg stuffs, and there were tofu sausages and sauces, and upon the old slave platform that had later become a butcher's table tarried many other breakfast goodies. It was no dream! Leon felt flooded with joy, and he breakfasted with his friends Jericho and Tinbuck, Gore and Goliath, Peter and Preston, and Mike the man who did magic tricks. As Leon ate, everybody patted his back and said nice things, like how they'd missed him, and they fed him strawberries, hand to mouth, and said the farm wasn't the same since he'd disappeared. They were so happy to see him again, once more, hell yeah! A dream come true! Leon felt the word *Yes* all inside his body. *Yes*, he was home, *Yes*, as home as home could be home, *Yes*, this *was* home, this *was* the place Leon wanted to call home.

6.

LEON FINISHED FEASTING. The kids whisked his plates away. They were dirty, the kids, and the plates were dirty, and Leon and the dirty people went out for a morning walk of smelly togetherness in the grass, and some rode mopeds with cats in baskets or on the seats, the cats too lazy to walk, or too fat, or charmed by the sensations of engines, the pull of throttle and release of brake.

Leon and the Dirties arrived to a gnarled oak tree. Below its branches, on the ground, a massive-ass piñata sat with the festive frills and sparkles. Leon said, "Is that a possum?"

"Do it look like a possum to you?" Potato asked.

"I guess it could be an armadillo."

Potato was dressed today in pink panties and man-sandals, the hair on his legs and chest very pubic-hair-like. He made all the sounds of a man laughing.

"Hellbender?" Leon guessed.

The rope attached to the piñata tightened. The thing was hooked to a pulley secured to the branch. It took two of the dirty farm's studs to lift it into the air, its crinkled legs dangling.

Ambrosia, the girl everybody knew as Uncle L's

darling, was blindfolded first off out of all the other
kids. They gave her a rusty club from a pack of irons
somebody found in a trash pile. Ambrosia was spun
'round by Windstorm, and let go, and the child
whacked at the air, missing the piñata time and again.
Come on, you can do it, Leon was thinking, but there
was a problem with her legs. Though some called it a
disability, it did not slow her down nor stop her from
having all the fun of regular kids. One leg looked a bit
like a clubfoot leg is all, and plus she had some bow-
leg in there, nothing big or nothing. It was from a injury
of old, and sometimes she limped when it acted up.

Alas the golf club made contact. Hell yes! A smack
to drop out caramels through the bitty slit. The
children scrambled for them, and another kid was
blindfolded, given a turn, and another. They didn't
make great hits. Leon thought they should quit now
and head back to the Great House. Beacon had been
banned from the group fun. Leon missed her. She was
nowhere. This was punishment enough. Poor thing
probably watched from afar. She didn't get breakfast.
She could be hungry. Beacon needed to be brought
back into the fold.

The adults took turns with the rusty clubs, the
seven irons and sixers and line drivers. Jericho went
up and, blindfolded, smacked the shit out of that
piñata. Candy spilled out. The children grabbed it.
The piñata rose and fell tauntingly, the adults
slamming it. What fun. Pieces fell off, a leg, another,
the thing's nose, its tail, all that candy raining down
in spurts and trickles. The guys working the rope were
clever.

Potato tried, and Goliath, and then Leon smacked
the crap out of the fucker. It was Sparrow, finally, God

bless her, who knocked off the creature's belly, it falling hard to the ground in a rain of individually wrapped Twinkies, the beast's undigested contests up there now revealed: a woman bound with ropes in the ungodliest constriction, boobs hanging down, duct tape wound 'round her face, each muscle of her body straining for release, even her toes. She was cowled by the creature's battered back, but did that stop Sparrow's next blow from making contact with her cage of ribs? That would be a nope, Mack. Strained veins coursed the woman's forehead, and Leon saw bruises on her, on his Beacon!

Sparrow slammed her again, a direct clip to the tit followed by a pain-beridden "MmMMmm!" and the rope guys raised her high to cheers. They bounced her, knocking Tootsie Rolls from hidden crevices, and lowered her into the dirt and candy, her body concealed by the creature's back. The wielders of the clubs closed in. They smacked the piñata, tearing through the colorful panels.

"Stop!" Leon shouted, but they tore the shell off and with bare fists now beat Beacon upon whose body, below the ropes that wrapped her, was a word that looked like PAT or SAT. Leon pushed some Dirties aside. He squatted beside her, but somebody's club came down on his neck. His eye, which was too small and sometimes popped out of his head, plopped into the candy where it blended with colorful mints and jawbreakers, his eye another butterscotch ball or ball of gum.

Leon swung his head back. "Damn y'all!"

The dirty people quieted, and stared down at him and Beacon, their faces removed of the joy they'd possessed two seconds before.

"I told you I'd think on it," their uncle admonished in a voice not altogether in control of itself. There had been a tremble when he said that, and they were noticing now, he noticed, that his left eye was not right, that Quizzleboon's gift, the symbol of Leon's heroic sacrifice, was not where it was supposed to be, that the socket was shriveled and empty and without the thing to hide his freakhood. Their faces bore a recognition of Leon's weakness, and they seemed to be realizing for the first time that a missing eyeball could be a handicap.

Leon stood and yanked the club from Goliath.

The dirt people scattered like a handful of bbs dropped on a conical birthday cap overturned in a parking lot—they were on the *git*—only Potato, the sonofabitch, looked like he wanted to come back to talk things over. Leon lunged at him with the club. Potato skipped backwards and tripped. The party was over. Leon was left with the rat woman whose pink asshole was visible—that's how they'd tied her, so that she was like a damn hovercraft, grab her sorrel mane for a ride. While you're at it, flip the zip for the midair screw—like filling a tank with gas. Make her go fast.

With spit Leon lubricated his eyeball. He shoved it into his damn face and leaned over to untie the yellow polypropylene ropes cutting into her flesh. This would take too long, though, so he whipped up his pocketknife, unfolded it and cut her free. He cut the tape across her mouth and eyes off and pulled three or four socks out of her mouth. She said Leon's name.

"Shhh." Leon lifted her and stood there with her cradled in his arms.

"I can walk," she said, wiggling.

QUIZZLEBOON

"I know."

"I'm serious, set me down. I'm not a invalid."

"Be still, bitch." Leon didn't want to set her down. He felt strong, like the I-Can't-Believe-It's-Not-Butter man on the covers of the romance novels you stumbled across in Wal-Mart. His mother had bought them now and then, so Leon was in the know. Fabio was his name. Fabio posed as model for the covers. That's how Leon felt, strong and manly and upstanding like Fabio. Had Leon not saved the very woman who'd fed him to the pigs? He'd done did that, and could you get any more noble? He'd used his body as a shield to protect the harlot from the blows of the Dirties. Her breath washed over his cheeks to cradle his ears. Her breath was all in his face, and Leon loved life very much.

7.

Across the field to the Great House Leon carried Beacon, her dirty-ass legs and feet joggling about freely. He carried her up the stairwell to his second floor room, the greatest of all of the dirt farm's rooms, and laid her on the mattress covered over with a beautiful Navajo blanket. Then at the window Leon stared across the land, the rich greens of the Rockies back there, and the fog. He said, "You hurt me."

He said, "You made me question shit."

He said, "I was a goddamn cook for a blind man. I been chased and beaten. You were my woman."

"Leon," came the voice from the bed.

Leon turned to the apple of his good eye. Bruises had come out on her neck and face and all over her goddamn body, and her breastbone, and just about everywhere you looked ugly bruises were materializing. She was blackened, made blue, a bit some green here and there, but mostly she was the woman Leon fell for those early days at the dirt farm, his summer of pussy and love, when he'd snake her down the lush hills in the El Camino, listening to the radio, tossing back Budweisers. The sight of her brought joy to Leon's heart. He could relive what he'd lived before!

QUIZZLEBOON

"You are the most beautiful woman I ever saw."

She seemed to smile.

"And I'll tell you another thing, bitch. I told Potato I was to consult Mr. Quizzleboon on what to do about the shit you fucked up with. We never decided. Potato canceled my word. I ain't had nothing to do with this here piñata bullshit."

"I deserved it."

"Shutcher fuckin face."

Just looking at her, shit.

"I need to tell you," Beacon said.

"Save it for later." Leon stared back out the window at the Rockies. He felt spiritual.

"Come to me now, darling," Beacon said, so Leon went over and sat beside her on the bed. In a second she embraced him. Leon's innards fluttered. Wet stuff shot from the good and bad eye both. Leon watched the shit race down into her ass crack, and remembered the day of the raid, how he'd grabbed a titty to get the info. What kind of man was he? There was no excuse for it, yanking on it thataway. Was that something Fabio would do? Leon reckoned not, Scott. Leon thought brief on the cop he'd done kicked in the face. He remembered his darling, how he'd left her in the shed that day on knees in the dirt with bicycle gears and chains and wheels.

It's the coke, Leon reasoned. Without it he'd not feel so goddamned sentimental and sissyish, but fuck it. Beacon was in his arms. Watching the tracks of his emotion evaporate off her skin, he felt he'd arrived at a long held destination, a fork to require of him a decision. In this fork he considered his arms that were wrapped around his sweet love. Take the left arm, which was his water arm, he could drown. Take the right arm, his fire arm, and he could perish in flame. Which was better? The drown or the burn? T'was a question Leon oft had pondered, for his life was a magic bag of water and fire. That was the story of Leon's tatts.

Leon's first two were sketched into his flesh by his mother when he was Ambrosia's age, to identify him, she said, should he be abducted, sexually assaulted, and thrown in a ditch with his head and hands nowhere to be found. These tatts on the toodler Sandra composed while they lived at the White Lady Motel in Virginia Beach, Room 14. On the bed together, not so different from how Leon and Beacon were on the bed together now, Sandra dipped her needle into the India ink bottle. As she dabbed at his arm, doing her hand like the sewing machine, he stared pondward out the window at the ducks that were later killed by the blacks to put to their dinner tables. Leon had been afraid it could hurt, but Sandra talked him through it as he watched the ducks in peaceful relaxation on the water. Turned out it wasn't nothing but a thang. Sandra did him four more toos the next day. When she was done, Leon had six black lines, each a half inch long, on various parts of his body. The lines marked his forearms, and one line graced his stomach below the bellybutton. Another scratched the backside of his left knee. One hit the inner side of his right ankle, and the other one nobody needs to know nothing about.

Leon honored Superscrub by not covering the tattoos when taking on new ink.

And Leon wondered was Beacon might could be a third choice? Seemed possible, so he hugged on tighter. If he chose Beacon, would he sacrifice the

collective powers of his arms? Could be, but fuck it—
Leon chose Beacon's uncertain world and called it a
day. He hopped down the stairs and returned with a
rag and mineral spirits can and scrubbed the word
RAT off her back, gave her the cotton dress he'd
cajoled out of Sparrow. Beacon slipped it over her
head. It was yellow, brown stains all over it. It was
likely the ugliest dress the jealous-ass dog woman
could find.

Beautiful on Beacon though! Leon's dreams from
Tallahassee had done got true on him. Leon fingered
her nub. "Baby, it's time for a skrunk, what say?"

"That's the what I wanted to tell you, honey. I
promised myself I wouldn't do it no mores."

"Hey, don't you remember how much fun we had?
How many times did I quit? It's easy. Pop you a squirt
in the afternoon then quit come night." Leon pulled
up the sacky-do, unfolded his knife, reached in and
drug out a drag of sniff. He sucked it up his left, after
which Beacon agreed it wasn't nothing but a thang.
She took a couple snorty-doos, but goddamn if it
wasn't enough. Leon gave her the shot. They spent the
afternoon in the fuck and the deep talk, and just
generally going back and forth between those two
activities. Leon knew she was the one, so along the
way asked her to marry. She said, "I will never fuck
you again," and the Rockies went to purple and pink
in the smoke. Leon and Beacon did some serious
promising on their hearts to each other.

So many folks had entered the Great House
kitchen to cook, and they sounded curious over their
Uncle of the L, was he up there? Doing what? When
Leon up and galloped down the steps and appeared
before them, they smiled small smiles and eyed each

other, acting weird. Was Mr. Quizzleboon alerting Leon to Danger again? Was Leon too dense to hear the sirens? "Beacon and me," he announced, "are to be wed."

Some folks said, "Hey, all right," but Sparrow came in with, "Her real name's not a word you could appreciate, Leon."

Sure, coming from Dog Girl.

"Her real name's Lucy Blue and she is from Alabama."

"I know where she's from," Leon said, and remembered his own new name, his official name that was on paper, how the blind man had teased him: *Lownote, Lownote, Cliff Lownote.*

"Lucy," Sparrow said, "don't you get it? Lucy, like she is loose, like she is a little bit loosey down in the goosey for everybody, see what I'm saying, Leon? Loosey as a goosey with a load of rocks to deliver from the quarry, we got limestone quarries, quartz quarries, quarries filled with crack rocks. While you were gone—"

"Stop that shit." Leon gave Sparrow the I-Will-Kill-Your-Ass-If-You-Keep-It-Up look he'd perfected in the joint.

"Opposites attract," Potato said, him still dressed in the pink panties and man-sandals. Leon had noticed the sonofabitch as soon as he'd entered the Great House kitchen. He stood by the front door fidgeting like with something to say. Leon eyed him now like *What's wrong with you?* and Potato came out with, "I'm real glad you're getting married, Leon, but we got some pressing shit to deal with. Gay Gary was busted for liberating the death metal cows."

The death metal people, or *Gothers*, as they were

more widely known by the people of Asheville, ran the farm some three miles up the hill. They were the dirt people's biggest competitors at farmers' markets and such, and worse than that and unforgivably, the Gothers raised meat cows. Gary had snipped some wires and one cow made it down to the freeway where she was hit by a eighteen wheeler. The truck jack-knifed and the driver's head was severed in the spill. During the crime, the little black book that had a anarchy symbol on it, where Gary kept his musings, including those on freeing the cows, somehow dropped out of his pocket. Said black book was gave to the authorities, who came out that afternoon and hauled Gary away. As Gary already had several warrants on him for doing gay stuff out in the world at large, chances were he would not be back for a good long-ass while.

"I hear what you're saying," Leon said, "but ain't a man's life worth more than a cow's?"

"That's presumptuous and irrelevant," Potato said. "What matters is the Gothers are denouncing us. They posted fliers of lies around Asheville. The liars claim we polluted the creek."

"But we got rules on shits to the creek. They live upstream. How could we pollute their water? Do turds swim upstream? How is it possible?"

"They want to destroy us," Potato said.

"Nobody can't shit within two hundred feet of the creek, that's the rule, so how is it a problem?"

"It's lies, I'm telling you."

"Who took a shit in the creek?" Leon asked the folks in the kitchen, and scanned their faces. By their quiet looks you'd think they might all could've done shitted in the creek water a time or two.

"People are liars," Potato continued. "That's just how God made us, but I don't believe in God, so what am I saying? They say we work human waste into our growing compost, ignorant assholes. I'm thinking we ought to do something here. I want some payback."

Leon felt right comradely with Potato at the moment and all. He liked to see the passion, so gave the boy a pat to the back. Leon intended to do something here to help out, but first he drove Beacon to Asheville to celebrate their engagement. They danced to the drummers at Pritchard Park, now and then doing a little snorty, and Leon bought a dozen gallons of Carlo Rossi burgundy. They drove the stuff home, and folks drank up, but were upset over Gary still. They talked of raiding the Death Metal farm. Leon shot another bunch of good stuff and, feeling great, said, "Round up the peds!"

The peds of mo got rounded up, the mopeds made ready to go.

And Leon made fine display of his love for Beacon, grabbing her to kiss at every fridge door, car door, front door, back door, and whatever door. He kissed her and hugged her, careful not to squeeze into her bruises too hard, and even though Beacon had near to been beat to death by a throng of golf-club wielding bubble-butts that morning, her now-demeanor was frolicy and spruce, ain't that right, Bruce? Blame it on the quarter gram Leon busted into her vein. Such aggressions swamped a body's blood with twinkle-stars, dumped joy into the limbs and flipped the organs upside down like beef shanks to fry in a pan of olive oil, throw on some oregano and don't forget the salt. Beacon was a happy soul, her bent of the positive.

By the barn door Leon with Beacon smoked

QUIZZLEBOON

Marlboro Reds, Goliath and Tinbuck and Preston here gassing the bikes, everybody in the gather of weaponry to use against the Gothers. Carburetors dropped into socks, yes. Hey, plastic tool cases were gathered for braining. Castle came up with the idea of pulling handles off umbrellas, damn stuff the umbrellas into lengths of metal pipe, then secure them with nails hammered in there, or sticks or whatever would clamp them steady. They made great lances, but, "You should keep the umbrellas in non-rain position until we get up close," Leon said. "It's more aerodynamic."

Despite the warm night the Dirties donned coats and helmets and painted their faces with axel grease. Some wore loin cloths and others moccasins. The flock of children went barefoot and carried pinecone wands, pretending they were wood sprites. Ambrosia, the queen of the pack, wore a sleeveless deerskin dress and purple headband with eagle feathers rising from her ears—those were her spiritual antennas. Under the light of the moon they loaded into the truck bed. Leon, squashed in with Beacon and Potato and Butterfly and Jericho, drove slow behind the vanguard of moped-riding lancers. The mopeds had ropes tied to their rears, and skateboarders clung to the ropes, carving the asphalt and shouting now and then like Rebels, Indians, hopped-up preachers of the Pentecost. Everybody brandished a weapon. Beer bottles were good, wires for garroting, lengths of painters' plastics for suffocating, glass shards for lacerating. Leon's weapon was nothing other than his fist, he had huge fists, he'd broken the noses of three separate people with his fists. Leon had no qualms in breaking the noses of jerks. The Death Metaling

Gothers were probably stuck-ups. Or worse, plain assholes who cared only for their own selves. Such philosophies clashed against the principals of the dirt people. How thrilling to crank your engine uphill to wreak havoc on what could have been a whole cache of fellow farmer friends. Instead over this that they were incapable of reason, incapable of harmony, the Gothers had a beat down coming on. Though Leon enjoyed meat and ate it aplenty, he'd learned from the Dirties that such behavior was not only disgusting, but selfish and cruel. Here was Leon's chance to lay down some shit on the matter, to cram a moral down the throats of ignorant souls in need of purification, or putrefaction, take your pick.

8.

THE DEATH METAL farm loomed up. Gothers poured from the property to crowd the road, their faces studded, and the chicks wore black lipstick and mean hats, tall boots and ripped stockings and collars. Had they known of the coming of the Dirtballs? Was a spy amongst them? Leon eyed Beacon with suspicion, but "What?" she said, her face too innocent. No, it wasn't no Beacon. Leon and the moped drivers were at a dead stop here in the face-off and Leon felt damned out of sorts. He'd hoped they'd surprise the sons of bitches, storm their farm, drink their booze, steal their veggies, makes slaves of the women, let go all their cows and pigs and chickens, and then torch the place. At least half of this was fantasy, Leon knew, but the scenario had sustained him throughout their preparation and three-mile journey. Now here they were, and the Gothers held shotguns, some. Leon saw a rifle or two. A bunch of Goth girls clutched branches that looked quite beloved in their pale hands, as if these branches, or *Nigger Knockers* as Leon remembered them being called in Virginia Beach, had been lovingly cut from the sprouts of crepe myrtles or scruboak trunks—peel away the bark, sand it so it feels good in the hand.

Each time you clobber somebody, make a mark, a slice in the wood to honor your deed.

"Check out those Asian chicks," Potato said.

"Yeah, Gary was talking on them," Butterfly said. "He'd seen them through his binoculars."

"We need some at our place."

"I agree," Butterfly said. "We need more diversity. Hey, is that a Jack Daniel's shirt she's got on? I always wanted one of those."

The moped men revved their motors. The wood sprite known as Ambrosia hopped pipe to pipe, unfolding the umbrellas of the mopeders, shouting, "You good to go!" each time. "You good to go! You good to go!" Then she climbed onto the hood of the truck and squatted, a human ornament.

"Get ye ass off there!" Leon shouted.

Ambrosia shot her tongue out at Leon, then faced forward in preparation for what was to come.

Leon felt a bit of déjà vu. Was this related to the dream he'd drumpt last night? What had the Quiz tried to tell him by giving him those pitiful visions? Oh, Ambrosia helps him look for a fucking rubber to poke Beacon with, but they end up in the woods where Kind Edward with a hard-on and bleeding mouth squats like some tropical gargoyle? A cat was in the dream. Ambrosia gave chase. Then Kind Edward clenched Beacon's arms, wrenched them backward so that her boobs lifted and spread and looked near to bursting. Leon could have given those titties a delicious rubdown, but instead he just cut out her eyeball with his pocketknife. Next thing he knew he had 20/20 vision and what he saw was Beacon in the dirt with her taco lips undulant and plaintive. Was that or was that not fucked up? Blood blotched her face. Weird scabs pulsated along her thighs and arms. "You can fuck me now, Leon." Just weird!

Leon eyeballed Beacon, his illustrious bride beside him. "I'm sorry, baby, for cutting your eye out in my dream."

"You did not."

"I did. I cut it out and put it in my head and then saw like I saw when I was little."

Beacon laughed uproarious, and Leon, pleased by her happy good old self, grabbed her neck and squeezed. She'd been humbled by her recent experience as RAT, but forgiveness and recovery were the orders of the day. Things were becoming nice and smoothed over and soon there wouldn't be a wrinkle to speak of on the bed sheet of their history.

"Listen here, guys," Potato said.

Leon said, "What say, Potato man? Should we storm them?"

"They got guns."

"At's a fact. What do you recommend, buddy?"

"Why don't you consult Quizzleboon?"

"You trying to be funny?"

"No, I'm serious. We need some out-of-the-world-shit to come at us now. They're starting to walk our way. Should we retreat?"

"I could treat a few of them to some down-home retribution."

"I think we should consider retreat."

"He's got a point," Beacon said. "What were we thinking?"

"I was thinking we would slay the men and make slaves of the women," Leon said. "Didn't you say you took a fancy to them Asian girls, Potato? We got some ropes in back, what say?"

"This be pure crazy," Jericho said, and he and Butterfly got out the truck.

"I was trying to be funny," Leon said.

"Consult Mr. Quizzleboon, hurry," Potato said.

Leon closed his eyes. Mr Quizzleboon came to him in the darkness. He said, "Cliff, make you some friends." Leon opened his eye. "Okay," he said.

"Okay what?" Potato said.

"He said make you some friends, but he called me by my alias. I don't know why."

"Make you some friends?"

"It's a shame not to slaughter them, but that's what Quizzleboon told me."

"That's the plan we're going to put into motion," Potato said, and Leon looked at him. He wasn't the rat neither. His face was serene and sincere. Potato was candid as a starving orangutan that moment. Leon felt touched. He pulled out his sacky, stuck his blade down there and pulled up a bump, said, "Go head."

Potato closed his left nostril with his index finger, and snorted the pile of coke off Leon's knife tip. Was this relevant to Leon's dream? Was Leon's dream a harbinger, as they say? No, a harbinger was a person who brought you bad news. This Leon learned in lockup. This was not no harbinger, but a portent, a warning. Leon's knife could have been the blind man's dick, in which case, since Leon had been offering it, the blind man's dick, to Potato who was the man Leon suspected of possibly trying to undermine him, maybe what Quizzzleboon was trying to tell Leon is that all his marbles should be delivered into Beacon's apron. If Leon would feed any man another man's dick, Leon was and would always be

QUIZZLEBOON

guilty. That was an interpretation. As Leon thought this over, he realized that later he would not remember it, and if he did remember it, he wouldn't be able to make any sense of it at all. It was the sort of thing one thought while away on good shit. It was, whatever it was, probably true, and that was the main reason you forgot it.

"I guess we'd best try make friends with em then," Leon said.

"Should we wave a white flag?" Beacon offered.

"Great idea."

"A white flag means surrender," Potato said.

"How else we going to party with them?" Leon said.

"I'm all about white flags," Beacon said, and climbed over Potato and let herself out of the truck. She ran into the spray of moped lights, peeled her yellow dress up over her head and waved it back and forth.

"She could be a . . . let's see . . . what do you call them?" Potato said.

"Politician," Leon said.

Lucy Blue, beaten down by her own people that morning, waved the yellow dress back and forth, giving the enemy to know that they were nonviolent dirt people, people who believed in reason and love and labor and good food and good will and passion and natural tobacco without the additives. Beacon waved her yellow flag, and as she did it, Leon experienced an empathy moment, a moment in which he saw Beacon through the eyes of the enemy, a woman baring her severely bruised body with grace and feminine charm, her statement a call for the putting down of arms. Leon felt what they felt: *Holy shit, look at that!* In their shock they were paralyzed, and through Beacon understood that these folks who'd come in the night were fellow compatriots in life and, *Holy Jesus motherfucking Christ, let's run forward to embrace each other with love. Hey, how are you? Let's get some fun going on between you and us right this minute!*

Leon and Potato took fresh bumps off Leon's knife tip. "Lookiter go," Potato said. They watched Beacon flow back into her dress. They watched her grab a tall Gother fellow and hold him close with a tight hug.

"Who's that?" Leon said.

"Nobody you need to study," Potato said.

Leon jumped from the truck and Ambrosia ran up and grabbed his hand. They walked past the armada of umbrellas, and stood in the headlights observing Beacon chewing the cud with the guy she'd just hugged. The men on the mopeds dismounted. Soon laughter was heard from all quarters. Beers were popped, bottles tossed back. Goth children spilled from the trees in black jumpsuits and miniskirts, and played with the dirt kids while Potato talked it up with the Asian girls. Under the bulbous moon the drink ran steady, all that wine from the back of the long bed Chevy, and the Gothers shared moonshine, and blunts were puffed on and passed. Clouds blew under the moon. The kids drank soda pops, yeah, but in the party of things one Gother tried to joke on Gary, saying by the time he got out of jail his asshole would be the size of a coffee can. The clever dude lost his teeth for that. Leon whopped them out. It wasn't like he cared a thing for Gary. Maybe it was over this here Kyle who entered Muskegon at seventeen and Leon never lifted a finger to help. Kid had fought hard, but they broke him, and the guards too made Kyle their bitchamoly. At night he'd hear the smack so now smack sounds, not always, but sometimes, made Leon think on Kyle, and it could mess up the flow of his fucking on whatever attractive miss he happened to be drumming with his disco stick at the time. He just loved the watery sounds of smack, the ankle-spank splash of cavernous gash, call it the boomstick—not the broomstick—smash of fat-faced chicken frowns and clown gowns from Florida to downtown Detroit, Virginia, and good ole North of the Caroline. Leon thought if he got hypnotized he might could be cured of the bad remembrances of Kyle, but of hypnosis he'd never had a chance.

Right then Ambrosia tackled a little guy. Girl pinned him to the street good. In a straddle she brought her fist up and dropped it in the boy's face. Then she pounded it, busting him up, not no playing around here, neither, but for real. Darlingest warrior you ever saw, fighting for justice and equality amongst men. Seeing her frenzied, Leon's heart near to swelled with pride. When Beacon and I have us a little girl, he thought, she will be just like Ambrosia.

"Let's go, people!" Leon shouted, and the Dirties retreated, stepping warily backwards from their new friends. All would've been cool, but the dude who'd hugged Beacon back when she was a nekid social relations expert, grabbed her again. Leon took a sharp eye on it, took a few clunky leaps the dude's way. The swing he swung was way too hard, but hadn't Beacon accepted his marriage proposal earlier that day? The dude fell to the road like a toad, and Beacon hunched down beside him. She said, "Bob ain't breathing," her voice in a panic. Beacon put her mouth to the dude's mouth, was trying to revive him. At that, Leon grabbed Beacon's arm, yanked her the fuck up. He didn't need to know aught more on the situation. He and the Dirties were out of there. Ambrosia, her fist red with blood from the little boy's nose, rode squatted on the truck hood the whole way home, laughing as the warm wind tussled her hair and feathers. Now and then she looked back Leon's way as if to say *Give it your best shot, Uncle L. See if you can make me fall off.* Leon swerved, and she wailed out joyful with some damn ungodful laughter for a child.

9.

BACK AT THE FARM the Bob business was a bummer. The Dirties thought Bob dead, so Leon said him and Beacon's honeymoon started right this minute. He counted out two thousand buckaroosers, and stuffed the money-wad into Potato's palm. "For the home fires," he said. Potato tried giving the money back. Leon slapped it away. He and Beacon left the kitchen, headed for the Camaro, but Ambrosia tugged Leon's shirt, crying, "Don't leave me, don't leave me, please!"

Leon knocked her away. She hopped back and grabbed his shirt and clung, causing a scene. Finally Leon said, "Bitch!" and raised his fist to clock her senseless, just as he'd done Mr. Bob on the Goth farm. The sight of Leon's fury didn't faze her. She just said if Leon did not take her she would hunt him down and skin him.

"Skin me?"

"I'm not playing," she said.

"Bitch, how old are you?"

"That's none yer fuckin business, bitch," Ambrosia said, and Leon noticed that her fist was bloody still. Seeing the blood up close grossed him out bigtime.

"She'll be ten in December," Potato said.

"Ambrosia honey, don't make life difficult for Leon," Beacon said.

"I'm going, that's all there is to it."

Butterfly, the child's birth mother whose weird dangling clitoris currently was concealed by some silky powder blue shorts, said, "Leon, come over here a minute."

Leon and Butterfly in the darker nightshade of the willow tree talked. By the flame of Butterfly's lighter, Leon opened his billfold. He peeled out ten Ben Franks. It wasn't hush money, but Ambrosia, now that Leon had considered the matter, would make a excellent thief and all around co-conspirator in crime. She might make a great bank robber too. She was a minor, and wouldn't go to jail if caught. That had to be worth at least a thousand dollars. Leon hugged Butterfly, this woman he'd done humped six or seven times in her yurt by the creek. Then he and Beacon and the child drove down the mountain.

Leon steered the car south, Ralph, and he and Beacon bumped white off the knife in the drive, stopped for snacks and pressed the gas, Beacon here slobbering on Leon's glob of blubber, call it a glubber, while Ambrosia slept in back. At about come three o'clock the next afternoon they rolled into Indianhead Acres in Tallahassee. Leon felt pretty fucking connected, driving up to the blind man's house with his bride and adopted daughter who still wore the deerskin dress and eagle feather headband. They walked up the walkway, stepped up to the porch, and knocked.

"I hear feet," Beacon said.

"They're going to love y'all," Leon said.

The door swung inward, and Edward the kind one

stood before them in boxer shorts, so many white hairs curling out of the peehole. Looked like he'd spilled some black bean juice onto his chest. "Cliff Highnote?"

"The one and only."

"Holy macaroni and cheese."

"Cliff Highnote?" Ambrosia said.

"Hey, who's that? I don't think I know you." Edward looked down her way with his whites. "Come here, darling, let me feel you."

"He's blind, go head," Beacon said.

Edward looked Beacon's way, took note of whomever she might could be, then cast his hands out in front of him, feeling around for the child's head. When he found it he squatted and felt the face and ears and said, "I'll always recognize you by your ears, darling. What's your name?"

Ambrosia said her name.

"And this here's Beacon," Leon said.

"Yes," Edward said, and Leon felt that dagblasted déjà vu shit going on again. Edward felt Beacon's face and ears next. Made him nervous, but what could he do? That thing on reading braille off a woman's bosom, it so turned out, was no joke. Back during his days as cook to the blind man, Leon had seen it plenty. "I have heard so much about you," Edward said, and invited the wayfaring trio into his home.

10.

DRUGGIES AND LOWLIFES graced the premises. One sick-looking flat-chested woman in a unbuttoned flannel shirt shuffled the rooms as if looking for her feet. The floors were wood. It was a nice house. Bookshelves of books in braille lined several walls. And paintings painted by Edward's mother showed a lot of women standing on beaches with backs turned to the painter. It was a theme. Edward told everybody his mother drowned herself when she lost her beauty. The hard-to-believe part was the way he said she went, jumping overboard off a pleasure cruise ship bound for Jamaica.

In the couches in the back room where the TV was three guys waited for the grand moment when the blind man might, upon a whim, get them high. One guy was Edward's new cook, and the other two looked like they might kill to get high, whether person or animal, it didn't matter. They would kill the thing you said to kill, but—and this is how it went, Leon knew their type well—they wouldn't kill *you* to get it. They were tailormade obeyers. As paid surveyors they would remain, if not by their own self-administrations, then for the shit they'd been clobbered with since birth.

"Holy fucking shit, I can't believe it," said one of the three guys. "If it ain't Cliff Highnote. Shit almighty, brother, where you been?" The man stood up to give Leon a shake.

"I been doing what I been doing," Leon said, but did not shake anybody's hand.

"I hear you," the man said. It was that lowlife son of Edward Rooks, a guy who could not stay out of jail, let alone tie his shoes as evidenced by the undone laces of his spotless construction boots. His name was Don, and he was named after Don Quixote by Edward's first wife. That was way before Edward met Leon's sister in Miami. Don anyway always brought girls home for his daddy to get fresh with. "I'm selling raw meat now, baby, door to door," Don said.

"Been there done that," Leon said.

"Don't knock it, man. I been getting some good commissions. You should come out with me tomorrow, Cliff. I'll hook you up with the owner of the company. I bet he'd let you rent one of his trucks."

"Ain't my bag," Cliff Highnote said. Or was he Leon Hicks? Leon and Cliff were having something in the way of an identity crisis. Leon-Cliff made a mental note to figure it out later, then sat down in the couch and partied 'til nightfall.

Leon and Beacon and Ambrosia shacked up in the concrete basement room below the house. They lived there, the three of them, and slept together on the futon on the raised platform. It was a good place over if the cops stormed in from the back, making it so that they could not escape, the three could crawl up the old chimney into a secret compartment designed special for such occasions. They didn't talk on Bob, the dude Leon dropped to the pavement with a dirty punch, but in truth Leon feared the incident could destroy him. Was the guy really dead? Too horrible to consider for more than three seconds, tops, but he'd felt a bit of give when his fist made contact. Felt as if Bob's headbone caved in, and then Beacon telling how she couldn't get a pulse. If Bob was dead, Leon was in a whole new country of sorry. Nothing to do on it now, so be happy. His fake identity was good indefinitely. From now on, Leon decided, Beacon was to call him Cliff. Ambrosia could call him Daddy.

Good home living commenced. The parties upstairs lasted all night, all manner of pill-popping and drink, and the constant light of joints, the poor-man's high. Sometimes, though, Cliff wished Ambrosia had been dished out to some other outlaw, for he and Beacon could not be intimate with her sitting over there staring at them with her beady eyes while picking her nose or chewing on crayons and shit. Seemed they were always having to get rid of her. Add to that that she all the time kept saying, "Let me try some too." Finally, just to get the little bitch to shutup, Cliff sectioned out a line for her. Once the stuff was in her nose she smiled like, *Goddamn you, Daddy, why did you keep this from me for so long?*

On coke, Ambrosia was a freaking performer on hyper-drive. Upstairs she picked up the guitar and learned to play in five minutes. And she kept on playing the *gitter*, and for each minute she played it, she was a bit more better. She figured out chords without never having been taught nothing before on it, and made up songs on the spot. "Eat my poop said the man in the big black jacket!" she sang to the top of her lung, and "Gimme high five on the top of the hill!" Everybody laughed, but it went to her head.

Child sang the songs over and over, and clearly thought she was much better than she was in the real. "I'm'a going to be a star when I grows up," she said.

Some got to wishing she'd shut the fuck up.

"Outside it was a rain," she sang, "middle of the night was a bloy with a name."

"Bloy? What's a bloy?" somebody asked.

"A blue boy."

"Well ain't you fuckin smart. You know what a purple girl is?"

"A pearl," she said, and sang, "Pearl and the bloy was in the road one day, and they came across a dog and said hey hey hey. Then they got married but the bloy said no. I gots to go, he said, and the pearl went crybaby, and then she ate his poop."

"Pretty good," the druggies admitted. They tried making sense of her songs, but whoever understood the mind of a child? Like every star, she had a hater, one or two, but most off Ambrosia was a hit to the druggies. They cheered, and when she left the room, they were sad.

Amber, everybody called her. "Get me a beer, Amber," they said, and Amber hopped to it, ran to the kitchen lickety-like and returned with a cold brewsky in hand.

"Pop it for me, baby."

Amber would pop it, and give it up, she the best beer popper ever, everybody agreed, and for Cliff the Highnote daddy of her, the top of the can she dabbed with salt, all around the keyhole with a wet finger— *tap tap*—that's how Cliff took his beer. Already she was quite the useful fetcher, and Cliff was glad he put the cash down. This thing on the coke, though, was a bad idea. She kept begging for more, saying it wasn't fair everybody else got to do it. "I want some, Daddy, give me some," turned into a refrain Cliff got sick of right quicklike. If his first mistake was doling a snort out for her, the second mess was the next dole he did. People did stupid stuff sometimes, but goddamn if he'd not felt good all over and generous. Cliff wanted to make the world happy wherever he went, just hadn't stopped to think is all. Then come to find out the druggies were letting her suck their backblow, not only of the Mexican Sativa they had going on, but of cracksmoke. Amber was falling into some deepass druggy type behaviors, getting too happy and jumpy, or falling down on the floor to stretch all over the world, rolling over and twisting and licking the floor like folks do after huffing up a double hit of great shit. Cliff hadn't seen it himself, but he'd heard tell on it, and wasn't much pleased on the score. He kept telling Amber it was bad, even though it seemed like it was good, and even mentioned Mr. Quizzleboon, saying you couldn't hide bad shit from his all-seeing eyeball. If she kept it up Quizzleboon would punish her, and when Quizzleboon punished you, you never forgot it. When she got older she might dabble a bit in the hits of shits, but right now, she was a fuckin child, and she'd best the fuck cut it out. "You understand what I am telling you?" Cliff asked her. He was kneeling, holding her by the shoulders. She nodded yes.

"Good girl," Cliff said, and figured that was the end of it, but a day later, right after a mess-around with Beacon, Cliff clomped up the stairs into the main house. Cliff had it in mind to write a letter to his mother, but when he entered the dayroom, there was Amber on the lap of Don Rooks. What followed might have turned out better had the damn child been wearing her dress like she was supposed to. Cliff should have paused longer to figure shit out, but he'd been thinking of his mother earlier, of the men always coming in to see her. He was a bit some angry. He was high. His mood was not always stable of late. After you'd been on the wave for an extended period, you always deteriorated.

Cliff swiped Amber off Don's lap so that she flew across the room and landed on her forehead on the floor. He'd meant to be gentle, but he'd clearly thrown her with too much force. Her feet hit the wall above her. Cliff slapped Don across the face, and plucked him off the couch by the neck. The druggies stood up and shouted as Cliff set Don onto the floorboards and raised his fist up, fully intending to slam him. He would have gone through with it, that's the sad thing. Good for him, Kind Edward's cook was in the room. Harmon tackled Cliff and a huge ruckus followed, so many druggies in the mix, all of them working together to restrain Cliff, and then to convince him that he'd picked up the wrong impression. They'd told her repeatedly to put her dress back on, they all said, but Amber was a stubborn little out of control bitch.

"Well, she still isn't used to the change," Cliff admitted. "Up at the farm everybody goes around buck nekid."

"That's y'all's fault," Don said, highly insulted.

Cliff and Beacon had scolded Amber over this shit before. Damn girl would pull her dress off at the worst places, like that time they were stopped at a Georgia gas station getting a fill-up. People looked at Cliff and Beacon like they were bad parents, but the girl had the feeling for the country is all. Up at the farm, when people dressed, it was for practical reasons, to fend off the cold, or to be decorative. It was not uncommon to see a young woman wearing only a belt and sandals, or maybe she had on one of those cabbage leaf bikinis that had been all the rage for about a month or so. Leon had seen many such unusual combinations, and usually there was dirt smeared all over the her, or the him, and the dirt more oft than not was put there on purpose. They took mud baths and shit and later didn't wash it off with water like normal people might would do. Once he'd seen Butterfly about with a goddamn hula-skirt of multicolored threads banded to her clit. He'd seen dirty men in kneepads, this for to grout tiles when the mood took up, or pick wild strawberries. Of such there was so much that nothing much surprised him no more.

"Goddamnit, man, I'm sorry," Cliff told Don, but Don shook him off, called him a fucking lunatic, and everybody agreed. Somebody said, "Tell the blind man," and in a minute Kind Edward came down from his room above. Meanwhile Amber was nowhere to be seen. She'd run out of the room at the first opportunity, leaving her deerskin dress, which had bits of deer meat still stuck to it in places. Cliff figured she'd done ranned downstairs and all was cool now, but the blind man wanted to know the details. Cliff was obliged to hung around, and he and the blind man smoked cigars on the back porch. Once Cliff understood Edward was tired of the shitty habits of his son, the air between them freshened. "The right thing is kick y'all out on your asses," Edward said. "You don't smack the landlord's babychild."

"Smack?" Leon said.

"Smack," said the king of the house, and laughed

out loud, and Cliff Highnote laughed along with, even though it made him to remember the boy Kyle whose ass got smacked by convict and guard alike inside the Muskegon Correctional Facility. The guards would come in and watch, or film it, and then, acting like they were to protect him, take him off someplace private, or put him in somebody else's cell for a few hours if he was "uncooperative." It was about Cliff's least favorite thing to think on.

When they finished their cigars, Cliff went to the dayroom to retrieve Amber's dress. He took it downstairs. The room was empty. He threw the dress on the bed and went outside. "Beacon," he called into the little woods in the backyard. No answer. "Beacon, Amber." He cleared the side of the house, and saw Beacon having a smoke while leaning against the hood of his Camaro. Cliff walked up.

"I heard the yelling and screaming," Beacon said.

"Amber disappeared. I think she ran off into the neighborhood."

"Half the time that fuckin bitch makes me about sick."

"Don't make me bust you in the lip, woman."

"Oh, I love her to death, don't get me wrong or nothing, but she whines over the smallest little dumb stuff you could think up. Don't tell me you haven't noticed it. Me, I get sick of hearing it. What? You want me to be honest, don't you? Don't you remember that time she kept saying Daddy, I need lotion for my elbows when there wasn't no reason at all for her to be asking such shit? She thinks that because we're not on the farm no more she can break the rules."

"She can."

"What about that time she acted like she would cry

JOHN OLIVER HODGES

if you didn't say you were sorry for calling her a selfish whore after she done ate all the meatloaf like a goddamn animal?"

"I called her a hog, Beacon, I didn't call her no whore."

"Same fuckin difference, are you kidding me? All the while, of course, she's supposed to be a fuckin vegetarian. You told it like it was, baby. And she going around insulting everybody such as she does, all eatin her fuckin boogers and shit. That ain't no way to act. Where I came up children did not speak their minds. They did not go around licking doorknobs and talking to their thumbs."

Cliff got in the car, and Beacon joined in, and they drove slow up Kolopakin Drive, looking for Amber, and every now and then they called her name out the windows. Maybe she'd gone and hid in somebody's bushes? Children did that. Ran off to find bushes or places private from the world, where they could hate freely, and cry. "Ambrooooosia!" Cliff called.

They drove up to Bill's Mini Mart for a six pack of Miller tallboys, then rode around the Indianhead Acres neighborhood, smoking and drinking 'til dark. They couldn't call the cops, so made a quick run to niggertown and came back to the house with an eighty-buck rock. Cocaine was good, but rock knocked shit up a notch. They smoked a bunch and fucked some, then lit the kerosene lamp. Talked of going upstairs for dinner, but took a few hits instead and fell back on the bed. They had forgot all on Ambrosia, *Amber*, as they called her now, when the sniffles and sniffling came down, this breaking apart of a child's held-back cry. Sobs to followed. Turned out the bitch had climbed up the chimney into the secret hideaway

70

space. She'd been up there in the dark all the while. When finally she slipped down, face-first, she was blacked all over with soot, and wanted to get high. "Please let me suck the devil's dick," she begged.

"I'll get you high," Cliff said, "but only if you promise to quit after this."

"I swear to God, Daddy, this will be the last time."

"No, don't swear to God on me, swear to Quizzleboon. Quizzleboon's the one who's gonna punish your ass if you act up, understand?"

"That's right," Beacon said. "Mr. Quizzleboon has been known to eat children who misbehave. First he starts on their toes, nibbling them and then biting them off and crunching them like pretzel sticks and you know it's gonna hurt, don't you? How you gonna like it when Mr. Quizzleboon rips out your hair and—"

"Shut up," Cliff said.

"Just telling it like it is."

"Swear," Leon said.

"Yes, Daddy, I swear to Mr. Quizzleboon."

"Do you give him permission to hurt you in the right here and now should you not follow through on your promise?"

"Yes, he can do it if he wants, but you gotta come through for me."

"Cover your body, goddamnit. I told you about that shit."

"Oh, you told her all right," Beacon put in, and mumbled something nasty under her breath.

Amber got into the deerskin contraption. It was pretty torn up by now, and smelled horrendous. Bits of meat were still stuck to the damn thing, and that's part of why she didn't like to wear it—it was rancid, a little scratchy in places. In any case, now that she was presentable and had sworn this to be the last time, Leon loaded his crack pipe for her. Amber brought it to her mouth and Leon flicked up a flame. Damn girl sucked hard and popped the carb. Was Leon a shithead? At least he'd given her what she'd wanted. Poor thing fell smack onto the floor and started writhing. Her being so small was good for her, Cliff guessed, being she would feel the white five times more than somebody grown. In looking at her on the floor in her magic high, Cliff realized that not only was he jealous now of this, of what he saw, her experience being high, but he'd been jealous of her earlier in the smiles of the folks in the room while she'd sat to Don Rooks's lap, her tater in clear view. Everybody loved Amber, but they sure did not love on Leon Hicks here, Mr. Cliff Highnote. Could that be why he'd swiped her across the room so bad? It was possible, he reckoned, but refused to believe it right here at the moment. Just over you made connections in things did not mean that they, those things, were connected. Was Cliff gonna accuse himself of being jealous of a goddamn nine-year-old? He didn't the fuck think so.

11.

THE COKE WAS near to cashed, so Leon took a spoke with Mr. Edward Rooks, the great blind man of such wisdom and compassionate generosity and druggy knowledge and connections. Leon paid Kind Edward the money he owed from before, and Edward made the call. Cliff met the dealer in a McDonald's parking lot. It came to pass. But Leon, shit, was low in the dough department already now again. When the last flake of snow fell through the waist of the hourglass-shaped lady, Cliff Highnote would have to grow a brain cell big enough to make a dime off what he'd done paid Butterfly for: Ambrosia—*shit*, girl was a robber of a bank at the bottom of a tank, pull her out and spank her into motion, she of the song and the butter-colored hair. Hadn't she'd proved herself reliable in character? You wouldn't think it, but she'd kept to her promise, had zero desire now for the skrunk, just over that she'd sworn to Quizzleboon. Was that a symptom of youth? Cliff wished more discipline like that was his for to use. In truth she might could be scared on what Quizzleboon would do should she break her promise.

First thing was the girl needed clothes. All she had was that dirty Indian smock, so Leon tidied his beard and borrowed running shoes from Edward. He made Amber took a shower then drove her to Wal-Mart for panties and socks and shirts and a few pairs of shorts she could wear, and some dresses and a pair of cheap sandals. They visited the Goodwill and Cliff bought his daughter a bunch of other great shit. The girl had a full drobe of war now, complete with purses and a choice for stockings and all other kind of crap. Her new clothes would help her blend in with the public. As a normal-looking bitch child she would avoid detection during whatever crime spree they happened to be on at the time. They needed to be nothing sore thumb going on in their attitudes and comportment realities. They needed to be one with the world's indistinct hordes.

Now Leon—or Cliff—bought Amber her first gun from the dude who sold guns at Brother's Bar. It was a .22-caliber cowboy gun, a Hawes six-shooter with a wood grip. Nice deal. Put Cliff out a mere forty bucks. From Brother's Cliff drove Amber into the Apalachicola National Forest, where he taught her to fire, nothing more than point and shoot stuff, but she picked up the feel for it. Now she knew of the pull of the trigger, the mechanical motion, the release of sound and hurt—ga*blam*, there you go, the world gone to confetti, Freddy. For an instant the future was uncertain, but then shards formed, small islands of matter. For Cliff the world was like this a lot, a handful of pieces, each a different shape, and upon which beach did Leon—no, Cliff—stand now? The constant question. Was Cliff on a boulder in the process of crumble? Or was this thing a solid plane? Had Cliff done fucked shit up for himself when he chose his Wing over his Wang?

QUIZZLEBOON

Shit it all to Hell! The nights in the boiler room with his new family, as he drifted off to sleep, or passed out if he was too high, Leon's mind drifted back to his days in the traveling carnival, to his uncluttered youth surrounded by strippers and freaks and the wise man who identified in Leon a "carrier of the Wing and the Wang."

The wise man was Ray Orbison, bastard brother, he claimed, to the singer Roy, a expert tattooist to boot. He gave Leon the mermaid with a red eel swirling around her body. On Leon's "water arm" as Ray called it, he painted starfish and seahorses and other strange, made-up happy creatures. Then Ray did Leon's right arm, his "fire arm." After several years of working the circuit, setting up tents and rides and taking people's money and doing whatever had to be done, Leon's fire arm was a flaming chaos of cinders and devils. There was a oven with teeth, and a slovenly woman with flaming hair, she tortured by demons with sharp fingernails and steaming pustules. These images of water and fire would balance Leon throughout life, Ray told the young man, and spoke of the opposing forces of the universe. If ever Leon got to feeling feverish, he could summon the cooling properties of his left arm, and vice versa, if Leon felt undone emotionally, he could call on the powers of his fire. As a carrier of both the *Wing* and the *Wang*, Leon might even, Ray said, heal people of diseases like sickle cell anemia. First, though, he'd need to access the power. As such powers did not come with instruction manuals, Leon needed to search the shit out inside his body as well as the world at large. "Through trial and error," the wise man said, "you can find the control room. You might get lost a bunch along the way, friend, but once you get the knack of using them powers, I don't know but that nothing you ever wanted won't be yours to have."

Cliff and "the Amb" as the druggies now called Amber, went out a good bit the two of them only, here while "The Beac," as nobody ever called Beacon, hung back for the in-house highs. In the byways of their new city life Cliff taught Ambrosia the tricks of the pickpocket. At the Tallahassee Arts Parade, women with open purses teemed the sidewalks, simply teemed them. When Cliff bumped into them—*Oh, excuse me*—Ambrosia, just some dumb kid stumbling about, plucked their wallets. Cliff slipped them one by one into his camera bag. The girl was quick in her craft, a natural thief, the sly one, plucking her clovers and flowers.

Ambrosia one day told her daddy about that goddamned Bob character. Goth Bob had been lovey-dovey, she said, with Beacon during the time he'd cooked Kind Edward his favorite meatloaves and whatall—that's what that whole ridiculous scene was about, why Beacon had dropped down to give mouth-to-mouth, and why the three of them fled North Carolina. Course, none of it would'a happened had not that one dude poked fun on Gary's asshole, saying it was to look like a coffee can. That Gary's asshole had dictated the course of Cliff's life bugged the fuck out of him, but what could he do for it now? The whole thing was a loose end about which Cliff cared not to dwell.

Instead Cliff spent his energies teaching Ambrosia more tricks, how to categorize people through their weaknesses. Take the lowdown characters to visit Kind Edward's day to day. They could be divided into three types: Never-Coulds, Might-Coulds, and Definitely-Wills. Beacon was a Might-Could. Might-Coulds were what most of the world was made up of. Unlike Never-Coulds and Definitely-Wills, Might-Coulds had the power to choose. Though not nearly as dangerous as the Definitely-Wills, the Might-Coulds were still to be looked out for. Quite often you came across a Never-Could. Those were life's sad sacks, hopeless individuals, the easiest to identify, but also the most potentially dangerous in that they had nothing to lose. Kind Edward's son Don was a Never-Could.

12.

CLIFF TREATED THE druggies to a huge crack cache to make up for his crazy blowout with Don Rooks. The druggers acted grateful, but in their hearts, Cliff knew, they would not forgive. They eyed Cliff and Beacon cornerwise, no longer begged Amber to play guitar and sing of pearls and bloys. Their noons were imbued by long silences broke here and there by the muffled peeps of bluejays, or the flick of a lighter, a hacking cough. Sometimes clipped conversations disturbed the quiet, or Cliff heard footsteps cross the hardwood floor. Cliff hoped this downer was merely the see of the saw, that the rhythmical seesaw of life would lift the other way soon, and things would return to how they were before he'd slapped the crap out of the landlord's son. Cliff should have been more prudent, more civilized. Slowing down on the coke might help. He should also, he told himself, make a effort to give Beacon "more space," which she complained about not having enough of of late. He could also take better care of the Amb.

Cliff needed to get his family away from Indianhead Acres is what he goddamn needed. Cliff's dream of buying a trailer out in the country where they could live the good life, just the three of them on a hundred-acre plot of land, was not so farfetched. They would raise chickens and goats and grow veggies and Amber would be home schooled. Cliff had talked to Kind Edward about giving Ambrosia the last name of Highnote so she could take the school bus and go to school like a normal little girl, but it was a no-go situation since the real Cliff Highnote, the one who'd been murdered in Colombia, had no daughter. Even if the real Cliff Highnote had had a daughter, they'd have to go find her and kill her so that Amber could take her identity. Either that or find some other Highnote daughter to slaughter. That was the only way Amber could take her "Daddy's" name, Kind Edward told Cliff, and laughed good and long.

Oh, their trailer would be far enough away from the road for Amber to play in the woods, nobody seeing her. Cliff would purchase a tractor for Beacon, and for himself build a barn where he could lift weights in the middle of the night while it rained. Cliff was about sick of not getting in the good lifting he'd grown accustomed to in the cooler. Pushups and situps didn't do jack, and besides, who could work out in this environment? In front of all those no-good mugs? They'd sit around making fun on him, and he'd have to bust somebody's chops.

Oh, it was a happy dream, a vision of domestic life into which, sometimes, Cliff oft inserted his mother, Sandra, who still lived in Virginia Beach, as far as he knew. Though he did not know her actual address, he'd been assured that the letters he sent to the White Lady Motel, where he grew up, would be forwarded to her. She was a much better cook than Beacon. Cliff hadn't spoken to her for over four years. It was his sister who'd informed Sandra of her son's incarceration. Sandra knew all about it, yet not once during his time in prison did the *super scrubba dubba lubby woman* send him chocolates or smokes such as happened for other inmates. Cliff didn't wanna criticize her, or be selfish by wishing she'd given him some attention during his difficult time inside, but didn't he write her three times? How many affections did he get back? Was the grand total in the zeroes, Zack? She was still pissed over Leon confronting her on his eyeball, is what he gathered, but she could fuck herself up a river to the place of hungry buggery muggers and maggots. All he'd wanted to know was what happened to him, so go scrub your ass out a toilet, beeeitch!

A wonderful dream. Thing is, Cliff had done jumped off the money cliff. The green from the Tallahassee bank ding—no *dong*, no *dang*—what he'd socked a woman's face on, was gone, spent, burnt, about squashed down in dirt by some-ass-body's big thumb. Cliff's dream was no dream he could reach for, wrap his manly hand around, and clutch to the breast. Soon Cliff and his charges would be expelled from Kind Edward's castle. Thoughts of them in the streets with no place to go, winter coming on, irked. Could they sleep in the Camaro? If shit got bad they could con it into the homeless shelter, but Cliff—no, he'd been Leon those days—had done time in the ways of the aimless. He knew the hand-to-mouth life of sunshine on benches, of drained minds and baloney sandwiches sucked ass. In its think he saw his future through the eye of the Quiz, not a actual picture but a feeling of bad breezes and pointless stale cheeses—Jesus! Cliff Xed the feeling out, and when Kind Edward sent a note down to the kitchen via Harmon the cook later, a note for Cliff, Cliff thought this was his eviction notice.

Leon carried the sealed envelope down to the boiler room where Beacon and Amber played cards, bored out of their minds. "I think we're being evicted." Cliff flapped the envelope.

"Is that from Kind Edward?" said Amber.

"His words has come down from on high. After all I've done for him, you'd think he'd show some respect, tell me to my face."

"That son of a bitch," Beacon said.

"Edward's maw, from what I remember, was a artist, rich, a influential society woman who sacrificed everything to join a band of gypsies."

"I don't care who the fuck Edward's maw joined. All you got to do is look at Edward and you know his mama was a piece a shit."

Cliff's impulse was to bang Beacon over the top of her head with his balled-up fist, slam her into the floor as if she were a steel cut masonry nail. That filthy mouth on her could be hateful and ignorant to the hilt. "I'm not gonna comment."

"Oh, are you making suggestions? Do you not even remember what I told you about a hundred times already before, that I completed two years in college? That I've been to fifteen states in the union? Here is a woman who has traveled around extensively in the University of Life. What have you done, motherfucker?"

Cliff slapped her.

"She deserved it, Daddy," Amber said. "Don't feel bad about it. She deserved it. I don't think you should put up with lip like she was giving you."

"Amber's right," Beacon said after a moment. "I

need me some blow, baby. You know how I get when I'm trying to quit. I turn into a goddamn monster woman."

Cliff held his hand out to her and she took it, and Cliff sat on the bed with her, and Amber came up close and Cliff opened the envelope. An old electric bill was folded inside, and to the other side of the bill was wrote: *Come upstairs ASAP, I need to talk to you.*

Cliff kissed Beacon on the lips, and gave his daughter a squeeze to the shoulder. "Keep your fingers crossed for the next ten minutes," he said, and grabbed his nickel-plated .35 from under the pillow. He pulled the back of his shirt out of his jeans where it was tucked in. He unhooked his belt, stuck the gun back there, tucked his shirt over it, then cinched his belt to the new notch. If Cliff bent over, or if somebody stared, they might see the gun, but the gun was merely a security, Shirley. As Cliff stepped up the stairs for his meeting with the King, it wasn't like he had it in mind to splatter the man's brains against the wall. The means would be there is all. Was Leon, or Cliff, or whoever he was, psycho? That would be a great big negative, Milo.

Kind Edward was a gracious dude. He'd been generous with Cliff throughout his troubles, and he always listened and was funny. He was about the smartest man Cliff ever met, and Cliff knew that as soon as he lifted his fist to knock on the door, the door would open. That's how it was with blind men—they saw the world through their ears. Even Cliff, after he'd lost his eye, way back when he was little, trusted his ears more. That part of his life was most faded, but he remembered the shift, where the ears picked up the slack of the lost eye. Kind Edward said a new sense kicks in, that when a guy goes blind, a big bubble surrounds him to where if somebody breaches his private space, the bubble pops. It's a great system of awareness and can be trusted so long as you're not too wasted.

The door opened. "My friend," the blind man said, and Cliff entered, and the blind man closed the door behind them. "I want you to steal a monkey."

"Is that a metaphor?"

"The monkey's on exhibit at the Florida History Museum, you know, where they keep the bears and snakes and mock slave quarters and shit for everybody to come marvel over? It's a special monkey. Barney. He's on loan from the Nicaraguan National Zoo in Managua. He was found in the Caribbean lowlands. A specialty albino type of monkey."

"Albino?"

Kind Edward said Barney caught the eye of a rich dipshit who'd once been a congressman in California, and was sometimes made fun of for having written a bill that made it illegal for guards to have sex with inmates in the California prison system. Behind closed doors it'd been known as Butler's Butt Bill, or the Tripple B. The ex-congressman was retired now, Edward said, right here in Florida. The dude had been a client of Edward's during his Miami days and, okay, he had a thing for albinos, what could you do for it? "I'd hire my son," Edward said, "but you know Don. If he was caught he'd lead the fuzz straight to me. I said, here is a job for Highnote. Cliff Highnote is already wanted by the law. By what reasoning would Cliff screw me in my butthole? He'll be great."

"I've never stolen a monkey."

"It'll be fun. You'll be paid."

"How much?"

"Twenty-five mothers."

"Is it possible?"

"I told you, it's a valuable monkey, didn't I say that?" Edward grabbed the collar of his showy Hawaiian shirt with both hands. He ran fingers down the slits on both sides, the moss of his curly white chest hairs wiggling like custard.

"How big is the monkey?"

"Let me ask you something, Cliff. If I was an albino, what would that make me?"

"A blind albino."

"No, I'd be an al-blindo." Kind Edward laughed. Was it funny? Cliff couldn't tell, but he laughed along with Edward, who threw in the words "Al Pacino" a couple of times, comparing himself to the Al in *Scarface*. That hundred-acre plot of land Cliff had studied on seemed more feasible now. All Cliff had to do, Edward said, was get the goddamn monkey, take it out to Coon Hill where an old hunting lodge sat in the forest like a barren woman. A week later, if shit looked cool, if shit looked like they would get away with it, Cliff was to deliver the monkey to Congressman Butler's mansion east of the city. That's all there was to it: an albino monkey for twenty-five grand.

"You got a deal, brother."

Cliff told Beacon and Amber and gave them to understand that the "caper," as Cliff was calling it, was their golden ticket. No words of it could be breathed to anybody. If all went well, they'd soon split Indianhead. Cliff drove his family to Barnaby's for pizza that night, and afterwards to Wal-Mart where he bought three watches, three flashlights, a leash, a dog collar, a pair of binoculars and some granola bars.

13.

PLANS HAD TO be made, details figured out for the caper to succeed. So Cliff dropped his family off at the entrance to the Florida History Museum where the albino monkey was kept, then drove around the perimeters taking note of access roads and the general layout. When he picked his wife and child up from the front of the museum exactly one hour and ten minutes later, he had some ideas, his best being to park at the Seminole Reservation, then row across the lake in the purple canoe he'd seen in the backyard of one of Kind Edward's neighbors, entering the museum grounds via the swampy shore.

"That's where the bears live," Beacon remarked, and a string of drool seeped out of her mouth. She was breathy, thinking on it. "Amber and I walked all around back there and we saw the whole exhibit, from the panthers and the bears to the goddamn cows and mules. I'm telling you, there ain't no way to get in there by boat. I ain't walking through no forest of bears."

"They got foxes, too, Daddy, and these cute-ass ducks."

"I saw the bears," Cliff said. "And I saw y'all walking around back there. The bears were in a fully enclosed pen. Did you think that bears could not swim? Would a place like this leave the pen open in back so all the bears could get out and do whatever they wanted? Sometimes you amaze me, Beacon. I think we should row in, and after we get the monkey, we'll just row on out like nobody was ever there but maybe a moth who come in the night to leave droppings nobody but a crackwhore like you would note."

"Aw, Cliff, I done insulted you again."

"We can't have negativity going on in this caper. We got to keep our minds glued to the basics and not get eager. That's what many a man did wrong to get thrown in the pen. If all you see is the prize, your securities blurs. That's when cops nab your ass."

"You ought to know," Beacon said.

"Damned straight."

She was afraid is all. When people were afraid they fucked up, so it was up to Cliff and Leon and Mr. Quizzleboon to provide the proper perspective here. Cliff asked for particulars, and Beacon explained that Barney was not all white as expected, but more of a bright orange color. "And he's sooooo cute," Amber said. They determined that he was kept at night in the glass building that had a trap door to a larger outside place where he could climb trees and stuff. A camera was trained on Barney's cage area from across the room. The glass doors to the building were thick as ham sandwiches. Beacon didn't see how they could break through them, but the tall glass windows along the walls were another story. Beacon hadn't seen any electrical wires running along the edges of the glass, so the place didn't appear to be rigged with security alarms.

QUIZZLEBOON

On the night of the crime, before they set out from Indianhead Acres, Cliff told Beacon and Amber that at some point Mr. Quizzleboon would come down from the moon and possess him. It had happened when he'd robbed the Tallahasee bank, though that time he'd worn a disguise. Did the disguise have aught to do with Quizzleboon taking possession of his motor skills and thoughts? Cliff could not say for sure. Best answer was said possession occurred over him being a carrier of the Wing and the Wang. In any case it seemed to Cliff that it might could happen again, and if it did, his family should be forewarned, and able to see it as a charm, and not get scared. All it would mean, Cliff said, is that Mr. Quizzleboon, through the greater vantage point of his all-seeing eyeball, wanted to keep them safe and help them succeed, for Mr. Quizzleboon took care of shit. It was Mr. Quizzleboon, after all, not Leon or Cliff, who'd slumpt his fist into the bank woman's face at the Southern Trust, dropping her onto the thin lobby rug. Leon reasoned it was Quizzleboon's payback for the eye Leon sacrificed for planetary goodness. If a dude cut out his eye for you—no, not just for you, but for all of mankind—wouldn't you owe him a shitload of favors? It made sense, didn't it? Beacon and Amber nodded yes, yes, it made sense.

Beacon was alarmed, though. She'd never met Mr. Quizzleboon. Amber picked up on Beacon's stress and was unsettled by it. She said, "What if Mr. Quizzleboon says I want your eyeball too? What should I tell him, Daddy?"

"Tell him you'll be fine with what eyes you got, thank you."

Cliff drove them past the airport and they

switched onto a dirt road dead-ending a quarter mile into the woods. Cliff pulled the purple canoe off the top of the Camaro and they dropped down to the water and got into it and paddled through the moonlight. About halfway across the lake, Leon felt the connection coming on, a tingling in his arms. His face started to twitch. He told his family to hold on, he was giving his mind and body over to Mr. Quizzleboon.

"I'm ready," Amber said.

"Go ahead," Beacon said.

Leon held arms up towards the moon and on came the calm collected feeling. He was Mr. Quizzleboon, and he said, in a much deeper voice than normal, "Monkey see, monkey do, monkey where are you?" and paddled them into the cluster of cypress trees rising from the water like so many monster boobs of the high-flying nips. Past the bear pen they paddled on over to an open place. He helped the ladies onto dry land and they walked up to the wood walkway that led through the woods. Here they took a moment to pull the paper bags down over their heads. As they made to the museum building where the monkey was, Mr. Quizzleboon watched himself through the eye that was his own eye up there on the moon. They arrived at the building for traveling monkey exhibits. Mr. Quizzleboon watched himself pluck a railroad tie out of some woodchips. The tie was being used as a boundary to mark the trail, how convenient. Being all-seeing had its advantages. Mr. Quizzleboon speared the glass wall with the tie, and the wall shattered, a great big rain of broken ice and diamonds. A few large pieces, weird triangles fell, razor-tipped slabs that could chop your arm off, looked like, but mostly it was hailstones, clarified shale shaped like the bits of a child's geometric puzzle. T'was very beautiful and worthy of pondering, but the Quizzleboons, wearing their paper bags, made careful progress over the border, lifting their legs up high so as to avoid the stuff that could cut.

Once in the room, they spraypainted the camera lens like robbers in movies do. Leon's eyeball recorded it from way up high on the moon, through tar and timber, yes, Amber—she had to climb onto Quizzleboon's shoulders for this. As Amber sprayed the lens, they heard the monkey grunting, going: "Ahwr ahwr ahwr ahwr."

"Monkey see, monkey do," Quizzleboon said, and Amber slid down his back onto the floor, and they shined their lights into the pen where the monkey lit up in triple beam, the first thing to note the small pink valentine-shaped face around which silky-looking Dorito-colored hair shot. Mr. Quizzleboon was relieved to see Barney wasn't huge like no gorilla, or one of the larger monkeys, an orangutan, say, or chimpanzee. This little orange dude was real monkey material, twenty pounds tops with a long-ass bushy tail to coil around the branch he was perched on. Looked kind of grumpy, and Mr. Quizzleboon guessed he'd look grumpy too if orange hair grew all over his body.

"Ahwr ahwr ahwr ahwr ahwr ahwr ahwr," the monky said speedily from his makeshift branch, his head jerking up and down with each bark.

The monkey looked curious. The glass wall Barney saw fall was a first. That wall was a shawl to bar his freedom, and evil. Now it was gone. Unless monkeys can't remember shit good, in which case the joys of the jungle with vines and rain and delicious bugs to eat may well have been rotted meat, nothing to think on for a monkey, Barney could'a been right happy here at the moment and shit. Barney seemed to know something good was going down.

Quizzleboon snapped his fingers. Beacon handed him the bolt cutters. Starting close to the floor, Quizzleboon clipped through the wires of the cage, opening up a square through which Amber could fit. She crawled through. Beacon handed her the leash and collar and she stepped over to the monkey who seemed very happy now that she was coming his way. The monkey jumped onto her from the branch, and knocked her down. When Amber reached up and put the collar on him, he seemed perfectly pleased. "Come along now, Barney," Amber said, and he followed her on all fours. Amber crawled through the square, and gave Beacon the leash. That's when the monkey took up second thoughts, started tugging backwards. Could the monkey feel that somebody else held the leash now? Beacon handed the leash back to Amber and the monkey relented, and crawled on through and jumped onto Amber's waist and clung. Amber nearly fell down again, so Quizzleboon grabbed her and carried her across the poking-up glass places while she held the monkey. Barney seemed to know that he was being stolen. It was a repeat of what had happened back when he hung out in the forest and shit.

They made it to the canoe, took the bags off their heads, and paddled back through the cypress trees. At about the time they reached the lake's middle, Mr. Quizzleboon said, "I'm going to head on back to the moon now, y'all."

"Wait," Amber said.

"What say?"

"I'd like to go to the moon."

"Ahwr ahwr ahwr," the monkey said. Damn thing sounded like a growly type of frog, just a whole bunch louder and more persistent.

"Talk to Cliff on it," the *Boon* said, again in the strange deep voice, and now Cliff came in with, "Holy crap."

"Oh, Daddy, thanks for coming back, I was afraid."

"No you wadn't," Beacon said.

"Yes I whas too."

"Looks like the Quiz came through for us," Cliff said.

"He was nasty, Daddy."

"He got shit done, just like you said he would," Beacon said, and they reached the other side of the lake and pulled the canoe up the bank and Cliff secured it to the Camaro's roof and they drove away. Leon wheeled the car south onto Capital Circle and drove them into Woodville, the monkey staring out the windows at all the cool stuff passing by. It was amusing to see the monkey's head turn, but the damn thing was stanky. Up at Natural Bridge Road Cliff turned left. Some five miles later, after passing the Saint Marks River and the monument marking the South's last victory against the advancing armies of the North, he pulled onto a sand road that led to the place called Coon Hill. The road was blocked by a cattle guard. He parked and got out and used the key Kind Edward gave him for the lock. He pulled the gate back, drove through, relocked the gate, and they were home free. Cliff drove another quarter mile, and turned, turned again—it was a maze back there—and he turned several more times until the cabin with its rough planks jumped out of the dark.

They'd come out earlier to ready the place. It had looked spooky then, but now in the Camaro's headlights it looked damned haunted, thank you Kind Edward. Upon handing Cliff the key, the king had told Cliff's gang a tale of "Southern Discomfiture," as he called it, where one of a group of five hunters took on the spirit of a Confederate soldier who'd died badly during the Battle of Natural Bridge. Said fellow blown the others to bits in the cabin while they slept, the first *blam* waking the others, but *blam* and *blam*, the others got it too, the whole place busted up with brains and blood, and the blood soaked into the floorboards to where it was down in there still, you could be sure. In the morning the hunter who'd been possessed, the one who'd done the killings, remembered everything and turned himself in to the Wakulla County Sheriff's Office, saying he'd killed his friends because "they crossed me over the breastworks." The interviewing detective pressed for details, and later described the killer as a decent kid who fell intermittently into violent fits of raging hatred, screaming "War is hell!" and "Stop it, you scoundrels!" Seasoned tough-guy hunters, Edward said, were afraid to sleep in that cabin, but fuck the dude to hell. They'd done a good-ass goddamned job stealing the monkey, and Cliff looked forward to spending a week in the woods with nobody to deal with but his own fucking family—and the monkey.

THE CABIN WAS a room with bunks, and another very small bedroom sort of thing, and there was what might be called a pantry that had a door to open and close. The main room sported plywood counters with cabinets above them, and upon the counters stood four kerosene lamps that looked to have been made before the invention of the hydrogen bomb. "God said let there be light," Cliff said, and lit a lamp, and another lamp. He lit all four lamps.

Barney still held tight to Amber, his long orange tail coiling down around her club leg. "Maybe Barney would like to run around a little bit now," Cliff suggested. "I bet he'd like to check out his new home. It looks a lot better to me than where he was living."

"Hey Barney, come over here." Beacon snapped her fingers from across the room.

"Ahwr ahwr ahwr," Barney said.

"Oh my God, he loves that girl," Beacon said.

Cliff peeled the seal off a new 750 ML bottle of Jack Daniel's. "I don't suppose he wants any of this," he said, and laughed a good one. He unscrewed the cap and tossed some back.

Then Beacon took a chug-a-lug.

"Look," Amber said, "every time I try to put him down, he won't let me."

"Oh, that monkey loves her," Beacon said.

Amber sat down in one of the chairs, the monkey's butt in her lap now, his hands clutching her shoulders.

"That is one ugly-ass monkey," Beacon remarked.

"Hey, don't say that," Amber said.

"I never heard of a monkey who knew how to speak English."

"He might not speak it, but he can sure-ass understand it."

"I told you about that ass business."

"She's right though, darling," Cliff said. "I can't barely stand to look at him."

"What he looks like is like he needs to have his balls cut off," Beacon said.

"We could just get him some pants."

"Smart girl," Cliff said.

"Every place on him's got fur on it but them balls," Beacon said. "That don't set right with me, and what's more is they look identical to a human man's balls. I don't take to the sight of it."

"Stop saying stuff." Amber ran her hand over Barney's head. "Don't let them tease you, my baby, it will only bring you pain and suffering."

Beacon laughed at that and Cliff laughed. It was funny how Barney acted like Amber was his mama. Cliff knew he would never stand for a monkey hugging him that way, albino or no. Amber looked like a mama in miniature.

Beacon lit a joint of some regs, puffed it a bit some extra heavy, then passed it to Cliff who puffed it light, thinking the room looked mighty spooky. At least they had water, though, and food supplies, including a lot of bananas for Barney. They had sleeping bags, and everything they needed, though Cliff thought back upon the barbells he'd left in Indianhead Acres. How could he have left them, here what with them going to be here a whole week? He'd have to find other shit to lift. Maybe he'd drive into town to get the fuckers. It wasn't like they were incarcerated.

"Here, gimme that monkey. I believe we need to get to know each other," Cliff said, and stood, and the monkey looked up at Cliff through bright fiery eyes that said *You stay away from me!* When Cliff reached his hand the monkey's direction, the most awful sound emitted from its mouth. It went: "Hgough Hgough! Hugga!"

It was the awfulest damn sound, louder than anything that small should be able to make.

Cliff started to back off, but the thing went, "HgoooooAHHHHhhhhh!"

"Goddamn that motherfucker!" Beacon shouted, and put her hands over her ears.

"HgOOOOOOOOOOOOOOO!" the monkey howled, but it wasn't no howl. Sounded more like a growl mixed with a vomit impulse, and the sound kept on going. "HGUUUUUUUUU," and the monkey's body was all rigid and strained. Barney looked to be trying to puke his stomach up, and then when he ran out of breath, the hideous noise continued when he inhaled, not so much as a pause here between the in and ex of the hale. "HgUUUUUUHHHHHH!"

"Shutup, goddamnit! Shutcher fuckin face up!" Cliff screamed at him, but Cliff's voice was no match for Barney's.

"HgooAHHHohhooooo!"

"Tell him to shut the fuck up!" Cliff screamed at Amber. He hoped she would hear him.

"AHHHHHHHHH!" the monkey screamed.

Cliff clamped his head with his hands and sat down to exchange knowing looks with Beacon: *Thank the blind man for this!* Kind Edward was probably sitting up in his high tower above the druggies, giggling to himself right this minute, thinking *Oh, boy, oh, boy, Cliff Lownote is sure up to his neck in it now, oh yeah, ha ha ha!*

When the monkey finally cut his racket, Cliff pulled his hands off his ears to say, "Listen here, don't think this is a habit that I am going to tolerate. Next time you do that shit I will smack you." Cliff gave Barney's pink-ass squinchy face a look of, *I know you understand me.*

"Damn monkey's a trip!" Beacon said, and accidental sucked spit down her throat. The spit went in her air tube instead of her stomach tube to cause her to cough. Her coughing turned to laughs.

"Calm down, Jesus, Beacon."

"You scared him is why he did like that," Amber said.

"Hey, I'm sorry if I scared you, monkey." Cliff put his hand out for a shake. Barney did not shake Cliff's hand, but Cliff sorta felt the monkey's hand in his. Cliff shook the air and the monkey and he seemed to have a understanding now. When Cliff stood up to step out to pee off the porch the way big dogs do, he looked at Barney like, *Don't you even think of trying to escape.*

Cliff and Beacon could not get close to Barney without him acting like he would start his monkey business. Therefore, the monkey slept in the bunk with Amber, all up inside the sleeping bag with her and everything.

Next morning, about 6 a.m., Cliff awoke to the monkey's bullshit. Old Barney had jumped onto the counter by the window where the morning light crept in, and was barking as if to get a message through to the other side—"Haoof! Haoof! Haoof! Haooof!" just loud as a motherfuck, and then, once again, the sustained grind came on, what sounded like a metal pipe scraped across a wall under an overpass, and put to microphone. Everybody was up now. Cliff would have grabbed Barney by the neck but he looked like he couldn't help it, poor thing. Something was in him. Barney, as far as Cliff could see, was a Definitely-Will, had no choice in the matter. Cliff felt compassion for the fucktard. All Barney was doing was what Barney was born to be doing, yet here Cliff was trying to think he was being a bad monkey.

Cliff put on boots and left the cabin to see was it so loud outside as it was on the in. Barney seemed to got a extra bone in his neck, some kind of crazy device to rattle and explode and make the sounds he made louder. As Cliff walked away from the cabin, the prolonged howl switched back to the bark. Cliff ran up to the tree line to get a check on how the sound traveled. He listened a bit then sprinted back to the cabin to shout, "Goddamnit, Amber, get him!"

"He peed on me."

Cliff couldn't hear her for the noise Barney made, but he read her lips. "What you waiting for, bitch?"

"Okay." Amber got out of her sleeping bag and went to the monkey. When he saw her come up, he stopped howling and latched onto her.

"That's some crazy fucking shit." Beacon lit a

cigarette. "I need me some vodka, some coffee, or some coke."

"Amber, make the coffee, what you waiting for, girl?" Cliff said.

"I got to deal with Barney."

"Don't listen to her, baby," Beacon said. "She can make coffee plenty well with that goddamn monkey on her back. He don't weigh but fifteen pound at most."

"Well, I ain't makin no fuckin coffee!" Cliff shouted, and went to the cooler and pulled out a can of ice-cold Busch.

"I never lit that thang before," Amber said. "I'll prolly splode the place. I'm scared of it, Daddy."

"There's bigger things to be scared of, child." Cliff took a long hit off his beer. When he looked back their way, Amber and Barney were looking at him like he was uncommonly cruel, or, to put it more simply, a sonofabitch.

"What I got to be scared of?"

"Nothing. Don't worry about it."

"No, Daddy, you meant it, I could tell it."

Cliff was remembering Kind Edward's laughter, and the stupid story he'd told on the man possessed by the Confederate soldier, him quoting newspapers and shit in his telling of it. Edward also knew of the Quizzleboon business, and had teased Cliff with it, saying shit like, "What does the moon eye see?" and "What would the man on the moon say about all that, I wonder?" Cliff hoped the blind man was happy, but shit if it didn't feel like something spooky going on here. Was Cliff a goddamn portal for fucked-up characters in the world, being he possessed a bit of *Wing* and a bit of *Wang*? Whenever Cliff looked at Beacon and Amber, they looked faded, like they were living in a old daguerreotype picture, washed in brown. They looked like the ones he was trying to protect his wife and daughter from, even though his wife and daughter—and the monkey now, too—*were* them, his very own family. Thank the blind man for this unpleasant experience. Cliff didn't much care to sleep on it, or eat or even think in a cooped up place like this that smelled of animals and old wood and fruit and other suspicious possibles. He told Beacon to make breakfast, and went for a smoke.

Cliff didn't like standing on the porch neither, he discovered. What Cliff liked was hanging back in the driver's seat of the Camaro, the door open. In his car he could smoke and look at the cabin and check things out and make decisions without distraction. Cliff decided the cabin was not good for him over that ever since he'd let Quizzleboon in his body he was susceptible to Daffy Duck shit. With each entrance and exit of the Quiz the hole through which such things could travel dilated. Before long he'd be a stopping post for spirits on the move. That could turn out bad if he wasn't careful, but right now what concerned him was the monkey's noise. What he'd have to do was drive to town to find some Styrofoam by which to soundproof the pantry. They could lock the monkey in there. Cliff was pretty sure that the monkey, when he started up his barking, could be heard from Natural Bridge Road.

Cliff's breakfast was a peanut butter and grape jelly sandwich. He ate it then kissed Beacon's lips. Cliff did not kiss Amber over this here that the stank-ass monkey was clutching her as if for dear life, but he snapped his fingers and said, "Teach that monkey some fuckin manners!"

15.

CLIFF CRUISED DOWN the hill and parked at Horn Spring, where he removed the purple canoe and tried to sink it but it wouldn't sink for some reason. Cliff had to put the canoe back on the car and return to the cabin where he was able to stuff it below the floorboards. His mood having soured considerable, Cliff said goodbye to the fam again and steered through the sandy maze, got lost a short spell but alas hooked up with Natural Bridge Road where he turned right. At the Woodville Inland store he stopped for a twelve of cold Busch beer then rolled into Tallahassee, passing by the fairgrounds where the carnies were gearing up for the evening. In a few days, they'd tear down the Ferris wheel and other great rides to hit another town. Been there done that. Leon drove on, but looky here, it was the bank Mr. Quizzleboon put a hurtin on only what? A month ago? Cliff was driving by the scene of the crime, sure enough, but he himself wasn't the one to commit that crime. It was Mr. Quizzleboon who'd done all that shit. Cliff wondered if he might could be trying to fool himself, rid himself of wrongdoing by passing the buck to the Quiz. He reckoned not.

Cliff eyed his eye in the rearview, and winked, a

fast black wall to slash down like the nights slashed down one to the other, then rose, ways made for bright days, what let men know they were alive. The blinks men blank in the turns of the earth were strung together—were identical: *blink blink blink*, and *night night night.* In their blinks lived things not apprehendable. That's why folks took to the psychiatric professionals for answers. In their blinks creatures washed up on beaches foamy and tangled in mysterious weeds; but fuck all that shit, Leon—*no, he was Cliff!*—told himself, and hooked a right onto Magnolia Street.

The blind man had said don't see me for a week, but Cliff needed his goddamn twenty-pound motherfucking barbells, goddamnit! If ever was a good excuse for going against a blind man's word, barbells were it. A blind man by his very condition was weak. A blind man would, by his very condition, understand the risk a one-eyed guy took to get the bells of bar back to keep up on the muscle.

Cliff parked and walked through the garden to the boiler room where a party, it here nothing more than ten in the morning, was full on fire.

"Ain't you supposed to be selling meats?" Cliff said to Don, who sat on the bed where Cliff and his family had slept throughout the last month.

"My dad said you was gone, Cliff. Don't you have some business in Georgia? What happened? The deal fall through?"

"Forgot my barbells."

The other four souls in the room were girls of the high school variety. They giggled but for one. The "one" wore large square earrings to dangle prissily from long lobes. She put the can to lips and sucked.

Her squares wiggled in her suck. When she popped the carb to inhale deep, she popped her lids Cliff's way, the lenses brown and sad and her eyes old-looking, lashes crinkled as if from the heat of yellow lighters, brows unkempt bridges over lakes of murk. In the smoke and sweet crack smell she was a vision of premature deterioration.

"I say something funny?" Leon asked the group.

"You know it, baby," Don said, it all too clear how proud he was to hobnob with *gorgeous young thangs*. The brunette to suck the hit up was a bit some flat of nose. Her long hair was done up in a bun that looked like a goddamn Cinnabon Roll, this to allow the square earrings to dangle free, Cliff gathered. He wanted her, but leaned over to grab his barbells. He said, "Nice meeting you ladies," and climbed the stairs to the back porch where through the glass doors he saw Kind Edward in boxer shorts guzzling down his glass of morning vodka. In Edward's guzzle Cliff slipped in quiet below the radar of the bubble. Edward's newest cook, Harmon, was pouring out the soak water from a pot of beans. Neither Harmon nor Edward had heard Cliff enter. When Edward set his glass on the counter he pulled the Marlboro box from his Hawaiian shirt pocket, opened the lid with his thumb and used his tongue to extract a cigarette. Cliff imagined *The Ed* tying the damn crack-smoking girl's tampon string into a knot with his tongue. It was not a made-up talent. Women druggies talked of it. Cliff wondered if after tying the knot, he'd yank it out with his teeth and slap it side to side through the air, chortling in staccato in his trademark way. It was the sort of gag Edward loved. Edward lit his Marlboro red. He dragged it and blew the smoke from his nose holes. "How's it going, Cliff?"

"Am I not quiet as the hawk? I got my running shoes on."

"My running shoes. Those are my running shoes, don't you remember? Are you gonna steal my running shoes?"

Harmon laughed. The beans he was washing were black, Cliff noticed.

"It's your cologne," Kind Edward said.

"It's oil. Beacon made it special. It's got sandalwood in it and cloves and a mess of other stuff. When it mixes with my sweat it makes a smell unlike any other." As Cliff spoke, he crunched the weights, one arm, the other arm, and so on, hippety hoppity, like Peter Cotton Tail hopping along the bunny trail.

"Cliff Cliff Cliff," Edward said, as if tsking.

"Had to get my weights."

"It's true," Harmon said. "He's lifting them right now."

"I know what he's doing, asshole," Kind Edward said, and Cliff was glad, once again, that he was not Edward's cook. Edward said, "I have to wonder what goes on in that little brainy pie of yours. I remember saying, and I quote, 'Cliff, whatever does or does not happen, you cannot make contact with me until seven days have passed.' What you said after I said that was, and I quote, 'If that's how you want it, that's how it'll be.' Now, as I reflect upon these facts, it is all too clear that you are either one, a liar, two, a sonofabitch, or three, an idiot. Which one is it, Highnote?"

"Are you sure we should talk about this with him here?" Cliff nodded at the cook.

Harmon laughed. "I know all about the monkey. I'm Edward's right hand man."

"Okay, then, well, we got the damn monkey," Cliff said.

"Did I ask if you had the damn monkey?"

"No."

"Do you even remember what I asked you?"

"I'm not a idiot, and I'm no liar unless I have to be. That, according to the way you set that up, would make me a sonofabitch, but problem is my mother is an upstanding woman."

"Okay, then it's settled, you're a figure-of-speech sonofabitch, not an actual sonofabitch."

"I just came to get my goddamn motherfucking barbells."

Cliff lifted faster, one arm and the other arm. He felt it, the heat, the strength inside him building. Cliff had more muscles than two or three Kind Edwards combined. As for Harmon, he was stringy and strong over the bike riding he did. Every day he visited the dumpsters and collected vegetables and meats. The blind man approved of it, and so did Cliff. That was at least one useful thing he'd picked up from the dirt people, that it was plain stupid to go into a store and buy food when the very same food existed in the dumpster out back. As Potato had explained it to Cliff: *That's alotta man hours gone to waste. What kinda fools are we, as a race, to work so hard then throw away the yield?* Cliff lifted, building up his muscles, *shit*—lifting always made Cliff feel better.

"So," Kind Edward said, "did that crazy spirit I was telling you about make an appearance?"

Cliff set the weights loudly on the counter and sat on the barstool across from Edward. "Why don't you knock it off on the spirit garbage?"

"Oh, does that mean you did feel the spirit?"

Edward asked, his face now lax with artificial worry, and genuine interest.

"Don't you want to know how the caper went?"

"Everything I need to know I'll get from tomorrow's paper. Did you feel it?"

"I felt something. Things go a little oddball when you quit. That's what I've—"

"I don't care about your ways of trying to make sense of shit, Lownote. Did you know that of the twenty-six Rebel soldiers that died at Natural Bridge, most were teenagers? No, I didn't think so. You don't know shit about history, so pay attention. Ghostologists have traced this quadruple homicide to a dude who'd been trying to be a hero. He'd snuck up too close to the union breastworks and was captured and interrogated and they found out his secret. It's come out through interviews and family histories. The poor kid had both sexes."

"I don't wanna hear about this," Leon said.

"Ha ha ha ha ha," from Kind Edward.

"Four men, each one blasted with a shotgun," Harmon said.

"Oh, that's not all," Edward said.

"You want an omelet, Cliff?" Harmon said. He cracked a dumpster egg into a large bowl. Already he'd cracked about a dozen. He was an eggs-pert cook. The blind man was in good hands.

"No."

"I admire your courage," Kind Edward said. "I don't think I could handle it, living out there like that, what with a violent hermaphrodite walking around sniffing for blood—"

"What're you trying to do? What is your point?"

"Don't listen to Edward," Harmon said.

"I was thinking Mr. Quizzleboon had a take on the situation. Mr. Quizzleboon records everything that happens on the earth, isn't that right, Cliff?"

"I reckon."

"But the all-seeing eye was only put into use when you lost yours, right? That means we can't see anything from way back in the past. That's a shame, but would you ask Mr. Quizzleboon something for me? I have a favor to ask. I want him to play back the time I made it with my only Asian. That was in 1981. I swear she was no more than seventy-five pounds. I still had my sight back then. Will Quizzleboon do that for me? I want him to hook it into my brain so I can watch it like a movie."

Cliff didn't know what to say, so he and his weights headed for the back stairs. "I'll bring you the monkey in a week."

"No," Edward said.

Cliff stopped. He'd never been able to walk out on the blind man, even though others did it all the time. It was not uncommon to come across the blind man talking along on some long-winded monologue to people who were not even there.

"Here's where to deliver the monkey." Edward pulled a folded-up rip of paper bag out of his Hawaiian shirt pocket. "The date and time are written on the map. There's a second house in back of the main house. That's Ex-Congressman Butler's private study. He calls it the Mutton House. That's where you're to take Barney. After that, come back here and I'll give you the cash for a job well done."

Cliff consolidated the barbells in his left grip, and with his right hand, the one on the end of his fire arm, snatched the paper from the blind man's fingers, slipped it into his back pocket.

"One more thing, Lownote."

"Huh?"

"The soldier's name, just so you know, was Opham Denyer. The blue bellies sent him back over the breastworks naked as a deer. When his fellow soldiers saw how they'd been lied to, that their friend had little boobs and was a freak from hell with a pussy, they dispatched him. The records show that his parents named him Ophelia, so when you tell the story, you can call him either name, Opham or Ophelia."

"Thank you for enlightening me," Cliff said, and hit the stairs, good to go, but paused in the crack-smell outside the boiler room. He could partake, he was sure of it, and who knew but that he could partake of the titty meat too. Cliff knew how such parties went, crack parties, they always ended up the same way, with the girls on the floor doing whatever the guys said to get another hit. With crack, once you'd acquired the taste and feeling, you pretty much made yourself a slave. Cliff had loved the face of that girl, goddamn him, and her sweet bod, but he felt sick to his stomach over the story Kind Edward had felt it his duty to divulge. Cliff passed it up, the potential behind the door, and made to the Camaro with his twenty-pound barbells.

16.

ON MERIDIAN ROAD Cliff picked a forty-rock up from a black transvestite in front of a 7-Eleven, didn't even have to get out of his car, then cut right at the fairgrounds. Here it wasn't but eleven and Cliff was headed homeward. It wouldn't do. Too early. Cliff drove past Natural Bridge Road on out past Highway 65 on into the woods where Gorch, the old cook Leon replaced the first time he was in the Sunshine State, lived in a trailer. Gorch was the one picked up in Frenchtown wearing a thong and shoe. He was trying to get his life back together after some forty-plus years of hardcore boozing and marijuana using—marijuana *abusing*, actually—that's how Gorch, who was also a Vietnam veteran and had about twenty million wrinkles in his face, put it, don't mention the pills and other drugs, the last this here crack that, according to Gorch, the niggers invented in a plan to overtake the world.

Gorch was happy to see Cliff, despite the humiliation he'd experienced when Cliff replaced him as Edward's cook. Being ousted from the Rooks Mansion was for the best, Gorch said, for how else could he stay sober? He really wanted to clean up this time, not temporarily such as was the case each and every other time he'd tried to clean up, but for forever so that when he died not the slightest smidgeon of drug residue would be found hiding out in some tiny little air-hole in his bones. Gorch wouldn't allow people to step inside his trailer if they had beer and weed. It was a plan, and Cliff wished Gorch well on it. He hung out with Gorch until noon, at which time he clipped back for Woodville, stopped at Beeps Bar for a burger and beer. While at Beeps, several ladies made their bids on Cliff. These were knowledgeable types, women who through experience could see what was coming. Good men were common in the boonies, but not great men such as Cliff. Cliff was not happy to turn them down, but he felt like a brick of gold on legs when he paid his bill and walked for the door. In sneakers, a pair of lawyer's slacks, a long sleeve shirt to hide his tats, and a beard, he was eye-candy for the ladies.

Outside the bar Cliff slipped on shades. He looked out across the highway at the stretch of bright pine forest. He wanted to return to the dark, to the beer and women's breath, the colorful jukebox playing a song by the Dixie Chicks. Outside in the sun he felt exposed. The Camaro might right this minute have an apprehend-suspect call out on it. The Camaro may have shown up the night before on any number of traffic video cameras, with a purple canoe on top! The stupidity of stopping here, of driving around Woodville and Tallahassee, of allowing himself to be seen by the general public, was too dumb for words— oh man. But maybe Quizzleboon would help Cliff out on this? The Quiz would warn him, sure. It was the least the Quiz could do, at least until Cliff figured out how to access the magic in his arms that, according to Ray Orbison, bastard brother to famous Roy, bore the powers of opposites, of heaven and hell, of ice cream and chili powder.

Cliff lit a Carleton. The traffic passed. He smoked half. He debated on should he get back in with the news, the forty-rock here burning yearningly in his pocket—*come get me, come smoke me, please, I wanna be smoked!* Cliff thought of the transvestite who sold it to him and how the guy's teeth had looked so huge and white and chalky when he'd leaned over to put his face in the window. Having teeth like that was great for selling crack, Cliff supposed. It made potential buyers think in larger quantities, but Cliff had actually wondered if the guy was a hooker. Maybe he was both? Cliff thought of the girl with the square earrings. Then Cliff stopped thinking about stuff and just got in his car. There he was, cruising north along 319, doing the speed limit. Cliff wasn't sure why, but he dreaded going back to Coon Hill. He'd made it through the gate, was driving the sandy roads now. He felt nervous, his ribcage a stew of butter and flies, or butterflies. Was Quizzleboon trying to warn Cliff of something? Was Beacon gonna betray him again? Was the ground cursed such as Kind Edward said? It pissed Cliff off a lot to think on it, the bullshit superstition type shit Cliff would not feel had the blind man not told such abominable shitbrained stories.

If I was double-eyed, Cliff thought, would I second guess myself on things I can't see? Am I filling things in too much, trying to rebuild the eye took from me by who if not one of the men who fucked my mother? Forget it. Better things to think on. What matter? Cliff wheeled by Horn Spring on up the road to the cabin, spun the Camaro's tires in the sand and revved for his minions to know the goddamn motherfucking big dog was headed their way, goddamnit, *shit*—he was driving back to his hearts.

Cliff was proud of his family—the *Quizzleboons*, he thought of them as. When the cabin fell into view, there they were on the porch in the sun, nekid and white and lounging about, the orange monkey in a squat on the crossbeam above them, chewing a banana with his tail hanging down.

"Daddy!" Amber cried, and flew off the porch for the Camaro.

Cliff parked, stepped out and she hugged him and Cliff lifted her and carried her for the shack where Beacon in flagrant womanliness waited, her back curved up against the pillar. She'd took off her jewelry, and her arms were crossed, a smile on her face, and in the lean of her to the porch beam a wiggle of pink shone in the snatch patch. It was a beacon that called him, but didn't it look like chewed-up bubble gum? Yeah buddy. It looked like Beacon had done chewed up several spearmint sticks then stuck the whole shebazzle between her legs in a sort of stretched out wiggle to tickle the fipple.

What a sight! In line with Cliff's vision of the ought of life it was. Here they were in Egypt of the bumfuck backwood, nobody to harass them. A feeling of deep red glow welled up in his brain, and he saw it, it glowing brainly like a planet flung into red heliosphere. He set Amber down and felt amiss, and blew the strange away with a brewsky with Beacon, whose hairy legs and pits he now was fully accustomed to be seeing all the time hairy such as they were in the open and shit. In some ways her hair was a turn-on, a kinky kinda thingum. Beacon's breasts had a light peach fuzz hair style here and there, and longer dark hairs grew from the annular spacejack waves blown from their nipular big-bangs. Sometimes Leon pulled the hairs. Such was his do in the now. He pulled her by the tit-hairs to the bunk bed, and there succumbed to the Bubble Yum, watermelon flavored, if you will, while Amber walked Barney. It was close enough after her period to where she didn't have to stuff the dirt in, of which Cliff was pleased, as the dirt sometimes irritated his pecker. When Amber returned, Cliff and the child bug-hunted, for could a monkey live on bananas alone? That would be doubtful, Malone. The thing'd been doing diarrhea sprays. They needed to feed the fucker some Phillips' Milk of Magnesia coming up one day in the near future, or else fix his diet up to how he'd done had it in the jungle.

Cliff in loose-fitting Wrangler jeans was barefoot, shirtless with arms out in the open, his tattoos on fine display for the Quiz on the moon, all that fire and water and the implications of what the two sides might one day, once wedded, have the power to conjure. The last thing Cliff wanted was to spark up a jealousy factor in the Quiz, but it was not to be denied—*shit*: Cliff's tats were badass, he was a walking work of art, a miracle, as Ray Orbison had prophesied. Cliff and his daughter walked up the sandy road through the pine forest.

Brakes and meadows and ponds peppered the landscape—a hunter's paradise. You could find worms and crickets here, caterpillars in the spring, but what of late October? They found a walking stick, a spider, a huge bright-colored ant. These bugs they imprisoned in a yellow coffee can—Bustello. On the bank of a green pool they saw what looked like about fifty snails.

"Oooh, I bet Barney might like those," Amber said.

"I couldn't tell ye."

"I know how to find out." Amber stepped into the slime all timid and pigeon-toed on one side over the dumb shit she'd tried some two or three years ago, jumping off a goddamn house with a opened umbrella. Stupid bitch'd thought she'd float down all peaceful like, but come to find out she slummed to earth to rip her *gracilis*, or maybe it was her *abductor longus*. That's what Butterfly said was her best guess on the situation after looking into a *Gray's Anatomy* book. Damn Amber'd done a perfect split and the shit ripped and she was took up to bed for over a month crying all the fucking time to where Butterfly about to lost her mind. She persevered, though, and said that one day, if she ever fell on a ton of money, she might look into getting the surgery for her, what some said was available for the ripped abductor condition. The good side on the whole thing, Butterfly told everybody, was the child had grown up quick. Since she had known pain, she was less likely to cry over stupid shit like so many other girls her age. One thing you could not say on Amber was she was spoiled rotten.

"Hey now, be careful not to slip," Cliff said, and she slipped onto her butt and slid down the bank to join the school of snails. Okay, it was kinda funny, but what if Amber splashed into the water and was attacked by snakes? What would Cliff tell Butterfly then? It was late in the year so water moccasins were not so active, but if a nest was down there, what then?

They would bite Amber on her nose and all over on her body. Cliff imagined Amber running through the forest with a dozen snakes burrowing into her with their fangs, not letting go. It'd be bye-bye Ambrosia. Cliff would bury her in mud.

Amber rolled onto her side and grabbed a snail. She looked in its shell, stuck her finger in. "It's empty."

She took up another shell and looked in it and reached her tongue in to see could she find it. Empty again. All empty. Amber threw the shells into the water where they floated then sank. She swept her arm across the mud, knocking a bunch over. They were all empty.

"Them snails must've wiggled down into the mud," Cliff said. "All that's left is the shells. You'd best leave the shells be for when the snails wiggle back."

"Oh no, did I mess up their houses? I'd hate to come back and not find my shell." She looked pained by the idea, and started righting the shells that she had knocked over. She was reaching out into the water with her club foot, trying to pull in several of the shells still floating out there, but this sound came in of a low-flying plane. The thing was coursing the treetops—Cliff couldn't see it yet. He didn't want to.

"Come back up here, quick!" Cliff stepped down to where the slippery mud began, and reached his hand her way. Amber stood but slipped. "Hurry."

Amber tried to stand. She kept slipping, so crawled to Cliff who yanked her off the bank. In the same gesture he slung her over his shoulder and hopped across the sandy road into the trees that were terrible trees, no place for one, or two such as the case was now, to hide from the sky. It would have to do.

Cliff set Amber in the needles up close to a scraggly pine, her back against the trunk, and sat down beside her.

The plane was above them, passing over. Had the pilot an eye out for movement or variation of color, Cliff and the damn mud monster had already been spotted, no need to hide. Or they might've been spotted the moment before, when Cliff leapt over the road, the monster's feet wiggling as if to say *Here is me! Here is me!* Was this messed up or what? At least the plane continued on its course, didn't circle around for another look, but who knew? It wasn't fair anybody could look down from the sky to take note on your business. Surely they saw Cliff's car parked beside the cabin. The plane didn't look like no cop plane, but who knew?

Cliff and Amber walked back to the sand for the can with bugs in it. Damn girl was blotched and striped half black from the mud, her face splotched, and stomach. Cliff said, "I could sell tickets at the fair. Come see the half nigger girl monster child."

Amber grimaced, showing teeth. She held up her muddy hands with fingers curled into claws.

"Only five dollars," Cliff said.

"Raaaaarah—ooooh!" Amber said.

"You been hanging out with Barney too much."

It was a good father-daughter time. They bonded. The mud on Cliff's chest did not worry him. It was that goddamn plane to ruin things this time around. Best case scenario was Mr. Quizzleboon would send down a laser beam and cause the plane to lose control as it reached the runway. Upon touchdown the plane would flip onto its nose. A propeller blade would crash though the windshield to pierce the pilot's neck.

The other people in the plane would be stabbed and beheaded and generally mutilated by the sheets of metal ripped off the fuselage, and hey there, is that the vertical stabilizer poking through Mary's chest? That would be a great big yes, Bess. But let's not keep these people bleeding in agony. A spark ignites the fuel tank and the whole thing erupts, a mean fireball to slide across the asphalt. Was it mean-spirited? The real best case scenario was the people up there had nothing to do with nothing. If they saw Cliff's car, all it was was a car, and if they saw Cliff run across the road with a girl thrown over his shoulder, all it was was a dude down there hauling firewood.

17.

BEACON ON THE porch was reading *Female Perversions*, a nonfiction book took from Kind Edward's plentifully stocked shelves. She was on her butt, her back propped against the pillar, one leg out in front along the ledge of the porch, and the other raised to form a white-edged triangle uncovered by the cheap see-through-ass purple hippy dress, what Cliff, back when he was Leon, first saw her in. Cliff loved that dress. When Beacon saw her family clumping her way mud-bespattered like creatures crawled from the Black Lagoon, she called out singingly, "Holy shit, what happened to y'all?"

Barney was beside her, leashed to the pillar. He jumped and scratched himself and went, "Hoo hoo hoo hoo."

"That monkey is a goddamn trip," Cliff said.

"I'm serious. What did y'all do?"

"I seen some snails," Amber said.

"Snails?"

"Them snails tricked me. They was laid out in the mud like come get me and feed me to Barney, but there wasn't nothing inside. They had slunk down into the mud."

"That plane made me nervous," Beacon said.

"I think them snails might'a been doing what like bears do, how when the winter comes they find someplace to sleep. When spring comes them snails will come out of the mud is what I think."

"What did y'all get for Barney?"

"Stuff," Amber said. "I don't think Barney's gonna like any of it. I think he might could be a vegetarian albino monkey. That's what I think when I look in his face." She handed Barney the coffee can. Barney sniffed it. He turned it over in his paws, or hands, more like. Damn fingers looked like human fingers from the second knuckle down to the fingernails. That's where the hair let off, and the color was too close to home for comfort. Couldn't see the damn things without making the connection. Evolution? Leon had no use for it, but Barney shook the can and thought stuff, and set it down. He peeled away the yellow lid and threw it to the side and peered in. *Bugs*, his expression said. Barney reached in and pulled out the walking stick by the tip of its ass, if a walking stick can be said to have an ass. Barney held it out in front of his eyes and was examining it, the walking stick's legs walking the air.

"Shit," Beacon said. "He's about to chomp that sucker like it's a gotdamn French fry," but Barney just watched it. He brought it close to his face and the walking stick stuck its front feet on Barney's pink nose. Barney blew on it, then set it down on the porch.

"I'll be a one-footed cat with a stick of dynamite up my ass," Beacon said. "Light the wick and watch me go meow, ha ha!"

"He might be vegetarian," Cliff agreed.

Barney peered into the can again, reached in and pulled out the furry bright orange and black ant, was it a cow ant? The ant crawled through Barney's fur. Barney and the Quizzleboons watched it.

"I got a bad feeling on this," Beacon said, and sure enough, when Barney picked it off his arm and put it to mouth, the bad of Beacon's feeling revealed itself. That goddamn ant bit, or stung Barney, whatever ants do. Barney's tongue, or the back of his throat, or his esophagus, which was the tube leading from the mouth down to the stomach, had to've been, shit, bit. Cliff wasn't absolutely sure about what that tube was called, the esophagus thing, though. In the past he'd thought it might be the vaginal tube because he'd once heard a man in prison say, "I stabbed her in the esophagus and that was the end of her baby." Cliff, later, said to a sexy short-haired woman in a bar: "I wanna stab your esophagus." The woman, after some confusion, then laughter, set him straight. Still, though, Cliff wasn't certain. Either way, if the esophagus was the throat tube, Cliff figured old Barney had been bit inside it over that he lit up like a gasoline explosion: "Ahhhhhhhhhhhhhhhhhhhh!" His wild-ass monkey voice could be heard throughout the lease grounds of the forest.

It was archery season. That's why the Quizzleboons didn't hear guns go off all day to let them know where the hunters snuck. Cliff didn't doubt that if a hunter heard that noise Barney made, he'd be curious and cross grounds in the criminal act of trespassment, thinking he could give, later, after the kill, the all-purpose excuse of ignorance.

"Amber, shut him up!" Cliff said. Amber tried to grab Barney, but Barney scurried up the pillar and took to roosting on the crossbeam, which wasn't a crossbeam proper, just a two-by-four nailed one piller to the other for to hang shit from. The monkey up there had the howl going on!

"That's it." Cliff ran to the Camaro, grabbed the roll of duct tape from under the seat, ran back, pulled out a long piece and bit it and ripped it and grabbed Barney's tail hanging down from the crossbeam. He yanked him off there onto the porch and held him down and taped his mouth shut. Shit wasn't easy over the Neanderthal shape to the head bone. Cliff had to run it up under the jaw where the orange beard hung down and around the snout, what else to call it? Even then Barney's lips flared as he tried to keep the beat of his bunk up. Shit looked disgusting, but at least Barney'd for the most part stumped his trunk funk. He tried howling through his pink-ass nostrils. Nothing doing, thank you Jesus! Cliff pulled back from the monkey, and the monkey got back on all fours. It flipped its head wigwag, trying hard to howl, but all he sounded like now was nothing to go worry over. Sounded like a damn squeak mixed with a moo from a Country Cow in a Can. Cliff was pleased to see a solution had been arrived at, only just then, to compensate for the stopped up mouth hole, the monkey's tail lifted up and out flew a shit stream to whap across Amber's foot. The loud fart sound scared the monkey so bad that he whipped his head around to see what was up back there, like was he bit by a wild pig or Florida panther? This caused the brown stream to whack Beacon's belly. Damn shit happened too fast for Leon to jump out the way, so the rank stream got Cliff's leg covered over in the good Wrangler denim.

The Quizzleboons took down into the sand quick and did what they could to get clean of the nasty stuff, all the while going, "Awww man, no way," and "That is too gross for school, bitch," and such things. After a bit, Barney quieted, but didn't look to be doing too well right here at the moment and shit. His eyes were popped out more than normal. Cliff felt sorry for the sentient creature. Barney could not relieve the sting of that goddamn ant by hollering. Hell though if Cliff was to feel busted up on it. To reassure the motherfucker, Cliff slapped his own forehead. "See?" he said, and slapped it again, slapped it, *slap slap*. Barney calmed down a little. Cliff put his finger up at his lips and went "Shhhh. Keep your mouth shut. You wanna be back in lockup?"

"He shook his head no," Amber said. "Come on now, take that thing off him."

"Sure enough did," Beacon said.

"You going to be good if I pull the tape off?" Cliff asked Barney.

Barney stared both eyes at Cliff, staring straight into his eyeball, those stares, and it was like the damn monkey knew that that was Cliff's only eye worth a shit. After more cooling down, the monkey seemed sorry for his idiot racket. To get the tape off, though, Cliff had to cut away at Barney's proud beard with his buck knife. When Baney's mouth was free at last, he rolled his lips around and, looking abused all to hell, went, "Ahwr ahwr ahwr," very soft, in the good-ass froggy-like monkey voice.

"Good monkey," Cliff said, and gave over a banana to cool his esophagus on. Barney peeled it, and began his eat, his human-looking balls swinging side to side all the while. Was that the way of the world? Give a thing a thing, a banana a monkey, or monkey a banana, and all things bow down in harmony? Cliff could not judge, but he was pleased by Barney's pleasure. "Good monkey," he said, and scratched the little guy's scalp. Barney was family, but somebody needed to clean this shit up. "Clean this shit up!" Cliff said, and Amber hopped to it.

Barney ate more bananas. Barney chewed banana while Cliff pumped his twenty-pound barbells in the sunshine by the car, a cigarette going in his mouth. He guessed they'd best head to the spring to wash off the mud and monkey dung good as could be done. Seemed the thing to do, but then what of the philosophy of the dirt people that said mud was the balm of the earth, said mud was the sweat of the planet, said mud was healthy, mud was good, mud was a miracle worker, a downer to mosquitoes, a replenisher to the skin, and Mother Nature's gift to keep your kin to a minimum? Cliff never would've thought it, but it had to be true over that the chicks that did it never got pregnant. What they did was mix rosemary oil in with it—a big pot of carefully selected dirt—we got orange dirt, we got black dirt—and mixed in other oils like pennyroyals and oregano and other stuff that they said was secret. The dirt they used was just plain old dirt, pretty much. They marked the grain sizes, and called it Dirt Control, like *Dirt Control #15*, and *Dirt Control Eu de Smoke*, and they had homemade labels that they put on the jars that they packed it in before putting it up on the shelves in the kitchen. It came in hot pink and hydrangea blue, too. They tried selling them at the farmers' markets but it never was a big hit, so they just used it themselves. The way it worked, Cliff was told, was just think if you were a sperm traveling through space in search of an egg. With the dirt up in there you'd have all kinds of asteroids and stardust to have to get through. By the time you reached the egg, which was unlikely in the first place over you'd be dead from the sharp edges of the rocks cutting you to ribbons, you'd be too tired to lick the vitamins off the egg's surface to get revived from the long journey, let alone rip off a bite so as to slide through and develop into a human being. "I mean seriously," Two-Stone had said, "imagine how big a grain of dirt is compared to a sperm creature?" Two-Stone was putting some in at the time, down in the dirt-floored basement of the great house where it was cool throughout the summer. The place was lit by Christmas lights only, and Two-Stone was plunk right there in the dirt, no problemo, Lieutenant Columbo. What Cliff loved about Two-Stone was her crazy storehouse of knowledge. She just seemed to know every damn thing, and her tattooes were also quite nice, done in black ink only. Had a theme of Nazis and Jews goin on, swastikas and all these baldheaded nekids being led to be fed the gas, German Lugers and tanks and Stars of David, her breasts done up as padlocks with identification numbers inked into the skin surrounding her coronas, the nips in the middles the knobs to turn to unlock the answers of her two hearts. Two-Stone told Leon if he ever was in a pinch, he could stuff any old dirt in there, and he'd be fine, just if he used the dirt with oils mixed in with it, less dirt was required.

The mud's black in its dry anyway had done turned to gray, and though Amber seemed fine with it all over her, Cliff wasn't happy too much on it. He set his barbells on the porch then went to the car for a red oilcloth that he dipped into the melted ice water of the cooler. He wiped the muddy spots off his arms to reveal, in full color, once again, to the world, to Quizzleboon, the fire and water that made of Leon—no, he was Cliff Highnote goddamn it!—a balanced man.

Check out the cooling properties of ocean on Cliff's left arm, the searing properties of fire on Cliff's right. Everybody agreed he was a walking work of art. The larger parts of Leon's chest—*no, he was Cliff*—and back were bare and Leon—*no, no, he was Cliff*—had meant to get new stuff put there, stuff meaningful and mighty, stuff that might could bridge his fire to the water, and free up, rather than dam up, the powers his body possessed. Cliff wanted no garbage on him, no sir. Some convicts at Muskegon Correctional had wanted to contribute their peculiar geniuses to what Ray Orbison created, but Leon said zip it. They wouldn't understand on *the Wing* and *the Wang*, how a bad tatt could throw off the balance to make Leon forever powerless. Had Leon told the story of the Wing and the Wang, what Ray, bastard brother to the singer Roy—may he rest in peace—told him one late night while it thundered outside the circus tent, the rain coming down so hard that it turned the grassy earth out there to mud, they would not have understood. They would not have believed. They were men of zero faithamoly.

That night Cliff and Beacon ate apples, and Amber too, sandwiches of cheese and mustard, old Barney up again in the howl. They put Barney in the pantry, which helped cut the sound down some, but it was way too loud still. Cliff made Amber go in there with him. Whenever Amber held Barney in her arms, he stopped his bull, and instead went "Ahwr ahwr ahwr," in the nicer monkey voice, the voice Cliff wished was the only voice ever to emerge from Barney's hole, which was a damn weird hole indeed, call it a mouth. When it put out the howl it opened up like the mouth in the famous painting called *The Scream*, but then the tone would shift and the mouth would squash down to the exact shape of a gigantic eye, with tear ducts and pink sclera over the thickness of lip pushing out from the inside of the mouth, the round black hole in the middle the lens. It was plain disgusting.

It was their second night in Coon Hill. In the morning there'd be five more nights to brook. On the seventh night they'd sell Barney into bondage and come away with twenty-five grand. So might as well smoke that forty-rock with Beacon right the fuck now, Cliff thought, but saved it, he didn't know why. Cliff drank Jack Daniel's instead, and thought of Ophelia, or what was the dude's name? Opham? Yeah, Opham. Made Leon think of Opie from the Andy Griffith Show, the kid who lived in a fantasy world, fuck that bullshit. This here Opham had lived a hard life, way back before black and white TV existed. Leon pictured her walking through the twigs in bare feet, the drippy trees of the Florida forest sort of cradling her from above, and her friends with musketed bayonettes finding her, and killing her, and he fell asleep in the bunk bed below Beacon's. Seemed like seconds later he awoke in a sweat with a palpitant heart—more bad dreams, Jesus. He'd expected, when opening his eyes, to see a huge Negro in a Yankee uniform with blood seeping out one corner of his mouth. In the dream, the man had only whites for eyes, no pupils. He'd come to the edge of Cliff's bunk and had leaned over him, had put a hand on Cliff's brawny shoulder and growled in a whisper: "Why you did this to me? I ain't done nothing to you."

Cliff carried his blanket to the Camaro, where he smoked some Carletons. It was some crazy bullshit. Had not Blind Edward told those stories, the ghost of the Yankee Negro dude would not have manifested. A man needs to close his ears, but Cliff was to his constant detriment polite. Was Cliff retarded? Seemed like yes. Whatever happened to the four men blown away in the cabin? Were they, too, walking around out there with hairs up their asses?

Cliff flicked his butt off and closed his lids. In his mind he said, "Mr. Quizzleboon, we go way back. Though I didn't discover you until the dirt people, that don't mean you weren't always there, waiting to hear my voice. I believe my eye is yours, sir, that you see me through it. What I ask, since you are my friend, is remove the bullshit superstitious-ass shit to come into my heart over this here Kind Edward bullshit-ass foolishness shit. Please, sir, give me the strength to ignore it and when you call I will grant your favor."

Cliff opened his eyes. Three deer hopped by the cabin. He smoked a Carleton and closed his eyes and drifted off. When he woke the next time, it was to the monkey. "Hgoo Hgoo HgoooAHHH!" it was going, barking, and "HGOOOOOOAHHHHHHOOOOO OOOOOOOO!"

Cliff grabbed the duct tape from under the seat and, groggy, ran up the cabin steps and flung wide the door. In there Barney howled desperate at the sight of the dawn creeping through the window. Was Barney trying to get a message to somebody out there? Seemed so, but Barney really looked like he couldn't help it. Barney's voice was so loud that Cliff wished he had some carpenter's earplugs in, but he stepped forward. Making sure old Barney was looking at him, he pulled a length of duct tape out and acted like he would tape his mouth shut if he didn't shut the fuck up.

Barney didn't mind Cliff. He howled onward.

"Goddamnit, Amber, get your ass up and make him zip it!" Cliff yelled.

Amber rose from her bunk. She went over to Barney and Braney grabbed her and wrapped his arms and legs around her and quieted.

So much for sleeping in.

Nobody could have slept through that.

Beacon had a cigarette going, a Doral 100, her brand. Nothing like getting up at the goddamn crack of dawn. Cliff grabbed a beer out the cooler, noting that there were only three left—how the fuck did that happen?—and lit his own smoke and smoked and drank. It was two nights down, five to go. So far so good, for the most part, but Cliff still worried over the plane, and wished that every plane in the world, from this day forward, would be deprived of the ability to fly. Cliff wished that the dirt people up in the Asheville hills were doing well without him, that Butterfly did not change her mind on selling Ambrosia into a life of crime, and that Bob the Goth guy, whoever he was, even if he'd been Beacon's lover, shit, while Cliff was down in Florida in the dirty work of things, was not dead. And, Cliff wished, goddamnit, that every child with a bad mom might wave a hand to make her go blind, watch the mother stumble into lamps and tables, pictures falling off walls. Cliff, as he inhaled some good Carleton tobacco, wished for a thing he was unable to put words to, but knew was there. The thing he wished for that he could not name, it had to do with Quizzleboon. Cliff felt as if he was on the brink of a great thing, as if soon he might realize the powers Ray, bastard brother to singer Roy, said were inside him.

Cliff shook his head, his dream of the big Negro coming back to him in greater detail. Maybe that's another thing I should'a wished for, Cliff thought, that I have no dreams no more, that I am dream free. On second thought, no, Cliff was glad he didn't wish for that. If that wish came true, Cliff might no longer have a eye into the future.

The eye cut from his child's body and left to hang—to swing, dangle, swung or swangle—by threads of nerves off the couch cushion, that was the start of Cliff's talent, the lost eye to give him visions in sleep, each a window into the future's dangers. Without his dreams, Cliff would be disabled.

"I had a dream," Cliff said.

"What was it? What was it about, hon?" Beacon asked, and slipped down off the upper bunk to sit beside her man.

Amber lit the Coleman stove and set a pot of water over the flame to boil it all up, first for coffee, then grits.

"Too crazy, too complicated," Cliff said, "but there was this bigass black dude who kept digging fingers into my ribs and his fingernails were going in and he kept saying I was his friend. Shit about scared me to death. I thought he was going to pull my rib out and beat me with my own bone."

"I bet he was the man who was hunged, Daddy," Amber said. "I bet he wants you to help him pull the hair out of his butthole."

"What the hell you talking, bitch? How do you know about him?"

"Kind Edward always talked on him, said he was a slave that turned into a soldier. He tried to save somebody so people got mad and pulled him into a tree by the neck."

"Did he seem like a friendly nigger?" Beacon asked.

"He might could'a been, but I don't wanna talk on it. Would y'all please shut up please?"

"You know, where I grown up in Alabama? Well, there's a old story on this one nigger man who drove everybody crazy in he always said, 'Yes kind sir, what can I do ye for?' He walked all up and down the streets, always was well dressed and clean and seemed like a nice person, but whenever somebody said, 'Hey you' or whatever they might've said to him, he always came back with 'Yes kind sir, what can I do ye for?' I don't know why that would make anybody mad. They took him out someplace and everybody stood around and they took off his nice clothes and set him afire and did what they had to do to make him burn good and they all stood around until he was nothing but char, you know, a black clump that was burning. This here was early in December. It was cold enough, you know, to where people went up close to warm themselves on the flames. That's when the nigger dude exploded and sent hot burning oils and grease all over the people that was standing around. After that, what my daddy told me, was all the men of the town had horrible burns, and that's why my granddaddy looked like he did, all messed up and burny-looking in the face, and blind in one eye. There were kids there too, and they too got the shit all whopped into their face."

"Your granddaddy was blind in one eye?" Cliff asked his darling.

"Yes he was, baby, but wait, don't interrupt me. All that burning grease had come up on his face from the nigger, you see? That nigger wasn't but a little eccentric like what you see with people walking around wherever you go. 'Yes kind sir, what can I do ye for?' We all called my granddaddy Poppy. That's what he liked to be called, Poppy. Poppy drove us to the Bear Bryant Museum in Tuscaloosa and took us to historical places and stuff. He loved his biscuits and gravy, but one day, it was just the two of us alone in the kitchen. Poppy said Lucy? I said Yes, kind sir, what can I do ye for? Poppy looked at me like I was the biggest piece of trash ever to live. He said, Pour me some coffee, girl, and later that day had a stroke. I figure that that stroke was on account of me. That was the beginning of the end of Poppy, and where I started to think that I'm a killer. I'm a woman who has murdered a man because I said Yes, kind sir, what can I do ye for? and that man was my own grandfather."

"We are a family of killers," Cliff said. "We will do what must be done to be in good harmony with all that lives."

"That sounds like something Potato might say."

"I don't give a shit about no goddamn Potato. I don't care what Potato says. Are you disrespecting me?"

"No no no."

"You'd best not to be."

"Here, Daddy." Amber handed Cliff his coffee.

"Thank you, darling." Cliff finished his beer, crunched the can and threw it, and sipped his good black hot coffee. The good brought to mind the forty-rock that might or might not could be sucked into the lung any moment of the day. Cliff had put it off long enough. Cliff had, shit, proved to himself he could have it with him and carry it around in the world with him and not smoke it. That made it all the more better in the now, this now in which he, Cliff and his family, shit, the Quizzleboons, the Quizzles, breathed. A forty-rock wasn't shit, but wasn't it enough to rush them out? It'd be a pop is all, not no precursor to a crack-down ho-down. It'd be a pop, a funtime hell-yeah, or let's look at our lives through different eyes. We've been some with the Wing. Now let's hook up with the motherfucking Wang!

"Hey, what're you thinking about?" Amber said.

"Huh?" Cliff said. He'd been staring into space, trying to make up his mind. Amber's hey had startled him. He'd been on the edge of the announcement of his prize, that hot forty-rock bocker in his pocket stock, a thing he might call "nigger tooth" were it not so politically incorrect. To smoke it, though, would be risky. Cliff needed to keep his head together. Eyeing Amber, he couldn't help but to feel shameful and low. Had he done included her, Ambrosia the daughter of Butterfly, in his vision of a morning skrunk out here after the child had done swore it off? "I was thinking," Cliff said, "I'd get some Styrofoam to soundproof the pantry. Then we can lock Barney up when he starts his monkey business."

"No you wadn't," Amber said.

"You're too smart for me," Cliff said, but they needed other things, too, like more bananas for Barney. Barney had only seven or eight bananas left, and besides that, it was important, Cliff said, that he get a newspaper to see what the cops were making of their caper. They needed beer, food. It was risky. So be it. "Another thing," Cliff said, "is I don't want y'all hanging around like snails with no shells on, you hear me? That won't do. Let's call it a rule, starting now. If we got to burn rubber, I don't want y'all wondering where the hell yallses goddamn dresses is and shit."

"That's reasonable. I won't fight you on it," Beacon said.

"It's archer season," Cliff said.

"I see what you're saying," Beacon said, and to Amber said, "Cliff thinks that if a hunter sees us, being we ain't got no clothes on, he'll think we're animals and send a arrow through our hearts."

"Like Cupid?" Amber said, excited by the idea.

"Then when we see you next, my darling," Beacon said, "we'll attack you by how crazy in love with you we are."

"Don't make light of it," Cliff said, and got into disguise: the slacks, the long-sleeved shirt, the fake glasses, the Nike running shoes and, for extra measure, a black beret—made him look like a communist art dealer, as Beacon had said, but these were the motions to carry them downstream in the river of uncertainty, and deposit them where? Oh, in the ocean of success, of course, shit, at least where their caper was concerned.

Before heading out, Cliff impressed upon the Quizzleboons the importance of what could not be seen in the world. "Beacon and Amber do not exist," Cliff told his family. "Therefore, if anybody comes around, any archers or muzzleloaders, or if a plane flies overhead, or if any army of dancing gypsies crawls out of a hole in the earth, you know what to do. You know that your job," Cliff told them, "is to be invisible."

18.

CLIFF **STOPPED AT** the Woodville Inland to purchase a Charleston Chew and *Tallahassee Democrat*—it featured a black and white photo of the Quizzleboons on the front page. When Cliff lifted the paper off the rack, he made no sudden movements that might alert somebody to his increased interest. He simply slapped the paper on the counter. He slapped the candy bar on top of her and paid and left the store.

Cliff's heart beat real fast now. It was that goddamn-it-if-I-ain't-busted feeling at it again. He got in his car, and looky here.

The picture wasn't bad. They looked like a happy threesome walking along, a regular family but for the crumpled grocery bags over their heads. Thank God they'd had sense to tape those on, even though it made them look ridiculous, and made maneuvering a bit more harder than normal. The picture had been took in infrared from a security eye secured to a tree. The monkey was in the arms of the little girl in the dress—Jesus. Amber had drawn huge smiles on the bags, and eyes where they'd cut holes to see out. Cliff's bag had only one eye—not good. Least it wasn't a picture of them climbing into the Camaro. They looked like trick-or-treaters is what they looked like. It was the first photo he'd seen of themselves. They looked nice, though the child's club leg was more pronounced than normal—*double not good*—maybe over that she'd been froze in motion, or that she'd been shrunk down to the size of a tumbler. Cliff marveled over the bonk bat crack nuts in the pan of the thing, and saw if you studied hard you'd see Beacon's pinky to be missing—*triple no good*.

Cliff drove on and parked to the Winn Dixie beyond the fairgrounds, where he'd planned to buy some supplies, and read the article headed: *Family Steals Rare Albino Monkey From Florida History Museum*. It told of Barney and the outrage of the museum curator. Said caring members of the community started a fund—the Barney Fund—to be give over to whoever supplied info that lead to the arrests of the perpetrators of this heinous crime.

Damn if it wasn't the whole FBI thing all over again, money for info should the info help get the criminal. The Barney Fund was started at 2,500 dollars, the paper said, due to the kindness of a individual who preferred to remain unnamed. The fund was expected to grow over so many people had loved on the monkey. People had laughed and cried over Barney's inquisitive personality. He brought joy to children. His hair was just so bright and inspiring— "like a fire with legs," the paper said—and his melancholy facial expressions won people's hearts. One woman claimed Barney helped her get through chemo treatments, and there was information all about the history on the monkey, and why its hair was bright yellow and orange and not white like you'd expect a regular albino to be. Damn things had been worshipped as gods by the ancient Mayan civilization, turned out.

Well I'll be damned, Cliff thought, and read about this here "hyoid bone," that the paper said was in the monkey's jaw and responsible for the "plaintive cry" that could be heard three miles through thick jungle vines.

And what's this? Holy shit if the Nicaraguan Government didn't issue a statement saying if Barney was not recovered, they would tell the World Wide Press that all the other countries of the world should not trust the USA to provide for animals delivered into their care. This was of special interest to the Florida History Museum over that a Bengal tiger was scheduled to arrive in January.

Cliff read through the article several times. He determined that they were in the clear. The Quizzleboons were comfy as bugs in rugs. Long as they stayed out of the public eye, what was there to worry on? There was no mention of a black Camaro—great news and more great news. Cliff anyway would be a fool to think that just because they didn't mention his car, that meant they weren't looking for it. Shit freaked Leon—*no, he was Cliff, get it straight!*—out. Cliff was Cliff. Cliff felt like a sitting duck, quack-a-doodle-doo. Cliff said to hell with supplies and drove on out of there, a driving duck.

The duck drove to Kind Edward's, where else? The king always had a sober take on shit, even though most of the time he was gone into the ether on the best drugs south of the Georgia line. Cliff parked on the side road, as he'd done the day before. He crossed through the backyard and passed by the Buddha sitting fat and smiling under the fir tree. Damn thing had bucked teeth, Cliff noticed for the first time, but he couldn't tell if it was a joke Buddha. It looked to him like that's how it was made, and that the bucked teeth were legit.

Cliff stepped past the boiler room, no party going on back there today, and up the stairs onto the porch where he saw, through the small square windows of the double doors, the blind man at the counter, lips in motion, he was talking, blabbing, but Cliff saw nobody else. Was Edward talking to nobody again?

Cliff set his hand on the brass handle and gently let himself into the kitchen. "Ha ha ha, she broke every window in my house," the kind king gloated. Then Cliff saw her, the girl of the square earrings, earringless today, the one from the boiler room, the dark-skinned quagmire who'd given him pause. She sat with her back to the fridge, bony feet flat on the glossy linoleum, face involved with a listen, she was a listener, the words of the blind swinging lazily on hammocks in the cups of her ears, which poked pointily through slits in the silky hair to run down over her shoulders on either side. When she saw Cliff, her expression shifted his way. She closed one eye so that, for the three or four seconds she kept it closed, she and Cliff were equal in the eye department—they were eye-to-eye. Was she letting him know she knew of his deformity? Why else would she do that slow motion eye wink thing? Cliff's normal response to such a rude gesture would've been to kick the bitch in the face. Or so he'd've liked to believed.

"They took a Polaroid picture of where she bit me," the blind man magpied. "She was in handcuffs on the porch. She kept yelling, 'It was a love bite, that's all it was was a love bite! Edward, tell them it was a love bite,' and she was crying and it was a terrible embarrassment and—"

"Edward," Cliff said.

"Aw, fuck, shit!" Edward said.

Cliff took courage in the girl's uplifting smirk. He said, "It's me, Cliff Highnote."

"I know who the fuck it is, asshole!"

She burst out laughing, and brought her legs up closer to herself. If she didn't have the pants on, Capri's as Cliff had heard them referred to as before, her puss would be quite the outward going Venus Fly Trap of the blind man's kitchen. Seeing her down to the floor this way, the loose fitting maroon blouse hung down off one shoulder, Cliff felt the tingle. Was a wrongheaded attraction, but men made choices in life. Choices came with consequence. What was rendered in the geometry of today's front page was one: *Family Steals Rare Albino Monkey*.

"This is really fucked up," Kind Edward said. "I'd love to tell you what a shithead you are, but what you need to know is only this: a man named Billy Waxman paid me a visit."

"Waxman?"

"A United States Marshall. He's looking to skin your ass like a softshell turtle, nail your head to a tree, then rip your back off clean."

"Clean?"

"Clean."

"Well goddamn. How the fuck he end up here?"

"Seems he had a talk with your cuntfuck sister in Buffalo, who I was just talking about by the way. Something is way wrong with her, and I don't know why I ever married her, and I don't know if Glinda ratted you out, but when Waxman found out she was once married to Edward Rooks, the famous Miami lawyer who cleared some big drug dudes, he put shit together."

"Billy Waxman is a total badass," the girl on the floor said.

"When was he here?"

"Left thirty minutes ago."

"What he look like?"

"Black," Edward said, and laughed and laughed and the girl on the floor laughed.

"Was he really black?"

"I don't know, I didn't ask him, everything is black to me. If you want some details, ask Deziray, she's my eyes. Was he black? Describe him for us."

"He was burly. I can say that without telling a lie."

"Burly, what do you mean, burly?" Leon said. "You mean to say Waxman has a fro?"

"No," she said, and stood. Of this Cliff was glad over it seemed disrespectful of her to talk serious matters while slunk to the floor like a goddamn slut. She wasn't the shortest girl in the world by a long shot. The top of her head was on a plane with Cliff's eyelevel, and she said, "By burly I mean he was a solid guy, muscle and bigness, a white dude with hair shorn down skiball style but for a long clump of it shootin out the back part like the tail on a Shetland pony. My best guess is he's a practitioner of the Hare Krishna religion. You know the Hare Krishnas believe that roaches are holy? If you step on a roach it's the same thing as being a giant and then stepping on a human being. Mosquitoes are considered sacred and of equal value with humans."

Cliff wanted to slap her. Not for the deliver of bad news she was on, what about this goddamn Billy

QUIZZLEBOON

Waxman. Cliff and Leon and the Quizzleboons could take care of that motherfucker. No, it was that already Leon felt himself, goddamn him all to hell and back, weakening, sort of becoming hollow inside at the sight of her mouth moving. Shit wasn't fair that she could make him love her without even doing a thing, just by being. Cliff did not care neither for having his foolishness shoved in his face. Hateful was the better thing to be, for as everybody knows, hate's the stuff of strong men. Love is for suckers.

Cliff did not the slapping of her do. With her, what it looked like was it would start something. If he slapped her. For her, what it looked like was it would be a personal victory, the little educated bitch. Cliff wanted to slap her for the pretty, and the long feet she had. He wanted to slap her over she was here to ruin his dream of a hundred acres and a mule, his happy family prancing about under the sun and moon and stars and whatever else was up there in the cosmos: *Leon, Beacon, Amber*—they twinkled and fumed in this vision like runaway comets and rocket fire. Cliff hated her for the what she was here to destroy. And her name, shit, Deziray, Cliff loved that too. It was great. And what in the motherfuck, come to think of it, was all that "tell a lie" business about? *Oh, I think I can say that without telling a lie*, as if it was granted she ought be telling one lie to the next. Was she saying that's what she was taught to do? Tell the lies?

"I'll keep a lookout for Waxman," Cliff said.

"It gets worse," Edward said. "Waxman has made the connection between you and the Tallahassee bank. He showed My Eyes a picture of you taken from the bank's security camera, and pointed out the ribbons wiggling down onto the top of your hand.

Waxman said they are the strands of seaweed hanging off a mermaid's tail, and I don't doubt it. In the picture the strands can be seen coming out of your shirtsleeve. Very sloppy, Highnote, I don't like the way things are going here, but all is not lost. Waxman has no idea that Leon Hicks has been laid to rest."

"I can't believe you've let this philly in on this," Cliff said. "Leon is a name not to be spoken."

"Oh, don't you worry about her," Edward said. "My Eyes knows if she breathes anything, a shadow will come along when she least expects."

"I won't tell anybody, Leon," Deziray said, and ran her hand down his forearm, looking at him all the while with her old sad eyes that were a darker brown, even, than Beacon's. Her smoker's breath washed up against his face, all delicious and shit, and he wanted to mash her flat nose in with his thumb for some reason, make it a tad more flat. "My eyes are crossed. If not for believers we'd all of us be smarter. I know I can say that without telling a lie."

"She goes on that way," Edward said.

"Is your name Deziray?" Cliff asked her.

"The one and—"

"Shutcher goddamn cocksuker. If I want a opinion from you I'll ask for it, does that sound reasonable?"

Deziray bit her tongue.

"She tries me," Edward said, "but I don't care. Last night I heard the shower go on. I went in there and read her left aureole that says, in braille, 'five orange trees,' believe it or not. Her right nipple doesn't say shit—it's just gibberish all around there. But I confirmed it was her. I pushed her down and she took me in her mouth and it was great blow. I said, Deziray I love you and put my hands on her head, but it was short hair. I said, What? That's when I heard the grunt that was my cook. My cock was in my cook. That's why nobody's here today."

"Is this something I need to know?" Leon asked.

"Hell if I was to stand for it. Me and My Eyes ran everybody out. When Waxman knocked, I thought it was Harmon coming to beg for his job back."

"Good thing nobody was here," Cliff said. "Waxman would have asked questions. Those bastards."

"Course, Harmon put her up to the whole thing, just like I suspected. He got her to do the switcheroo. To call her a jerk wouldn't even start the discussion, but it's pretty clever, you gotta admit. I'd always heard guys were the best cocksuckers, ha ha ha!"

"I'm sorry that happened to you."

"Ha!" Deziray said.

"What?" Leon asked her.

"Just the world, it's crazy."

"I hear you," Leon said. "Thanks for keeping this shit inside your panties, don't let me hear otherwise."

"Hey, I wouldn't do otherwise. Do you think I want a cap in my ass? That's what Edward meant by shadow, did you pick up on it?"

"What, you don't believe it?"

"No, I do, that's what I'm saying."

"From what I could tell on Waxman," Edward said, "is he is a narcissist of the negotiator variety. That could be good news. The best news of all though is he hasn't connected you to the monkey."

"The Barney Fund is at twenty-five bills," Cliff said. "I've heard on this before. Next thing it'll be ten thou. Then we'll have a hundred motherfuckers on us, everybody and his grandmaw trying to pick up the reward."

"This is America, don't worry," Edward said. "The only thing that matters in America is if you kill somebody. You didn't so don't worry."

Cliff felt grateful to the blind man, and like he was doing him a disservice by being here. Should Waxman be casing the place, all plans could burn to shit in a flash pan. It was Cliff's duty to go. He eyed Deziray. She seemed to know what Cliff was thinking, and said, "Edward, I'm going down to check the laundry. She screwed her face up at Cliff then left the room through the back door.

"It's not fair for me to be here," Leon said.

"Damn straight," Edward said.

"Goodbye," Leon said.

"Goodbye," Edward said.

19.

IN THE BOILER ROOM Deziray puffed a cigarette, her bronze clavicles long and musical, spreading out from below her neck in the way of a cormorant drying its wings in the sun while perched on a pilon—that's what Leon saw when he entered the boiler room, she at the round white table smoking. Her loose-fitting blouse hung down low off a shoulder—her inoculated one. It was like she'd set herself up that way for Cliff to see when he walked in, and he saw, too, that she wanted rock. If Cliff didn't smoke his with her what would that make him? A boy who'd done growed up to be a man who could not admire his face in the mirror? Fuck that. "So what's your story, bitch?" he asked, and looked into her left eye direct with his right, his seeing laser beam.

"My story is for friends. You my friend?"

Cliff sat across from her, lit a Carleton, dragged it, a lot of good nicotine going on. A hand-shaped ashtray sat between them, there was the love line.

"How'd you get messed up with Kind Edward?" Cliff asked.

"He likes to get high. So do I."

"You can say that without telling a lie."

"God was in a good mood when he gave us drugs."

"I thought you didn't believe in God."

"I believe in good. Only difference 'tween the two is a single o. You ever thought about that?"

"What are you, some kind of artsy crackho?"

"I'm a thousand years old, Leon, that's the truth. You wouldn't think it by looking at me."

"Don't call me Leon."

"You're not the only Leon. Why do you think my appearance pleases your eyeball, even though I'm a thousand years old? It's because I met this dude whose name was Leon. He showed me a magic fountain and I jumped into it and became young and now my whole body is filled with rejuvenating waters. That's one thing they left out of the official story. Once you've partaken of its gift, your body reproduces it. When I pee, out comes the fountain of youth. That's why I no longer get urinary tract infections."

"Okay, so maybe you're an artsy crackho. I've met a few."

"My parents are artists and intellectuals." Deziray snubbed her cigarette out in the hand, a quick-witted snub-out if ever Cliff saw one. You could tell some things on a woman by her snub. When the woman dabbed the tray with her butt, twisting it and playing around with it five minutes before she got it out, you pretty much knew she sucked in bed.

"You wanna smoke some weed, Leon?"

"Fire it up, bitch."

Deziray slipped a Scooby Dooby Doo from her Marlboro red pack, and lit it, and took several bigass massive tokes. Her face clouded over, the smoke sticking to her cheeks and temples and hair like bolls of cotton candy. Then she blew, and the air turned gray. She leaned forward to hand Cliff the joint, so

QUIZZLEBOON

Cliff—no, he was Leon for Deziray—took it and puffed it ginger and gave it back. Leon wasn't big on weed. He only enjoyed it when drunk. When he was drunk, weed knocked his skrunk up a notch. If he wasn't drunk, weed made him paranoid, or muddled his brain to ruin the day. More often than not he smoked to be polite. This one here with Deziray they passed back and forth. After a bit she acted like it was too much trouble to reach across the table, so eased around into Leon's lap, draped her arm over his shoulder, set the spleef backwards in her mouth and blew. Leon sucked the thick in, but only into the foyer of his lungs. He didn't wanna seem like a sissy so held the smoke a bit before letting it go. In his let-go the tongue of her pushed out for some reason, and was all red like she'd just ate beets or some shit. Leon looked it over, wondered what could be wrong with it. Had some black splotches there like what you see on rottweilers. Was she in some fashion diseased? In a second the tongue moved his way. She was tilting over is why, the eyelids of her drooping as if she might nod off. Her damn tongue slipped into his mouth sorta accident-like.

Damn tongue was hot and grew long and fat. Brought to mind a thing Cliff cared not to know on so of it knew not. What with the wet Leon squeezed up on her, here took the shapes in of her strong leg muscles while bearing down on her tongue, feeling around on her ass and all. Her heart got to beating fast, so he lifted her, set her on the bed, pulled her cotton pants off inside out and her legs opened of their own, *hey hey*, her jigamoly bare for the absorbent powers of the ball—could anything beat it? "That's what I'm talking about," Cliff—no, he was

Leon at this particular moment—said. Next step was to take the plunge. "You mind if I put some dirt in there?" Cliff—no, he was Leon at this particular moment—said.

Deziray lifted her head, raised onto her elbows and observed Leon through her old sad stoned eyes that matched the color of her hair. "I beg your pardon?"

So you don't get pregnant, Leon thought of saying, but did not say. In truth she more likely than not was on a prescription of baby-killer pills. He did not wanna spoil the moment.

Deziray said, "Hey, I heard you knocked Don on the floor and were gonna hit him in the face."

"I don't like violence."

"Had you done that, his nose would've broke and blood gone everywhere. I can't stand people who pick on children. I wouldn't be at all unhappy if you broke Don's nose. The world needs less Dons and more heroes. Would you like to get with me?"

"I'm engaged to be married, bitch."

"I'm the fountain of youth, Golden Man." Deziray lifted a tan foot Leon's way, something wrapped around her ankle—leather shoestring, looked like. Leon didn't take it. She set it back to the blanket.

"I like you, bitch."

"And I you, Golden Man."

"Did you know I got a rock?"

"I knew nothing of the sort," Deziray said, and closed, slightly, her legs, the smallest increment. "Do you really?"

All good sense told Leon to grab the ho's ankle, swipe the dust off the bottom of her foot and make love to her this instant. He could whop his wiener out and plug her before another word could be thought, and Beacon would be pissed, sure, but was not free love the philosophy of the dirt people? Should Beacon fuss he could accuse her of hypocrisy. Spread your love around so it don't go to wasting, is what they said. Since they'd left the dirt farm, Beacon had shown signs of being your typical jealous shrew. Cliff wanted to preserve his dream of the happy little family. Was not Deziray Kind Edward's eyes? What a time for a conscience prick! The only place Cliff's prick belonged was inside Deziray's body that was half his age and smelled pleasantly of old books and pesticide. The smell drew Cliff closer. A little drink is all. He didn't have to fuckalucky like a ducky with her, but screw it. Cliff sat on the bed. He pulled her up into a sitting position so her legs hung down, and put his hand on the back of her neck. His other hand he set on her thigh and drew it up to where a finger came to a rest atop the bald man's head, nothing intentional going on here, it was just a coincidence.

Deziray closed her eyes.

Cliff said, "You wouldn't believe what I been going through with that goddamn monkey." Cliff waited a second for her to say something, but she didn't saying anything, so he said, "Did you know monkeys bark? I never saw nothing like it in my life, and it taking shits all over the fucking place. I thought this was to be easy take, but here come to find out the monkey is a treasure to the Nicaragua country. Who knows what all kind of stuff I got into, and the place I'm staying at is haunted." Cliff shook his head. In doing so his fingers kind of pulled her vagina open, nothing intentional going on here, it's just where his fingers happened to be in the side-by-side sit they were doing. The dark peach color was right nice, and her feet were really dirty. The toes looked kinda crowded together. The dirt people up in Asheville would love her. He said, "I was this close to strangling the little bastard," and Cliff noticed all the sudden like that Deziray's face had grown sadder than its regular sad look. "Did I say something?" Cliff said, "what did I say?" She sniffled. "Come on, say something."

"The airplane, it's that damn airplane. I keep thinking about it. I don't want to, but I can't get it out of my mind."

Cliff thought of the plane he willed to explode after it flew over the trees to invade his privacy.

"I'm sorry, I just can't help but to feel crushed inside. It happens to me whenever stuff like this happens in the world. Be glad you didn't see me in April when Columbine High got shot up. My therapist says I'm a depressive realist."

"What plane?"

"You haven't heard?" She looked at Cliff like he was some kind of heartless mammal. "It's been all over the news."

"What plane?"

"AirEgypt Flight 990. It crashed into the Atlantic Ocean last night with 217 people on board. I just hate when people die for no good reason."

Kind Edward cried out from above: "My Eyes, My Eyes!"

Deziray jerked away from Leon, but Leon grabbed her arm and yanked her back, he didn't know why, exactly. He'd thought he'd had something important to say to her, or ask her, but now that he'd pulled her close, he couldn't think of a thing.

"Not that I care or anything, but you're hurting my arm," Deziray said.

"Oh, sorry," Cliff said. He let her go.

Deziray slipped into her Capri pants and hopped out of the room like a long-haired cheetah.

Cliff left the boiler room behind her. He felt as if he'd dropped a precious doodad, a glass unicorn, say. It had landed between his feet and shattered. "Forget her and that goddamned plane," Cliff said and, stoned, went up to his car and drove along, thinking of the needs of the day: get bananas, get beer; but Leon—no, he was *Cliff, Cliff, Cliff*—was fevered in a ditch, was not in control of his brainwaves. Could his wish for the small plane to crash have been redirected to take down a jetliner? He ran a red, Jesus Christ, how often did that happen?

20.

CLIFF TURNED INTO Wal-Mart's lot, parked, walked down and grabbed a cart. The old greeter man said, "Happy Halloweeny, friend," and Cliff wheeled into fruits. He dropped some forty bananas into the cart and pushed on, then considered: shit, what if the cops are looking for banana buyers? Too late now. Put the bananas back, they might see it on video, get suspicious. He pushed on. To de-emphasize his banana load he grabbed a couple packs of salted sunflower seeds, a bunch of apples, and a sack of oranges. Cliff put all kinds of shit in his cart, just whatever moved him as he cruised the aisles, his mind flashing back to Deziray's mellow brown hair and the feel of her and the what he'd wanted to get into 'til the voice of the king came down from above. Plus she told that shit on the plane. Might his eye on the moon not see shit as good as it thought it could do? Could his eye've made the wrong plane crash? Could this mean Leon's Wing was in its find of its Wang? The powers were manifesting, so who knew but that before long he could fly, but *no no no, what am I thinking?* Leon—*no, he was Cliffamolio*—thought. *None of that stuff is real*, he thought, and thought, *please, brain, quitcher moutharrhea.*

QUIZZLEBOON

Cliff tossed cans of sardines in there, a jar of pickled artichoke hearts—Beacon loved pickled artichoke hearts, Cliff didn't know why, they were weird and obliterated in brine, but she did, crazy woman.

Cliff put in four cases of Busch beer, and a bunch of other shit he considered necessary for the days to come. All that, and a king-sized Butterfinger for Ambrosia, child of Butterfly.

And why, Cliff wondered, did Butterfly's cunt not affect him the way Deziray's did? Why was that? Cliff didn't think it was over the dangling clit thing, though that was weird, he had to admit. Damn thing was about two inches long. When she got excited it shot straight out from her body like a pencil stub. When you went down on her, the natural thing was to suck it, a gesture to grow weirdsome in three seconds.

Why am I even thinking this? Cliff thought. And he thought, *I wish I wasn't so stoned. It must be for the stoner. Don't never get stoned no more.* Cliff grabbed a big can of kidney beans. He threw it into the cart and remembered some women he'd heard talking on about how, oh, all vaginas looked the same, but no, they did not. Some were tall and they all had different colors and stuff and there were variations in hair styles and some were spooky with special flaps and secret compartments inside. Not all were created equal. Some made juice whereas others made nought. Some made nougat whereas others made gray paste. Some were loose enough to stuff a turducken in, whereas others were so tight you could barely get your index finger in there, and when you did, the damn thing might squeeze down with all the pressure of a regular pair of jaws, just with no teeth, like a bite of gum, and you couldn't just yank your finger out over you didn't want to hurt the damn thing. Who knew but that if you gave the yank, a bit of the inside of it might come out with? Best to wait 'til the woman, who was probably showing off her special gripping powers, let go. Two-Stone's was one of those.

On the other hand, there did seem to be a flavor in common to run the gamut of the pooki world. Call it *the base*, like what you had with this here *roux*, the bacon fat and flour you mixed together to mainstay your sauces and gravies and whatnot. As Cliff understood it, you could put all kinds of other things into the *roux*, like rosemary and spices and seafood. What gave a particular pot four hats out of five was not the *roux* itself—it was the *other* ingredients . . . or was it the *roux*? Turned into a riddle if you thought on it more than five seconds, like the thing on the chicken or the egg, so best to say *fuck it*, and push your cart on over to the bread and peanut butter aisle, throw in some blackberry jam, Sam, some English muffins to go with, Smith.

Though stoned, Cliff was respectable in appearance, him here in Wal-Mart in his fancy clothes and beret. He made his way through checkout, then once more was in the Camaro, the place he recognized as home, not in matters of the heart, but in terms of place. The Camaro could slide, groove. It needed gas to go, sure, like people did food, but the Camaro went where Cliff wanted it to went. It went here, it went there. Though it could be stolen, it could not jump up to run off on legs like a woman. Where it went was up to Cliff. It had a good engine under the hood, and had come with a number of cassette tapes, so in a way it sang. The dude who'd owned it before Cliff had had a thing for Prince. There were many tapes of Prince, including the one with a song about let's party like it's nineteen ninety-nine, which the Quizzleboons loved singing together while rolling through the woods, it here the year 1999 right now! The together-sing was fun, but a Schubert was in there, too, a George Michael, Cheap Trick, and Fleetwood Mac. Was fair to say Cliff's car was reliable. Was fair to say Cliff loved his car.

Cliff drove, him the Santa with a load of goodies, drove leftward, drove eastward. Cliff knew new houses were being built out this way, new communities, places called East Gate and South Lake, all these houses upon whose grounds goods stood, stacks of wood not even covered over with tarps, and all sorts of supplies kicking back in the shade like *Hey, haul off with me!* Cliff drove through the hoods to see stacks of what looked like good Styrofoam insulation, but he'd have to get out and break it to stuff in the car, so said fuck it, and drove on.

Cliff drove back to 319, hooked a left and passed the fairgrounds where the great Halloween action was in high gear, the Ferris wheel the thing one saw while approaching this land of chance and stuffed tigers and, if you knew where to look, great wisdoms. At one such fairground Ray Orbison told Cliff—*no, he was Leon then*—of the Wing and Wang. The shit went down before Jesus was born, before the great flood when angels ran unruly and got on rudely with such pretty gals of the earth, who could blame them? When these women impregnated by angels tried to give birth, they exploded in heaps of smoking guts and body parts, like what to could happen if a Rottweiler fucked a Chihuahua. You can't have something so fierce and powerful come to life through a thing of lesser business. Sometimes, over a strain of weak to the angel plus one of might in the earthling, a supreme beautiful creature was born, sometimes with wings.

The official story says the men of the earth were wicked but for Noah. In truth a man of Uruk much beloved by God, a surgeon and scholar blessed with great physical beauty, a half-breed who'd flown to heaven on many occasions, too was good. He and God played board games and drank wine and conversed in the towns when God came down to walk around. God loved the guy like a brother. To God the guy was like Maxwell House, Ray said, good to the last drop. The guy healed people of diseases and never took their money.

When God brought on the rains to flood the world, the dude tried to save himself. He lifted into the air and settled into a glide, but he was too heavy, see? His wings got waterlogged, so he unsheathed the sword strapped to his waist, and slammed it over his shoulder, cutting his body diagonal from the shoulder to hip. The right wing, along with the man's lower half and legs, fell into the flood, that's the Wang. It's down there now in the ocean flapping about amongst the lanternfish and bulbous dreamers. As for the Wing, that's the piece to sport the neck and head and beard that has continued to grow throughout these thousands of years. The Wing wings above the earth. In the separation of Wing and Wang, God's beloved friend became part retarded.

"Now, why do you think," Ray asked Leon, "that God would do that to his friend and brother?"

"I can't say as that I rightly know."

QUIZZLEBOON

Ray said he was pretty sure the unnamed half-breed might be the real reason God flooded the earth. "Something don't add up," he said. "God had to've had a better reason to kill everybody, one not mentioned in the bee eye bee el eee. At first I thought God could be jealous of that sonofabitch underling, but then I thought on it more, and I thought, Shit, who's to say God didn't find a personal attraction on them womens he done made? I mean seriously, Leon, if you were God and looked down and saw all that fine-ass pussy running all over in the hills, and all the other mens getting it on withem, and the angels too, wouldn't you be tempted? Would you just set there alookin?"

"I'd be sore pressed I guess."

"I think you'd take your ass a fuckin bite. That's just human nature, and what is human nature if not God's nature since men are modeled on God? Can you answer me that? I'm telling you, man, I got to thinking on the shit and it came to me that if God were to fuck his daughters, I call them daughters, I don't know what else to call them but daughters since it was God to make them, well, he wouldn't want them to explode like what happened with the angels and shit, how after sex they'd leave the blow-up woman in a field by a rock or whatver, I mean, what I'm getting at here, Leon, and maybe I'm giving God the benefit of the doubt, is that God is a good God at heart, so what he did was temper his juice, you hear me? He tempered his juice so the women would not explode."

"I think I know what you're getting at."

"That's right, Leon, that's right. The man from Uruk was God's personal son, and what God did was just like what Hitler done when he bombed them towns that he grew up in where all the evidence could be on his true daddy. God was destroying the evidence. It's the best explanation I can think of."

Leon anyway, what with his fire arm and water arm, might be the man to bring the two halves back together, Ray said, for Leon was a conduit between them. The closer Leon brought the Wang to the Wing, or vise versa, the stronger he would become.

Ray told the story while tattooing flames on Leon's fire arm that night of the rains in a small Arkansas town, under the main circus tent after the gates had been closed and the carnies were drinking wine and smoking cigars and playing cards and eating fried chicken at a nearby table. That same night another carnie was caught fucking Baby Geraldine the elephant with his head. Dude'd done put on goggles and a swimming cap for it. The Baby Geraldine incident, though it bore no significance on the story Ray told, did anyway taint it. Leon could not remember the golden man of the wings without also that he thought of Baby Geraldine.

Ray was a good man. He drowned one night in a bath in Georgia over this heroin he did around about throughout the counties they traveled through. Ray was imaginative. As bastard brother to the famous Roy, he was friend to unwed mothers, children and convicts and dogs and grasshoppers.

Cliff felt nostalgia whenever he passed a fairgrounds, but was too amped up in the feeling, right now goddamnit, of that bitch Deziray, he couldn't shake it. Her bare coot, all the while as he drove, floated over the roads. It turned sideways in front of him like a whispering eye that glistened, and he was driving into it. Whenever Cliff brought his cigarette to his mouth, he smelled it, it mixed wonderfully with his burning tobacco. Her damn legs had been shaved, too, and her armpits, goddamnit, none of that weird hippy dirt-smear shit going on except for around her ankles, and her feet whose toes, contrary to the rules of the dirt farm, bore traces of old red paint on their nails. Cliff caught himself giggling over how wonderful she was. Perfect. He was proud that she'd offered her affection. Not only had she spread herself wide like a plate of Swiss hors d'oeuvres at a convention for housemaids and plumbers—*come on and get you some pink taco!*— but she'd called him hero and Golden Man. These were names Cliff could embrace.

Cliff still had the forty-rock bocker. It burned in his pocket. How easy to turn this ship around, drive back to the blind man's, have a smoke with Dez down in the boiler room then fuck the bitch silly. Did this rock not have the sockless one's name spelled across it in bright flaming letters? All Cliff would be doing was delivering the rock what was hers.

Forget it, buck your ass up you stupid sonofabitch! Such damn ridiculous shit of a grown man to carry on this way could only dirty up the brains of the waves. He was on his way home, getting closer to his dream that called for lots of shit to be done according to plan, no time for funny business here. Forget her, Cliff said, and pulled onto the Coon Hill road, opened the gate, and let himself through.

Once again Cliff's Ambrosia, the rose of Asheville, jumped off the porch shouting, "Daddy Daddy." Damn girl wore a dress now, and Cliff hugged her and swung her as any good daddy would, round and round, and set her down in the sand, and he and

Amber and Beacon carried in the groceries and stuff. Then Beacon told Amber to take Barney down to the spring.

"Why, what for?"

"You know why," Beacon said.

A few minutes later Beacon stuffed some dirt into her pussy. Cliff ran some fuel rods into his nuclear babe. She reacted. So did he. What a relief, there was the release, but Cliff felt feverish still over Dez, a bit some contaminated. He'd blotted her out, but as he lay there postcoital on the bottom bunk with his woman, goddamnit if Beacon didn't catch on. She said, "I swear to god, Cliff, I been smelling it ever since you came home and I didn't want to believe what I thought it was but now it's done growed stronger."

Beacon was nudged against him, her head on his shoulder, her nude leg wrapped over him, hair on it from the knee down, not thick hair, but hair. She grabbed his right wrist, brought it to her mouth and smelled his fingers.

"Okay, so you did, you fucked somebody then came home to me, not caring if you was to give me AIDS or warts. Thanks, Cliff." Beacon slid over him and grabbed her dress off the floor and yanked it down over her body, more to hide it than put on an article of clothing. "This is the first time you cheated on me. I don't know what to do. I think you might have broken my heart but I don't even know it yet. I'm in a daze."

"You're barkin up the wrong tree, woman."

"I am? Tell me the truth now, don't lie to me."

"The only woman I did it with today is you, and I can honestly say that without telling a lie."

"What? What? You're acting weird, Cliff. What did

you do, stick your hand into a woman? You think that's any different?"

"If all you care about is warts, you should be happy."

"Oh oh oh! Is that beautiful? Holy shit!"

"When I met you you said you was a Freebird-style woman."

"So I could get into your pants, Cliff, didn't you figure that out? I swear to god."

"I believe what a person tells me. You want me to think you're a liar?" Cliff pulled on his jeans. Hell if he was to sit here having a talk like this while nekid.

"Tell me, tell me, what's her name? You better tell me."

"Or what, you'll call the FBI?"

"Never know, right? I did before. Was she good, Cliff? Did you cunnilinctus on her? No, you didn't, I woulda smelt it in your beard. Ha ha! She prolly had you going then turned your ass down. Is that why you were horny when you came home? I tasted come on you, baby. That was come meant for another woman, wasn't it? Don't lie to me, just tell the truth." She sat on the bunk beside him, covered her face with her hands and cried and wept and blubbered.

"Just what I need," Cliff said.

On she blubbered.

"You need to give me a break here," Cliff said. "You haven't even heard the story and you're jumpy for conclusions."

"All I wanna know is her name, motherfucker. Tell me her name and I won't cut off your balls! You think I won't cut them off, bitch? Try me!"

"You best shutcher fuckin face up. How dare you

talk like this to me?"

"I'll cut your balls off, motherfucker!" Beacon screamed.

"Shhh, stop that."

Beacon gritted her teeth. She growled, and paced back and forth inside the cabin fast, then went out on the porch. Cliff heard her say "Scrotum" and then she came back in. "Tell me her name," she said calmly.

"Well, I don't see any good in it."

"You don't tell me her name you'd best to keep them balls under lock and key. No telling when I will do it, but I damn sure will, when you least expect it, too. I ain't no fuckin whore motherfucker that you can just treat me this way whenever you feel like it, do you hear me? Do you understand what I am saying? Didn't I call the FBI on you? Do you really think I won't cut off your balls? I thought we were together."

"Why can't you forget about it? I'm telling you it was nothing. Did I question you on Bob?"

"You mean the man you murdered?"

"Okay, let's not go there."

"What's her name, Cliff? Tell me her name this will be over. What's her name?"

"Deziray."

Silence.

A minute went by. Beacon wiped her face. The air felt fresher. This wasn't so bad, things could be worked out, it wasn't nothing but a thang. Poor Beacon was jonesing for rock is all, as was Cliff. It'd been a full week and a half since they'd sworn it off for better things, to see the greener pastures up here directly in the future. All was good, it was a little slipup is all, a pothole in the zippity dooh dah day sort of road they were trying to cruise down. Cliff set his muscular hand on Beacon's back to comfort her, promising once more that it wasn't nothing but a thang. After Beacon thought on it a bit she said, "When I find that bitch I'm'a rip her titties off, you know that, don't you? I'm'a throw'em into the street to see them squashed by tires. If I don't rip her titties off, it'll damn sure be your balls in the middle of the street."

"No need to be rash."

"What, are you sticking up for her?"

"No, nothing like that, I'm just saying."

"So am I. I'm saying when I find her she'll be sorry she was given a hole to put shit in. I'm'a fill that bitch with a few things she ain't never dreamed of accommodating."

"That's downright cruel. Pains me to hear you talk this way, Lucy."

"Lucy? What are you saying, Cliff? What is the point you are trying to make by calling me Lucy?"

"Lucy as a goosey's what Sparrow said. I think it's strange you would talk this way on another woman who's got so much in common with you. Didn't I save you from the golf clubs coming down on your back? Those folks were going to tear you up. I think I deserve a little gratitude."

"Yes, I should get on my knees, shouldn't I? You want me to suck your dick?"

"You should respect me more because who knows but that if you keep it up like this I could lose control. I might clock your whiney ass back to Kickback. Then where will you be?"

"I'll be in Kickback, motherfucker!"

"Where will you go from there? You'll end up some cheap crackho selling fucks to niggers and rednecks. Weren't you telling me rednecks was something you've been trying all your life to get away from? The truth hurts, don't it, Beacon? I can say all this shit without telling a single lie because you and I both know it's true."

"Stop it."

"Lucy as a goosey, spreading it around all over the godddamn place. Without me, who would you be? I don't think it's right for you to begrudge me whatever fun I see fit to have. You need to calm down, and get with the program. I thought we were in this forever. It upsets me to think you are so flighty that you can, over just nothing, say shit about mutilating me, and did you threaten to call the FBI again? What kind of woman for a man are you that you can talk that way? Am I supposed to respect you?"

"I'm crazy for crack, baby."

"I know." Cliff hugged her close, and they rocked together, and Cliff was happy. He thought of that damn bitch who'd thrown her slop shop in his face then lowered the curtain. *My Eyes*—oh, she really had it coming, Deziray, and Cliff was tickled. Beacon's anger was a token of the true love she felt for him. True love and ownership could be tricky when drugs were in the mix. Cliff was glad for the talky talk.

"There there." Cliff stroked Beacon's head, running fingers through her beautiful hair.

"I'm still going to rip her tits off," Beacon murmured, and Cliff kept on being tickled. His inclination was to say: *Babes, you know I love tits with a bit of sag. I don't like firm tits, they rub me wrong. I like a tit you can grab on, a thing you can twist around and play with and use to pull the woman closer. I think Deziray's tits, even though I haven't seen them, are too firm over this here how young she is. I much prefer yours.* Cliff knew better than to say it. Thing would've blown new life into Beacon's wrath. Shit woulda got urgent, and who knew but that soon they'd hate each other. It could happen like snap a bean and throw the two ends over your shoulder. Best to blow the house up on that one, so Cliff kissed Beacon's temple, and called her the apple of his one and only eyeball.

Upon Amber and Barney's return, Cliff laid out the stuff of the day, what his family needed to know on Billy the Wax Manhunter whose want was to put them in manacles, and that they were caught on video exiting the scene of the crime. The front page of the *Tally Goddamn Motherfucking Democrat* showed it all, a newspaper that, like all newspapers, was not good enough to wipe your ass with. Newspapers were too crinkly and had ink on them. Did you want a bunch of ink smearing into your asshole? Cliff didn't think so, even if the shit was about the new war in Kosovo, or, say, the news on what happened to the Mars Surveyor Orbiter that disappeared the month before. What they were saying was the people who built the 125 million dollar space robot used Japan's measurement system for its trajectory guidance software. As a result the probe got too close to the planet. Instead of going into orbit like it was supposed to, damn thing was destroyed by the violent atmospheric conditions.

Oh, but people all over the handle of the pan—the *panhandle*—read the mofo effering demon of the crat. The fucking *Democrat* readers would see the front page picture. Was there anything the Quizzleboons could do to make themselves less like the people in the picture on the front page?

Why yes. Earlier in Cliff's wheel through Wal-Mart he decided some things. Whoever saw the picture would be looking to make connections. That's what people did, they connected shit, even if they didn't want to, it was natural, they couldn't help it. So Cliff bought cheap scissors, a six-pack of kids' t-shirts, a pair of boy's jeans, and a hoodie with a mutant turtle with a sword pictured on front. It was a obvious safeguard.

"No," Amber said.

"Don't start," Beacon said.

"It's a disguise," Leon said.

"Outlaws can't go around advertising theyselves," Beacon said. "You don't want us to get caught, do you? If we get caught just think how bad you'll feel."

"But I ain't no dude."

"Take some pride in it," Beacon said. "How many little girls get to go around being outlaws?"

"I don't care."

"Shut your mouth," Beacon said. "Come on, girl, it ain't nothing but a thang. You'll be two whole sexes rolled into one."

"A hermaphrodite?" Amber said, a frightened tremor in her voice.

"No, a hermaphrodite ain't neither man nor woman. You'll be a professional, somebody who fools people. Don't you want to fool people? It'll be like dressing up for Halloween every day of the week."

"I ain't no boy!"

"You lucky thang." Beacon scratched Amber's head.

And so it was. On the cabin porch Cliff smoked while Beacon cut Amber's hair, all that gold silkiness falling down into the sand strand by strand. A minute later Amber was quite the tyke with a crew cut. Her head was good to go, but what of the duds? "Take that motherfucker off," Cliff said, and threw the pants out there. He pulled the cheap sneakers out of the bag and threw them out there. A minute later Amber stood on the porch in her new clothes. "Not bad," Cliff said.

"I need me a wiener," Amber said.

"What you need is a name," Beacon told her. "How about Andy, that sounds a little like Amber, don't it?"

"If I'm gonna be a boy I need me a wiener."

"No, that ain't true," Beacon said. "All you need is a attitude. Walk your ass over to the tree over there like a boy and see if you can do it. We're gonna grade you on a scale of one to ten."

"I don't like Andy. I wanna be Fred. Can I be Fred? Let me be Fred."

Beacon looked to Cliff.

"I wanna be Fred! I wanna be Fred!"

Cliff nodded.

"Okay Fred," Beacon said, and Fred jumped off the porch and ran to the tree.

"No no no, that ain't it," Beacon said. "You got to put some rough into your stride. You ain't no goddamn ballerina, bitch. Walk over here but make it look like you're stupid and heavy, that's what boys is like, stupid and heavy, just remember that and you should be all right."

"Okay, is this better?" Fred walked with legs spread farther apart from each other, as if he needed to do that to stay balanced. With his club leg and the bow of the other he looked kinda girly and messed up.

"Hell yeah, that's a lot better." Beacon clapped. So

did Cliff.

Cliff told the Quizzles that Billy Waxman, the marshal who wanted to nail their necks into trees then rip off their backs, was a vegetarian in a ponytail, not no regular ponytail neither. This particular ponytail shot out the back of his bald head like the tail of a Shetland pony. You could grab onto it if you wanted. On some special arrangement with the U.S. Marshals Service, Waxman crossed state lines and traveled down here all the way from New York, which was a good indication he meant business. Waxman would not be satisfied until he had them in custody. "So we got to be special careful. In five days we deliver the monkey."

The Quizzleboon family played cards and long-walked through the woods, smoked cigarettes to pass the time and went down to the spring where Cliff swung Amber—no, Fred—'round and 'round, holding her—no, him—by an ankle and wrist. He'd let go to see Fred fly higher and high, rising and twisting in the open air like a star, a snowflake or some shit, then down, there she—no, he—goes, splashing into the spring, gravity's will. Whenever Barney barked and jumped, Fred took him up to solve the problem.

Fred loved Barney like a brother. Barney was filthy, hell yes he was, just the filthiest animal, but Fred slept with him. Fred spoke to Barney all the time, acting like a math teacher one minute and the next minute telling Barney wild stories about her friends up at the dirt farm. Over this new turn of the screw Beacon was pleased in she had more time to herself, and felt less stressed out.

Barney was better behaved now that he drank a lot of beer, and Jack Daniel's. Booze turned out to be the perfect cure for Barney's morning and evening sicknesses, crazinesses, whatever you wanted to call them, shit, thank the Lord, praise be unto Him, unto Quizzleboon, Jesus, praise them all, the luminaries and lunatics and Lucifer, those men in the heavens who had a few simple powers that could make or break you. It was nice when they helped you out and gave your monkey a cure. Not only were Barney's barks not so constant no more, but his habits in the rivers of shit shot from rectum found closure in their discovery of Barney's love of leaves and flowers. How it happened was quite magical. Ole Beacon had found some kind of wild begonia whose stem she'd slipped behind Fred's ear. Fred had been holding the monkey, and the monkey just turned his head and took a bite. It was a *Hey Mikey, he likes it!* moment, just with a monkey instead of a dumbass. Next thing they knew they were feeding Barney leaves and picking up pecans from under the trees to smash open and feed the orange thing the stuff what came inside.

Life was good. Life was real sweet but for the dreams that came at night, the damned Yankee Doodle Dandy Dude chasing Cliff through the haunted forest, calling out, "What I did to you?" and begging for help until Cliff woke up. Cliff didn't like running from people, especially people who weren't even people. Whenever it started to get dark he always got nervous, and then sometimes in the dreams he'd see the angry nekid bleeding chick-dude step out from behind a tree. She too, would run after Cliff, and he'd wake for the terror. What would happen if she caught him? Would Cliff do like the poor hunter who killed his friends in the cabin? Cliff had had a vision of himself braining Beacon with his barbell while she slept, and then turning to the child, but Quizzleboon would save him, right? There's nothing to be scared of, Cliff told himself, but was glad that soon they'd be leaving the forest where the battle was fought.

At least I'm off the coke, Cliff thought, and thought a lot of Deziray, his heart crying out like a howler monkey. It was so stupid but what could be done for it? As for Beacon's budding friendship with the scissors he'd bought from Wal-Mart, Cliff hoped she only was trying to be dramatic. He doubted she would snip his testes off, just she kept the scissors within reach.

The day before their delivery of the monkey to Ex-Congressman Butler, Cliff journeyed to Woodville to buy a paper and found out that the Barney Fund was up at nine thousand dollars. That made the Quizzleboons more wanted. More people were mad over the albino monkey bullshit. How could anybody steal a monkey? What unsupportable treachery! Reading on it made Cliff's mouth curl up like a goddamn sour grape mid-shrivel; but they, those pissed-off monkey lovers, were the upholders of a shitty social system, were they not? Those wicked people bought and sold for greed, instead of necessity, and were the ones the Dirties of Asheville hated and stood stoutly against. The monkey-lover assholes drove Saabs and Volvos. Paper said the "Monkey Thieves" might be a normal family. Might live across the street from you. Several fams had been investigated, the paper said. At the moment, more fams were under investigation, but there were no strong leads as of yet. The deplorable abduction of the albino monkey was a great unsolved mystery of modern times, the way they talked on it, right up there with alien abductions in Idaho and the Bermuda Triangle disappearances. Was there water on Mars? Did the Virgin Mary appear in Mexico? What of O.J. Simpson? He'd been acquitted, but nobody agreed on did he stick a knife in the wife to cause the larynx of her, whatever a larynx was, to be seen though the hole if you looked down it.

21.

THE QUIZZLEBOONS THAT night arrived at nine at the place on the map Kind Edward gave Cliff, a lakefront property on Lake Shore Drive. They slipped down the slope and skirted the house proper, and took under a stone archway to a small wood of pine tree and oak. The path was of brown needles, and dim, lit each fifteen steps by a lantern hung from a hook on a pole. The Mutton House, as Kind Edward called it, loomed up lonesome and creepy, a castle lost in a fog. Was made of stone. Had a crenellated tower. The path took over a pseudo moat of goldfish to end at a large bullet-shaped door. Cliff lifted the knocker, which was the trunk of an iron elephant's head, and dropped it once hard to the wood. Door opened without delay to reveal Butler's butler, or that's who Cliff guessed the man to be, for he wore a bow tie and sported the demeanor of a loyal old man. "My name is Stanford," Butler's butler said with a slight bow, and made way for their entrance.

In the bigass foyer the head of a albino rhino greeted them. The albino rhino jutted not so much *from*, as *through* the wall, that's how the rhino had been put, as if the stones were crashing to the floor that very moment. An iron chain hung from the high ceiling, and Stanford, whose brows looked bleached and were the thickest brows Cliff ever saw in his life, like two huge albino caterpillars clung to his face they were, told Fred to pull it. Fred gave the yank to a warped trumpet sound, a gravel roar and gallop of beast here coming in—a rhinoceros stampede. Snuffle sounds followed. Sounded like huge lips flapping dirt. There came squeaky hollow sounds and a sound to sound like some baby clearing her throat through a kazoo.

They followed Stanford through a hall on into a spacious room with a fireplace with a fire in it burning. On the walls paintings of hunting scenes hung, like windows into a past of safaris and champagne picnics on the banks of reedy lakes. The walls held rifles, and enlarged black and white photos of albino men and women in fancy clothes, black suits with top hats, hoopskirts, ankle boots. Cliff figured these were Butler's progenitors, but some pictures reminded him of the Freak Exhibit of his younger years, when he traveled around with the carnival.

The main thing to grab the Quizzles were the heads. This here Congressman Butler dude appeared to have collected the things since birth. Cliff saw hog heads and deer heads and a moose head, all albino. An albino bear head, unless it was a polar bear head, was placed above the fireplace. He saw an albino dog head—what kind of freak would cut off a dog's head?—and a cow head and what looked to Cliff like a albino seal head, its whiskers white and personable like the skinny Enoki mushrooms folks fried in butter at the dirt farm, sprinkle you some salt in there. The room was laid with white carpet, but throw rugs of albino animal hides were placed strategic throughout.

To the middle of the room, kicked back in a white leather cozy chair, white bare feet on a white ottoman, was the ex-congressman of butt proclaim. He was dressed in white. By his looks one could take safe guess over his underwear color. Old Butler acted like he'd been kicked back, all hum de dum, just another quiet evening in the Mutton House, right? When Butler finished reading whatever paragraph, he set his *New Yorker* on the table beside his chair, peeled off his reading glasses, and stood.

Butler was a mid-sixties man. First thing you saw was the bright white wrinkle-free complexion from which a pink witch's nose did protrude. He was thin, Butler, but strong, a weight-lifter who sized Cliff up, then took Beacon in. The man was exercising great restraint in the not-look-for-Barney-straight-off-the-bat business he was doing. He was withholding gratification, as they say, but oh, when he saw Barney clutched to the boy's side, the monkey's fox-colored arms wrapped around Fred's neck, his face near to burst a blood vessel. "Barney?" he said, and Barney, who knew his name, took up eye on the congressman whose long nose began to salivate in a mouth-watering flavor-lusting kind of way.

"Hoo hoo hoo," Barney said.

"Oh, Barney," the congressman said, more of a heave than a said.

"Hoo hoo hoo."

"Don't you worry about those heads on the walls, Barney," Butler said. "That is not what I brought you here for, my good friend."

"That's right," Cliff said. "Mr. Butler wants you for a pet, ain't that right, Congressman?"

"Oh, he'll have a lot more fun here than he did in the jungle."

"He's going to feed you bananas and green beans and whatever else you wanna eat for supper, ain't that right, Mr. Butler?"

"Please, call me Butt," the ex-congressman said, peeling his eyes, for the moment, from Barney. Butler straightened his posture in what struck Cliff as a political manner. The Butt here needed, Leon conceded, to keep his excitement concealed 'til the tape was cut. "All my good friends call me Butt," the ex-congressman continued. "When they speak of me behind my back, they reference me as *the* Butt. Didja hear that *the* Butt bought a Jaguar XJ6? Didja know that *the* Butt was friends with Tom Cruise? Hey, is it true that *the* Butt built a castle in his backyard?"

"Oh, people do find it interesting that I built a model castle in my yard, but I've always been one to have my way. I passed a law, you know, that made it a felony to kick a turtle in California."

"Yeah, I heard about you did some real cool shit for people in California," Cliff said.

"Usually when I tell that story I say I made it illegal for people to kick turtles in their butts, but in truth all you gotta do is kick the turtle anywhere on its body and you still get the penalty. I've always been a strong supporter of animal rights."

"I heard on the Triple-B Bill, or, what was it called? Let me think a second."

Butler laughed and gave Cliff a brotherly—*or was it a fatherly?*—pat to the shoulder. "That's it, the Tripple-B, the Butler Butt Bill. I did that."

"That's damned decent of you, Congressman."

"Butt, just call me Butt."

"I'm sorry, but I won't call you Butt. We're here to deliver the monkey."

"Okay, give him here then."

"Fred."

"No," Fred said. "Barney said he don't like this place. He wants to stay with us, Daddy."

"Go over give the good congressman the monkey," Cliff said.

"You got to understand," Beacon told the ex-congressman. "Fred has done builded himself a relationship with this here monkey."

"Yes, I'm sure she has," the Butt said.

Cliff noticed that the Butt did, actually, have a pretty big-ass behind.

"No, he ain't no her, he's a him," Beacon corrected the Butt.

"If you say so."

"Hand him over, Fred," Cliff said.

"I ain't got to." Fred turned as if to walk away from the Butt, leave the premises of the Butt, no big deal here on what the Butt might think on the renig of the Butt.

Beacon grabbed Fred's arm. "I ain't playing," she said, and took to peel the monkey from Fred. Barney barked up loud now in the long-ass Barney-bark to travel for miles. His damn mouth was wide split in the ovoid scream thing going:

"HgoooooooooAHHHHHHHHHHhhhhhhhh."

"Beautiful!" the Butt cried, loud enough to be heard through Barney's noise.

Barney was not happy on the situation, but Beacon handed him over to the white man in white clothes. The Butt clutched Barney tight to his chest, Barney's hands and legs sort of squirming and kicking all over. Talk of pathetic, but the Butt smiled on, not the least concerned or distressed over the poor monkey's discomfiture.

"The family," as they were known to readers of pap smears—or *newspapers*, take your pick—all over the Florida Manhandle—or *Panhandle*, say it how you please—followed Stanford back through the hall. When they got to the foyer, Cliff said, "Goodbye Mr. Rhinoceros," thinking it would cheer Fred, but no such doing. They passed back through the woods with its mystery lanterns hung from poles and Fred, even though he was a boy now and supposed to be strong, wept in the step of his dumdumbness.

"Oh, stop yer gotdam sniveling," Cliff admonished the idjit. They were moving up through the manicured lawn, headed for the car. Cliff would have said more, but what's this in the eye? A old woman—Cliff saw her through a window on the house's side—with curly orange hair in a white nightie. On her knees before a towering crucifix she was. The woman, like Fred, appeared to be weeping, but why? Cliff never would have pegged the Butt for Catholic, but who the fuck knew anything on anybody? The people of the world were impossible to figure. All but for that they were blobs of want. Were people blobs of want? When they didn't get what they wanted, they wept, and did want obliterate decency in the pops of elations? Did populations make monks buy monkeys, or skunks steal poodles for ransom? Cliff didn't care to be a slave blob. Like everybody, though, he maybe was. If he thought on it, he might could admit he was a blob.

"This ain't right," Fred said as they reached the car.

"Shutcher fuckin cocksucker," Cliff said.

"You shouldn't talk that way to a child," Beacon said. "I don't care what she did."

"He."

"Okay, he, same difference."

"He knew it all along that Barney was our ticket. If he had doubts he should've said something upfront and not waited 'til the last minute to drop a bomb."

"You can say that," Beacon said, "because you don't understand what it's like to be a child. You don't understand how a child's mind works. Fred lives in the moment. He won't recognize danger 'til it drops on his head to make him go splat."

"I don't care," Cliff said, and they climbed into the Camaro, and Cliff drove them to the blind man's to collect their money.

22.

BLIND EDWARD TOOK the Quizzleboons upstairs. He handed Cliff the Ziploc sack with four rubber-banded bricks of green in there, a clean twenty grand in Ulysses S. Grant heads. "That wasn't the deal," Cliff said.

"This is true," the blind man said, "but there were unexpected expenses."

"Unexpected expenses? I bought all kinds of crap to make this operation happen. I paid fourteen dollars for Fred's hoodie with a turtle on it. I bought bananas and flashlights and all kinds of shit."

"I never said you had an expense account. If you bought stuff, that was on you. As per our agreement, such expenditures are completely meaningless. Those are expected expenditures, not unexpected expenditures, learn the difference."

"I'm not complaining, I'm just saying. I don't know what expenditures you could have to run so high as that."

"Twenty-five hundred went to the Barney Fund." Kind Edward held up one finger.

"What?"

"The Butt was the anonymous donor, guilt notwithstanding, who started the Barney Fund. It's called an expenditure, Highnote. Every job has expenditures that come up unforeseeably, quit acting like an amateur."

"It wasn't part of the deal."

"What about the other twenty-five hundred?" Beacon wanted to know.

"That was money paid out in blackmail fees, another unforeseeable event."

"Blackmail fees? What's that got to do with my end?" Cliff said.

"She told me you fucked her, Cliff. You fucked My Eyes, but I'm not holding that against you. It's an expenditure."

"Daddy, who did you fuck?" Fred said, looking at Cliff like she—no, he—might weep again. Fred was sad to be without Barney, and now this—*goddamn!*

"Never trust a blind man," Cliff said.

"Well, that's not fair," Kind Edward said. "Billy Waxman returned, if you really feel the need to know stuff. Billy and Deziray struck up a friendship. Waxman left her his card. She threatened to spill the beans, so I gave her the money. I said don't come back."

"I'm'a kill," Beacon said.

"Who Mama? Who you gone kill?"

"I won't say her name."

"I believed in her," Edward said. "At heart I'm a romantic gentleman from antebellum times. If a woman says she's my eyes, I gotta believe. I tied my Tommy Hilfiger sweater around her belt and she walked me to the Chevron store for a six-pack of High Life, pulling me along behind her like she was my seeing-eye-dog. She didn't mind being seen that way in public like most women. Deziray doesn't care what people think. I like that about her. I was hoping she'd stick around."

"When I find her she'll be sorry," Beacon said.

"Good luck," Edward said.

"Are we going to hit her with the golf clubs?" Fred asked.

"Damn straight," Beacon said. "I have it full in mind to rip her titties off and throw them into the road to where they are run over by wheels of trucks and cars and eighteen-wheelers."

Kind Edward smiled, and some beads of sweat instantly popped out on his forehead. "Hey, there's an idea," he said, his eyelids blinking rapidly.

"What was your cut in the deal?" Cliff asked.

"A clean ten, why?"

"The right thing would've been to take that money out of your own."

"Do I believe what I'm hearing? I just handed you twenty thousand dollars and you are accusing me of wrongdoing? You know something, maybe if you hadn't gone behind my back and fucked My Eyes I would be more in the magnanimous frame of mind."

"I didn't fuck your goddamn eyes."

"That's what you say."

"That's the truth."

"If it is, I guess I don't really give a shit at this point," Edward said, ending the conversation. All would have been done did here now, but the blind attorney, as an afterthought, put in, "If you come across her, tell her I want my Tommy Hilfiger sweater back, that if I don't get it she'll be cursed. Not everybody knows this, Highnote, but if you steal a precious object from somebody, it curses you bigtime, even if you know nothing of the preciousness of that particular object. It's got nothing to do with what you do or do not know."

"Okay, sure," Cliff said, and he and his family went downstairs where a party was going on. All the druggy lowlifes who'd been run off previously were back to stay. They smoked crack in the Don Quixote room, and played guitars and sang and told stories and joked. When they saw "The Family" standing there, everybody quieted.

"There's a ten-thousand-dollar reward out for y'all," Don said.

"So why ain't you running for the phone?" Cliff asked.

"Shit, who you think I am, some bumfuck redneck from Whoville?"

"No, I think you're a real upstanding solid guy."

"Which is more than we can say on your daddy," Beacon said. "He ripped us off five motherfucking thou."

"That's alotta breeze," somebody said.

"Hey Amb, play us a song," somebody else, name of Earl, said.

"My name is Fred," Fred said.

"Oh, ha ha ha, you in disguise, that it? Shit, girl, how long you gonna keep it up? Anybody can see what I can see."

"Long as I gotta," Fred said.

"A time comes for every girl," Earl said.

"Why don't you shutup," Fred said.

"I'm talking fried eggs and peaches, baby." Earl winked at her.

Cliff dropped into the couch, lit a Carleton. The can was given over and he whopped a ghost down into the lung. Once more he was in the zone. It only took one for the mood to rush in. Cliff loved it, was in paradise, but Beacon refused it, was mad. That Deziray stuff had pissed her off. Twenty-five hundred bucks was a lot to lose over some crackho's wiles. Plus, she no longer associated with scumbags such as these—she was beyond it. What did that make Cliff? Well, he didn't care at the moment what it made him. The twenty grand under the belt felt better than a slice of hot apple pie with a scoop of vanilla ice cream on top. If somebody wanted to skrunk him out, bring on the skrunk!

"I'm going down to get the rest of our shit from the boiler room," Beacon said.

"Okay, once you load up we'll be gone."

Beacon and Fred left. Cliff breathed in a new ghost. He fell into the see of the jam he and the fam were in. Just everybody knew. Cliff's heart puffed up with love to think nobody had turned him in yet, and he blew out the ghost and watched it twitter. A second later his heart grew harder in the sea of their smoke, and the know of that right now, in the put-on of their friendly faces, the want was to fuck the fam straight up their ass and out their mouth hole. The wanteds and the wanters. Everybody was both of big or lesser degree, but right now the fam was more wanted than Sting who sang not to stand so close to him. Leon's arms, both fire and water, were supposed to balance him out, only right now they were sleeping on the job or some shit.

Well, old Ray Orbison, bastard brother to singer Roy, had told Cliff, warned him back when he was Leon, that he needed to make a conscious effort to use his arms if they were to help him live life. Whatever magic Leon's arms held could only be harnessed through constant effort. A man did not hop a horse to ride without that he'd rode the horse before. Man had to know the horse, understand horses, and hang with horses a load before he could ride like the I-Can't-Believe-It's-Not-Butter-Guy rode. Now that boy could straddle a horse! Cliff remembered how that March he'd seen the news of the flying goose to smash Fabio's face while Fabio partook of a rollercoaster ride in Florida. Damn goose broke Fabio's nose. Cliff had felt concern. Had Fabio had to cancel a modeling job over this here goose? Cliff wondered was the goose yet alive.

Cliff had fallen behind, he knew it, in his efforts to harness the magic in his arms. If bad things happened to his family, it was on him for being a slack-ass fool. Cliff knew he ought split town, not tomorrow, but tonight, this minute, like the song says: *take the monkey and run.*

23.

BEACON AND FRED appeared in the Don Quixote room after clearing the boiler room of their stuff, some trash bags filled with clothes, a boom box and hammock and various useful objects such as forks and candles and an interesting book with pictures titled *Caring for Tortoises*. Cliff's family stood before him and the druggies, and were the most beautiful things in the world, too beautiful, even, to be real— were they apparitions? They reached their arms Cliff's way, and his heart swelled with pride. It was time to go. Cliff said goodbye to all, and minutes later was behind the wheel of his 1970 Camaro, matte black, awesome as fuck.

Cliff was a bit some skrunked, not totally wasted, but roasted enough to be adventuresome of spirit. When Beacon and Fred started in about how, oh, since they'd been ripped off, the original deal was changed, Cliff saw the logic, and agreed that the right thing to do was bust into the Butt's castle to save Barney. Barney was family. Would a Marine or Green Beret leave Barney with the Butt? What would Rambo do? Was the Butt a man to trust? Was Cliff a self-respecting babe magnet? What kind of man would leave his monkey behind in the hands of the enemy?

What did the Butt want Barney for anyway? To stuff? Kinda seemed like it.

Cliff parked where he'd parked before, up on the shoulder under the moon. The Quizzleboons stepped down through the grass, circumvented the house as before, but this time skirted the woods, and made to the lake and walked along its shore 'til they were behind the castle. Huddled together in the moon shadow of a live oak tree, they saw up through the windows of the Butt's lair, Barney, he was secured to a cross in the middle of the room, arms outspread like Jesus's had been during the crucifixion atop the hill they called Golgotha. Cliff lifted the binoculars to see Barney's feet cinched together down below, not nailed in like the way of Jesus's, but it was weird, and Barney was not no happy monkey, no sir. Good thing they'd had the sense to retutn.

The Butt was bowed down before the whole thing, in prayer, looked like, but they watched him stand up and stick Barney with something. The monkey's body stiffened even more, but Barney didn't cry out, which was disconcerting. Cliff watched the congressman kiss Barney's forehead. The congressman got back onto his knees. Looked like the congressman was smelling Barney's feet.

The Quizzleboons climbed the stone stairs to the back porch upon which there was a table and some rocking chairs and a telescope on a tripod. Cliff tried the knob. It didn't give so he nodded to Fred to slip the clicker up and shoot out the window. The music of sound followed—wasn't glass made of sand?—an avalanche in suburbia. Cliff reached his hand through, unlocked the door, and the Boons rushed in.

"Don't do nothing!" Fred said, and pulled back the hammer of the Hawes.

Butler stayed to knee, and just looked at Fred. But needles were in Barney's body stuck all over. Cliff started yanking them out, one by one, and throwing them into the animal throw rugs where they might could later stick somebody's feet. As Cliff plucked the needles out of the monkey he remembered the old curly haired redheaded woman he spotted when they'd first delivered *the Barn* to *the Butt*. Sounded like a song that might be written and rapped by a famous black guy like Busta Rhymes and played on the radio. *The barn to the butt, the barn to the butt, the butt to the barn and the barn to the butt.* Cliff wondered was the woman the Butt's wife. *The wife to the barn and the butt to the bible. Betcha five dollars she's a crack in the crockle*, hell, Leon didn't know. He wasn't a great rap artist like Fresh Prince or Busta Rhymes.

"Man, you're into some sick shit," Beacon said.

"Acupuncture," the Butt explained.

With each needle pulled out, Barney got a little more animated. Finally Cliff cut away Barney's fetters, and Barney dropped down into the carpet, and jumped for Fred, sprung up onto him and hugged him and started humping his flank.

"Wait," the Butt said as the family left through the door they'd just come in through.

Cliff looked back at the congressman, not pleased. Cliff was pissed off over he'd had to come back and do all this shit, but right was right. The Butt was wrong.

"I'll give you more money," the Butt said.

"Tell it to the Moon Man," Cliff said, and the Quizzlers went down and ran up through the woods to the Camaro and drove away. The road wound back and forth along the edge of the lake, and then they were cruising west on I-10. They passed turnoffs for Chattahoochee, Sneads, Cypress and Marianna known for its caves of bats. And just where did they think they were going to, Henrietta Pussycats? Did it matter?

Chipley, Bonifay, Ponce de Leon—Cliff thought on Deziray fondly as they passed that one—and Defuniak Springs and Crestview, these signs, one after the other, enough backwater towns to where if you gathered them up in the palms of your hands then slammed them together, you'd have half the alphabet—*no, the whole damn alphabolio*—asparkle before your eyes—*twinkle twinkle*, a crest here and a view there, a back and a water and a Baker and a Blackwater River. They crossed it, that river, and passed through Milton and Gonzales, and hooked a left toward the Gulf of the Mex. Outside the cole of the Pensc—*Pensacola*—they booked a room at the Brokenhearted Woman Motel. The motel was named in orange neon glass tubes curling around through the darker parts of night.

Their room had two big double beds in it, and was quite satisfactory. Had cable TV and a round table and relaxy kind of atmosphere. The painting above the beds showed a scene where two guys fished by a stream with mountains in the background. The colors in the painting were mostly of brown hues, such as everything else in the room: the table, the bedspreads, the rug, the cushioned chairs, it was all sort of brown, and the Quizzleboons slept well until Barney woke them at dawn with his barking. Quick, Cliff taped the monkey's mouth shut. He'd brought the tape in from the car as soon as they'd arrived the night before, thinking ahead. It didn't take Cliff long to shut the mother up.

Cliff tried to sleep after that, but couldn't. He stepped outside onto the walkway in his bare feet, the sun coming up behind the trees, and rubbed both eyes. He pulled his left eye out to put to mouth, rolled it around in there, then stuck it back into the socket. Felt better. Now what he needed was a tall cup of Joe, or a beer. Cliff looked to the check-in office. This was a cheap motel, no Joe for patrons, so he went around and popped the Camaro's trunk, thinking he'd grab a cold one from the cooler. When the trunk popped up, what he saw down there was too weird. It was too early in the morning to see stuff like this so he shut the trunk. Went back over to the walkway by the motel room door and rubbed his eyes more, and watched the orange light flood in through the pines. Made him think of a stack of pancakes poured over with hot maple syrup. He lit a smoke, but was it fair for him to stand out here with no beer? Fuck that shit. He went back to the trunk, popped it, grabbed one out the cooler and shut the car up. He sat in the driver's seat and drunk, or drank, in the think of the eyes to shift his way each time he'd popped the fucker. They'd cringed from the light.

Poor thing—wasn't fair she'd been in there all during the time they'd driven, or druv the interstate, and then all night long, the duct tape wrapped around her face, hands taped behind her back, and her knees duct taped together, and ankles taped. She was wedged between the cooler and various bags, Leon's weights and what, the back of her skull wedged to the spare tire so her neck must've hurt like hell by now.

All she could do was wiggle. Her eyes, each time as he'd closed the trunk on her face, had registered alarm, all begging out for help, cute in some ways. She'd obviously pissed herself. He knew she was thirsty.

Cliff snubbed his Carleton in the tray between the seats then got out, left the driver's door open, and went back there and used the key, unlocking the trunk for the third time that morning. He said, "I didn't know you were in there 'til just now. I'm'a drive us out someplace. Hold on." Cliff dropped the trunk, started the Camaro and drove out of the lot. He wasn't sure where to go, but a powerline road popped up. Cliff pulled in and crested a hill and drove another half a mile through the sand, the world gone to pretty, and Cliff could have gone on, the morning light so nice, the pines and shrubs decked in dewdrops and spider webs and strung with morning glory necklaces.

Cliff killed the car in the shadow of the tree line, got out, popped the trunk. Bitch hadn't moved. Cliff said, "You look uncomfortable, you lying, blackmailing piece of shit." Cliff grabbed her out, had to squash her into a kind of ball to maneuver her through the narrow trunk opening. He set her on the hood, legs to dangle over the front tire. He pulled the blade halfway out, flicked his wrist and it locked into position. "You ought to've known I'm a convicted felon three steps backward from desperate."

Deziray shook her head. "Mmm."

"Best thing is to slit your throat. You said I stuck up for kids. You called me Golden Man."

"MmmMmmMMMmm." She had something important to say, but Cliff cut through the tape around her ankles anyway. He cut the tape above her knees. He cut the tape doped around her stupid-ass face of lies, inserting the four-inch blade below her left lobe to draw it up. He peeled the tape from across her face, took some lip skin with it, then pulled the underpants from her mouth and tossed them aside.

"Leon."

"Hey baby, how you?"

"I'm happy to see you."

"Can you say that without telling a lie?" Cliff—no, he was Leon for Deziray—said.

"I blackmailed Kind Edward for you. I told him if he didn't pay me I'd tell Billy Waxman. I used that money to buy drugs for everybody so that they wouldn't tell on you. Everybody in the acres knew about the Barney Fund. I was trying to get in good with Billy so I could send him off on a wild goose chase."

"You did that for me?"

"I told Billy you and I were lovers, but I hated you for dumping me."

"Did I dump you?"

"Listen, I'm telling the truth. I told Billy, I told him, I said you split town the day before for Asheville, that you were going back to that farm you lived on."

"Did Billy take the bait?"

"I don't know for sure. I can't say but that Kind Edward contacted Billy and reversed all my hard work. I know it sounds crazy."

"I think you shouldn't go around lying about fucking people."

"It's not a lie, Leon."

"Okay, sure, it's not a lie. You dreamed about me, is that what you're saying?"

"No, just time is precarious."

"Precious?"

"No, just what I'm saying is since you're about to, it's the same thing."

"Bitch."

"If you don't now, you will later. I knew it was no lie when I heard Edward speak your name for the very first time. I never lied to you, Leon, I won't."

"We'll see." Leon ran the knife blade across her neck, barely, to see what it was like, that gesture, that motion, to imagine how it would feel had he pressed in hard to slit her throat. He didn't mean nothing by it, but his blade was so sharp that she took up to bleeding. In several spots along her neck red beads emerged and dripped. "Oh no."

"I don't care."

"I don't like to see it." Leon grabbed the length of tape he'd cut from her legs and wrapped it nice and tight around her neck. The blood that had traveled down beyond the width of tape he wiped away with the neckline of her flowery green dress. He yanked the damn thing down then, over shoulders and boulders to the waist of her, the fucking bitch, her wrists taped behind her still, and the duct tape in her hair dangling from one side like a silver-ass dreadlock. Her tits had some sag in them, he saw, which was way nice. They were not jam-packed with fat. He liked that. Her clavicle bones were pronounced, almost like you could grab into them like a pair of handlebars. Inspiring, the sight of her this way. Leon stepped back to take it in a bit more fuller, and pictured the come across it in the walk of a misty morning, the matte black of the car and the sand and sizeable tits hung down for whatever hungry animal to come along and chomp, her muss of hair a Motel 6 for field sparrows and centipedes. Check out the close-up here of the freckles to the cheeks. Part Cherokee, the blind man had said of her, too good even to touch, ask Leon, but he weighed one.

Did Deziray move? That would be a nary from Thelma's roasted hams to Melba's toasted yams. Wasn't like she could choose, could she, Coochiecoo?

"It's nice," Leon said on the hoopdie hoop. He checked its grab-action then ran a hand to and fro across the two, sorta slapped them, and ran hands over the shoulders, felt her nodules of spine. She had sweet breath, and birds chirped in the air all fresh and watery. Not even thinking hardly he undid the pants and pulled her closer and there it was. They were still under the sky, some deep looking into the faces of each other. In this posture Deziray stretched her long neck to set mouth to eye, reached her tongue into the socket and sucked it in, and knocked it about against her middle-class teeth. No woman ever in the world had done Leon this way. It wasn't a thing to tolerate. Here she was his weakness damn near to already now, this "daughter of artists and intellectuals"—that's what she'd called herself when Leon first met her. Her mother made pottery, her daddy wrote books. Sounded like some kind of fairytale land.

"Don't swallow it." Leon reached around and cut free her hands. Deziray gripped Leon's shoulders steeped in muscle and smooth and nearly hard as polished concrete. Leon didn't have time to set his knife down. The girl had closed the gap and was at it as was he. In the smack and spackle she grabbed his face. With lips and tongue she expertly replaced his eye.

So how'ya like that, Mr. I-Can't-Believe-It's-Not-Butter Man?

Driving back to the Brokenhearted Woman Motel, Cliff laid down some basics. "Most of all you got to remember you ain't shit. Nod your head yes you understand. And ye best not to start shit up with Beacon. She already said about how she wants to chop yer damn titties off and throw em into a swimming pool. Bad idea to mess with a jealous woman."

"I know. She put me in a headlock and slammed me with knuckles. That girl you saved from Don Rooks bit my leg, and when I kneed her, just as like a gut reaction, you know? That I couldn't help? Beacon said I did it on purpose. She punched me."

"You got off easy."

"My arm fell asleep. I was so cold last night."

"Are you going to act straight when we get back?"

"I about need a cigarette now. Can I have one of yours, Leon?"

"Help yourself."

Deziray grabbed the pack off the dash.

"But don't call me Leon. I'm telling you, if Beacon hears that you'd best to cover your titties. She also threatened to cut my balls off, just so you know. If you see her coming at me with the scissors, will you lend a hand?"

Deziray blew her smoke.

"Light me one too, bitch," Cliff said, and she did and they drove around smoking awhile and small-talking. In a bit Cliff steered the Camaro into the lot of the Brokenhearted Woman, and parked. Beacon burst through the door with Fred close behind. Beacon was going, "Hell no, you can forget it," and she yanked open the passenger side and pulled Deziray out by the hair.

"Beacon!" Cliff said.

QUIZZLEBOON

"No, goddamnit!" Beacon shouted, and had her in a headlock. As she dragged Deziray into the room, Fred kicked Deziray's legs. Cliff eyed around to make sure nobody had seen that sloppy interaction, then followed them in, closed the door. Deziray was on the floor now, facedown, and Beacon and Fred, and Barney too were all sitting on her.

"Beacon!" Cliff said.

"No, don't you dare!"

"I'm not going to tell you again," Cliff said.

"She's a rat, Daddy!" Fred said.

"Who told you that?"

"She stole our money!"

"No, no, it was Kind Edward stole our money. Deziray was helping us. She's one of my double agents. Get your ass off her, Beacon."

"What, did you just say what I think?" Beacon said.

"Get off her."

"Okay, fine," Beacon said, and stood. Cliff had Beacon and Fred sit on the brown bedspread on the bed. He explained how Dezzie told Waxman they were headed north, how she took Edward's money to bribe the druggies into not turning the Quizzleboons in just yet. "She was buying us time," Cliff said. Beacon didn't buy it, so Cliff told Deziray to stand the fuck up. "See her neck?"

Beacon and Fred saw the duct tape wrapped around it. Cliff grabbed an end and ripped it off and the cut started bleeding again.

"I damn near slit her throat. I made pure certain she wasn't no rat."

"You tortured her?" Beacon said.

"Damn straight."

"She still owes us twenty-five hunnerd dollars. I'm'a set that bitch on the strip. She can sell it!"

"That would draw attention to us, dipshit. Besides, we're rich. We don't need money, and that don't hardly sound like you neither. What happened to the good Beacon?"

"It's the principle."

Cliff was about to tell her a few things on principles, but Deziray lifted her hand. She said, "Beacon's right. I should not have presumed. I used the money to keep y'all out of jail, but I had no right."

"Oh, pat yourself on the back, that it?"

"I'm saying if that's what you want me to do, I don't know that I'll fight you, Beacon."

"Did you say my name? Did I say you could say my name?"

"Sorry." Deziray stepped back against the wall. The blood driblets had made it down through the neckline of her dress. Cliff could hardly stand to see it, so went into the bathroom to alas, finally, shave that goddamn motherfucking beard off. He did that, and felt a hundred times better, like Leon Hicks again, good old Leon Hicks, that's who he was. He was tired of being Cliff Highnote, or Cliff Lownote, however you took a look on it, take your pick. Had not Deziray called him Leon? Sure as hell had, and he loved it. Was it unwise to undo the disguise? Take a guess then hop on the bed, Clive. *Yes*, for the wherefore of the motherfuck might make Leon a duck, dead. His face was on post office walls.

Leon felt confident. He was proud of his encounter with Deziray. Talk of romance! He had the I-Can't-Believe-It's-Not-Butter guy beat, hands down like to shut somebody's coffin lid. Cliff stepped into the tub and promised himself, under the hot stream showering down, no more garbage. No more! Fuck em all! He was high, a fierce bulldog, a impressive con. Leon was king to two brown-haired ladies of the jungle, each with unique sensibilities, don't mention the dipshit child or monkey. Was there more to life? Holy Jesus H Yes—Leon was the man of the magic eyeball.

24.

LEON CLOSED HIS eye in the shower to see Quizzleboon on the moon. The Quiz had grown large like a flowering Magnolia tree, and with outstretched arms held shining swords, kabobs upon which were skewered the wiggling bods of the vengeful hermaphrodite and black Yank soldier man. Behind the Quiz a sea of stars glittered in the deep, and there was a sunburst and foggy space clouds floating. It was glorious, and Leon felt secure in the knowledge that his tormentors from Coon Hill had been reined in by his benefactor. He could look at the colored black Yank now and not get the heebie-jeebies.

Oh, the dude had dug fingers into Leon's side, quite nastily with his long sharp fingernails so that it hurt, all while Leon—*no, he was Cliff back then*—had been trying to sleep. The Yank had been desperate to tell Leon a story about something or other that he thought was real damned important, but *Tell it to the Quiz*, Leon had thought. *I'm not interested.* Since leaving Coon Hill the visitations had stopped, but Leon, in his running from the Yank, and hearing his urgent calls echo through the forest, had figured out that the Yank and Herm knew each other, in some capacity, and were not friends. The Yankful man, Leon guessed, had tried to stop his Union buddies from doing cruelty on Ophelia. Somehow, because of Ophelia, the man was pulled up by the neck into an oak and left to hang.

It was from Amber, who'd heard it from Kind Edward, that Leon learned that the Yank was a Carolina slave assimilated into the army by a General Newman. In his buttoned uniform the Yank was right spruce. Leon understood that the Yank and Herm had some probems, but why did their problems have to be his? He wasn't into it, so Quizzleboon just took them bitches up as his playthings. The Quiz drew the sword tips together and watched as these lost ones from the past, the Yank and Herm, flailed at each other, kicking and trying to scratch each other's eyes out and bite and kill. The Quiz found pleasure here. He was amusing himself in the way a child might a cat held by the tail—let the cat run some, think he's getting away, then yank back. Old Quiz was teasing them, and it seemed downright cruel, especially since the hermaphrodite was nekid and had that weird, you know, situation that had caused her friends to butcher her, or him, Ophelia or Opham, take your pick. Leon's own personal pick was to call her Ophelia. She was actually a very good-looking chick, though somebody needed to wash the blood off her body. You could hardly bare to see her without that you felt sorry and sick to your stomach.

Old Quiz shifted his head, his gaze lining up with Leon's face where he stood in the shower. Quizzleboon winked. Leon shut off the water.

Leon dried his legs and stuff, and wiggled into his jeans, and knocked a Carleton from the cigarette pack he'd left on the fake marble counter there. With his fresh smoke he left the motherfucking bathroom, and said, "Beacon, get my duffel bag out the back seat."

"Holy shit, Cliff," Beacon said.

They were staring at him.

"Don't call me Cliff no mores."

"But you shaved."

"The better to eat your pussy with, bitch."

"Does that mean I can be a girl?" Fred said.

"Hell yes, motherfucker." Leon clapped his hands and snapped his fingers and pointed at her. "You a girl now, girl."

"Yay yay yay! I'm a girl, I'm a girl," Fred—*no, he was Amber*—shouted, and she jumped up and down, waving her arms like to fly, and old Barney, seeing Amber excited, he too jumped up and down. He went, "Ahwr ahwr ahwr," though not too loud. Barney knew if he went "Ahwr ahwr ahwr" too loud, Leon would shut his ass up. Barney jumped from the bed to the dresser then hopped to the TV, his long tail whipping this way and that, him so excited, old Barney, over this shift in the wind. From the TV Barney jumped onto Amber who climbed onto the bed and jumped up and down while clutching the monkey to her bosom as he humped her excitedly.

"Are you sure about this, baby?" Beacon said.

Leon inhaled the fine tobacco smoke.

"I don't want ever to be locked up," Beacon said. "I'd go crazy."

"I say we have bigger bones to crush," Deziray said.

"Who the hell asked you, you pukeweed whore? Did I say you could talk?"

Deziray kept her eyes on Leon. She was admiring

his arms, he could tell, his cool-ass tattoos, fire on one side, water to the other. This arrangement was a thing Dez could appreciate. Leon was not quite as muscular as he liked to be, but he was damn cut, especially if you considered what type of guy she was used to, shit. Leon had the abs, the pecks, the tats, the sculpted jaw. His neck was wide and sturdy. He was no brainy man, or hairy—his chest was not bald, but close, which he'd been told by one lady was a aphrodisiac. That had been up at the dirt farm. It was Two-Stone. After fucking her in the Great House basement, she ran her hand over Leon's badboy pectorals to say, "This here is a aphrodisiac." Leon said, "What the hell you talkin, bitch? I ain't got no fro!" Two-Stone laughed. "No, silly," she said, and explained to Leon what a aphrodisiac was. Leon, with Deziray's eye on him, felt like the most aphrodisiacest dude to put on long pants.

"Bitch, I'm talking to you," Beacon said.

"Goddamn, Beacon, knock it off," Leon said.

"What?" Beacon looked injured.

"Would you please get my duffel bag from the car?"

"Fine." Beacon left the room.

"Don't worry on her. I got ye covered," Leon said.

"Hey Leon, you remember when I told you I'm a thousand years old?" Deziray said in a sweet voice she would not have used had Beacon not been in the fetch of his duffel.

"Yeah, your crazy business, sure."

"Well don't you think after living that long I would have figured out how to deal with people like her? Edward told me she called the FBI on you."

"Don't mention none of that." Leon stubbed his

Carleton in the tray on the round brown table. Beacon came in and threw his duffel bag onto the floor. Leon picked it up, hit the bathroom and brushed his teeth and dressed. He took his old pants off, put on a new pair of briefs from Wal-Mart, then pulled up his favorite pair of Wrangler jeans, freshly washed, tight fitting. Next came his IF YOU CAN'T PISS WITH THE BIG DOGS STAY OFF THE PORCH shirt. Leon looked himself in the mirror. None of that goddamn History professor bullshit going on here anymore. How nice not to be in disguise. That incognito shit messed with a man's pride. Once back in the room Leon pulled on some tube socks and stepped into the cowboy boots, completing the picture of the man he was what? Born to be? Born to become? Born for why? What kind of asshole looks behind him when trying to explain what's up ahead?

"Uhm, OK, listen up," Leon said.

His minions awaited instruction.

"I hate to say this," Leon said.

"Say what?"

"Barney," Leon said.

"Barney what?" Amber said.

"Barney's got to go."

"Hell yeah," Beacon said. "I'm sick of his ass."

"No," Amber said.

"A monkey belongs outside swinging in the branches. We've got to let him go for his own good, and ours," Leon said.

"Let him go?" Amber said.

"That's a great idea, Leon," Beacon said. "He's a liability. We get caught it'll all be Barney's fault. We won't have nothing to say for ourselves, and besides that, I really don't want to have to hate this monkey."

"No," Amber said.

"He's a liability," Beacon said.

"Beacon's right," Deziray agreed, "but I don't think he'll do too good in these woods around here, do you?"

"Goddamnit!" Beacon shouted.

"Stop your crazy bullshit, woman!" Leon shouted back at her, and balled his fist and gave Beacon to understand that he might use it, just keep pushing, you've been warned.

"Okay, you're the boss, Leon."

"Goddamn straight, bitch. That's a fact you keep forgetting."

"What Barney needs," Deziray said, "is to be let free in the jungle he came out of."

Beacon let loose a nasty put-on guffaw.

"I'm serious," Deziray said. "We should drive him down to Nicaragua and let him go."

"We? Did you say we?"

"That's his home," Deziray said, and Leon noticed the passion creeping into the whole thing of her voice. The girl was passionate, and sort of regal and sad with a sapped-out used-up look that came over her from time to time. The blood on her neck, though, was making Leon sick.

"Put something over that," he said.

"Here," Amber said, and handed Deziray the blue bandana she sometimes wore on her head.

Deziray thanked the child and remedied the situation. Leon saw that Deziray had a lot she wanted to say, that inside her a bunch of squashed-down input frustrated her and festered. It wanted to get out. Deziray held stuff back due to Beacon's jealousy factor. Such were the demands made on her now, but cut her loose and who knew but that she might perform a miracle, especially with that special piss she manufactured that, according to her, was the Fountain of Youth. Leon wondered if he might not grow backwards a little if he drank some.

"Hoo hoo hoo," Barney said.

Everybody looked at Barney in Amber's arms, his gorgeous long tail curling down to her ankle.

"Nicaragua's a long-ass way away from here," Leon said.

"What, you ain't considering it, are you?" from Beacon.

"If we can make it down to Mexico, who says we can't drive to Nicaragua?"

"Hell no, I ain't going to no Niggeragua. You can forget it."

"I'm hungry," Amber said.

Leon put a think down. Was it in their interest to let Barney go? The worst to could happen was Barney would wander onto some highway, like what happened to the cow Gary cut free from the Goth farm. Barney could be made road meat, a thing of orange to peel off the asphalt to eat, chop it into hamburmonkey patties, fry up some hamburmonkey, put some Heinz ketchup on it, and a pickle, go ahead, take a bite. On the other hand, somebody might find Barney in a tree, or rummaging through somebody's garbage, or taking a walk. With all the barking Barney did it could happen right quick. Barney would be returned to the Florida History Museum, then dispatched to Managua via United Airlines, first class. The political shit he'd started would iron out nice and cute. Or a hunter might take aim on Barney and shoot. Barney would be dropped dead, or made the cripple, see him in crutches, but was he a liability? That's what mattered was the talk Beacon talked and was talking. She had a lot of the power of persuasion going on with the talk she talked on.

25.

THE QUIZZLEBOONS HIT the Camaro hungry, only they needed to toss Barney off in the woods somewhere. Coming up on the powerline road, Leon hooked a left and drove over the hill. He watched Deziray's face in the rearview mirror as he pulled up to the place he'd damn near slit her throat. When they got out of the car to dispose of the monkey, there were Dezzie's footprints in the sand,

"Stop acting like you don't want him to go!" Beacon said.

"I ain't," Amber said.

Beacon pulled Barney off Amber and tossed him some eight feet into the palmetto scrub. Barney bounded back like with bedsprings hooked to his feet—*boing*. He jumped onto Amber and wrapped his arms around her shoulders and went "Hoo hoo hoo."

Beacon pulled him off again and threw him out there. Barney stood up tall on his legs and sniffed and turned his head around looking at things.

"He don't want to be free," Amber said.

"Like most people," Deziray said.

"I love you, Barney," Amber called out, and Barney bounced back, boinging onto his beloved, damn wrapped his arms and legs around her and started humping.

"She's his mama and he's her baby," Deziray observed.

"Well," Leon said, the ought of the motherfuck that they should leave Barney here. Might give Leon a guilt-feel, though, so they packed back in the car, Barney included, and Leon drove them to Pensacola City, where a nice old-time place called The Miracle Diner popped up. Before the turn-in to park, Leon pulled behind a shopping mall. Though a bit some inhumane, he peeled Barney off Amber like a piece of skin with balls of dangle, and threw his ass in the trunk all plentiful of banana. Were some Nature Valley Granola Bars in there. And some figs from Spain and lettuce of romaine. Leon gave Barney a baby bottle filled with watered-down tequila.

Eggs, bacon, cakes, coffee, grits, it was the full-on menu, eat your fill, though the menu did not have no tits. If it did, Leon would order his with a bit of dangle, some jiggle in there, and stretch marks, wow! A real damn nice-ass thing to grace a titty, ask Leon. Things were like tiger scratches—*reeahwrrr*—and looked damn nice of ass. Of the belly they were like rays around the sun. When they took up to the inner thigh, we talking trickle-downs of holy water.

As no dirt rules here said NO MEAT, one and all were in the eat of it, why the fuck hell not? Oh, bacon, sausage patties, links. Deziray ordered a country fried steak, and Leon had a nice pink slab of ham to a plate. Amber done chomped into the bacon like it was a old friend she was happy to reunite with after all these years. Leon felt relieved. Damn bitch had acted like some kind of uppity purity woman not yet grown. If you ate steaks or invertebrates did that make you a sonofabitchful ingrate slapped to the grates laid over the fires of Hell? Even people in the bible ate animals, Rashanel.

The Boonquizzles, four in number without the quadruped, feasted, and talked on stuff, and it came up on how they ought hit a Salvation Army for groovy clothes.

"Salivation Army?" Amber cried out.

Deziray said, "That is so smart, that is so cool, I love how you misheard that, Salivation Army, I can just see it, a whole army of people folding clothes and placing items with drool dripping down."

"Salvation, not salivation, stupid," Beacon said. "Do you even know what salvation means?"

"That's what Jesus did they say."

"Ain't but a bunch of bullshit," Beacon said.

"It can also be for things," Deziray put in.

"Things, what the fuck you talking, things?"

"Things can be saved too."

"That's all what we do at the farm. You gonna act like you telling me something I don't know?"

"No, I didn't mean it that way," Deziray said.

"Y'all shut the fuck up," Leon said, and back in the car drove his gang through the downtown part of the city. Everybody looked out the windows at stuff. He gassed up at a Shell and bought smokes and asked the cashier where a good thrift store was. The mother looked Leon up, and the mother looked Leon down. Leon's feel was to smash the mother's nose. The mother may have sensed it coming on, so thought better on the make of a comment. He said, "Go down to Fairfield, turn left. A mile on the right you'll see it."

Leon thanked him, drove over to the warehouse

style Salvation Army full of appliances, furniture, clothes and general doohickeys. For Amber Leon found a pink ukulele, but it was the clothes they were there for, not a bunch of crap they'd have to carry around and look after for God only knew how long. Amber just tried on some dresses and wigs. She picked Jesus shirts off the racks, and got shoes, chintzy jewels and socks and a aluminum water bottle. It was neat how she could flop and flip back like now I'm a boy, now a girl, a boy, girl, boy, girl, take it up Busta Rhymes: *hip to the hippety hip hop, a bee bop, now I'm a girl, now I'm a boy, gimme gimme five, gimme ten, gimme twenty, if you mess with my monkey, all you get is a penny*. It was easier if you were a child, Leon guessed.

Beacon found clothes for Deziray. Even with Leon's say of it out of the question, Beacon held to the *We gone pimp the Dez* idea. Dezzie needed a attire to attract lowlifes. Beacon picked out items to make her look cheap. Damn shit about to pissed Leon off. You'd think Beacon'd not do that over the what she'd gone through at the Vanderbilt. Bitch told him of it early for spring while a snow fell slow through the glass of the Great House. They were nice in the coke of the high, comfy in bed upstairs, somebody out there chopping wood. In the splinter Beacon said she'd learned to sew. She got good at it and made her own clothes and wanted to be a designer—that was her dream. Come twenty she moved to New York City, got on in Soho as a fashionista's assistant. Damn near to next day, it seemed, she agreed to sex stuff with the gay designer, a important black guy whose fang she harbored in her gobble bay, or choral portal—*take a sing on this action, Janet Jacskon*—and did the knee on him as he brushed out minx coats, other gays in the room. He told stories as if she wasn't there, and Beacon—*no, she was Lucy Blue back then*—tried toughing it out, but the guy was crazy. At some point he started in on the stank shit, said she'd better apologize. She'd go back to the Vanderbilt Y, and wash herself the best she could, but next day it was the same. He'd pinch his nose and say, "I thought I told you to wash that shit out. Geeez, girl, why you do this to me?" and the gays, his employees and clients and such, laughed a bunch. "Fuckin *staaaaaaaaank*," they said. She left the city after three months total. For Lucy Blue it was back to the Bam of the Alacazam.

The Amb left the Army of Salivation in a flounced powder blue dress. Even with short hair and zilch in the tilt for Milt department she looked more the girl, a fairy tale child of magic power and concealed ability. In the green-ass flip-flops to cost Leon a dime, who could accuse her of wishing for a goofy goober?

Beacon wore faded blue corduroys worn through to the knees. The Dez Beacon had decked out in a tight green miniskirt with silver sequins sewn into the hem and up the sides in places. Now Dezzy looked more leggy of a Saturday morn. Of Deziray's feet the chintz straps of gold high heels a size too big, stained, were, and the red berries, some kinda fake gemamoly of glass pomegranate cluster looked crusty, like pancake batter spilled onto them and dried and then somebody tried to wipe it off but couldn't get down into the crevices very well. For a shirt sort of thing Dez wore what Beacon called a "boob tube," an elastic purple strip wide enough to cover a pair. Along with the leopard-print purse on a gold chain, Dez looked down for business on the Bobbit in the rain, some slurp going on here in the gherk and gobble of Hussein. Whoever said a gal could not get spider in the sport of Jericho's Ladder? Was it by chance the Jimmy of the swagger? Leon cared not for any of it. Beacon was plain weirded out. Once back on the road it wasn't but a minute before she said, "Pull over. We can pretend to wash clothes."

"I told you it ain't gonna happen," Leon said.

"Pull over!" Beacon shouted in his ear.

"Go head," Deziray said.

Leon pulled over.

"It's cool," Deziray said.

"I don't think it's cool."

"I was raised humanist," Deziray explained. "People always are concerned about doing wrong things. They think they're so important and—"

"Cutcher goddamn bullshit!" Leon said.

"Being alive means living, Leon. If I don't do this, I'll regret it forever. The road is here before me now."

"The road?"

"You disrespect yourself when you deny experience. You can only know donuts if you eat every flavor. You gotta eat the chocolate and powders and blueberry ones and cruellers. If I deny myself this I'll be half a woman. I'll be an asshole when my goal is to be an expert."

Leon thunk on it. He reached for his Carletons, but Beacon and the Dez already were out of the car. They stepped to the curb where the traffic rolled by, and shared a word, and Leon saw Beacon smile at Deziray. Could they be becoming friends? Leon liked that idea. He'd pictured the three of them together in the sex throes, why not? Leon saw himself on his back in the middle of the bed, arms out like Jesus, upon each shoulder the head of a beautiful woman, fire to one side, water to the other.

"I'm worried about Barney," Fred—no, his name was Amber now—said.

"Barney's fine. We gave him plenty of tequila, didn't we?"

"But what if he can't breathe?"

"He can breathe. Don't you remember how Dezzie was stuck back there all night breathing? Barney can breathe. Don't worry."

"What if he died or something because of us?"

"Then he's a dead monkey."

Beacon brushed back into the car, from which they had a clear view of people doing laundry in the Washarama. To the right of the building, Deziray stood in her new whore's clothes. She struck poses for the cars and trucks. She reached her arms above her head, sexy with a leg out sideways, the skirt rising higher.

"We ought to peel out and leave her ass," Beacon said. "She's a liability."

"You think I would do her that way?"

"Don't eye me. I'm just saying."

"You guys are crazy assholes!" Amber shouted.

"I don't do people that way," Leon said, but a car pulled over and Deziray got in it and the car drove away.

"Damn," Beacon said.

"I was just getting ready to run out there," Leon said.

"What would you've done?

"Slammed him."

"That's you for you," Beacon said.

If not for Beacon's blabbermouth Leon would

have stopped the thing. Nothing to do now but wait, so they waited. Each time Leon looked to Beacon he saw the smile she was trying to hide. The gloat in the face. The woman was happy.

Damn near thirty minutes later the car let Deziray off at the curb. She stepped over not the least bit upset and got in. Leon peeled out, headed back for the Brokenhearted Woman, where they had a room still, and beer. Nobody spoke. They passed through the city to head north. While Leon drove, Deziray handed two twenties up front. Beacon stuffed them into the front pocket of her new corduroys.

"All I gotta say is it won't happen again," Leon said.

"Pull over here," Deziray said.

"What?"

"Pull over please."

She was talking about this here two-story cinderblock building with bricked-up windows. A sign up high read TITILATIONS.

"Fuck you," Leon said, and sped past, disgusted by Deziray. How could she? Leon was not ignorant as to street prices. He knew people paid pretty much the same for hot young thangs as they did weathered whores. And people didn't pay no forty dollars for a damn blow job, neither. The fellow in the Lincoln Continental had fucked her. Leon had caught a glimpse of the dude, about forty-five he would say, hairline receding bigtime and the hair combed backwards, a few deep wrinkles in his forehead, and a winning smile. Wore a white polo shirt, sort of a fat guy of thick neck, looked like he could be a football coach, or math teacher, who the fuck knew? Dude looked cheery and personable, and was Deziray fucking with Leon's mind? Leon eyed her in the rearview, and their eyes met and she smiled, the cum-sucking whore. Hadn't to yet washed his own garbage out of her. Now up in there were the minnows of the coach all swimming along mixed up with his own piss-ass rugrats.

"I love to dance, Leon," Deziray complained. "There were cars out front. I could get an audition. I want to earn back the money I took from y'all. I want to prove to you that—"

"Forget the goddamn money!" Leon shouted.

"Damn, Leon, what the fuck?" Beacon said.

"Welcome to whoredom," Leon said.

"Holy motherfuck, what're you talking, Leon?" Beacon said, her shocked look to say he was a asshole for giving a shit on Deziray's damn just got fucked over bullshit. Beacon's want in the blob of her thingage was for him to feel dumb for the give he'd guv the Dez. Damn shit would not have happened had Beacon not egged her on, so up flipped his arm, fist-back to eyeball.

Now Beacon may not have looked to give him the guilt trip, but hadn't Leon promised the soul-ass crapamoly of the self of him: *no more garbage*? He'd put up with such a bunch of it. What man was he to deny the word he gave himself? What man was he to not keep his word? What turn to a day? It'd started out funnily with promise and love—he'd been the guy on the covers of the Wal-Mart romance novels. In the silence now a goo gooed around, the invisible sub of stance what emanates from unhappy cats. The engine sound intensified the feeling. Amber picked now to turn into a snuffling crybaby bullshit sonofabitch. Damn pathetic-ass shit was so pathetic, a sniff first off only. In Leon's inside self of him he said *Stop it you motherfucker!* but the child's sniffs grew and the tears came, the nasal wetness there, and then—*no, goddamnit, don't do that*—the full on sobby wobby mobby shut the fuck up if you got a brain slob on my knobby!

It gave Leon sickies. The unwanted child's cries took up tenor to the rhythm section of Leon's goddamn motherfucking Camaro's pistons and plugs. Did he have a carburetor? Sure, and hot rubber and a muffler.

Was Leon supposed to apologize? He might be willing to admit he'd been rash, but why was Amber trying to make him feel like dogshit and a goddamn abuser to children? Wasn't that the opposite of why Deziray liked him? That Leon was the protector? "Golden Man," she'd said. Would Deziray think less of Leon for his make of the dipshit to cry?

That goddamned dolorous music was the sound of what Leon wanted not to be. Amber wasn't trying to hide it, neither, just cried on like a stupid bitch.

And here the Brokenhearted Woman Motel popped up on the windshield glass.

And was Leon a lowdown dirty dog?

His women of the luscious brown hair, sorrel if you will, left it up to him on the take of it back, if he could, the business of the crapamoly smack-out of a niggling-ass pimp-faced rat style woman before a child.

Leon parked.

Leon killed the engine.

Amber sniffled on, and they listened. It began to got a soothing effect on Leon. Maybe it soothed Deziray and Beacon too. What could you do? Was there something holy here? Anybody of half a bug's brain told it, and in this world honesty charmed the dickens from the chickens to squander in the yonder, ain't that correct and quite accurate and true, Jeffrey of the Dahmer? When she'd had her good cry, the sniffles petering out, Leon cleared his throat, him the bigdog as ever. The child's sniffles stopped. The ears of them waited for Leon's command. The ears of them waited for the words of the Golden Man.

"I ain't saying shit," Leon said.

Beacon leaned in for a hug, but Leon pushed her away.

"I deserved it," she said.

"To say you zerved it don't mean shit."

"I'm jealous, goddamnit! Look at her."

Leon's heart softened immediate. He remembered his promise, that he would never not smack her no more upside the head like she was a piece of shit again, just never ever after what he'd done did to her in the bike shed that time at the dirt farm with a fucking bike pedal.

"I know you like her, I got eyes, asshole. When you like her I hate her, can't you understand? Have you never been jealous?"

"I don't care to think on it," Leon said.

"She's young and I'm an old fucking maid!"

"Beacon."

Beacon flipped her face to her enemy. "What?"

"You should never be jealous. It means you don't respect yourself. There's nothing in the world worse than jealous. Cast it far away from you, throw it into the deep blue sea and hope with all your might it sinks to the bottom and is buried in sand forever. I believe in hope. I don't believe in jealous. I believe in hope."

QUIZZLEBOON

"Oh," Beacon said, and sounded resigned, beat down. It was sad. Was she putting him on? She might could be acting, so Leon eyed her, and their eyes met. He saw what damage had been done to her eye, and wanted to find the bitch who'd perpetrated this crime. A man who could hit a woman didn't barely deserve to live. A woman was by Nature's Decree, or God's Proclaim, weaker. It was by nature an unfair fight. Only cowards hit women.

Did being a bitch mean you ought to be popped in the eye?

Not no more than being a dog meant you ought be kicked in the rib.

How many times did Leon see men push his mother? What did Sandra do to deserve it? You could not stretch the word BITCH to fit around Sandra Hicks, go ahead and try, yet Leon saw many a black eye on Sandra H. Mr. Quigley gave her several, for what? Not scrubbing out the toilets good? Maybe it was for fucking around on him, good for her, but did he own her? He was the boss of her was all he was. He was her boss and nothing but her boss, and that was the truth, the whole truth, and nothing but the truth.

Leon didn't care to think on it, so why the fuck was he?

He was heartsick and sad. Could not go find himself to beat the shit out of himself because he himself was right here in the motherfucking car with himself. What was he gonna do? Slam his fist into his own face over and over?

"Beacon," Deziray said, and put her hand on Beacon's shoulder. The normal Beacon thing would've been to slap Dez clear to Sing Sing. Beacon's eye was bloodshot and swole and purple already and would be pure black come the new hour. Leon still felt the squashy soft collapse of her eye against his fist-back. It was a nasty thing to do to a body, but fuck it. Leon had sworn away garbage. Garbage was a thing that, if he took himself serious, he could not nor would not tolerate.

"Leon is beautiful," Deziray said. "Don't hold his beauty against him like the Jews did to Jesus. Don't be jealous like the Jews, and have murder in your heart. To this day the Jews have not forgiven poor little Jesus. They forgot about their jealousy, that's the worst of it. They never forgave him for making them kill him. It would be very hard, don't you think, to forgive a guy who made you kill him?"

Beacon and Leon looked at Deziray.

"What?" Deziray said.

Beacon and Leon laughed, couldn't help it, it was funny the way Deziray looked so sincere in the stupid bullcrap she talked on, and she dressed in the whore's clothes such as she was, the purple boobtube slipped down sorta lobsided across her chest. It was a nice change to the goo in the air, but Amber again sniffled up. She was tired of the privy to the fishy. What Leon had heard people call The Adult World must've been so damn stupid to her. "Barney," she said. "Where's Barney? What did you do to Barney? Why did you do that to him? Why did you say he could die? He didn't never do nothing mean to you. Why did you—"

"Shhhhh," Deziray said, and ran fingers through the child's hair. "He's fine, I guarantee. Just because we haven't heard him banging back there doesn't mean he's dead. He's drunk is all. Even monkeys get drunk. You saw all that tequila. If you drank that much tequila you'd be flat on your ass, I guarantee, Amber. What's your last name, Amber? I don't even know your last name, what is it?"

"Spoonbill," Amber said.

"Well, Amber Spoonbill. What do you say we get Barney out the trunk and find out how drunk he is? People can be real funny when they're drunk."

"Barney ain't no people," Amber said, but was excited over this new friend in Deziray she was beginning to have.

"Aw, come on, monkeys are people."

"You're a monkey."

"I'm a fuck monkey," Deziray corrected the misguided child, and scratched herself and said, "Hoo hoo hoo," her lips going out funny like a monkey's. Amber laughed, and Deziray said, "I'm a ambidextrous fuck monkey. I can scratch as good with my left hand as I can with my right hand." Deziray demonstrated, scratching her ribs with both hands at the same time, going, "Hoo hoo hoo."

Amber giggled, and followed suit: "Hoo hoo hoo."

Beacon, looking to Leon for support, rolled her eyes. "Looks like she's a humanist over children, too."

"I reckon," Leon said.

They got out the Camaro. Leon popped the trunk. There was Barney, pretty as lemon pie, on his back with pink feet took to the air. He was looking up at them, scanning their faces while squinting at the light, his face framed in orange bristle. Damn drank all that was in his baby bottle is what, all the tequila—*drink, drank, drunk*. He was dazed up too much to fuss. Deziray lifted him out to give to Amber and the five Quizzles stepped through the doorway of Room 14 of the Brokenhearted Woman Motel. They closed themselves in, or closed the world out, however you took a mind to see the situation.

26.

CLOSED AWAY IN the hideaway, Leon said, "Take your ass a goddamn shower, bitch. I don't know what your problem is."

"Yeah, I been noticing some stank coming off her," Beacon put in.

"I'm not talking about no stank," Leon said.

"I told you," Deziray said, "I'm a humanist," giving him sass. Leon looked the other way for the moment, for she'd put into motion what he just now told her to go on with. Next time she sassed him though who was to say he might not black hers too, a complement to the line he drew across her throat with his Buck 110, the thin cut now looking, come to think of it, sorta sexy like in its beginning stages of scab.

What Leon needed was a beer, right now at this very goddamn motherfucking moment and shit in time, so he hit the car and brought the cooler in and did what? Popped himself a goddamn motherfucking beer. He didn't worry about the salt that he liked to have dabbed around the keyhole. He drank the mother down, squashed the can and threw it at Amber. The can bounced off her shoulder and hit the wall and fell to the floor. He was mad at the little cocksucker for crying like a goddamn baby, but the beer made him feel better. Plus, the sound of the shower soothed him. That was a good thing, wash that shit out, what's the matter with you? Whoring your goddamn body to some piece-a-shit motherfucker, doing the dog with a complete stranger in a goddamn Lincoln Continental. "Get me a beer, please, would you, Amber?" Leon said.

"Me too," Beacon said.

"No, you don't get a beer," Leon said, and Beacon knew she'd best not to fuck with him while he cooled off. If Leon said she didn't get a beer, she didn't get a beer, not one sip. Things were gonna be different from here on out. *No More Garbage* was Leon's motto.

Amber took a beer up out of the cooler for Leon. She wiped the can dry with a bathroom towel, popped it and set it on the table. She ripped the end off a paper salt packet from McDonald's, eased the opened end of it along the brown tabletop, the salt spilling from the cylinders like two readymade lines in miniature—*tahdah*. She licked her finger and pressed it into the salt. The wetted crystals she dabbed around the aluminum keyhole. Before she'd finished dabbing, Leon grabbed the beer and drunk a bunch. Amber licked her fingers while he swugged the Jack, or jigged it. Over on the bed Beacon sulked like a busted-mannequin-looking motherfucker, a thing might could've been hit by car then drug in to prop against the headboard. Wasn't his fault. She'd done made him to hit, said so herself, so no booze on you.

Leon swiggled more Jack, lit a Carleton, thought on Mexico, of driving there. Be lots of work, but if he wanted he could dump these lame bitches, the burnt remnants of his dream of a hundred acres and a mule, what he'd held onto as some sort of purpose in life. Without them he'd likely escape detection longer. Or did Leon have a pen-wish? Was Leon like some say happens when a convict is freed, that in the deep-down where you don't know what you are thinking you wanna be captured and put away for life? Ted Bundy Syndrome, he'd heard it called, or TBS. The dude'd been a divided soul. Was his division reflected in the hairstyles of the girls he killed? Their parts went straight down their middles. If the part was to the left or some tiny bit to the right, the power distribution lost its equilibrium, and the Bundy side that liked to bite behinds and shove branches up in there, lost its power. Was Leon anyway in the TB of S? Did he have a unconscious desire to be conquested? Took down and locked up and blocked in the exercize of his will? Hell naw, Paul, not no Leon Hicks. Was he a dumbass hick motherfucker from Whoville?

That would be an absolute I don't think so, Bill, or call it the love of the freedom of the voices of the world, the sun of Belson in Burgundy in acapella, can you hear it, Nelson Mandella? Of the slice of machete, we gone get some Freddy Flintstone, ain't that the truth, Jenna Malone?

What Leon wanted now, right now, as a matter of the factamoly, was a little bit of pussy and a lot of good fun. To the other hand, he might like to be respected and loved by people he was familiar on, loved and respected by people he saw everyday: *Hey, how're you?* Those folks at the dirt farm had shit going on good, didn't they? To work the land and grow shit, did it get any better? Leon had been happy there, up in the penthouse with all the great views. He could look out the window at the gold light aslant upon the yurts and sheds, the happy splash of mater and such, and the purple coneflower crops arched by rainbow. Sometimes the kids loaded into the outside tubs to stomp grapes saved from the Asheville dumpsters. They stomped and sang to the mountains and sky, the fog, and the toads, and the yonis opening up all over the fields like so many rare tulips. It was like how in the *Wizard of Oz* the Tin Man came to the field of them in their bloom, a clam addict's dream: *Poppies!*

Leon drank a new brewsky. He shook his head. Here he was with two gorgeous babes on the premises. Leon didn't want to come across as a big softy, but he couldn't help himself. Before Deziray had finished washing the junk out of her body, Leon told Beacon to grab a cold one.

The bitch hoppedy-split licked to it.

"Can I get one too, Daddy?" Amber asked.

"Go head," Leon said, him the good-feeling kindly king who doled shit out to poor-ass jokers and desperadoes. A guy or gal did not need crack to get high. Jack Daniel's, beer, and nicotine was all a body needed for the feel good or get happy. Maybe they would head out for Mexico tonight, what to stop them? Just get in the car and go. The map from which he could plan their route was in *the Cam*, but Deziray stepped out from the bathroom wearing the stuff she'd been in before, while they'd been in the car and all that stupid shit, what Beacon had picked out for her so hatefully at the Salvation Goddamn Army Fucking Thrift Store.

"Uh uh," Leon said, "Not in here. We ain't gonna have none'a that going on."

"What my sposed to wear then? Beacon threw my

dress in the trash top some baked beans and chicken bones. That was my favorite dress."

"What?"

"I tried to pull it out to save it but she—"

"Goddamn girl, shutup," Beacon said. "You know that's a distortion of the truth. What are you trying to do? What is your point?"

"Beacon, you need to put some ice on that eye," Deziray said.

"Deziray is honest," Leon said. "She doesn't say stuff without telling lies."

"Do you mind if I fix you up an icepack?" Deziray said.

"I think it'd be a good habit for you to try and copy," Leon said. "I don't want you being mean to Dezzie no more, got it? The way I see it, you owe her them pants you're wearing, so hand 'em over."

Beacon resisted, but tough titty, bitch. Beacon had other shit she could wear. She took off the new corduroys with holes in the knees, and gave them to Dez and Dez took them to the bathroom and came out a minute later in them, and a button down left over from Leon's history professor days. That was more like it. Leon didn't like women looking cheap. "Grab a damn beer, bitch," Leon said, and complimented her on how nice her ass looked in the new pants when she bent over the cooler to collect ice for Beacon's pack.

"Thank you, Leon," she said.

The Quizleboons spent the afternoon watching TV and talking and drinking and smoking and opening the door now and then to let out the smoke. Leon was not one to become drunker than a skunker, but today he lost track. It happens after the coke ditch. You overdo the bottle in the pinch. That's your body's making up for the loss, but it was Amber too, she was drunk and once Deziray's hair had dried she ran a comb through it on the bed, singing Prince songs stupidly like a drunk little bitch. She was the first to pass out like a drunk little motherfucker. She lay on the brown bedspread beside Barney who was on his back with his tail curled up around his own neck. She curled up beside him, and they hit a touch of pot then, and blew their smoke over the faces of the open-mouthed children—oh, one was a monkey, sure, but what of it?—and Leon came to find out Deziray and Beacon, or Beacon and Deziray—however you wanted to arrange the two in terms of which one you said first—now that they both had shoes off—were the exact same height. What the hell? They were face-to-face by the window when he noticed it, and this wasn't nothing about no same height in general, neither. Deziray was giving Beacon a shotgun, which was a thing of hers, putting the joint backwards in her mouth to blow the smoke out the other end into the mouth of somebody else—*Suck it in! Suck it in!*

So Leon went over there and pressed them to the wall and double checked and saw it was true. They were the *exact* same height, and their hair was colored after coconut shells. Leon considered which of the two was his Wing, and which was his Wang. In Deziray's hair was a bit of a wave, whereas Beacon's hair was plain straight. Deziray had brown freckles each side of her nose, whereas Beacon had none. Beacon's body was hairier. A bit of a mustache grew from the outer ends of her upper lip. In his hold of them to the wall Leon sucked its hairs, then kissed the Dez. He pulled back from her to see Beacon's black eye in the head beside hers, and was drunk, damn for sure, so said he was sorry, but he was going to bed. He lay down, and woke to the TV on, a infomercial over this thing you turned ordinary bottles into drinking glasses with. *Well, I'll be damned*, Leon thought. That was a thing the Asheville Dirties might could appreciate.

Now previously Leon had thought if this happened, him to be took in bed with both, Beacon he would find to his conflagration side, just come to find out it was Dezzie who'd lund—landed or clumbed—natural to his right, and felt most comfy there. Beacon was Leon's water in the moment, sure enough, his *Wang*, and as he lay there still drunk, the smell of Deziray came to him from some far off place he could not remember. Her smell was a rich sulfuric nast with cinnamon and spices thrown in—*cumin*, that's what they ate a lot of up at the dirt farm. Cumin and allspice and this weird powder they called paprika. You sprinkled it into a pot for the nutritional qualities of red stuff, and it ain't had nothing to do with no papsmear, neither, just so you know. The smell of the Deziray deepened. Were clouds in there of smoke and a smidgeon of death milled. The smell of the Dez was of rats after decomposure in a wall for six months—had that unique flavor. You snuffed hard to smell it, and got closer to the wall to smell it more better. It drew you in. Before long you found yourself with your face to the wall, sniffing hard.

Leon breathed her in and got like Adam when he saw Eve to the bank of the river. He was a man with a club. He smashed the Dez with it, she his fire while in the bed beside them his water bubbled with snore.

Sure, Leon was drunk, but what of it? The tongue

of the Dez shoved into his mouth. Leon felt like he was falling while flying apart at the joints, or flying while the screws of the plane came loose due to vibrations. Though Leon had never been in a plane, he'd often thought of women like them. They had wings to spread out and light up in the sunshine, even when you were in a dark bedroom, and when you were on top of them, you were like the middle part where the people were kept safe. Leon was flying over a sea of cloud with her, a few runaway thoughts in his brain. In the fly of this flew, in the flap of this fluck, he saw Beacon's black eye, and the Continental Lincoln, and the dive of AirEgypt Flight 990, the 217 lives trashed into death some sixty miles East of Nantucket, their bodies all sinking in possible due to a error in the eye on the moon, to the bottom of the ocean to join the Wang. Leon multiplied 217 by two, and stood under a table that said in this loss were 434 eyeballs. That was a lot of eyeballs rolling around in the sand, but not so many as if everybody in the world had a camera to took pictures of everything of note. Then you'd have twenty-four billion eyeballs at work, recording the shit Leon's one right this minute was up to the thick of it in. Leon still shook his head on it, when he thought of it, how the month before, on October 12 to be exact, the sixth billionth living person on the planet was born—so he'd heard Paul Harvey say on the radio while waiting to place his order at a Wendy's drive-thru.

Her cunt had a million muscles in it, undulant waves to pull and pulsate like the suction-cup underbellies of a legion of snails.

Oh, Leon fell back to sleep. His number two wake passed to Andy's whistle, Andy the sheriff in the *Andy*

Griffith Show, if you ever saw it, the old time black-n-white country bumpkin shit where the deputy acts up being goofy while Andy spouts out the wisdoms. Leon's family was up. Barney, they said, had howled, as was his custom, come dawn, but Leon had laid there like a frog.

Leon rubbed his eyes. Was all of what happened in the night with Dez a dream? Leon pondered it. Dez came out from the bathroom and, in the see of her there he knew it was true. The thing was *in time*, in the way Dezzie liked to say. When a thing happens, it exists *in time* forever. The Quiz, through the eye Leon gave over, recorded all. All was etched into the databanks on the moon.

So what else was *in time?* What else could not be took back from Leon? A few bad things from the White Lady Motel, sure, all the shit with Leon's sister, Glinda. That was way early in Leon's life, and mixed up with Mr. Quigley and the eyeball situation.

Leon's eyeball?

Oh, this man came down from the moon and Leon gave it over, his eye. Leon wasn't sure on what happened, but remembered a man in the room with him. His preferred memory was that the man in the room was Mr. Quizzleboon, like what he'd told the kids at the dirt farm. The eye was a gift, and the Quiz held it between thumb and finger, and turned it in the fluorescent light, admiring it, appraising it as a jeweler might a diamond dug out of a bluff in Tennessee. The expression on Quizzleboon's face was like: *All that seeing, Jesus, it's locked in there. All that seeing!*

27.

LEON ROSE FROM bed to see two cashed Jack bottles. He lifted the cooler lid. Nothing but ice particles floating in water. Damn women had cleaned him out. That was fucked. They should've left their king a beer for morning. Leon stared at the watery emptiness, then closed the lid. He sat back on the bed, his back against the headboard, crossed his feet at the ankles and lit a Carleton. He closed his eyes. His head ached. On TV that guy Barney, the sheriff's helper, said, "Andy, I think it's time we make a move."

Leon thought on it, on all of what his, or *their*, it was *their*, not no his, options were, and what they could do, where they could go, what might result from whatever move they made. In truth he could not make his mind up, so thinked and thunk and thought, thinking he'd know come noon, but the answer never came, and then he thonkulated *Fuck it, let's buy a case and pull up a skrunk*, and the same thing happened the next day and the next. Now it was many days later and Leon felt like they could stay indefinitely at the Brokenhearted Woman Motel. Life was good here, and Deziray played ukulele and sang songs with Amber and for some reason Beacon let up on the jealousy factor. For a bit there Leon had thought it was an act. Beacon was too nice out of nowhere, with unnatural smiles and stuff. Oughtn't she be pissed over the smack he'd smuck her? The eye had come out crazy black—looked like she'd been hit in the face with a brick, her eyewhites on the blunked side bright red—despite the ice she kept putting on it. She looked the woman with a grudge. There was that thing, too, of how she'd gone out to the car for the scissors he'd cut Amber's hair with back when they were shacked up in the spooky woods. What did Beacon need scissors for? She pretended to need them to trim her own hair with, "to make the ends look nice and healthy," as she'd said, but was that Beacon's style? Could she be waiting for the right moment to try and snip his balls off? Leon knew it wouldn't happen so easy as her threat. She would make a huge mess, maybe cut through half his scrotum before he knocked her senseless. She wasn't competent enough to get them both cut off, no matter how drunk Leon might get, not with no paper-cutting scissors like those. If she managed to get one off, what then? Leon didn't care to ponder it, just whenever he caught Beacon staring at him as if lost in dream, he wondered: *Is she plotting to cut my balls off?* With her black eye with its bloodshot white it damn sure did look like she was plotting shit.

Mostly though Beacon was cheerful, and seemed happy, and took Amber out in the Camaro for groceries. That was Leon and Dezzie's private playtime. Beacon and the Amb would return and smell the sex and sniff around, Barney too, and they'd giggle. You couldn't keep secrets here, and the way shit was set up, what with Leon being king and all, the bitches had no choice but to come together in a

unified purpose of pleasing their Lord. When Leon
was a boy, was not his purpose to please his mother?
His mother was queen. So it was for the Quizzleboons
now. To the her that was his mother was the him that
was he, and the him from back then was now the they
that they were. While Barney rubbed his nasty
human-looking balls all over Amber while she in one
bed slept, Leon in the other loved on his bitches. He
was a romantic guy. The Quizzle Girls called him
Hottie and *Rocky Balboa—Come over here, Rocky
Balboa*—and they complimented Leon on his
muscles. His tatts, they realized, as every woman who
scrutinized them did, were out of their league, but he
kissed them passionate to lip and eyebrow and
delighted in his mop up of their cocker spaniel
exercize pens.

Of course, if it was the middle of the day they
would blindfold the Amb first, or make her go in the
bathroom where she hung with Barney in the tub
stuffed with blankets. In there she drew pictures and
drank lemonade while listening to the transistor
radio, Leon rubbing his darlings beyond the door,
kneading their muscles and boobs with his great
strength. He made them comfy and loose. With knees
to the floor one day he spit-shined Beacon and
Dezzie's birth cannon, them side by side on the
bedspread, each taste different, a sort of sweet and
sour pork combination going on here and everything.
Through the eye of the Quiz Leon saw himself in
prayer, and thought on how people who tasted wines
cleared their palettes between each flavor by chewing
bread. His mental note was to bring home bakery rolls
from the market. As Leon wanted to be more
romantic, even, than Fabio, he brushed their hair,

squeezed their feet, and bought flowers, a dozen in a bundle for the both of them at once, Barney here to eat them before the end of the day, and chocolates, cheese and crackers, celery sticks, and can I get some cans of sardines in there too, Mr. Cliff?

Oh, at first Beacon had been particular, standoffish, would not let Leon stick her after pulling out of the Dez, but she came around. Leon liked to lie on his back in the middle of the bed, hands connected to the mounds of his brown-haired women who, together, were a pair of wings. With fingers in their caves, his wings fluttered, his erection grew larger and he flew. Leon found that with a witness on standby, he loved better, and was higherly in demand. When he stormed the cotton gin of the one, the other was desirous of his stormage. Beacon acclimated. She approved now, or seemed to. It was nice, a new kind of trust. Leon felt her deflate whenever he pulled out to swack the Dez. It wasn't like he was rejecting the one for the other, just those feelings of rejection, Leon noticed, kept them interested. His lovers competed. They pushed the limits of what they could do to Leon, and get away with. Deziray bit Leon's arms, ears, was crazy with her tongue. She stuck it in his eardrum, reached it up nostril and down dickhole. Beacon in her compete tried licking his ass on the hole, but he swiped her away. What did she think he was? Some kind of Quigley, a man to delight in another's lowering of herself? Hell naw! Leon Hicks was a kindly king, not no shit-for-brains to delight in the humiliation of some bitch motherfucker. Leon Hicks believed in democracy and equality, and set fingers to Deziray's axe wound one day to pull the two sides opposite directions, as far apart from each other as they could go. Her legs were stretched back, toes hooked under the open rectangle of the headboard. In Leon's hold of it open he noticed the familiar. He puzzled on its symmetry and then yes, it came to him. It was shaped like a security officer's badge, just turned upside down so the wave-like pinch to the bottom matched the rise each side to the pearl. *Fuckin goddamn*, Leon thought. He'd done a stint in security so knew he was on target, not making shit up here in his mind. He'd seen the badge pinned to trooper uniforms as well. Was it possible the design was ripped off the vagoo? Somebody'd done got smart here to a trick, Leon reckoned, and knew his feminist friends would take a interest over what'd gone down.

To make things equal in the do of the done, Leon spread wide Beacon's soggy box later that day, eager to see would hers too stretch to reveal a badge. It did, just it wasn't the security officer's badge he was familiar on. Looked more like, honest to god speaking, what the Detroit cop wore to end him in lockdown.

A bit some here of mystery, two upside down badges, hey? Leon kept the knowledge to himself, and tried for them to French kiss. They weren't into it, did he press the issue? The Dez seemed like she might could be okay on it—she was, as everybody knew, an eat-every-donut-known-to-man kind of gal—yet Leon wasn't sure. Should he turn them into cunt-sucking lesbos they might change their feeling, not find him quite so valuable. Instead of bringing his fire and water together, as Ray Orbison had said was the ticket, they both might roll off into the hills like a tumbleweed of woman. In their tumble their tongues would bounce in and out of each other.

JOHN OLIVER HODGES

It was complicated. Leon's indecision in bedly matters made him feel incompetent. In his tie to the Wing and the Wang was he neglectful? For only through the coming together of them could he activate the prowess of which Ray Orbison, bastard brother to the singer Roy, spoke those nights after the carnies laid their heads to rest, the moon hung above the tents and rides like a paper lantern. Leon knew of the waste of opportunity, so said: *Ain't but the fancy of the skrunk*, and absolved himself of consequence. Ray Orbison would've been sore pissed over Leon's lame-assed attitude. In simple terms the haves of the man from Uruk might've come together by now if not for Leon's aimless tampon tunnel tangents. Here Leon barely took the shit serious.

Leon Hicks took pride, though, in the knowledge that, as king, he outshined Kind Edward. Leon thought this on himself in the tell of no lie. What his sister ever saw in Edward was hard to see. Granted, when she first married Edward in Miami, the man's eyes both were seeing. Edward may have been different, more refined like what you thought of on bigtime lawyers. Now he spouted vulgar rarities one after the other all day. Kind Edward's claim to fame was what? That he could tie a girl's string into a knot using only his tongue?

In the carefree life on the Pensacola City outskirts, Leon did not feel the pressures of Danger. He took the Boozlequins to the beach, Barney drunk in the trunk, where Amber danced crazily in the sand, to her heart's content, and they picnicked on artichoke hearts and tater logs and watched the dolphins play. They watched the Blue Angels put a spectacular show on over the gulf in their F-18 Hornets or whatever, and what was this shit here about the first man who walked on the moon? Come to find out Neil Armstorng had been trained in Pensacola, so said a fellow in a straw hat who they met on the beach. Dude had some serious face cancer he was dealing with, and was also interested in the situation at hand, this here tough guy—*that would be Leon*—with two brunettes and a child. Even the Quizzles had to admit that they were interesting. Together they made up all kinds of lies for the man about who they were and where they'd come from.

And the Lee of the On—*Leon*—played cards with his girls, lifted his barbells, watched cable TV, drank beer, and laughed at Barney hanging upside down from the overhead light. Before long shit stained the ceiling, fancy that. Damn monkey was taking shits on it. All around the light were shit stalactites that developed in thickness daily. They began to drip. It was funny, but once the smell came on a bit more strong than could be tolerated, no, it wasn't no funny. Good thing Leon paid the maid to not enter their room.

Two weeks into their stay at the Brokenhearted, Leon still could not make his mind up on what to do next. Beacon's great idea was Deziray should hop a Greyhound, along with Ambrosia, to Asheville, go be a member of the dirt farm where she would be much loved, Beacon assured her. Beacon hammed it up, talked on how great Potato was, and mentioned the other great men of the dirt farm, good Castle and Grootika and Gay Gary who was in jail still for his criminal mischief charge, this here snipping he did of the fence of the Goth farm to free the cows. "It's the greatest place on earth," Beacon said to the Dez.

"Didn't you say you wanna experience the world? At the dirt farm you can do anything you want but wear a tampon or shave your pits."

"That ain't true," Amber said. "We don't allow tons of things. If you wanna eat a egg you gotta ask the chicken first. You gotta get on your knees and hold the egg so the chicken can see it. Can I please eat your babychild? you gotta say. If the chicken scratch dirt, then you can eat it, but you got to fit the egg in your mouth. You got to hold it in there and lick it and kiss it before you can fry it. One time Potato was out there doing it for hours to save the eggs up for later. He almost died when a egg broke and went down the wrong pipe."

"Amber's homesick," Beacon argued. "Think how her mama and friends feel to be away from her so long."

"It sounds awesome, but I wouldn't feel right," Dez said, and Leon was proud of her, for she was his *fire*, and was loyal, and lived for Leon. If Leon wanted her to go, she would, but otherwise she would stay. She was a damn good bitch.

"Why don't *you* go?" Deziray asked Beacon, and Beacon fumed for the rest of the day.

Something had to change though. Deziray was tired of being a "bimbo in limbo." She was a sinner by not adding more variety to her life, she said. Now and then her depressive realism condition acted up. She went around crying a bunch for no apparent reason at all, and once, when she and Leon were alone, she said she'd thought hooking up with him would be an adventure. She'd learn shit and discover the purpose cut out for her from the fabric of the possible. Come to find out she was turning into some kind of party girl, some kind of fuck doll, which were fine things of themselves, Deziray said, just not activities you wanted to linger in lest they grow roots. "I wanna dance," she said, and King Hicks consented. King Hicks drove his fire to Titillations, the building of the gigantic plastic cigars out front, and waited in the car while she auditioned. Such places were not always in need, Leon imagined, but if you were hotter than a jumper cable at a Mexican family reunion, he betted you could always find work, especially if you'd been trained in ballet such as Deziray the humanist had been done to. And was she agile? Was she wild? Was she tasteful and classy and mysterious and sassy? Could she trot like a pony? How about breakdance like a tomboy? Or flow like a waterdrop across a elephant leaf, and over the edge, the light alive inside her as she falled, or fell, an explosion upon contact bright enough to get a job fit for a daughter of a mob boss or cob of corn in the corner of a smoke shop. Was she the opposite of a coward? Check all of the above, Howard. Her audition blew the skullcap off the owner. He called her Hellenic, Deziray said later. He asked her to light his cigar, and she did it with great poise and finesse, even while wearing no pants. The dude's name was Ezekiel Rosenthal. He was a one-time professor of classics at U of F who'd lost his tenure for selling four hundred hits of LSD to a undercover agent in a Panama City Beach motel room. He'd done time for it. Titillations was his new venture in lucre. Everybody called him EZ.

Dez shaved her snatch, and the next day, come three, danced the Titillations stage in the wobbly berry heels Beacon selected for her from the Salvation Army Thrift Store floor. As Florida law forbade women to show the boober in public establishments, it was all about the puss or the bleeding meat socket if you happened to be in your menzies, or, if you wanna call them womenzies to be fair, please do. EZ was strict on the exclusivity of the Sir Rumpled Slit Skin. "If you show your tits, you're fired," he said, so Dez showed her quiff, tugged its lips. Didn't know what she was doing. Nobody cared. She got some nasty looks from other strippers. In the prep room one said to the other, "What a fucking joke," but later, coming up on around midnight, a woman named Beatrice, stage name Mamajay, gave Deziray a breath mint. Beatrice showed Dez how to put on fake eyelashes, and gave her pointers on her dancing and makeup and bedside manner. She told Deziray to bring tampons with her should Aunt Flo make a surprise visit, and to always have baby wipes on hand, and feminine spray and condoms.

Leon said. "I'm glad she's helping, but still, she ought not to've made that bitch-ass suggestion to you."

"She means well," Deziray said.

Leon wanted not to see Dezzie in the dark bar. Wasn't sure how he'd respond on the whole self-administered degradation thing. A few days later he went, though, and drunk a beer to her abs. The song on was "Welcome To The Jungle," and Dezzie rocked out with air guitar on it, and flung her hair in circles like a banger—looked to Leon like she'd ought best be careful not to get whiplash. Leon was surprised to see her do all that shit on the pole, too, whipping legs up to spread wide while in the upside down position. She anyway was in the get of the mooch, and Leon respected that. Hard work for good money, we talkin sweat here. Sometimes she got ten dollars for lighting a cigar, sure, but mostly she was in the physical shit of things, like what farm work might do on a body or some damn shit. Leon knew she lap-danced and got paid for those, but give a girl her money! Sometimes in a single shift, after EZ took his cut, she came off with as much as four hundred bonkers. After seven days in the dance business she'd done paid Leon fifteen hundred of the twenty-five she owed. These monies Beacon kept hid in a sock.

Most off Leon drove Dezzie home after the pick of her up from Titillations, but sometimes he drove her up the powerline road to their special spot, and Leon thunk the Quiz for the nap of the kid and stuff of her in the trunk, Jesus. In the spot Dezzie hit the ganja and told Leon of her day. Quality time here under the moon. They'd drink a few and Leon would massage her shoulders, and lightly massage her arms that had become so sore from working the pole. In their private bonding Beacon was a bit some in the fade of shit. The together-all-three-of-them-stuff had gone down maybe eight times, then stopped to the edge of the dime.

That was stuff. Before the drop-off of Dez on the Tit, Leon oft took her for grub to the Mick, or Miracle Diner. One day in the munch of their burgers, extra mayonnaise for Leon, a huge bald dude in white dropped into their booth—Dezzie's side.

28.

LEON WAS TO jump to the bone-busting task, but Deziray nodded to the dude, whose presence was likeable and warm and looked to have the power of the put—just how some people put people at ease at first sight. The guy's bigness was one thing, but he wore gold-rimmed glasses, the type you buy at drug stores to read books through, just you could tell he wore them always. The glasses made him look smart in combo with the weird shirt buttoned up to the middle of his fat neck. The outfit looked took off the Hollywood set of *Lawrence of Arabia*. Leon saw Dezzie nod to him, and did he see a tiny smile in there? Oh yeah, they looked to be friends, all right. A braided ponytail jutted from the back of big baldy's head bone. Leon ran a fry through his ketchup.

"Do you know me?" the man said.

Leon put the fry in his mouth, his thoughts on Deziray. Why did she smile? Her mouth hadn't curved upwards at both ends like a regular smile. Instead her eyes twitched and she'd looked to be holding back wild joy. Her face had impulsively smiled. What's worse is she'd tried to conceal it.

"I do," Leon said.

Waxman scratched his fat neck. "I didn't ask you

to marry me, baby," he said in his deep-ass voice that was like how you'd expect a devil's voice to sound in a Christian rapture movie, low and scratchy, full of gravel, yet smooth. Waxman's voice was, Leon admitted right then to himself, not what you bought off a rack like the glasses on his face. If Leon was a woman, he realized with some discomfort, he'd wanna keep on hearing that voice. It was friendly. Leon raised his eye to Dez, who seemed sorta empty now and free-floating and without will.

"There's something I gotta tell you," Waxman said.

Leon eyed his fire well now, took note of the ripple to course her face, the flicker of lip, and muscle grown taut along the jaw-line, a pulse of vein in her temple. How about the tremor of nostril, or miniscule flex of lash above her left ball, and the right eye too? The stuff damn harmonized, and the lipstick, her chorus of personable detail thick with talky birds, but what anyway were this song's words? Were they, perhaps, "Billy Waxman is a total badass"? Had Leon forgot it? That would be a big fat no on the River Yeocomico, Joe from Machipongo, but Deziray had said it. It was the first thing she'd said to Leon while in the presence of the blind man. "Billy Waxman is a total badass." Leon had thought on it once or twice.

Waxman scratched his fat-assed neck more.

Leon flicked his eye Waxman's way.

Waxman looked peaceful.

"Another moneygrubber look to me like," Leon stated.

Waxman's face darkened. He sighed and sorta frowned and looked devastated. It was funny how Leon's money comment needled Waxman. Was money a mother? It made lowlifes of otherwise respectable citizens. In Waxman's case, the money idea was not only odious, but odiferous, for why else would he flare his nostrils as if he'd been sprayed by a skunkamolio hid below a table in a diner in Pensacolio? Billy Waxman did not like to think he was a slave to cashamolio, all that bread and lucre and booty—call it a bootalicious molio, which was kinda like polio—or a mayonnaise-boysenberry sauce or aught else you might buy to a Dollar General Store from here to San Antonio where the Montezuma Cypress trees were quite beautiful.

"I am a trained professional," Waxman said.

"Did you say professor of a urinal? I ain't never heard none on no professor to the urinal."

"I am experienced in the investigation, identification, and apprehension of individuals wanted for bank robbery."

"That's nice," Leon said.

"Maybe you should be afraid of me."

"I reckon you like when people are afraid of you, right?"

"Listen, friend, did you know that a thousand Jupiters will fit into the sun?"

Leon ate another fry.

"Do you know how many planets the size of earth that translates to?"

Leon ate another fry.

"Over a million," Waxman said.

"He quit the deputy marshal business," Deziray said.

Leon squinted his eye at her. She looked out the window at the weather.

"Would you like to know why I mention this, Leon?"

"Just tell me what you want," Leon said, still eyeing the Dez.

"Have it your way." Waxman pulled a cellular phone up. He opened it and showed Leon the buttons. "See the one next to my thumb? That's the thirty-five thousand dollar button. All I have to do is press it and I'll be that much richer. Twenty-five from the marshal service's reward, and ten from the Barney Fund." Waxman smiled, showing his teeth.

Leon looked to Deziray, who shifted under his eye. Could she do more than grin stupidly? Or blink real fast, pulling farther away from Leon as if thinking what? He might reach out and touch someone? Might he could reach out and break every tooth of her?

"I'm good at what I do, baby," Waxman said. "The fact that we are having a civilized conversation proves it. The easy thing would be to press the button and collect the money, but I'm spiritual, you feel me? I like you, what can I say?"

"Are you saying you got twenty men out there waiting to raid me?"

Waxman went ha ha, and looked to Deziray, shit, as if expecting her to go ha ha too. Dez had better sense than to go ha ha too. Had Deziray gone ha ha too, Leon would have damaged her caca stew. He might not would've ruptured her bowel with a *kaplowel*, McDowell, so her caca turned to diarrhea in an instant and squirted uncontrollably out her ass like the way Barney's did sometimes, causing other people in the diner to eye them like they were poor white trash scoundrels of an as of yet unseen lowly variety, Piety, but he would have damaged her somehow. There were forks to the table, knives. Leon could blind her with his butter knife, though it would take repeated stabbings and maneuvers. She could run then—no, stumble outside with arms out like a zombie's in the sun, shit flying out of her ass with a prolonged fart sound, and in the parking lot fall down. How's that for a *ha ha ha?* After receiving medical attention she could *rah rah rah* back to Kind Ed's for the be of the what? The fuck of the Wetsy Betsy? That's what Dez complained about all now about how Leon was turning her into some kind of a fuck doll—pull the string and watch her pee some Fountain of Youth, Ruth from the *King James* version. Her destiny was not of that, but of a superwoman. Fully blinded, her dreams would be dead, so instead of shouting, "My Eyes!" Kind Ed would go, "My Fuck Doll, where art thou, come here now!" and she would stumble bandaged into his arms. Do you see him pull the string? It sucks into her back and she kicks and clucks and pisses and scrambles like a duck to sneak under somebody's truck to fuck a monkey wrench or celery stick, say, or maybe a ham sandwich with Dijon mustard and Swiss cheese? Would you like some coleslaw to go with that?

"You got it right," Waxman said. "I'm a moneygrubber, but not a crass grabber for the cash. Can't you see me and see we are brothers? My years in law enforcement have refined me, friend. Not everybody sees the friend, but I'm thinking you can because you are smart, and also because those are some of the best tattoos I've seen in my life."

Waxman stopped talking, as if waiting for Leon to say something so that he could continue talking, so Leon said something. "Hardy hardy har."

"The world is brand new for me every moment that I am alive. What I want you to know, Leon, is that we brothers are the antidote to the prescription, you feel me? I want you to join the Mother Brother Sisterhood. You're a man of your word. Give it, I close my cell."

"I won't ask for details," Leon said. "Just say what you want."

"Brotherhood."

"Oh really? Then why do you call it Sisterhood?"

"That's what I was trying to tell you before, all about how many Jupiters will fit into the sun, but you didn't want to hear it, remember, my brother?"

Leon thought he should eat another fry. He considered the four or five left on his plate, if you could call them fries. They were more like scraps of grease.

"I want you to swear allegiance to my cause."

"I don't swear to causes that I don't know what they are."

"Our cause is to break the cycle of planetary ignorance."

"You mean you believe there are people on other planets? That sounds interesting. I might could get with that program."

"Excellent." Again Waxman smiled.

"But I'll have to think on it."

"I'll give you thirty seconds." Waxman checked his gold watch. "If you don't join us I'll have you arrested right now. If you do join us you'll owe me thirty-five thousand dollars. I'd rather collect the money from you, and have us be friends, see? Why should I turn you in, just answer me that, Leon?"

"Only you can answer that question."

"Let's take the fact of your sloppy unprofessionalism. Don't you see that I'll be taking a big risk by taking you on as a brother in my sisterhood? On the surface the smart thing would be to press the button and collect my money. When I consider your horrible cruelty streak I see how kindhearted I am. That frail woman you thought so little of as to punch in the face at the Southern Trust Bank, remember her? That's brutal, dude. You know how to not give a shit. You've evaded the law for over a year. There's something to be said for that. I wouldn't say that you're one of a kind, but I like you, Leon. I think you're planetarily aligned with me."

Leon lifted his face.

"I'll give you a year to pay back the money you owe. That ought to sweeten the deal, right? Just contribute little by little or in a big blast after a good job well done. Will you join the Mother Brother Sisterhood, Leon? Will you rob banks for Mother Brother? Will you sign up to tear down the walls of ignorance between planets? Or should I press the button?"

"Hey, hasn't thirty seconds gone by?"

"It most definitely has, Leon, but didn't I say I like you? I think you deserve an extension. I have a strong hunch that once you join me, you will want to double if not triple your purchase price into a life of spiritual richness and reward. I had some nice conversations with your friends in Asheville. They told me all about how generous you are, and that's part of what persuaded me to respect you. That, and all the good words Dezzie put in, but listen here, Leon, did you know that proof of the great big joke of the world is told in the story of the Tower of Babel?"

"Beg pard?"

"If God suddenly made it so nobody understood

other people due to a sudden chaos of tongue, what explains race?" Waxman smiled, his upper and lower lips parting in plenty, revealing what? A bunch of white piano keys? Yesamoly. That's how all of Waxman's smiles were. For a dude making a claim on the spiritual, his teeth were awful white. Old Waxman had done put veneers on his goddamn teeth. He was, old Waxman, another vain sumbitch preaching Man's inner goodness or something close enough to it to make a sane man sick. Leon, through his years, had met a few.

"Sound to me like a bargain," Leon said, and crossed his fingers under the table.

The piano keys grew in size.

"Sign me up," Leon said, and crossed his ankles.

"I'm real glad about this." Billy Waxman snapped shut his phone and lips at the same time with a smack and a clap. He inserted the device into a secret fold in his Lawrence of Arabia shirt, then reached his big-ass hand across the table for a shake.

Leon smacked his hand into Waxman's for the trusty squeeze. In Waxman's squeeze Leon felt the notch of a thing higher than what his own hand gave off in a squeeze. This baldheaded Waxman man was a muscle. What with his Mother Brother Sisterhood goal and passion, who could tell how deep his power went? Or how long the run would go? For all Leon knew, Waxman held a hundred devils back, whereas all Leon could claim was the Lynched Yankee Negro Dude and Vengeful Hermaphrodite. The Yank and the Herm seemed like interesting cats. Now that they no longer harassed Leon in his sleep, he was curious over what they were like in person. Might be fun to get high together, or grab a bite.

Billy Waxman released Leon's hand winkingly, not no gay winks here, nothing like that, but Leon wasn't accustomed to such winks from men. The winks seemed to be Waxman's last effort in establishing dominion over Leon, his cross of the tee, as people say, his dot of the eye. Leon felt good when they let go of each other's hands. Next thing for Waxman was to disappear.

But Waxman did not disappear. Waxman did not even stand up. Waxman slid a card across the table with his hotdog index finger. The finger withdrew to Waxman's side of the table, and the card was left beside Leon's dinner plate of unfinished stuff, some gravy in there, and ketchup. Leon looked at the card. BILLY WAXMAN GETS SHIT DONE. There was a number. Leon slipped the card into his back pocket. "I see you're still here," he said to the Wax.

"You should know that Robert Butler wants your blood."

"Beg pard?"

"Robert Butler wants your blood," Waxman repeated, and left his mouth hanging partway open, his lips paused above and below the pearly white keys of pianos cruising his mouth. "By the way he talked. I know he wants blood. And Grant Whitelaw is coming after you. When you double-cross people like the Butt, they sick dogs on you, dog-people whose arms are knives and guns. They'll use dental floss to garrote you, whatever works. I'm sure you're familiar with the type. Your whole family must die is their mentality."

"Okay, thank you for the tip," Leon said, and they shook hands yet again.

In this last shake Leon shook, he did, actually, feel a bit of bonhomie going on between them, but when they let go of each other's hands, Waxman said, "As regards to—"

"Don't," Leon said, knowing the what of Waxman's mind—some kind of apology over the what of the Dez.

"I understand, I think," Waxman said sadly. Was he trying to push Leon's murder button? Was it the final test to see was Leon good enough to enter the Mother Brother Sisterhood? The consoling quality in Waxman's voice was just mean, just damn if it didn't contain the sympathy a man might feel for a brother upon learning said brother's wife had done fooled around behind his back. Leon was hard on the try of the tame of his molecular stirfry here, just keep shit together in one piece a moment more, he told himself. Leon needed time to think. That's why he'd played along with Waxman, to buy the time to bide, that's all he'd needed, some think time.

"Okay then, brother," Waxman said, and stood. He hit himself on his left pec with his right fist, then hit his right pec with his left fist. "A brother is a brother no matter the mother." He nodded and turned. Leon watched his bulk walk off, exiting the Miracle Diner into the sunshine that caused him to light up. Through the glass Leon saw the Wax duck into a brand new light blue Toyota Corolla.

"Nice for long distance," Leon said.

"Leon," Deziray said.

"But I prefer mine," Leon said, and the old fries were there, the puddle of ketchup beside them, two elements in perfection that depended each one on the other for completion. Fries and ketchup were natural partners, inseparable by their togethery goodness.

"He came in one day while I danced."

"Don't."

"I told him—"

"Shhhhhh, did I say to shut it?"

"I don't want you to think—"

"Shhh."

Then finally, Jesus, shit, Deziray shut her trap. It took long enough, but at least she was quiet now. From across the table Leon eyed her. Part of him wanted to pick up his plate to smash into her face. Another part wanted to hold her close, pat her back and smell her ears and tell her he loved her more than Dutchmen loved beers, or bears loved honey. He knew Waxman was pernicious, a persuasive man. His power of the put drew you in. He'd entered Titillations while Dez had danced. Leon gathered as much. She gave him attention, a lap dance maybe, in the back room, big deal, a private show. He'd paid her, but the mother had done got bewitched on her ass, was took down by her feminine magma, gone to pieces by her velvet yoni and the natural tan on her phenomenal can, ain't that the correct of the matter, Lieutentant Dan? The mother could have done did the dog with her too, couldn't he have? Leon flashed upon the Wax nailing the Dez from behind. Had the Wax a pin-the-tail-on-the-girl kind of mind? Leon pictured Dez bent over the hood of his Toyota. Was he plowing through her cinnamon ring like a Pit-bull dog into a Chihuahua's thing? The condom on the condo fit tight, right? Was this the what for which Waxman's console was brought to the light?

Leon was of two minds, or three, and as had happened of lately, didn't know what to think. His ability to make his mind up on garbage good was in jeapardy. To stay safe he said nothing, just said fuck it and paid the bill and drove Dez in the direction of *The Tit*—Titillations, yay! They didn't speak during the whole drive, and Leon pulled into the parking lot at fifty miles per. He slammed the brake and the car skidded and stopped and he said, "Get out!" Her eyes watered up. "Goddamnit!" Leon shouted, and brought his boot up as if he would kick her. She knew he wasn't playing, so left the car. Leon watched the slut-ho-show-on-legs high-heel it for the door. She had dressed the part, but beyond the dress was the soul that abided in the frame. Her bunched up shoulders as she walked got to Leon, he felt like the royal assamoly. How suave, pushing her away without no hug or no kiss. Once inside that place, the box locals called *The Tit*, from the waist down she would strip. She would prance, work the pole, dance up close to the edge of the stage for assholes to slip fivers and tens between her garters and thighs and, sometimes, right up between her ass cheeks. So Dezzie had said. As Leon scallywagged back for the Brokenhearted, he felt slimy for the do of what he'd done did. He felt bummy for the bad of how he'd bummed out the Dez, she having to step into that situation without the feeling of some great man like Leon Hicks—*the Golden Man*—patting her back all the while. Now, Leon imagined, she would feel like a hole with a body all around it to guide it through space. Women had told Leon of such feelings. Leon had heard of black holes, wormholes, holes in the ground out of which stinging bees could fly. A hole did not seem like a thing a body would wanna be. To be a hole with flesh to support it? How could that be aught but humiliating? I'm a hole everybody, look at me!

29.

LEON PARKED, upset over Waxman's Waxmania, him with his Mother Brother Bulimia, and goddamnit if he wasn't pissed over Deziray's Deziraynia. To fathom—had she not kept Billy Waxman secret three days?! The girl by now had got bandy with her panty, and could be tamping her clit to the steel pole, a rub-a-dub up and a wiggle-diggle down, EZ the Jew's eyeballs behind their big-ass lenses rolling with her awesome squat-drops and booty bounces, the handstands and upside down randy shit she did, and this here thing where she got on hands and knees to whip hair across the mugs of the men at the edge of the stage, them with smiles, and drinks, and hand-rolled Cubano cigars.

Was Leon a man from Mars? That would be a great big yay, Lars. Was Leon muddled in his brain? Call it a big yessie, Bessie or Cain, an affirmative, Germaine. Leon wished he could think clear. He hoped the Quiz would blast air across his brain's floorboards. Did brains have corridors? Long tubes to stretch east to west? To drop down like somebody's esophagus? Or shoot up like a narrow-hipped woman's hole then curl—fallopian tubes, they were called, Leon had seen diagrams—around about and swirl? A brain's corridors dripped memories like a woman's clams did mirthful things. Not all throughout the nights and day, but when stimulated.

The brown door Leon looked at now, its number fourteen yellow of color. When Leon tired of eyeing it, he got out of the Camaro, and shut the car door right polite like. He walked for the number, him in the know of Ambro soon to greet him, going *Daddy Daddy*, and Beacon here with *Leon baby, sit your ass down, take a load off*—that would be next, the stress would linger, but Leon would relax in the chair while Amber on knees on the floor pulled his boots off, one then the other. She would bring her daddy a cold beer and they would laugh on Barney's shit stains on the ceiling that dripped, what the maid would think once they'd cleared out for the hightails of the upper take. Leon might do several sets of eighty pushups, and a few sets of twenty with Amber cross-legged in the *lotus position* on his back. It was a daughter-daddy thing. They called it spiritual calisthenics over Amber, having grown up amongst hippies, was in the know on the scotch and splotch, call it the hip and the scrotch, the music and puke and spirit of the forest. Leon rose up, in his mind, on his hands, lotus-legged Amber going, "Ohmmm," and sometimes she spoke in tongue, stuff like, "ombabada labba da bay"—she'd learnt that from some religious hicks who'd stopped at the farm once, having come down from Kentucky with a blanket of wild ginseng for trade. They stayed a week, and told of the fires of Hell and a fellow called Lucifer. Amber picked up on their methods in religion. She was a beautiful speaker in tongue.

Danger—Leon intuited it as the door and number came closer. It was the buzzy feel—call it the

Twizzleboon Quingle—that more oft than ever Leon blew off as imagination, the squirt of weird juice into the ditch irrigating his brain. Leon felt it up on top of his head. He felt the quingle in his palms and the prinkle on the bottom of his left foot where a plantar wart had grown since the time before he left Muskegon Correctional. Probably picked the damn thing up in the shower.

Leon grabbed the knob. The door was locked. The door had never been locked before, so Leon wiggled the knob, and Amber from behind it back there went, "I'll shoot your black ass!"

"Open the fuckin door, bitch!"

Amber unlocked it, her face wet all over with smeared tears. She held the .35 with both hands, the barrel pointed at Leon's scrotum. "Where's Beacon?"

The child sniffled.

"Amber?"

"Yes, Daddy?"

"Did I teach you how to handle a piece?"

"Yes."

Leon squatted, the barrel now pointed at his nose. "Baby?"

"He took her and Barney."

"Why you pointing that gun at me?"

"I don't know."

"Do I look like me?"

"You look like you."

"So put the gun down. It's okay, you don't have to worry about nothing now."

Amber let the hammer down easy and poked the gun down into her shorts pocket. "I'm sorry, Daddy," she said, and jumped over the threshold into Leon's arms. He hugged her. The hug made her start to sniffling afresh, so Leon patted her back like any good dad would do. He stood up then with her in his arms and entered the room and sat on the bed, and the story came out. The Butt's lowlife muscle dude had come in and frightened the bejesus out of Amber, had flicked up a switchblade, grabbed Beacon's arm and *doinked* her in the side a quick three times—*doink doink doink*. The man kept saying he wanted the Butt money.

"Did he really say Butt money?"

"Yes, that's what the nigger said, Daddy."

"I thought I told you not to use that word."

"I know, Daddy, I'm sorry. It was a skinny nigger who done it."

"I'll let it slide this time," Leon said, "but don't let me hear it again, you hear me?"

"I would'a kilt him but he backed me against the wall and made me sit."

"Did he lay a hand on you?"

"He put his hand on my head and squashed me down so I had to sit. Then he put his foot on me."

"I see," Leon said.

"I'm'a kill him when he comes back."

"No you ain't, know why?"

"The cops will come?"

"Good girl." Leon scratched her scalp.

Leon paced the rug, it helped him think, but Amber said, "Don't do that. Why are you moving so much?"

"Okay." Leon got on the bed with his back against the pillows piled up against the headboard, his legs jutting across the mattress like two legs wrapped in jeans with boots on the ends of them. In a second Amber jumped onto his lap and wrapped her arms around him. He patted her. "Don't worry," he said.

"I wouldn't put it past him," Amber said.

"Put what past him?"

"What he might could do to Barney. Don't you remember what the Butt was fixin to do to Barney?"

"What should I do, baby?" Leon ran his hand up and down her back, absentmindedly patting her and scratching her scalp.

"Get him back."

It was fucked up. Everything had been going along fine. Now this, all this stupid shit dumped onto their family. There was nothing funny in it. And the girl was not acting right, Leon noticed. "Oh Daddy," she kept saying. In her grief she kissed his neck and jaw, and scooted up on him like she might want to ride the flagpole. Leon ignored it, at first, but then she reached for his mouth with her mouth. Turned out the damn thing was not his imagination. Talk of stupid-ass crunk. Leon whipped his legs around, and the dipshit bounced off the mattress onto the floor. The gun slipped out of her pocket.

"Don't try that shit with me." Leon pointed in her face.

"What?" She started crying again sort of.

"Don't do that neither." Leon offered her his hand. At first she wouldn't take it, the pouter, but then did. Leon helped her stand. To smooth things over they drank brewskis. Amber felt better. So did Leon. The brewskis helped. They were across the table from each other, feeling better by the second. Amber asked Leon for a smoke, and he lit one for her and handed it over. Wasn't like she'd not smoked before. Wasn't like Leon was corrupting a child's innocence, running muddy boots through the snow of her soul or some weird shit like that. Where Amber came from, everybody smoked tobacco. Tobacco was a god. People worshipped it. Amber's mother Butterfly smoked constant, and whoever her daddy was did too you could be sure. Amber just was a bastard sonofabitch like Leon was a bastard sonofabitch. Their bastard sonofabitchdom they held in common.

Oh yeah, Leon was a bastard. He was a bastard in all the ways a one-eyed guy could be a bastard. He was mean to women. He was all up in the selfish mindset of things, and did he know who the goddamn motherfuck of his daddy was? That would be a great big no, Flo from the show *Alice*. Didn't Alice from the show *Alice* have a bastard child for a son too? Ask Mel, the man with a spatula. He's the one who could tell you, just Leon, when he was Amber's age, and asked the Scrubbersoup all over on his damn daddy and shit, what she said is, "Your daddy has better things to worry over than you and me. He is friends with George McGovern."

"What's he look like?"

"What you're gonna look like when you're a sonofabitch."

"Where is my daddy?"

"China, but might could be in Japan or Australia. You never know with him. He is a bigtime scholar in the United States government. He was in Vietnam for a while. Got a whole shoebox filled with medallions for the brave shit he did, risking his life, all shooting out the brains of all kinds of weird people over there in the jungles."

Amber thanked him for the cigarette, and Leon marveled at her eyes. He liked looking into them. They were like his were before somebody cut one out. Amber's eyes were more beautiful even than Deziray's badge of shame, come to think of it right here at the moment and everything. Maybe he'd change his mind tomorrow, but Amber's eyes, when it came down to the nitty gritty of it all, had a different kind of light in them than did the sleeve of the wizard, a piece of life closer to what? The whatever it was to give a person feelings of purpose? That didn't seem right, since it was the beef curtain a man popped his head out through when he first encountered the world. Whatever it was, Amber's eyes were filled plum to the tippy top with it, each eye a promise to spite the naysay gloom Leon's mind was bent for.

"What did he look like?" Leon asked the ditzo from Planet Skitzo.

"His teeth was gold, his face was black, him in a black hat. He comes I'm'a bust a hole in his head."

"No you won't. I thought we discussed that."

"Ho yes I whill."

"You a drunk little bitch."

"Haint neither. I know all about drunkards."

"Okay. You too smart for me."

"He stuck his knife in three times."

"Damn shit had to hurt."

"Daddy?"

"Yes, child?"

"Have you ever kilt somebody?"

"Not lessen that dude Bob got killed. It's possible. I can't say for sure. I just know I never hurt nobody more than what I thought they could handle. I ain't no sadistic."

"I'm glad."

"But I will."

"I don't think so."

"There goes your mouth again."

"You ain't a mean stomper on life."

"Oh yes I ham."

"No you hain't."

"Yes I ham."

"No you hain't."

Leon grabbed a couple brewskis from the cooler, popped tabs on them both, sprinkled salt around the keyholes. They knocked cans and drank. Amber was trying to be a bigshot by drinking down half the can. Good for her. Leon clapped. "Go girl," he said. She tabled it, lips wet, and went, "Mckhaaaah."

"Mckhaaah," Leon echoed. He saluted the drunk little bitch.

"I'll kill him next time."

"Oh no you won't."

"Yes I whill."

"Cut that out," Leon said. "You ain't no killer."

"Hey, can I ast you a question?"

"No."

"I need to know what to do if the skinny nigger comes back."

"I told you about that shit!"

"I need my monkey!"

"That monkey has caused me so much goddamned trouble."

"Daddy, don't disrespect Barney. It upsets me. Will you do me that kind favor? I'm not asking for much. Just don't disrespect Barney."

"You got it, sweets." Leon got the cowboy gun from the car. Back inside, at the round table with Amber, he cracked it and emptied its bullets out. The bullets bounced on the shiny brown surface, and slid around, each a possible dead man, dead woman, dead monkey, or dead dog, or frog or mosquito even if you had great aim. Every day folks got snappy over the puppies. Dumbass Amber had said Leon was not no killer, and maybe she was right, but if Leon believed his momma, his dad had done killed many a man, Gooks, she called them. If you believed the Christians Leon in his lifetime had butted heads with, FIRE awaited every killer. "Them flames'll burn the skin offen yer pecker, and the skin'll grow right back. Them flames is hungry, brother," the prison preacher had said.

Leon picked a bullet up and blew it. Felt like he was blowing lint off Grant Whitelaw's head. Bullet had Whitelaw's name on it, he guessed. Leon shoved it into a chamber.

Amber swung out the other clicker's cylinder. She pulled the ejector rod and the bullets plopped out and they reloaded the guns together. They spun cylinders and clacked them into place in the Russian roulette kind of way. The parts were in good working order. When they tired of that they spun the guns on the table, sorta like spin the bottle, just nobody asked for truths, nobody asked for dares.

In the spin of things the remembrance of that damn forty jobber came to Leon, what he'd bought the day he'd first laid eye to Deziray, *the Dez*—wasn't not yet burnt, not yet cashed out. Wazzy was, as a matter of actual fact, in the pocket of his jeans bunched up to the duffel bag—thank God they'd not been washed. Must to could be true, so hot damn, motherfucker! Is we talking on a flat triangle to melt the heart here?

30.

LEON BUSTED A HOLE in a Busch beer can. He
pinched a bowl up and jabbed a screen in with a
safety pin. From his Carleton he ashed the bed for the
chunk of white, and laid her down, a virgin plucked
from the wood and slapped into dirt, see her
surmounted by evil! She was damn pretty down there,
and Leon wanted her, but Amber pulled first, lifted
her thumb off the devil's dick and cleared his
chamber. Her eyes dimmed. Leon grabbed the can,
careful not to spill any, and slammed her, heard bells,
the snakes of crawly clawing lovesomely through his
bloodstream. In a minute Leon sucked down the last,
Amber on the floor in the writhe, her mouth opening
wide then closing, like a nurse shark gaping for water,
suffering on some sandy shore in Capetown, or below
a Florida pier, just trying to make you feel all guilty
and shit to where the best option was to kick the bitch
in the face, or club her with a bat, do you got one of
baseball or hockey or golf? If not, a tennis racket will
do. On this here Amber you could not tell if she
needed help. If she did, she was too gone to ask.

Back on the bed Leon closed his eyes to make
contact with old Mr. Quiz whose burden in the
wandering of the Herm and the Lynched Yankee

Negro Dude needed release. Leon said, "Smack them down," and the Quiz obeyed. The giant Quizman slampt his left arm out, and the Lynched Yankee Negro Dude flew tumblingly into space. Quiz slampt out his right arm, and the Vengeful Hermaphrodite rocketed off the kebob of the shish.

Like watching a movie, seeing two dudes flying through the nether hungry and looking for trouble, but the Rebel was a girl. She had tits, a pot, a ladle. They tumbled toothily through ether into the earth's bright atmosphere, catching fire and screaming and baring gums. Gross, but when the Lynched Yankee Negro Dude slammed onto Billy Waxman's back, it opened its mouth up way wide and chomped into the mother's neck. Waxman slapped his shoulders, trying to fling the Lynched Yankee Negro Dude off him. It was funny, just here seeing how the Lynched Yankee Negro Dude was invisible to the Wax of Manchuria.

Next came the Herm with her flapping flag of the Confed, the burning cape, the hair grown down for a hundred years—it was on fire. She slapped hard upon good Grant of Law, unprincipled uncouth white mother who'd called Leon's money "Butt Money." A man to call money "Butt Money" was freak-o creep-o, and Leon was pleased-o to see the Herm pound knuckles-o into Whitelaw's face-o, beating the crap-o out of the turd-o mofo.

If that didn't take care of Leon's problemo, something was wrong here in that Quizzleboon owed Leon motherfucking Hicks a thing or goddamn two or three or four or five or six or seven or eight or nine or ten or eleven or twelve or thirteen or fourteen and so on and so forth into the future. The time had come for Quiz to eat Leon's laundry, fry Leon's bacon, take out his garbage and lick his organic egg.

Beautiful! Funny! Delicious! What a vision! What a funny knockdown comedy, better than Jerry Seinfeld. Leon wanted to watch on, but the voice of the Quiz came on with *Git yer ass up!*

Leon rose, knelt beside Ambrose who writhed like a catfish thrown to dust. He grabbed her clicker off the table, opened the child's fist and set the gun handle into it. He went to the door. Somebody had been softly knocking. He cracked it. A mouth in a brown face opened. Beyond the lips a showing of gold bricks was displayed.

Leon flung the door way wide, bowed deep like a gentleman in tuxedo, and motioned for Whitelaw to enter.

Whitelaw stepped in.

Leon did not close the door.

"She ought not point that shit to me," Whitelaw said.

Leon snapped his fingers to Amber, said, "Now's not the time, Sweets," and to Whitelaw said, "She's got a bone to pick with you, Mr. Whitelaw man. She wants her monkey back bigtime. Is Beacon in the car?"

"Hell naw she ain't in no car. I come here for the Butt Money, motherfucker."

"I spent it. Give Beacon back to me and you can keep the monkey."

"No!" Amber cried in a crazed slur. She set another foot forward, the gun again pointed at Whitelaw.

The bruv—more brown than black—raised his hands in mock fear. "Ho now, girl, do like you daddy say."

"Tell Butler we're sorry for what we did," Leon said, "but you know, there's a difference between a monkey and a woman."

"No there hain't neither," Amber said.

"So where's she at?" Leon said. "I ain't kidding you now."

"Safe in a place. Where the money at? Hand it over we can quits it."

"You got the monkey back so why don't you split?"

"I ain't splittin 'til the money right heah." Whitelaw held his hand out and slapped it. "The Butt done changed his mind on the monkey. He want his money back over what y'all did. He don't take to no double-cross."

"Okay, well, what if I tell Sweets to plug you?"

"I'm a good bullet dodge."

"Can I ast you something, Mr. Grant Whitelaw?"

"Ho now, you calling me Grant?"

"I know all about you. I been meaning to ast."

"I ain't here to convenience."

"I was wondering," Leon said, "have you felt anything biting your neck or slapping you on the back or anything strange thataway?"

"What kinda shit you talking, man?"

"Any weirdy tingle feel or anything like that going on?"

"Don't mess with me, man. Just gimme the goddamn Butt Money. Where it at?"

"I told you I spent it. You want a beer?"

"Do you want your lady?"

"I have many ladies. Where is she?"

"Safe in a place I said."

"Keep her."

"Gimme the Butt Money, I go."

QUIZZLEBOON

"Whore the bitch out, Grant."

"I ain't no pimp, man."

"You look to be like one to me."

Amber's snicker was contagious, it caught on, Leon snickered, laughed, couldn't help it. The Grant man plain looked to have a pimped up style going on right here at the moment and shit. Funniest was how Grant looked self-conscious over the pimp thing, like he spent his off hours worried on did he look the pimp. Grant's eyes shifted to the side, his buttons pushed in serious here now. He was nervous, looked uppity like to blow a brain gasket. The snickers turned to laughter.

"Stop," Whitelaw said.

"You look concerned," Leon said, and gave the ha ha ha.

"Yes he do, Daddy!" Amber cried. "He looks real concerend."

"If I ain't ever had met you I'd take you for one," Leon said.

"That how you wanna play?"

Leon slapped the dude and the dude's feet flew up and he landed on his back. Leon to the quick hopped onto him and pinned the fellow's arms to the floor with knees, gave him the Chinese Torture in the sing of, "Wedding bells are ringing in the chapel!" Leon wasn't the best singer in the world, but that was one song he sang on key. It was the song Mr. Quigley sang while working the office of the White Lady Motel. As Leon sang it, Grant Whitelaw laughed, that was the nature of the Chinese Torture, it made you laugh. As Leon sang, Amber went through Whitelaw's pockets, found keys and a wallet and a sandwich bag filled with stuff to look like cocaine, white sort of but yellow and powdery and a little wet. Amber waved the sack in the air with, "Looky here."

Amber tossed it on the table and squatted and put her face next to Grant's and shoved the barrel to the temple. "Where's my monkey, bitch?"

"Amber," Leon said.

"Stop making him laugh," Amber said.

Leon stopped pounding the tips of his fingers into Grant's solar plexus.

Tears on Grant's face. Grant rolled his jaw, squinted his eyes and winked at Amber like he had some nasty plan for her later.

"Did you wink?" Amber said.

"Amber?" Leon said.

"He winked at me."

"He likes you."

"If he did he would give me Barney."

"You stupid sonofabitch," Leon said. "If he told you where Barney is, what would you do?"

"Get him right this minute."

"That ain't true. You'd look up to me to go get him for you."

Amber said, "If this nigger don't tell me where Barney's at, I'm'a shoot him, Daddy, I don't care." She cocked her canned heat up nice and firm.

"No," from Grant.

"Tell me." Amber pushed the muzzle into Grant's ear cup.

The room held its breath.

"You better tell her," Leon said.

"No!" Grant's mouth remained open, his gold-plated teeth aglitter. A drop of Barney's shit fell off the ceiling and landed in Mr. Whitelaw's mustache. The man was about to spill the beans, but right here a vehicle pulled into the lot. Its shadow touched into the room. Amber moved back from Whitelaw and set her aim at the open doorway.

Good girl, Leon thought. A fast thinker, Amber, Ambrosia, the Amb, she had them covered, but in walked Billy Waxman, and *looky looky looky*, what's this here? Why, *it's Deziray*.

31.

LEON WAS ASTOUNDED. Girl was supposed to be shaking her goddamn pussy hole right this minute at her chosen institution of gainful employment. Here it wasn't but five or six, dark coming on, and Dez was home. She wasn't due to get off work 'til ten. Billy Waxman, the bonehead, wore a wife beater now and was quite the upstanding heroic figure of iron muscle and trustworthy pectoral. The man's nipples poked out like a woman's almost, only they were hard as steel, Leon could tell, and looked more like the snub-nosed barrel-ends of a Chuck Wagon duo—*bang bang* they might go any minute. The man had done shoved his white teeth into Leon's business a second time, the mother! In a flash Leon saw Waxman drop in at Titillations when Dezzie felt rejected and cowed by Leon's irritation. In that flash Leon saw the comforting, *Oh thank you, Billy, that's so sweet of you!* Did Deziray run her hand along Billy's forearm as she'd done his when they'd spoke in the blind man's kitchen? That was a powerful run of a hand over a arm. Shit had activated Leon's groin, she all looking into his eyes with her sad brown ones a thousand years old. At the Tit with the Wax, the man of the year, did a tear drop into Dezzie's beer?

"Fancy fancy," Leon said.

"Oh, Amber, what're you thinking?" Dez said, and knelt beside the child, took away her gun, had to pry loose Amber's fingers while pointing the thing at the ceiling.

"Looks like we arrived in time to make a difference in the world," Billy Waxman said all self-congratulatory and shit.

Leon kinda sorta wanted to hug him, truth do tell. Billy Waxman looked all muscular, just damned muscular. Must've gone to the gym since lunch.

And Waxman was looking down at Leon, sorta judgmental-like with arms crossed, a smirk on his mug, a look to say *What're you doing on the floor?* Why, Leon was straddling some skinny black dude who looked like a pimp, or a huge dressed-up worm. Was Leon a jockey in the Kentucky Worm Derby? Did Leon care to explain? That would be a great big double negative, Blaine. Leon stood, and for whatever dumb reason held his hand Waxman's way.

Leon noticed, as he'd noticed earlier that day when they shook hands at the Miracle Diner, that Waxman harbored a few more notches of strength in his grip. Leon was about to ask Billy how much he could bench-press, but Whitelaw shot to his feet like a vamp. He grabbed Amber's neck with long fingers and whipped her to him, switched out his blade and jabbed her ass.

The child screamed.

Whitelaw was a stabber. Had the child skewered on the end of his knife. "Shutup!" he shouted.

Amber whimpered.

"This not be good," Waxman said.

Whitelaw yanked the knife out of the child's butt

cheek and stuck it up by her throat, acting like he would stab it in and rip out a hole. There was blood on the knife blade. It was very gross, too gross, and the fingers of the man, the fingers of Whitelaw, were sweaty and orangey and looked eager to cut the little girl, just give him the excuse, *please, go ahead, make me do it!*

Leon and Waxman exchanged looks of *Okay, this dude is up there in the thing of things.* They were in agreement. Grant must be stopped. To distract Grant, Leon stuck his index finger way up his nose as if trying to dislodge a booger of unheard proportions. Grant was looking to see what kind of booger Leon pulled out. He'd slackened his attention. That's when Billy rushed him. In a finger-snap Billy tackled Grant, Amber flinging off to the side like a goose feather out of a busted pillow. In the tussle the Lynched Yankee Negro Dude, who'd been gnawing on Billy's shoulder, reached out and bit the Vengeful Hermaphrodite. It was very dim, but Leon saw it, just barely. They were locked at the face, mouth to mouth, each huge mouth biting and ripping and tearing at the enemy. In the mix of it did Billy raise his big-ass fist? That would be a superlative yes, a gift from Billy to the Grant. The slam splattered blood up onto Billy's white wife-beater and he-man's girthly neck.

"Lord," Billy said, and stood as Amber, curled by the bed, struggled for breath. "What I just did is against the values of the Mother Brother Sisterhood."

"You knocked him senseless," Deziray observed.

"Is he conscious?" Waxman asked.

Amber got to her feet. "Motherfucker!" she screamed, and kicked the man's head with her bare foot.

QUIZZLEBOON

"Amber, no!" Deziray cried, and stopped the dork from kicking him a number two time. She pulled Amber over by the bed where she broke out hysterical with sobs. "Shhh, come on now," she said, and shook the dimwit's shoulders.

Amber stifled her cries, made the effort, but really sounded some like a tiny weasel to got its guts wrung out, a ferret, like if you grabbed the two ends and twisted opposite directions, the Indian Twist is what they called it when you did it on somebody's forearm. Somebody in the hood had more like to've heard it, and become alarmed, called the cops. Worst was Grant Whitelaw was out to lunch. Could a out-to-lunch guy say where Beacon was? Call it a fat nary, Perry. Leon told Dezzie to revive the sumbitch.

"Why me?"

"I ain't going to touch him," Leon said. "You like touching people. Slap him, hurry up now. I'll get some water to throw in his face."

"But Amber needs me. She's bleeding."

"He stabbed me!" Amber screamed, and the thought of it, of having been stabbed by that man, got her scream-crying all over again. Amber tried freeing herself so that she could kick Whitelaw more, but Deziray held her back. A lot of butt-blood had soaked into Amber's shorts. Leon watched a red stream of it trickle down the inside of her thigh to her ankle and hit the floor.

Billy Waxman cleared his throat. "Leon, I've got a First Aid kit in the car, I'll get it." He left the room, shaking his head like he simply could not believe what was happening.

Leon stretched his arms out, thought, and thinked, and thunk real fast. Nothing came to him. He just wished he had not puffed that rock bit early on with Amber. He wanted stuff to slow down now. His thoughts could not keep up with the tick-tack-tock forward of the march. What to do?

Leon looked to the door Billy passed through, and thought *I could disappear*. T'was the second time that day he'd thought that thought, this to press the eject button on the whole deal, say goodbye to all and start over someplace new like he'd done in Asheville after his release from corrections in Michigan. What a time. Within a week of his release he'd robbed three banks, ding dong dangle a carrot in front of your own nose why don't you? Old Quiz would keep Leon straight this time around. Quizzle*boon* would protect Mr. Leon Hicks. Where was the Quiz now? Hey Quiz, where you at, buddy?

Deziray squatted beside the black—actually, he was more brown than black—man on the floor. In her short-ass skirt and high-heeled glittery sandals she placed hands to his shoulders, shook him gentle, said, "Hey, mister," and Leon was aroused. Girl was in a squat, good Dez to the rescue, her hands on the worm awesome! Was like looking at a girly mag. Leon didn't care for it, so moseyed to the sink, filled a plastic cup with water that he fully intended to slap down into Whitelaw's face. Dead or no dead, Whitelaw deserved to have his body defiled and dragged through the streets behind the back of a jeep. Whitelaw had a lowdown temperament, was so lowdown that stabbing a child in her ass was not beneath him. What Whitelaw was was a lowdown ex-pimp who thought he'd done climbed the ladder a rung in he was on the payroll of a ex-congressman. In some ways Leon commiserated to the dude. They were both cons, in the same game give or take a pineapple—but fuck it. Whitelaw deserved it.

Whitelaw had nerve.

Whitelaw was a fearless mofo.

Whitelaw had been playing possum.

Whitelaw whipped a hand into his crotch. He brought a thingy up and let it go. The sound blossomed and bloomed and wilted and died. It tossed Dez on her back with legs flown up. She tried to recover. Blood poured out of her neck so she clutched it with both hands. Gory runlets came through, and she looked like she was choking herself. She twitched, and kicked the floor so hard her high-heeled sandal strap broke and she was barefoot on one leg. Her look of disbelief was changing into some other kind of look.

"Deziray!" the child cried.

The blood all over brought down Quizzleboon. Like quicksilver poured into a test tube, the Quiz entered the man that was Leon, his transformation immediate. The agony that had barely had time to register was drowned in a rejuvenating flush of calm bubbly watery stuff that tickled his brain and thickened in his ears and trickled around all over everywhere inside his body. It was the Quizzleboon buzz, and the Dez was a shape now is all Dez was, the brown hair in the rug slopped up with redish liquids, and looky looky, is that the strawberry cookie?

Was the world interesting?

Was the world a thing?

The world was both a thing and interesting, interesting as a purple squid addicted to iceberg lettuce, ain't that correct? Bits of it twisted and turned and sometimes fitted together like jigsaw pieces, a puzzle of the Milky Way going on here. Do we got satellites bound for collision pictured here? And hey, look over yonder! Why, it's Interplanet Janet! Check her out, zooming past moons and asteroids. Good luck, girl! And good night to the light. The shape the Quiz watched now, now that he had put on flesh, was kinda fascinating—*a work of art*—and the Quiz above it stood, drinking the water Leon—bless his ignorance—had intended to throw in Whitelaw's face, to what? Revive the sonofabitch?

Billy Waxman burst through the door with wiggling jowl-flesh. The funny expression revealed the contents of the brain of the man. The dude saw himself as a David Koresh mofo kind of guy, a Waco wannabe wacko with a scalplock a la ridiculo. Mother Brother Sisterhood? Is that what Waxman called the organization he was trying to start? Ole Waxman, through the eye of the Quiz, looked weak, and slovenly, and pretentious and not bright. Before, through the eye of Hicks, he had looked intimidating and brilliant. Oh, was the Wax here to cringe at the sight of a bleeding lady? Some dumb dancer whose hands had gone lax around the neck while a shrunken Yankee soldier and hermaphrodite, like dolls, licked at her blood? It was pretty pathetic, and the hole there visible. Once the blood stopped pouring out of it, you might look inside to see the larynx like the people did on O.J. Simpson's wife. The Quiz looked up to see what Deziray saw. It was all that good monkey shit around the light fixture. Then looking back at the art of her he watched the tension leave her eyes, her body meat-like of a sudden, a thing bred and raised for consumption.

Waxman of the Billy, the big sissy, the mouth of

him was open way wide in the watch of it. It was open and stayed open.

"I said I wasn't here to play," Grant Whitelaw said. Ole Grant, after popping the Dez in the neck, had hopped to his feet to stand in front of the TV, the guys on the painting on the wall above him still fishing by the stream up in the mountains.

Quizzleboon only could laugh, it's all he could do was laugh.

Waxman's face sucked inward. The what Waxman was behind Waxman's face was tried hard in disbelief. But Waxman had to perceive it. Facts were asteroids of destruction, and could not be denied. The girl was shot so bad that nothing could be did—it was over— or done—and Quiz registered in the nuance of Waxman's face a dwindle sort of thing of love and hope. What would come of his Mother Brother Creaturehood? Waxman, Mr. Quizzleboon saw in the plain, had loved the Deziray, no surprise in the Cracker Jack box. The Wax had hoped to have Dezzy in a everyday cluckalong sorta way, Dez a cluckalong smart one in his mother load freeway.

Amber—no, she was Ambrosia in the eye of the Quiz—was a bit some too scared to barely move. Would that time did not budge, but it bulged, so the scream she'd held to bay caught up—it issued full-bore into the room.

Quiz swallowed more tepid juice. He watched the Wax Mandrake Man tackle Whitelaw, *ha ha ha*, the Vengeful Hermaphrodite and Hanged Union Soldier at it once more, gathering strength in their fight from the blood they just drank, and tumbling towards the sink as they hit each other and fought, here to stay and haunt the lives of whoever checked in next.

Quizzle gave Amber a respectful nod, grabbed the sack of white shit off the table and, careful not to bloody his boots, stepped over Deziray—she was dead, so fuck her—and left the room and stepped down to Leon's Camaro. Quizzle opened the door and set down in the bucket seat and stuck the key into the ignition and turned it. Engine came to life. Quizzleboon entertained himself on if you stuck an engorged wiener into the dead girl's ignition switch, then turned it, would something happen? Sometimes people underestimated the medicinal values of hot beef injections. Could the combo of one and the Fountain of Youth juice in her produce a miracle? Could it bring her back? Maybe, but Quizleboon had not the time nor wherewithal to discover the damns of these matters.

Siren sounds had been making their way their way. The siren sounds came closer. They moved in quicklike, the first fuzz buster sliding into the lot as Amber—*no, she was Ambrosia*—limped into the slackened light of day. The Quiz would have left her too, only he was curious on what the cops would do in the confront of some pigeon-toed kid with blood running down both legs, them no doubt thinking Amber—*no, she was Ambrosia, goddamnit!*—had been split in two by some fellow's long dong silver. Sure enough, it was a bit some funny. Cops hopped out screaming the usual shit with guns up. Their gums dropped at the sight of her, guns atremble, their eyes rolling in their head holes like cartoon cops. Just then Billy Waxman emerged from Room 14 with muscled arms held high, some kind of badge or identification card in his hand. The cop who'd been shouting at Mr. Quizzleboon finally let off a round to cut through the

Cam door. Thing lodged into the driver's seat. The Quiz smirked at the fellow as the Amb—*no, she was Ambrosia, goddamnit for the last time!*—got in shotgun.

32.

THE BOOT OF the Boon slammed down hard. The Quiz of the Boon and the Amb of the Rose—Am*brosia*—slammed back like a truck sucked off a road by a quake of earth in Asia. A quick shift into first whipped the Cam up perpendick to the bubblegum machine. Quizzle slipped up Baby Boop to fire out the tires of the geeks. The cop car was rendered *debilitato*, its front and back tires on the left side deflated squash-o funny-o like overly ripened tomatoes, or Mr. Potato's nose if you were to stomp on it with your boot heel. With a beaming smile Quiz peeled rubber out of there, and headed north for I-10, but looky here, brother mother man, it's the powerline road, same one Leon Hicks had done squirreled onto the morn he popped the trunk to find a cute brunette tied up like a sex slave in transport. The Quiz had watched the whole thing from his vantage point on the moon. The details, thanks to Leon's eye, were in the machine, her hair and the sand and twigs and the light that danced through the forest like piggies. There were hawks in the sky, purple flowers, and was that blood on them thar titties?

Quiz slowed, bumped through the grass to the side of the road, into the sand, then gunned up to the special place to kill the Cam. An absence of sound. But the child had some complaints. No sooner had they stopped but that the silence gave way to her box, the one containing her voice. "She's dead," the child said, and just sniffled and snuffled and complained and worried about shit out loud to where Quiz had to give her his *I'll-kill-your-ass-if-you-don't-shut-the-fuck-up-right-now* look.

"Don't," Amber—*no, she was Ambrosia*—said, and held her hands up at her face as if protecting herself from the ugliness of the Quiz, like she could barely stand to look at him.

"Didn't that boy Leon say I would whoop you if you acted up? You want me to bite your head off, that what you want me to do?" Quizzleboon asked the annoying idiot.

Ambrosia looked forward out the window and swallowed. It was a gulp of nothing. She did not sniffle now.

The Quiz felt himself grow tired. The smell of the woods floated in though the windows and it was very beautiful here on earth, with the scrub palmettos and slash pines and some kind of flower blooming in the high trees, even here in mid-November. The scents floated down and entered Quizzle's nostrils and he felt a pain in his chest.

"I know what you're doing," Amber—*no, she was Ambrosia*—said.

The Quiz looked at the poor child, her face the color of sand, but polished, smooth, glossed over and moist with glazed irises a shade of blue never seen up close and personal on the moon. Her bright black pupils emanated intelligence, and the puckering weird hovering fluctuating red hole below them—that would be her mouth, Ralph—lulled the Quiz into a peaceful trance. Some seconds walked across the dashboard with smiles on their faces, like ants up on hind legs. The child seemed to know what was happening. "Come back, Daddy," she said, and *yowza kadoodle*, the Quiz took off like a moth from the mouth of a drunk-ass poodle. Leon was Leon. The shit from the Brokenhearted Woman Motel flooded back. Leon saw Dez on the floor, leg twisted to the side, the glittery shoe half on her foot and her sex exposed in flagrance. There was the blood, and was she staring at the monkey shit on the ceiling?

"Damn," Leon said.

"I heard that."

So what now? What of the dream? And what of Amber here bleeding, her legs red with it, and Leon didn't wanna see it. "You okay?" he said. Amber leaned to the side. She pulled her shorts down. The damn stab hole could be stitched up easy, but since no doctor lived in the Camaro, unless he was hiding under the bucket seat, Quiz—*naw, he was Leon*—wiped her ass down with yellow napkins from Wendy's. He pulled out a length of duct tape, ripped it free with his teeth. He placed a folded napkin over the wound and taped her up.

"You're good to go," Leon said. "We'll stop at Eckerd's for Superglue. I'll bead it along your cut and the cut will grow together like it was never there to begin with."

"I'm so glad you're back, Daddy. I don't like that Mr. Quizzleboon man no more. He threatened to bite my head off and I don't know what he would'a done if I gave him lip."

Amber hugged Leon, her Uncle L. Leon patted

Amber's back and stroked her head and called her stupid and slapped her gently across the face to try to get her synchronized. The horror of the situation was too much to cope with for both of them, so Leon slapped his own face too, then asked Amber to slap him, and she did right there in the car. "Harder," he said, and she smacked the crap out of him. They had a laugh on that one, but Leon was pissed at Quizzleboon for not grabbing Whitelaw's wallet. In the wallet of Whitelaw could be clues on how to find Beacon and Barney. The cops had Whitelaw's wallet now. What was wrong with Quiz? Quiz was the smart one who knew how to manipulate shit and make provisions for the future, so why did he get so careless and tear out of the Brokenhearted like a goddamn lightning bolt on wheels? How could Quizzleboon be so heartless?

"I'm hungry," Amber said.

"We've been burning calories by the dump truck load," Leon said. "Whenever you are emotional you burn tons of calories. There might be some bananas in back. You want a banana?"

"Why'd you make me think of Barney by saying the b-word? You shouldn't'a done that. Why me? Oh, why me, why me, why me?"

"You want a bump? It'll curb your appetite."

"Bump?"

"From the sack we took from Whitelaw. Least Quizzle boy had sense to grab the bump. It's burger meat for hungry girl, makes hunger to go way."

"I want it."

Leon reached into the sack with his knife, pulled a little bit out on the blade's tip, and snorted it up his left nostril to check it. It was pretty refined, a hell of a lot cleaner than crank, which his biker buddies used to mix up in a bathtub in Detroit. That was when everybody called him One-eyed Leon, back when he was a naïve springtime bunny rabbit boy, before he'd been to prison for knocking the damn cop's front teeth out.

Leon took another bumpy-doo, then lifted one out for Amber who, holding one nostril shut with her index finger, looked like a scientist or some shit. Girl sucked it straight up her nose, and through the woods to grandmother's house did go. Her damn face turned pink, and Leon said don't worry, it was supposed to burn. Count to ten they'd both feel better, and they did. They got calm, calculated, felt smarter, and saw here the best thing for now, at this point, was to *git*, say goodbye to Dodge City, Smitty, but first they had to squitch. "Excuse me," Leon said, and walked up into the trees for the dumpy doo dah day.

Leon wiped with spindly fern leaves, then wiped his hands in the dirt, cleaning them. Once back in the driver's seat he felt ready to go, but Amber had to "excuse herself" too. "Be careful not to pull the tape off your butt," Leon said, and reminded her not to use poison ivy to wipe with. He watched her return to the car, smelling her hands, then drove them out to I-10 to steer west. Soon it was full-on night, less danger of spottage by Highway Patrol. Leon drove through the Alabam on into Mississippi, feeling sick like a sissy over how things ended in Pensacola. The crap-o feeling was so strong that he'd best to relegate those memories to a lonesome corner within. Leon made it happen, but still felt the sensation, the nag, the bunk of the business left undone. What if Beacon was locked in a trunk? A refrigerator? At best she was cuffed to a cozy chair in a room, her mouth plugged so that she could not scream. Was Barney monkey-cuffed to her ankle? Was he tugging on it, maybe gnawing through his monkey leg to go find help? The maybes were trillion.

"Fuck it," Leon said, and clapped once and was done with it, sort of. By midnight through the Lou of the Anna they drove—*Louisiana, baby!*—and as Leon drove, he and the Amb talked, with the help of *the crissss*, on many a wild varied scientifical thing, astrology and literature, and reminisced over great times they'd had up in the dirt farm hills. Their connection was more mind-related than before, more intellectual. They talked like two geniuses without the big age difference. The crystal snow was at work, hats off to the *crissss*.

Amber wanted to know on Leon's childhood. "Tell me about when you was little," she said.

"All my childhood could do for you is make you puke."

"How did you lose your eye?"

"You know how I lost my eye."

"You gave it to Mr. Quizzleboon so he could watch everybody on earth?"

"You know it."

"You got to come clean with me, Daddy."

"You believed before, didn't you?"

"I was pretending. How did you really lose it? I need me to know."

Leon said Mr. Quigley of the White Lady Motel came into the room while his mother was in another room cleaning, and pulled out his wiener. The Quig, as everybody knew him, tried to stick it in Leon's mouth, so he ran, as any self-respecting nine-year-old boy would, but he tripped and fell against the foosball machine that the Quig was keeping in their room until his new bar and grill opened up. Leon's eye slammed against one of the steel rods poking out. The rod pushed into Leon's eye socket and popped his eyeball out so that it hung on strings. The medical people tried to save his eye. No luck.

"I don't believe it," Amber said.

"You calling me a lie?"

"I knew use a lie when you talked on men on the moon. I don't like when you act like the moon man. All that is is you lying to youself."

"Maybe you're right." Leon tried to change the subject, but Amber was back at it, asking Leon questions and making comments. Little home-schooled bitch was talking like an adult. She was about ten or some shit, Leon didn't know, he forgot, maybe nine. She was cocky.

"Something's wrong," she said.

"Lots of things, hundreds of things, thousands, millions."

"I mean about the story."

"I know what you mean, but you need to stop harassing me. I told you what you wanted to know, now why don't you let me be? Tell me about your own damn bullshit childhood why don't you?"

"I'm not big enough to have a childhood, but I remember my babyhood."

"Tell it."

"I 'member when I was inside my mama I always looked out at the world through the hole in her bellybutton."

"You a goddamn lie."

"No, I really do remember it."

"What did you see?"

"People and colors, and I always got mad when she put on a shirt. Then I couldn't see nothing. Did your eyeball see?"

"Did it see?"

"When it hung on the strings? I was wondering could it see stuff still."

"No, it couldn't see stuff still, you happy?"

"Don't get offensive."

"I ain't offensive."

"I was wondering," Ambrosia—*no, she was Amber*—said. Or actually, maybe she was Ambrosia now, but did it the fuck matter? That would be a big fat no and a never, Chester.

"I don't remember if it saw," Leon said.

"That's what I mean by something's wrong."

"If it saw I should know if it saw, but no, I don't think it saw."

"Did it hurt?"

"Okay, well, how do you think you would feel if you slammed your eye into a foosball thing?"

"I wouldn't stop screaming, but I ain't sure that's what happened."

"Boys don't scream. Maybe that's the difference between us and y'all. I don't know, but as soon as my eye popped out my mouth went dry, I can tell you that without telling a lie. The dryness went into my bones and made me stiff all over."

"What did they do to Mr. Quigley? Did they put him in jail for molesting you?"

"I didn't say he molested me, bitch. What's this shit you talking? What happened, if you really got to know, is Superscrub told the cops she and the Quig were together at the time of the accident. It all came down to boys will be boys."

"She was mean to you, wasn't she?"

"Naw, she was a good mamma. She was afraid of the Quig. I never could figure out why. All he was was her employer."

"And her lover?"

"Listen here!"

"Either she was or wasn't. I think it matters for the story to be told right."

"She was, I guess, shit, I don't know."

"I know all my mother's lovers. You and Castle and Potato and—"

"Cut it out, girl, things are different where you came up."

"But you would know."

"Maybe I didn't wanna know."

"That's called making ignorance a virtue. Think back and remember, Daddy. Close your eye and see it. I'll take the wheel."

Amber grabbed the wheel. Leon closed his eye. The mottled dark enveloped him, and gave way to pleasant flashes of light. In the sound of the engine Leon traveled back in time, for eyes, if anything, were blobby recording devices. They had that stuff called vitreous humor in them—it somehow etched reality into the soft tissues of the brain. What was in the brain was in the brain. It could not escape the brain. When the memories took up on the screen, Leon wanted to open his lids to call it a day, but his daughter—no, she wasn't his damn daughter, she was Butterfly's bugger—might think him lily-livered.

A bright slit split the dark, and Leon peered through to see himself walk up to Vauss Buckner's house. Vauss had a four-wheeler and the plan was to saddle up with cane poles and ride through sandy forest on down to the fishing hole. Vauss's leg though was broke. He'd been hung onto a rope attached to the bumper of his dad's truck is what, riding his skateboard. Their speed got up too high and Butch flew off the road into a mailbox. He was drugged up now useless, so Leon walked home to the White Lady.

Leon sees the hand reach for the knob. It's locked. He hears stuff going on back there. He pulls his key out of his pocket and lets himself in. The Quig on the far bed is fully dressed but for the hairy butt cheeks bouncing. Under him Leon's sister Glinda, dress raised to the neck, is going, "*thank* you," to each bounce of the mother, just going, "*thank* you, *thank* you, *thank* you."

Leon opened his lids. He pushed Amber's hand off the wheel.

"What did you see?"

"Nothing I didn't know."

"You're lying. Tell the truth, bitch."

"The Quig was fucking my sister, bitch."

"That sonofabitch!"

"It ain't nothing but a thang, bitch."

"What else did he do, bitch? What happened when you seen it?"

"Take the wheel, bitch."

Amber took the wheel and Leon closed his eye. Over there Mr. Quigley and his sister were so lost in the make-the-baby thing that they hadn't noticed him enter the room. Looked to Leon like the Quig was hurting Glindy, choking her or, if not trying to kill her, at least making her feel uncomfortable—so why was Glinda going *thank* you, *thank* you?

Leon walked up to the edge of the bed and set his hand on Glindy's foot for some dumb reason. She screamed and kicked. Mr. Quigley rose to his knees and his wiener looked like a damn gaff or some shit, like what you drag a gator up out of a swamp by. Leon hadn't known wieners could be so large and strange-looking. Leon thought Mr. Quigley must be a monster who hid within a human shape. Leon had caught the Quig with his guard down. Now the monster was going to destroy Leon. Leon turned and ran smack into the foosball machine.

Leon opened his eye, took back the wheel from Amber. "Wasn't for him I'd still have both eyes. I must've been trying to protect my sister by saying to the cops he got fresh on me, you know what I mean? I ought to go find him. He can eat my Lady Chatterley."

"No, Daddy, you ain't no killer."

"I killed Bob, didn't I?"

"That was a accident, and it ain't never been told if he was dead for true."

"The Quig's got it coming." Leon switched on the radio. Golden Oldies played as they cruised below the stars, songs by Frankie Vallie, Elvis and The Supremes. Leon and Amber drifted about in their own worlds.

An hour later, or maybe it was twenty minutes later, Amber said, "I'm hungry girl. I want a bump." They were approaching Baton Rouge.

"I think it's time we get some food, baby."

"I told you before not to call me baby."

"You a long way from grown, Amber."

Amber eyed Leon like hey, don't worry, and they sped past Rosedale and other Louisiana towns. These towns, their names Osprey and Hutica and Quence and Born were breadcrumbs to lead back to Deziray on her nasty rug, staring up sadly at the shit-stained ceiling. What a thing to behold! Brought to mind the dream Leon dreamt way back at the dirt farm, where Beacon in a clearing on a hill in the woods, on the ground, legs took back like a damn peeled open baloney sandwich, said, "You can fuck me now, Leon" over the eyeball exchange they'd done done, which Leon guessed stood for the rubber they'd been searching out, it now found, her eyehole drooling blood. Damn dream was vivid still, and Leon relived the gross sensation of cutting her eye out and replacing it with his own dud ball of plastic. He'd been made to see in stereo! Did that mean he was supposed to see something new now, some new thing he'd not before seen? Some wisdom, a revelation? Was this a think of the meth? The dream was so powerful and disturbing back then, visionary, like it'd meant something important, and was a window into the future that Leon had done already drove his ass into. Blood drizzled about in the dream. It drizzled about at the Brokenhearted Woman Motel that evening. Deziray's blood was darker and thicker than he would have expected, as if mixed with molasses or brown sugar. Maybe, Leon thought, had I interpreted my dream of yore, my Dezzy would still be mine.

Leon cared not to think on it too deep right here in the moment and shit. Their need for nourishment was the better thing to think on, so Leon dropped the Cam off the Interstate and pulled into a Chevron. Amber stayed in the car as Leon gassed up, and inspected, for a moment, the hole the copper's bullet made through his door. Then he purchased Cheetoes, Moonpies, Snickers Bars, Mountain Dews and Charleston Chews. Leon bought new smokes, a tall cup of black coffee—yummy-delish. He drove them down to a lake where they ate then snorted up some lines of the good Whitelaw meth.

Leon and the Amb took a walk, the sky a fast black sheet of spattered fiery pinholes reflected in the lake. Bugs and flies bounced off the water in the moonlight. Amber grabbed Leon's hand, and they crunched through the leaves down to the small beach. A jetliner flew overhead. Amber asked Leon if a monkey'd ever got a woman pregnant. "Hell no, what the hell?"

"I was just wondering," Amber said, and waded into the black water. She splashed her thighs in the wash of the butt blood that had dried to her.

33.

AMBER WAS THE woman you wanted behind the wheel of the getaway car when you pulled off the tough job. She had drove since five or six years old, was up on the press of pedal and handle of stick. And did Leon teach her a cool trick back at the spooky cabin? In Coon Hill he taught her of spin, how to make donuts in sand, and back up and whip the car sidewise to shift into second in a single fluid motion. Leon adjusted the seat forward so she could work the pedals. Long-legged for her age, she had no problem there, but she needed a little extra ass. Leon thought the 400-count pack of fifty-dollar bills might help raise her up enough to see out the window better, but when he reached under the passenger seat, nothing.

"We been ripped," Leon stated, the words crisp and final. On that moolah their plans were built. Mexico? People said you lived cheap there, but Leon's wallet was not maxed out—all it held was about some two hundred in paper. The bones Dez had brought in through her Shake 'N Bake Crusted Parmesan Pussy business, all what she'd done at Titillations, was with Beacon who'd been the family pimp, their secretary treasurer. In remembrance the shit had been crispy on the outside, juicy on the in, and was under 500 calories, could you beat it, Jim?

"All that trouble for nothing?" Amber said.

"Last time I checked had to've been what? Three days ago?"

Shit was about funny as dogshit if you studied a pile of it for no particular reason. It anyway was unbecoming to obsess over money. Had to be Beacon, he thought, but no, dead Dezzie had been giving Billy Waxman lap dances, hadn't she? Behind his back? Putting up all kind of deceitful attitude? Lying to his face? The Dez may have done it, sure enough. And where had Quizzleboon been during all that time? Wasn't The Quiz supposed to see shit like that and warn Leon?

"Let's do a bump for the road," Leon said.

Again Leon dipped into the meth sack with his knife tip. Father and daughter snorted some up, then Leon remembered the Asheville phonebook in the trunk. He'd seen it for weeks, kept telling himself to throw it out. It wasn't much, but it would help Amber with her driverly duties. Leon retrieved it and she sat on it, brought the Camaro to life and, reaching her legs way down to press and release the clutch and brake pedals as needed, using her toes, drove them back to the interstate.

So no money it was, but at least they had guns. Leon's .38 rested under the seat and Amber's long barrel .22 took a nap in the glove compartment atop Cliff Highnote's pink slip and registration and insurance papers. The ship was legal, baby. Leon guessed he could rob another bankaroozie, but whenever he thought on Quizzleboon now, a bad taste formed in his mouth—bitter spittle and moldy cheese.

QUIZZLEBOON

Leon felt swindled by the Quizzle. Leon even suspected Quizzleboon of stealing off with his twenty grand. It was an impossible scenario to figure out in his mind, but some things defied understanding. He wanted his eyeball back is what he goddamn wanted so he just closed his eyes. Colors blobbed about like amoebas in space, a nice show. After some minutes Leon found himself in front of a mountain with a door stuck in its side. It being hard to breathe and all, Leon figured he was on the moon. Not only that, but he was starting to float so he grabbed a big rock. He lifted it out of the dirt and carried it to the door and just dropped it and opened the door and let himself inside where he could breathe and stand fine, only it was pitch black in there. "Hey Quizzleboon!" he called out, and his voice echoed back as if from the far end of a wormhole, the dark broken now by a flickering of light that seemed to have been activated by his voice. The light flickered in the way of those old coiled fluorescent bulbs that sometimes take forever to turn on after you flip the switch. After some flickering the place lit up at once, and holy gazoly, the whole inside of the mountain was resplendent with light. The uneven walls, if you could call them walls, moved upwards and to the sides and stretched out every direction, for miles, looked like, and were comprised of millions of pale slimy interconnected discoid thingamajigs, each ranging from about the size of a dime to the size of a schoolroom clock. Upon the thingums were dingbats and doings that danced, images that were, Leon assumed, stuff his eyeball saw that very moment, it recording according to the plan laid out by the Quiz. The jig-jaggy sky of the place—or call it a ceiling—was covered by nummular slime coins too, and from it hung wiggle-drippy thingawhickeys, huge skyscraper-sized stalactites—or tentacles—or call them cumulonimbus-cloud-shaped danglers covered in crystal balls.

Leon saw a funky contraption in the middle of the mountain, some several miles away. He needed to see it up close and personal, but all over the floor of the place were those damn round slimy things with the moving pictures on them—it was like a weird-ass damn carpet, and the whole thing looked to be like smeared over with spermatozoa. Leon would not have wanted to step on it. Luckily a path ran through it, and Leon walked for the thing way over yonder— he could tell it was the place to matter—but for some reason he didn't have to walk the whole way to get there. He just suddenly was there, presto, and he saw what was going on with his eyeball now, the one he cut from his head for the Quiz. It sat on a wet purple pillow placed on a block like what museum statues of nekid ladies are set upon. In front of his eyeball was a copper pipe, and the eyeball was looking into the hole of the copper pipe, and the copper pipe branched out into more copper pipes, first hundreds, then thousands, like one of those family tree diagrams, as it reached into the sky of the mountain. The branchy copper thing had algae growing all on it and the thing sparkled in copper hues tinged with greens and blues and silver drools like from the movie *Alien* where Sigourney Weaver battles the monsters.

The eye on the wet purple pillow pulsated. It expanded a little and contracted, as if it was breathing, and now and then a device squirted mist on it to keep it hydrated. Damn thing looked to be in the suffer throes. Coming out from the back part of Leon's eyeball were the gut strings, of course, attached to whitish vein things that led to the floor where the damned eyeball carpet or whatever you wanted to call it, began. Somebody had either 1) expertly spliced his eye together with the thing, or 2) the thing had done growed naturally out of the backside of Leon's eye. Leon preferred to think of the former option as true.

All the while, across the walls for miles here inside of the moon, the circular screens moved with pictures of everyday shit going on. Leon had took a peek at a couple of them when the lights had popped on. In one circle he'd seen some dude in a tuxedo walking along on a sidewalk. In another he saw a woman looking into a mirror, dabbing shit onto her face. Another circle showed somebody in a forest somewhere doing something or other, Leon didn't know what, or where, nor did he care. Was Leon a Care Bear?

Well, it was Leon's goddamned eyeball! It belonged in his head! He was going to grab the sonofabitch and shut down Quizzleboon's *looky-here* business—what did Leon care if "the sins" or whatever the fuck of people all over the goddamn world were recorded or not? What business of it was his if a jetliner crashed into the ocean, killing 217 people, or if a thousand Albanian women or whatever the fuck got raped last month in Kosovo? His eye might provide the means for accountability, but that's as far is it went, as far as Leon knew. He just hated the shit, and wanted his eye, only it seemed like a pretty serious thing to shut down an operation so big and important as this. He needed to pause and take himself a think. He wondered if maybe he might could see his mommy, good Superscrub. He wondered what she was doing.

Leon noticed a nearby table upon which there was a keypad. On the table was the largest of the circular sperm-covered things he'd seen yet. It was about the size of a car wheel and propped up so that you could see it good. There was nothing playing on it though, so Leon typed in "Sandra Hicks." Just then a door slammed. He hadn't even had time to press enter. Leon turned to see Mr. Quigley step up from a hole in the floor, gussied up as he always was in that stupid yellow tweed suit, and smoking a Blackstone cigar. "You," Leon said.

"Don't look scared."

"I came for my eye, bitch."

"Look over there, boy," Mr. Quigley said, and nodded to a nearby mound of thingamajigs that showed his sister in each and every thingamajig. Here Glindy was undressing. In another she danced nekid with her damn bigass boobs flapping side to side. In another she was on her back with penny loafers in the air. Leon did not recognize the guy banging her, but was that Kind Edward and her in the one over there? Why yes, it was their wedding somewhere in Miami with a fountain going off in the background. Leon saw his mommy in there too, and wanted to get closer, but Mr. Quigley distracted him with his laughter.

"Where's Quizzleboon?" Leon demanded to know.

Quigley lifted his hand up to his face and smelled his fingers, which were wet and glistened as if sprinkled with diamond dust.

A balloon of panic expanded inside Leon's manly chest. He felt terror. He had to get out of there, now! He turned and ran smack into a rod that stuck up from the floor and curled around. For some reason he hadn't noticed it before. The rod entered Leon's good eye. It reached up deep into his eye cavity. He felt his eyeball shoot from the socket like a cannonball, and he screamed, but then realized that he *was* his eyeball, and he was hurtling through space, and the universe swayed back and forth and broke into blotchy deep blue colors and red and crazy midnight brown and he heard the sound of the engine and the voice beside him of the child.

"A good one?" Amber asked.

"That sonofabitch!" Leon placed his hand on his heart.

It was growing light out. Amber drove on and the sun flipped up from behind them. The sun cast their shadow far ahead, for miles it looked like first off, but the shadow shrunk down. The trees lit up bright in places, the heavier light nauseating Leon. The dark had staved off figuring out what to do next. Leon wanted to either 1) jump back into the dark, or 2) bump up. Paranoia and other such garbage was trying to wiggle into his *here*. Leon had already hallucinated once—he wouldn't call his experience on the moon a dream—so he denied himself another blow of *go-go-getcha*, or the *crisssssss* or the *crassamoly get-down-to-business*, bitch.

What they needed was money, honey. Uhhhhhh, and some deep sleep coming up here pretty soon here in the world and all if they could. And they needed peace, joy. They needed a picture of what happened after they left the Brokenhearted. They needed Dezzie back from the dead, way the fuckamoly goddamnitall and shit! And Bob even too, what the fuck? Barney? What had become of Barney? Where was Beacon?

With shades on even Leon felt daunted by the sun's bright light. Was aught more intense than it?

An exit in Texas called Beaumont offered Amber a cloverleaf to cut down to the intersection, and she took it there. They waited for green. She drove south then, hooked a left into Wal-Mart and parked at the far end. On their trek to the entrance they noted the cars that might could be good for stealing. It was habit, most, but they needed to switch cars out soon. If they stole one from here, what point? The trick was to steal a car nobody would miss.

The blood that had soaked into Amber's shorts, staining them red in hearts and paisleys and clovers, had dried long ago. The red stains looked intentional, as if her shorts were manufactured that way and available to other little girls across the country. Though she had left her shoes at the Brokenhearted Woman Motel, along with her other worldly possessions, Leon doubted it would be a problem. Though Wal-Mart may have had a dress code, in his experience it wasn't enforced. He'd seen all kinds of dirt-footed girls traipsing about the place. Once he saw a anorexic old lady in a tiny bikini, more of a g-string, really, squatting with a box of Ritz crackers, reading the ingredients. Least Amber wasn't in some crazy obnoxious thing what like she'd been known to wear in the past. In her pink *Jesus Died For Me* shirt she lent them respectability, even, so through the sunshine they stepped quite presentably, Leon thought, as father and daughter. They passed by some Girl Scouts setting up their table for a day of cookie selling. Amber nodded respectful to one of the girls, Leon noticed. He grabbed her hand and pulled her inside the superstore.

Superglue they purchased from the superstore, and a bottle of hydrogen peroxide, a jar of Jif creamy peanut butter, a box of Saltines and pair of child's flip flops. Leon would have bought regular clothes for Amber. Child needed sneakers, socks, long pants, a coat. They'd be most broke then though, so they quit it and hit the car. Leon drove them to a Dairy Queen behind which a big cow field stretched out. There wouldn't be any goddamn cameras here like there'd been at Wal-Mart. He parked with the trunk facing the field, and went around and opened the passenger door and Amber got out. Leon sat in the passenger seat while Amber stood with hands on the ledge of the opened window. The cows in the middle of the field had noticed them, and were walking their way. "So cute," Amber said.

"You say that about everything."

"No I don't."

"Pull your damn pants down, bitch, hurry up."

Half concealed by the opened passenger-side door, Leon peeled the tape off Amber's ass. He sloshed hydrogen peroxide onto the cut and the white bubbles foamed up.

"Mooooo," Amber called out to the cows, and some of the cows mooed back.

"Don't do that." Leon dabbed the thing with napkins. People walked in and out through the glass doors of the DQ, and rolled by on their way to the drive-thru, so Leon felt exposed. One blond guy looked down at them from an opened truck window. You could tell how arrogant he was by the way his forearm rested along the windowsill. Dude gave Leon a look like he thought something suspicious was going on here. Leon had to rethink on could he have seen aught more than just Amber's shins and feet coming down from below the door. Wasn't like she was frowning, but the last thing Leon needed was some kind of AMBER Alert put out on him. Damn needed to split this shit quit, so he popped the aluminum seal on the Superglue tube, attached the plastic nozzle, and glued Amber's ass the fuck shut.

A few minutes later they were on I-10 again, driving.

"You ready for your bump?" Leon asked.

Amber pulled the sack from the glove box. Using Leon's knife she bumped up, then pulled one out for Leon. "Hey, thanks," Leon said, and took the knife from her and did it.

When they'd first started doing it, Leon felt confident, slung headlong into the cool zone, as if he knew what he was doing, but now, even though he felt smarter each time he freshened up, he wasn't sure. He lost track. The world was electrical, buzzy, its wires shorting, the planet tilted, screwy. Leon trusted himself not, yet here he took bitty steps into weirder waters, and the Quiz was a fraud. The Quiz would not warn him when Danger lurked, such as he'd thought all along. And who the fuck was the Quiz anyway? Was the Quiz the Quig for real?

Leon hooked the Cam onto a northward going highway for no reason really. Fuck the Mexico shit. Mexico was *no-go*. Why not Asheville? Leon steered the boat homeward, for the Ash of the Ville, where he was loved by Sparrow, by Soil, by Lichen, by the children and by Butterfly of the dangling *clitori*. The dirt people lusted for life. The dirt people believed in love and a better world. At the dirt farm Leon was loved.

34.

IN BLEAKWOOD LEON bought Whoppers to fries to chocolate shakes, then onward for North Carolina drove, for the Fly of the Butter who must've been missing her goddamn daughter something scorchous by now. When Leon to Amber said, "I bet you can't wait to see your mamma," the ingrate frowned.

"What the hell?" Leon put in.

"She never beat me or nothing."

"What's this shit you're mouthing off on?"

"In a community every woman is your mother. Maybe I don't like being everybody's daughter."

"You don't like everybody looking out for you?"

"Hell no, would you?"

"I can't say," Leon said, and remembered his mother giving him the attentions, her kisses to him goodnight and the useful things she taught him, such as how to make a oil funnel out of a plastic soda pop bottle—just saw it in half. Five or six mothers fussing over him was hard to see. Leon missed his *Superscrub*, his one and only.

Signs popped up for Tuscaloosa. They'd be up on Kickback *soon-ah-loosah*. Alabama? Beacon was born there and raised. Her name then was Lucy Blue. Leon figured he could look up the Blues, look up

Beacon's daddy, drink a beer with the dude. Leon saw himself say, "What can I do ye for, kind sir?" and the face of the guy go sour.

Leon rolled off 59 into Kickback, passed through downtown and found a quarry. All kind of dirt roads shot off back there, looked like a place one might could ditch a car. Leon took note, then drove on to a neighborhood that wasn't dirt poor. Leon would call the hood middleclass, and one house caught his eye. A heap of newspapers piled up at the end of the drive said the owners were dead or out of town. In the open garage a lonely green dust-covered Pinto sat, about the lousiest piece-a-crap-looking car ever seen up close or from a distance. Wouldn't be missed. The car had been a bright lime green once, Leon could tell, but the dust had darkened the paint color to that of a Picholine olive that had been sitting in its juice for a decade or more. When Leon went to inspect, he found the keys hanging there in the ignition. The owners might be glad to hear, he thought, that somebody took the damn thing.

Leon drove the Pinto. Amber followed in the Camaro. They drove to the quarry and along the sandy road that coursed the edge of a cliff. The road wound off into the trees, but they found the spot they were looking for and parked. A dry sinkhole, Leon guessed, some forty feet deep. At the bottom Leon saw washing majiggers and water heaters and other shit folks had dumped. Shrubs grew up around it all. Looked like nobody'd been down there in years. Leon unscrewed the Camaro's license plate, and he and Amber transferred all their shit into the Pinto. They ran wet rags over every surface that Leon might have touched on the Camaro. When they figured the car was fingerprint-free, they rolled it down the bank. The car sort of took off at a gallop then jumped into the air and went down. The front windshield splintered upon contact with a water heater. Leon's first thought was, *Why?* His second thought was: *Stupid*. His third thought was: *Why?* Seeing his car thrown down there with so much junk by his own hand plain disgusted him, but such was the life of convicted felons turned loose upon the world. Sometimes they fucked shit up. Amber, good girl, looked about to cry. "Hey, don't sweat it. You know it ain't nothing but a thang." Leon ruffled her hair, and they climbed into their new craft. Leon opened up the sacky sack and reached in with his knife tip, a little something to get them started on their new stretch of road, but Amber's nose started to bleed. She wiped her face with the back of her hand, smearing the blood.

"Don't do that," Leon said. He felt sick already from what he'd done to the Cam, but the bloody face knocked the sick feeling up through the roof. Leon wanted to tear out, get away, Jesus!

"What makes you think I can help it, Daddy?"

"Snorting's dirty. I been thinking I should do this shit the right way ever since we started, the clean way. You want me to stick a needle in your ass?"

"Yes."

The needle was wrapped in oilcloth. The oilcloth was enclosed in the duffel bag. The duffel bag was in the back of the Pinto. Leon got out of the car. He popped the damn hatchback, unzipped the duffel bag, found the works and brought it up front. Using a spoon and lighter and piece of cotton and all that, Amber helping, he prepped the shot with enough for them both. He said, "Could you get me a beer please."

Amber twisted over so she was on her knees and reaching between the seats to get at the cooler. That's when Leon pumped a blast into Amber's ass. Damn bitch didn't have to pull her shorts down or nothing. He just jabbed her when she wasn't expecting it, straight through her shorts and panties, and she sucked her breath in. Leon withdrew the needle. Girl fell back weirdly against the dash, legs back like the way infants do like, all *goo goo ga ga* and shit. As she'd sorta fallen into the foot space, Leon had to help twist her back around. He then leaned over her and pulled the lever to draw the seat back so she could relax. Now she looked like a doll what like to buy from Wal-Mart for the *rugrats*, made in China. For thirty seconds she was froze, glass-eyed, plastic-faced. Her nose started up on the blood again, and was gross as fuck. If Amber was a doll sold in stores from Miami to Anchorage, she'd be called *Bleeding Amber*, and packaged with bandages, no doubt. The little boys and girls lucky enough to own her would wipe her nose, such as Leon was doing now. Whenever Bleeding Amber went dry, they would insert a tube into her ear and fill her back up with fresh blood.

"How you feel?"

"Mmmm."

"You buzzing good now, girl," Leon said. "Is it clean?"

"A million midget people scrubbing me, oh!"

"You're rushing. In a minute you'll want more. I know about speed crash."

"What did you do to me?"

"I filled your ass with some high-octane gas you ain't never tried before," Leon said, and couldn't help but to laugh.

QUIZZLEBOON

"Shhh."

Had it been with anybody else, Leon would've switched out needles, but damn if the Amb wasn't nothing but a fucking virgin and shit, so why bother? Wasn't like he'd catch AIDS from the fucker. What was good for Amber was good for the gander, but what was a gander? Do you even know? On second thought, maybe Amb and the Barn had got together, it was possible the way Barney always was humping her, and them sleeping in the same bed, and hadn't AIDS come from some dude fucking monkeys out in the jungle or some shit? It was a risk, Leon knew, but damn if he'd spoil the mood by asking his daughter did she fuck a monkey. So fuck it. Leon pushed the shit in. This was the thing. Should've done it this way the whole while long. The map said three hundred or so miles of road left to travel.

35.

OUT FROM THE quarry grounds, back through Kickback whose buildings by Beacon were known, Leon the man of no money, drove, nice and steady, the Pinto lolling along like a giant hollowed-out stinkbug. Whenever he and Amber passed people, the pedestrians of the world, Leon looked for their facial burns—*What can I do ye for, kind sir?*

Leon saw no burns, but where was Beacon? Where could Beacon be? He'd gone and failed her. Yet *What can I do ye for, kind sir?* he kept hearing in his head, and then he would imagine "the black piece of char" as she had called it, exploding and all the dumb white guys that had been warming their hands on the poor fellow, suddenly they'd be screaming in pain, slapping at their faces and arms, trying to get the gross stuff off them. Damn sure got what they deserved, Leon thought, and *What can I do ye for, kind sir?*

The metal stinkbug moved up onto the highway. After a bit it rolled down into Tuscaloosa, where Leon found a Publix. Even though they weren't hungry, his thought was to buy a rotisserie chicken from the deli for later, that, and some ice and a case of beer for the cooler. Amber, though, looked too much like a

Bleeding Amber Doll. Wal-Mart was one thing, but Publix? Publix was more high class, with concerned mothers that were teachers and you saw lawyers there sometimes and other important people—no, not people, at Wal-Mart you had people, at Publix you had citizens—and suspicion was a thing to avoid. As such, Amber should stay in the goddamn Pinto bean. "I want you to hold down the fort," Leon said, but Amber would have none to do with such thinking. Little bitch slipped her hooves into the new flip-flops, peeled her cowboy gun from the glove box, and stepped out of the car. She slipped the clipper grip-first into her back pocket. Extra ass on her now. Her shirt came down enough to where citizens might not notice the barrel poking up. They'd be more concerned over the mess of her, the dirty blood-soaked shorts and shirt, and some of the blood was still streaked across her neck and face, and a bunch of it had gotten into her short blond hair that, because it hadn't been washed in a while, was punk-rock-like, like that dude from the Sex Pistols. She'd been losing weight. She was pale. All skinny and ribby she was, a lot of dark intensity around her eyeballs.

The supermarket was plum out of chickens, so they got the beer and ice and milk pint, and some Lay's Flamin' Hot potato chips and, citizens were in the look of them, as Leon had predicted. The citizens talked to each other, leaning over to whisper shit in each other's ears and shit. It was clear they needed to go, so they hit checkout station number three whose cashier, too, gave them the scroot eye. Leon felt like he should smack her a good one for existing. He wanted to, but the poor woman, Mildred as her nametag told her to be, was fat. Her green vest, whose top button was plain gone, appeared to be suffocating her.

Mildred smiled, and said to Amber, "Honey, that is soooo true. Jesus did die for you. He died for you and me and everybody else in the whole wide world, even the people in Japan, isn't that wonderful?" Her lips were the only things on her face not fat—they wiggled like worms into a kind of frown when she saw that the blood on the Jesus on Amber's shirt was not Jesus's fake blood, but a real person's real blood. In Leon's mind he ripped the frowny worms off her face, and tossed them onto a mulch heap, where they wiggled near some other worms poking heads or asses, either one, take your pick, up out of the moist compost.

They were halfway to the car, on their way, in the clear, but Amber out and said, "I been thinking."

"Oh shit."

"I want you to drive over there to Radio Shack to wait for me."

Leon started to protest, but she held her hands out for him to shush.

Leon knew it was crazoe to let her go do whatever she had in mind to go do out of the blue, but he'd made some mistakes as boss. If Amber wanted to try out her boss-being skills, who was Leon to say she would be no good at boss-being? She deserved a chance, so he nodded bye, and went up to the Pinto and started her and exited the lot then hooked a right into the Radio Shack strip where he killed the engine. A few seconds later Amber's clicker went off, two snappy claps like some sumo wrestler banged his hands together twice. Leon tensed up, but here came Amber hauling down the grass slope in flip-flops and messed-up legs, gun in one hand, a brown grocery bag in the other. Leon started the Pinto. Amber hopped in. They putted on like two old ladies with colorful bonnets on their heads, on their way to a picnic. In a minute they were back on 59, doing the speed limit.

As Leon drove, Amber counted her take—so many twenties and tens and a gazillion ones. Leon kept asking questions, him in the need to know what went down exactly, but it caused her to lose count. She kept having to start all over, so Leon listened: "Three hundred and eighty-seven, three hundred and eighty-eight . . ." The final count was four hundred and twelve.

"Well ain't you about the shittiest little sonofabitch," Leon said.

"We got plenty of money now. Who's it thanks to, bitch?"

"You did good," Leon admitted, and toasted her and swallowed. It was his second Busch since Tuscaloosa, since the child had robbed the Girl Scouts at gunpoint—*you did good, girl*—and had made Leon an accomplice in a felony—*you did good, girl*—and she'd even come out with half a dozen boxes of cookies! Leon's favorite were the Do-si-do peanut butter sandwich motherfuckers, but she'd done scored some Thin Mints and lemon-flavored cookies too.

Who would've ever thought it up if not for Amber, Amrosia from Planet Zambonia? "Did you kill somebody? I heard the shots. You plug that fat mamma lording over the table? I seen her munching on them fucking cookies. You best not to've done something bad."

"I shot the cookies."

"What?"

"I shot the cookies."

"Why did you do that? What kind of goddamn?"

"They wasn't listening, Daddy, so I shot the cookies."

"You little motherfucking sly devil. Damn shot the cookies. Damn if that ain't the story of the month. She shot the cookies. Naw man, did you hear what I said? I'm telling you she shot the cookies. A motherfucking eleven-year-old."

"I'm nine."

"Whatever," Leon said.

And they drove. And bumped up the right way, a nice fresh load of celebration, and blipped through Birmingham into the dark, and drove by Annison and Atlanta. They hit 26 and steered for Asheville, *the place with all the grace*, as the local punks called her, *the place with all the grace*, and Leon agreed. If a place had grace it was the Ash of the Ville.

As Leon drove, Amber fell into power-sleeps of smile and lip-licking and tooth-grind. Looked like a snake or slug or some shit awiggle in the seat, and she snorted through her nose, growling, and scratched her arms and neck with her nails. Having fun, the damn girl. Leon was envious, lookiter go, but his job was to drive, so onward he drove, onward he druv, onward he driv.

Asheville popped up like bake a cake and pull it from the oven, Muffin, thar she blows, Rose, good Asheville, holy shit, Witt. Leon wound them up, up into the hills, he and Amber two peas in the Pinto bean that rolled up into the fields of home, the farm. While still driving Leon killed the lights, and turned onto the road to wiggle down through the pines to the junkyard. Leon parked, but didn't seem right to head up to the great house yet. Leon felt sad. Did he want to announce his failures to the Dirties? His loss of Beacon? Though the dirt people knew nothing of Deziray, the fact that they would have loved her was enough to make Leon wish he'd never been born. He just did not want to think of Deziray or any of the shit that had gone down. Amber appeared to have the same sort of things in mind, so they spent the rest of the night sitting there under the sleeping bags, thinking their thoughts. Come dawn they watched the light pour color onto the pines, whose bristles had frosted up during the night. The whole world sparkled and was quiet and beautiful, but they left the Pinto and walked up and entered the Great House where Barney, squatting on the edge of the kitchen table, was finishing off a banana.

When Barney saw Amber he stood up straight and threw down the banana peel. He leapt into the air, and landed on Amber and wrapped his arms and legs around her. He clutched her tight, switching his head back and forth with a paranoid look of terror and glee. He was afraid, and Leon didn't blame him. What if this bliss was withdrawn, as it had been before? Old Barney was scared shitless, even as he adored Amber—or was she *Ambrosia* now, now that she was back on the farm?

Leon narrowed his eyeball on Barney and said, "Hey there, little partner."

"Hoo hoo hoo."

"Where's my Beacon?"

"Hoo hoo hoo," Barney said, not loud as a motherfucker like Barney used to hoo all the damn time back at the spooky cabin and shit, but softer, less obnoxious. Damned monkey was growing wise to the world.

Now Potato, who'd been holed up in the penthouse, clunked down the stairs. He entered the kitchen in a orange jumpsuit and combat boots, and was followed close behind by two young ladies in prim dresses, black stockings, and chunky-heeled Mary Jane shoes. These ladies, girls, held big bibles. One was blond, the other dark of hair, and they both were cursed with acne on their faces. The sight was unexpected, but then, such were days at the dirt farm. Potato scratched his thickly bearded face, which made him seem all scuzzy and not worthy of the company of the two young bible girls. "Holy piebald cows of India," Potato said slow in monotone, as if he was not exactly too pleased to see what was going on here right at the moment and shit.

"Freaky freaky," Leon said.

The monkey had started humping poor Amber's side as he clung to her, his human-looking scrotum with its veins running all over it slapping against her hipbone.

"This is fuckin surreal," Leon said. "I feel like I'm in a dream."

"I know, I know," Potato said. "You must be flabbergasted."

"Flabbergasted?"

"Flabbergasted."

And the human-looking balls did flap and flop.

The bible girls laughed. The blond was missing her two front teeth. Leon's mind could not help but to imagine what happened. Some man knocked the girl's teeth out with his fist, didn't he? Was the same as what Leon did to that cop in Detroit, what put him in the pen for two years. Leon wished he could find the fuck who'd done her that way, make things right, distribute some two-fer-two. The chick gave him a fine vibe, but fuck it. "How'd Barney get here? Where's Beacon?"

"Beacon's at the Goth farm hanging with Bob."

"Bob?"

"Bob."

Ambrosia sniffled.

"Hey," Leon said.

Amber rubbed her eyes.

"Guess you've been tossed about in the high seas, eh?" Potato said.

"Low seas and high."

"Not to worry," the blond bible bitch said, and when she spoke, Leon saw again in her mouth how her front teeth were gone. Made her look the vampire. The deformity turned him on. Went hand in hand with her bible and the intense acne. "Call on the Lord for the remedy."

"That's Wolverina," Potato said.

"And all will be made righty to the tune of his promise to ye."

"That's Mouse," Potato said, pointing the other out. "Those aren't their real names. They arrived yesterday afternoon. We named them. We tried to get rid of them, but they shared their thoughts on the bible, see. For that they put up some collateral. We named them. That was our trade."

"I thought this was a welcoming place of dirt," Leon said to nobody in particular.

"Huh? Bible thumpers and squares? They wanted to save us, Leon."

"Hey, I love your shirt, little girl," the one called

Mouse said. "Why are you crying? Don't you know that Jesus loves you?" Mouse set her hand on Amber's shoulder. At that, Amber slung her face around and bit Mouse's wrist.

Mouse yanked her arm away with a scream, and dropped her bigass white bible on the floor.

"You stupid woman!" Amber screamed.

"Ahwr ahwr aughhhh," Barney said, and howled: "GHHHHOOOOoooooooooo AHHHHHHHHHHH."

"Wha'd I do?" Mouse cried.

Barney jumped off Amber onto Mouse, and Mouse thought Barney was attacking her. Mouse peeled Barney away and sort of threw him and Barney bonked his orange monkey-head on the table.

Such was their homecoming. By noon Ambrosia had hooked up with her old children pals. They hung on her words and followed her and did what she said. By the third day Amber had a gang going on. They called themselves the Black Monster Kids and made the mopáge their clubhouse. The children wore black armbands and made necklaces and anklets out of black strips of leather to adorn with copper washers and bolts and shiny scraps of tin. When they walked around you heard them, and you heard them in the dark late of night when the Dirties were asleep in bed.

36.

LEON DROVE UP to the Goth farm in the humble Pinto hatchback car, parked to the shoulder, and walked up through a tobacco field to the three-story farmhouse, and knocked. A brown-skinned Asian girl answered, but she spoke English, so hardly could be called Asian. She remembered Leon from the night of the raid, and let him into the large living room where people hung around. Over there Beacon reclined on a plush red couch reading a book, in black stockings, a black skirt, and weird black blouse with buckles on it. Her hair had been dyed black. For some reason she wanted Leon to think she didn't know he was in the room, even though she'd heard his voice when he'd talked to the fake Asian chick at the front door. Or was Beacon waiting to get to the end of the sentence she was reading? How rude. Her book, Leon saw, was the one she'd done stole from the shelf of the kind blind man, the intellectual book called *Female Perversions*, by Louise J. Kaplan.

Seeing for true that the woman on the couch was Beacon Blue, Leon's sworn bride-to-be, his heart leapt her way with love and long and lee, which is to say lovingly and longingly, but stopped short when her feet swung down from the couch arm. Leon saw the black toenails, the black brows and shit. Damn woman had smeared on black lipstick what like here with her new Goth friends, her face powdery, which bashed the dirt farm rules that said makeup was anathema to the spirit of Venus, abracadabra here on the left side of her head—it was *shaved*, and Leon remembered the dude who got the lobotomy in *Planet of the Apes*. That scene had scared the fuckamoly beezie shit out of Leon when he was a boy, but the main thing to give off the unwelcome feeling was that, when Beacon stood up, she reached her hand out for a shake. Right then Leon saw in her eyes that she no longer loved him. She was Bob's girl now. Bob was Beacon's sugar daddy. Leon did not even deserve a hug.

Beacon did agree to spend some time alone with Leon though. Was the least she could do after what they'd been through. Beacon got into some Doc Marten boots, what must've come from Dezzie's dance money, unless Bob was buying her all this crap, and they walked out past a Quonset hut in which somebody practiced keyboard and groaned into a microphone. Leon wondered was that Bob in there singing eerie. They listened to the dude moan as they walked down the path into the woods, talking some in their cross of a bridge and walk at the side of the stream. After a while they climbed onto a boulder and lit up. Beacon undid some buckles on her blouse. She lifted it at the bottom to show Leon where Grant Whitelaw stabbed her three times in the side, right up there on the ribcage. The cuts were not nearly so bad as Leon had imagined in his mind. They were just dinks carved out of her—ga-*doink doink doink*—or more like busted into her, nothing to need stitches, let alone get your panties wet up about. The *doinks* of scab were healing fine, though if you'd wanted you could rip one open, Leon saw, and they would bleed again.

What happened, Beacon said, was Whitelaw took her and the Barn to the Holiday Inn in downtown Pensacola, where they got high on meth and made friends. Beacon felt safe enough with Leon to say she'd sucked Grant off—not in those words, but he got the picture—and she left it open on whether or not Whitelaw boinked her, which Leon thought was cruel. He suspected Beacon of doing that shit intentional, but let it go. "Whitelaw turned out to be really cool," Beacon said, "once I got to know him, I mean, he kept harassing me about where the Butt Money was. That's what he was hired to go get, you know. He was just doing his job, like we were when we run off with Barney, I mean, you got to admit that that was a bold move, Leon. Ain't nobody ever heard nothing about stealing no monkey from Nicaragua. Grant kept walking around asking how he got himself into this shit, and he said—"

"Hey, I wanna say something," Leon said.

"Okay, what?"

"When we were walking over here your voice sounded different. I thought you were trying to be high class, but now it's gone back to normal. You sound like your old self just you're dressed up like a crazy woman."

"Fuck you. I was trying to tell you how much I loved you and then you wanna throw in suggesting how you think I'm white trash?"

"Sorry."

"Hey, you apologized, what's the matter with you, baby?"

"Maybe you ought not call me baby."

"Sounds fair to me."

"And I won't call you lovey dovey terms neither no more like what I used to call you?"

"Oh yeah, I remember your names. You called me Fire. I liked that, but then suddenly once you—no, I don't even like to remember it—but once you did what you did to me you done started calling *her* your Fire! How do you think I—"

"No, no, that ain't how it—"

"Shutcher fuckin face up, bitch! I know because I'm the one who lived it. You called me Firehoney and then you were calling her shit like that and suddenly I was Water. You called me Waterdog, Leon. Do you think Waterdog is a thing any woman in the world would wanna be called? Do you remember that you wanted me to suck your dick at the same time that *she* did?"

"To get the balance right."

"Do you remember that straight in front of me she would talk about your dick, saying shit like it was getting bigger every day, and then laughing about it? Think back on it, Leon. Did I laugh when she said shit like that? What did I look like? Tell me!"

"Without water you can't live."

"What?"

"I said, you cain't live without water." He was thinking of the other nice names he had called her that he wasn't ever gonna get credit for, in all honest to God truth, back early when they were first falling in love, names like *Dirt Muncher*, and *Funny Ears*, and *Baloney Sandwich*.

"Don't try that shit with me, don't even try it, Leon."

"Fine."

"I don't know why I'm even talking to you. You only know how to do one thing, and that's be the boss. I caved in with you. I ripped out my soul, but Bob ain't like that. Bobby respects me. He wants to teach me my potential. Did you know Bob bought me a sewing machine? I got plans to start my own business."

"Sounds good."

"The owner of the Honeypot promised to put my stuff on consignment."

"I didn't know you hated the setup so bad."

Beacon flipped her face his way to look him over close. She flipped her face back for the stare of the birds out there, and squirrels to hop about.

Leon saw she could give him a earful should he say more.

And the sounds the creek made rightly were nice in their sit of the side-by-side smoke they shared. The day: overcast. Looked to be bad weather coming up here in the near future.

Leon felt the pour of hateful vibes from her pores.

He waited a minute, then said, "Somebody took the Butt Money. I don't know where it's at, but the Butt Money is gone."

"Huh? What're you talking? Did you check under the spare tire?"

"Why would I check under the spare tire?"

"I knew somebody would steal it."

"Steal it?"

"Where you put it was not the brightest place to put a thing like that, Leon, so I put the money under the tire in the trunk to keep safe. I could'a told Grant where it was, but I wanted to pay you back on calling the FBI. Damn shit scarred me for life. When I think on it I get the answers to why I said go ahead and degrade me, asshole. Do you remember telling me I needed to kiss that bitch so you could realize your magical power? I did all that shit for you, and I wanna tell you something else I never told you before. When I called the FBI it wasn't just because I was greedy. In my heart I recognized that you were a dirty sonofabitch no different than that damn nigger dude in Soho who fucked my life up forever. My plan was to use that money to start my business, motherfucker! I was to get back at some of the assholes of the world!"

"Well I'll be goddamned," Leon said. His poor Camaro down in that dumb damned hole in Kickback he saw.

"I know I was greedy, but I've changed. Bob is compassionate."

Was dumping his car down in that hole the stupidest thing he ever did?

"I want to grow as a person," Beacon said.

Leon could smack her upside her Goth-ass cup, not for the took up with Bob after so short a while she'd done did, for messing around sexual with Whitelaw and all that excretion, but for fucking with the Butt Money! Leon was slow these days to anger by the look of his not no do shit attitude. He mellowing out bigtime, Jude. He guessed he was about cowed after all the crap he'd been through, seeing Dezzie murdered in the very own ball of his eye, for one, enough blood in the pupil to cry a lifetime by. Did he feed the worst drug known to man to a moppet? And what of the Quizzleboon manure to open up on account of the mind-altering drugs he'd took down like something tasty when you was getting hasty and hadn't washed your body for a long time so it was getting pasty? "It's all in a day's work, I reckon," Leon told Beacon, "but there's something I need to tell you, bitch."

"Oh, what could it be? I'm dying to know."

"You ain't gun like it."

"Just tell me, Leon, for Chirst's sake."

"Dezzie," Leon said, and his mouth trembled. He closed his eye to steady himself, and said *don't cry* to himself. He was just thinking of that damned stupid slut who'd gone kaput.

"She ditch you?" Beacon put in, but then, after thinking on it, came in a bit more honest with, "I'm'a find that whore and rip her titties off! That's a promise I made before I ain't held true on. All those times you made me touch em I wanted to rip em off and throw em out the window, but I smiled, didn't I?"

Leon did not speak.

"That's just lowdown dirty. After all you did for her, she breaking up our lives how she did. Bitch deserves something super bad, I mean, like maybe a pit-bull could attack her. Do you know any people with pit bulls? I'd love to see her get torn apart by dogs."

"No. It's not that. She . . . I don't know, she just, you know, she got caught in the middle." Leon threw a stone into the creek. "I can't say for sure if Whitelaw meant to, but she took a bullet to the neck."

Beacon shut her trap at that. They sat in the brook sound and call of bird, Leon didn't know what kinds of birds, but he'd seen crows about the place, had recognized their voices, and saw bluebirds and brown birds. What was the deal with birds? Were birds supposed to fly south or some shit about right now? Leon didn't care. He just felt as if he'd known Beacon all his life. She was family, even though she was with Bob now and done up like a goddamn street whore come out the future. Leon hoped they would remain friends. He turned his face to hers and said, "Man," and hugged her. In the hug of the her he felt the skronk-a-donkle-in-the-pronkle-urge, but let it slide. Seemed things could go either way, like maybe if he reached up and squeezed a titty good he could make her his again. It might could be done, but Leon didn't wanna mess up the good thing Beacon had going on with Bob. Leon was glad Bob was not dead. At least now he knew he was not no damn murderer of a guy named Bob, and he told Beacon of the Camaro, what he and the Amb had dropped into a sinkhole in Kickback, her hometown, *What can I do ye for, kind sir?* Now he had to go back there to retrieve the money from under the spare tire, did Beacon wanna go with? No? Okay, well, you and Bob enjoy your fuckin selves!

Leon headed back for the dirt farm, during which time a cold rain fell, ice mixed in with it. He flipped the Pinto's wipers on but nothing transpired. If having one eyeball wasn't bad enough, Leon had to squint, scan the windshield for spots he might could see the road through. He slowed, and finally pulled over to wait out the rain. The sound of it washing over the car mesmerized him, put him in the mood for a bump, a nice little bump, sure, a little bump would enhance the enjoyment of the sound of the rain, a *bumpty boo bah* batch of beauty—*bumpty bumpty bump*—and help Leon reflect over current events. Bob. Beacon and the goddamn Goth business she was up to. The Butt Money. He'd gone a few days without, had even managed to sleep, so fuck it up a tree and grab you some kumquats. Leon Hicks from Virginia Beach popped the glove box.

Okay, this was weird, the sack was gone.

Leon stared straight out the window.

Leon waited, and he thought about things.

Leon was glad when the downpour thinned. He hauled ass back to the farm, and parked, and ran through the sprinkle to the Great House, entered it with wet hair. What he saw in the large main room made him wonder had he yet risen from bed.

Amber, Ambrosia, Queen of the Black Monster Kids, stood barefoot on the table slab upon which animals once were butchered and upon which, as the story went, slaves were auctioned off way long ago, *ten* dollars, *twelve* dollars, *fifteen* dollars, *sold* to the man in a stovepipe hat. She wore a ripped-up Easter dress no doubt plucky duckied from the Cloth Shack's teeming rag heap. Her crown, a twisted up clothes hanger fashioned together with aluminum foil, twigs and chewed-up bubblegum, glimmered weird in the chandelier light—and her eyes were closed, legs an overturned V, Barney in the clutch of one with a sketchy look. Was the monkey on meth? Black bands secured to Amber's ankles made her look militant. Below her on the floor the other Black Monsters kneeled, about ten smeary-faced kids with hands clasped in prayer. They were speaking in tongue.

"Ambrosia!"

The girl's eyes flipped open, the nonsense chatter of the kids rose higher and high and even the rank smell of them seemed to grow.

"What's going on here?"

If she heard him, she didn't let on, though she was staring straight at Leon, unblinkingly, her eyes wide and wider. Leon said, "I know you took the sack, bitch. Where's it at?"

The child remained upright and headstrong.

Leon eyeballed the others, a lot of new piercings going on here, and some wore dog collars. One boy in one-piece spaceship jammies wore a pair of shorts on his head. Some wore dresses and weird combos, like the boy in a checkered skirt and sheepskin coat. Others were buck nekid here in the indoors heated up hot by the wood-burning stove that ticked and sorta vibrated, the clothes they'd peeled off in a pile by the door. When they left, they'd put on whatever came to hand, looked like. They'd leave the Great House dressed different from how they'd come in. The kids were raising big ruckus over damned Amber who'd decided to be a leader, yep. The talk she'd heard of celestial kingdoms, of Doubting Thomases, Pentecostal fires and Jesusy characters—it had infected her brain, poisoned her. Leon was guilty of a bit of "fantasy" himself, so couldn't much hold it against her, but this shit was ridiculous-ass dangerfied-looking. Did Rodney Dangerfield ever deal with shit like this?

"Amber!" Leon's king's voice went unacknowledged. "Goddamnit Amber, gimme some skin, bitch!"

Amber raised her eyes to the chandelier, the light pouring over her face, and she opened her mouth, but nothing came out. Then she went, "Yi," peeped it sorta like a bird. Where was the mama crow with a worm to deliver? "Yi yi yi," the child continued, and raised her hands up with outspread fingers and spun in slow circles, revolving steppingly, making that sound, "Yi yi yi," and then "Ya ya ya," and her gang members clicked in. "Ya ya ya," they went. It was a goddamned madhouse. Leon had once lived behind one, so knew the sound.

Amber turned in circles three or four times, the monkey in silent swirl around her ankles, and then Leon saw the marks on her arms. The little fuckface had been shooting the shit. Leon decided to yank her ass off the table and run upstairs with her to the penthouse. Leon would go the mile for his partner in crime, like Powers Boothe did for the dude who'd been hooked on heroin in that movie where Powers plays Jim Jones, the man who tricked a boatload of people into drinking suicidal poison juice. Powers hugged the dude when he was going through the withdraw symptoms, and held on tight until he was free of the monkey on his back. That's what Leon would do for the Amb.

The Amb, though, read Leon's mind. She was tuned into his thoughts and the thoughts of the world. That's how it went when you kept up the meth. You became a bit some omniscient, a bit some Spallanzani a la Lazarro, and knew shit you wouldn't otherwise know. Shrinks call it paranoid, but of meth were benighted. Whatever they said on it was by the nature of the universe suspect. Ambrosia was about goddamn seventy years old at the moment.

Leon could not reach out to her—too many tongue-speaking brats between them—but here came a shriek so bad that Leon covered his ears. The Amb leaped off the table to slap Leon's right shoulder with her foot, here launching herself across the room, above the children, to the shelf that she grabbed like a supernatural freak bitch, Wuzzard, call her, half witch, the other part buzzard. Herb jars and jars of

Dirt Control and dry beans crashed to the floor in the scatter of glass, but she clung, face backward-flung, eyes burning with a tooth-bared nasty. Again she screamed to the top of the lung, or scrum, Barney here up a-howling on the table, *Hgaaaooooooh*, and jumping up and down. The Black Monster Kids then rushed Leon, grabbing on his belt, all yank here on it. Damn were trying to take his clothes off. He pushed them away, had to kick a few. They sprung back, and then one Kickapoo, the little shit in spaceship jammies, bit Leon's calf.

Leon lunged from the Great House for the meth sack to find. Damn shit ought never to've been invented. While in prison Leon heard Hitler was the sonofabitch to come up with it. Something like that could only've come from evil. Having seen what he just saw, Leon might empty the sack into the creek—*gone!* Leon ran across the field, under the apple trees. He passed the Home Schooling House, and ducked down the bank and crossed over the bridge, boots pounding the planks. The clubhouse of the Black Monster Kids, the mopáge as they called it, was a big old barn with tons of junk in it pushed to one side, plus the dozen new mopeds Leon purchased with his bank robbery money, *ping pong ping*, three banks in a row in a single day in upstate New York, first Schenectady, then Saratoga Springs, hello Amsterdam—*kablang, kablong*, and *kabling*. Talk of productivity. That was the most productive day of Leon's life, a crime for which no atonement could he give. Why? Over the money did more good outside the bank than in. It bought wine and made men happy, put gas in Leon's car and, one thing to the other, helped save a monkey from the needles of an ex-congressman known as Butler.

QUIZZLEBOON

The doors were punt black to about the height a child could reach, painted but padlocked. Leon lit a Carleton. To the side of the barn he jimmied the glass, clumb through—or climbed—and dropped to the floor where Mouse over there was on her stomach, dozens of wadded up pieces of paper all around her. Toilet paper, he thought at first. Sorta smelt like shit is why he thunk it, but then he saw the overturned bible. Thing was split open like a broke bird.

37.

LEON DRAGGED HIS BUTT and thought stuff. He threw his butt down to squash underfoot. He eyed the mopáge good and well, checked for weird shit like eyes in the junk. They were alone, so he slipped the Buck 110 from his front pocket, unfolded its stainless steel blade, and knelt. The duct tape wound around her wrists and ankles was a repeat of what Beacon and the Amb had done did Dezzie back in Tally the night they delivered the monkey into bondage, then stole him back a few hours later. Leon cut through it where it held her ankles together and helped her stand, her small pointy boobs scraped up something horrendous, with bits of grit and dirt all over them, and her face too was bruised, looked like two black eyes developing above the silver tape that had been wound around her face several times to keep her quiet by. Some of the zits had done got scraped off and were drooling, and she had scrapes on her legs and stomach and hindparts, and one of her knees was bleeding. Mouse looked as if she'd been dragged over concrete. "They got you dirty," Leon observed, and brushed some of the grit off her chest. He then slipped out of his Mr. Cool jacket of soft brown leather, and draped it Fabio-like over her shoulders. "Damn kids've gone bonkers. Don't think this is like normal behavior for us."

"Mmmm," she said. Leon was mad. Just why did she come here to complicate shit up for everybody? Damn girl had goose bumps on her forehead—no, no, those were tiny little zits, Leon realized, but he'd seen them elsewhere on her bod—and here she just shivered like that little fuckin bitch in *Frosty the Snowman*. That girl, because she'd been so cold, Frosty put her in a greenhouse, but then the magician locked them in and Frosty melted. It was all the girl's fault. That's what happened when you got all soft and nice on people. Damn bitch probably needed water right now, but the water would have to wait. Right now Leon searched out her dress and shoes, and searched for the meth sack—a *twofer* operation going on here—rummaging through cardboard boxes filled with mechanical parts and checking behind stacks of old books.

"Where's your friend?" Leon said, knocking the contents of a box of doodads back and forth. The sack didn't reveal itself.

"Mmbbmmm mmbb," she said.

Leon climbed the ladder against the wall to the loft and looked around then unclimbed the ladder to the floor, and went back to her. The dark pupils above the strip of tape sorta widened, made her look like what you see in a horror movie after the bad man has lifted the knife and the woman, who's already had her blouse ripped open, the brassiere showing, knows she's gonna get stabbed in the damn chest.

"Where's Wolverina?" Leon asked her.

She shook her head a little.

"You want me to take the tape off, that it? I guess

that's it, ain't it? Seems like I'm always doing this shit for y'all. I didn't ask for it. Believe me, I did not ask for it." He pulled his knife out again. This time he started with where the tape was stuck to the back of her head, cutting off the hair there. As he sawed, he spoke to her, saying, "Part of me hopes that when I get this shit off yer fuckin face you won't know where the sack's at. It just pisses me off. I need that fucking sack." Now he ripped it off her mouth. She made a pained expression, and bent over dry-heaving and coughing, her face dripping pus from the injured zits. When she finally had collected her wits, first thing she said was, "Praises be unto Jesus!"

"Shut the fuck up, bitch! That's not what I need to know."

Damn girl started breathing fast. Her hair all messed up made her to look wild.

"Start talking! Tell me what I need to know."

Leon guessed the weird breathing was normal. After breathing through them nostrils for so long she probably got a little retarded for lack of air—that's why doctors spanked babies when they were born, in case you didn't know, so that the brain didn't grow retarded. "What's the matter with you? Are you okay?"

"My hands. Please."

"Holy shit, I guess I forgot," Leon said, but in honest wasn't sure he liked the way she'd said please. Made it sound like she'd the need to ask, like it wasn't what he'd do all natural of his own without haved to been asked or thunk for it. Was it the sort of dunk women did in the want to give you the guilt trip thingy? Sure enough, Leon took his jacket off her to drape over a moped mirror. In the thing of the free of her hands here he noticed how fine her legs were, wow!

"Hey, what's your real name?" Leon asked in a softer tone, more friendly like, but damn if her pussy hair wasn't trimmed nice, too, a real polite self-contained patch, a garden with a fence to keep out the rabbits and mice, so unlike what one saw at the dirt farm, pussies gone wild, call it, just hair taking off all over the goddamned place, growing out of control like Kudzu or the beard by the man named Marx, way down the inner thigh and up into the stomach and shit. Maybe Mouse was all tidy in the puss department over this here that she was a Christian, glory hallelujah. Leon didn't know if he'd ever took horizontal refreshment on a true Christian, though many a one had claimed to believe in the big J. It hardly mattered. Leon just felt sorry for Mouse. He helped her into his jacket and drew her close by the lapels and zipped her up. Now her upper half was protected from the elements. Mouse pitched her head into Leon's manly-ass chest and grabbed onto him and sniffed.

"I know," Leon said, but now was no time for weak behavior. He pressed her away, and stepped back. "Come on now, be strong. Do you know where the Black Monsters keep that sack of white?"

"White?"

"Talk to me. What happened?"

"Wolverina, she . . ."

"Yeah?"

"She went to Asheville with Potato and the others to an Anarchist meeting."

"Uh huh."

"I wanted to go, but Wolverina said uh-uh, I

should stay here to proselytize the children. I tried. I said Jesus died so you could be happy and not burn in Hell, but they unbelieved me. The little girl kept saying I should open my eyes."

"Open your eyes?"

"Open my eyes."

"You done offended the Black Monster Kids," Leon said, and pictured them getting madder until they went to ripping off her dress and socks and shit and dragging her over the concrete. The kids had done took to some action. Damn kids had done took up with a Hitler vibe. Leon would bet that Amber held a grudge over that Mouse freaked out when Barney attacked her. Don't fuck with a woman's monkey, that's rule number one.

"They were paying you back for what you done to Barney, I reckon."

"They said the world hadn't been saved yet by nobody, that it was all a lie, and they wanted me to speak in tongue. I tried. They laughed. They said I was faking. They took my bible, and poked me with clubs and ripped my bible pages out." She sniffed again, and went over to her white bible and picked it up and was brushing off the dirt that had got on it. "They read stuff I underlined. They laughed at me and called me stupid. I tried to reason."

"It amazes me, that you went along with it."

"They talked about killing me, sir!"

"What? Did you call me sir? What the fuck is the world coming to?"

"I was scared! They kept saying a sacrifice had to be made. I thought they would black me out, but they made me sit on the floor and they all had steak knives. They put a rope around my neck and I thought they were gonna stab me, but the queen said no, don't hurt her. She said in the new world slaves would be needed, so they made me pray on my knees."

"Pray? Who the fuck were you praying to, bitch?"

"The queen. I didn't understand. They said for me to pray for her to die, so I prayed for her to die. I just did what—"

"Shutup. I don't guess I need to hear more."

"They said if I tried to escape the monkey would eat my boobs."

"Hey, what did I just say?" Leon wanted to knock her lights out, truth told, or do something to shut her fucking face up right this second. Instead he hugged her, like Jim Jones would've done, and patted her back all looking over her shoulder and shit at the nice ass poking out below the jacket hem. No pimple to speak of. Thing split into whitewater rapids, but didn't women with acne on their faces have acne also on their asses? Mouse's patoot was the full-on cheese of cute, no real fat to hamper the flow, and not too skinny neither. Leon wanted to grab that shit with both hands, warm it up for her, smooth away them goose bumps, and he'd been too many days without a woman. He needed to take some payment here was his feeling for all the shit he'd gone and had to do for her. "Don't worry about them fools," he said.

"I couldn't believe how mean they were. I never met children like that ever in my life before. I think they were possessed by demons."

Leon rolled his eyes, and figured it was time to get the fuck out of the barn. His damn fire hand, though, as if disconnected from his brain proper, a renegade motherfucker here, slipped down to her hip. Mouse made no change in posture, so the hand sorta clawed up onto the hill there, caused Leon to lean over. His water hand took up with her other side. He pulled the damn shit apart, then released, pulled his hands away saying *no don't do that* to his hands, but his hands went back.

"Hey, what're you doing, sir?" Mouse said.

"Mind yer own business," Leon said, and lifted her.

Mouse took to silence, the little zitfaced fuckhead, hung in the air such as she was with her ass pulled wide apart, Leon here getting riled up and all. She had that power on him, and what he feared, that he would start to get mad, appeared to be happening, he felt it. To combat the mad feel his fire hand fell away like burned—her left foot touched down to earth—and his water hand fell off—and the other foot touched down. Leon was to split like a peach pit smashed by hammer was his intent here, but goddamn if his fire didn't go back for senct, or seconds as they licked to say—or liked to say—*hey, hand, what're you doing?*—or was it thirds? Hard to know for sure, but his hand took up with another grab. *Should I say I'm trying to get some weight lifting in here?* he thought. Would explain things, but no. He wanted to whisper something Fabio in her ear, like "I will do you the way Jim Jones done the drug addict." After that he might turn things up a notch over the damn girl was light, Dwight. He could pin her to the wall and have at it five seconds from now, his dude piston gone to *kaplinka*, ain't that right, Treblinka?

Outside some commotion was coming on.

"They're coming," Mouse said.

Leon stepped back to some fuckwad beyond the double doors to scream, and more screams came.

Sounded like a full tribe of Injun warriors stomping in with raised spears.

Leon wheeled a moped to the middle of the room, and gave it life. By the time the padlock had been keyed free, the doors here in wide swing, Mouse was astraddle the seat of it. In front of her Leon wound up full throttle, and they advanced through the angry mob of drugged-out children, knocking several down and running over ankles and toes.

Leon putted over the bridge to the Cloth Shack where Mouse found a pair of baggy pants fast, and slipped into them. Before the pile of shoes then she searched out suitable fits. "Hurry," Leon said, and wanted Chris, or *crisssssss*. On meth it was easy to decide shit. Off it, you felt like the biggest goddamned idiomoly, and here came the sounds of ankle bells again. The moped had been idle out there, await for Leon and Mouse to get their shit together. The engine was killed, though, and the doors whopped free in revelation of the Black Monster Queen who stood barefoot and panting in the cold, the orange monkey clinging to her leg, his prehensile tail doing an S up through the air to the hand of her. Together they were like some space travel team walked from a wormhole, check out the Babylonian goddess whore with her magic ogre, her army of munchkins behind them awaiting her orders.

"Fucking methhead," Leon said.

"We need more," the queen replied.

"More?"

"More!" the queen repeated in a very loud, angry, impatient voice. The monkey let out a bark, and scowled at Leon.

"That bag was fuckin—Hey, earth to Ambrosia!"

"You must get it for us!" the child insisted, her voice now robotic of sound, and then she went into her crazy tongue-speak talk again. Her Black Monster friends started up too in the tongue, and the thing they tounged in tongue on, this plea to the *Holy Ghost*—yeah, he heard them calling on the *Holy Ghost*—had to do with Leon going out in the world to buy a fat sack of crystal—that's what they were pleading for, for Leon's cooperation. Now and then the garbled made-up words were sandwiched between clear words and phrases such like "meth," and "Leon buy meth!" and "Daddy" and "Uncle L" and "crystal." It was so stupid.

Ambrosia stepped closer. Screwing her face up, she screamed, "It's your fault!" and looked at Leon through her stupid eyes, eyes of which she had two, not one, but two of the stupid fuckers.

"My fault? What's my fault you lying piece a—"

"You kilt her!"

"I know you ain't talkin bout no Dez."

"Dezi*ray!*" Amber shouted, and the monster kids stopped the tongue-speak to shout it. "Dezi*ray!*" they cried, "Dezi*ray!*" and spoke again in tongue with "Dezi*ray!*" thrown loud and sporadic—*han dan tada da boodie boo*—into the mix. Little fuckers never even knew Dezzie, so what were they complaining on? Did Amber tell them Leon was responsible for the death of the Dez? Leon didn't wanna think any over on it, just their voices moved him. He understood where they were coming from. He wanted to help, but couldn't, so balled his bigass fist up, unaware of what he might could do next. He pictured Dez in the clutch of her neck on the floor. He cut the shot up with scissors in his mind, and the pieces fell, and Leon thought *I'm'a bust you a new asshole, bitch!* but to whom was that thought thunk? He thought of the large meth sack that somehow had been emptied into the bodies of these children.

Leon damn to near wished the Quiz would possess him now. With the Quiz it always was like *Calgon, take me away!* but it smacked of the cowardly. So Leon looked to the Mouse, as though she might could hold the answer as to what to do. Her bleeding zits were sure to distract if nothing more, but Leon only saw fear there. He smelled it coming off her body in waves of festering nast. The what to do was look at the dumb little slut calling herself the Black Monster Queen, and hope she'd back off on account of the evil in his eye. Leon said, "Listen here, why you got to act this way, Ambro? Can't we be friends?"

"More!" she cried.

"More!" the children cried.

The Black Monster Queen raised her hand and snapped her fingers and a little boy in furry slippers and Winnie the Pooh pajamas stepped up with a pile of money. This would be what Amber won hard off the Girl Scouts of America.

"I don't know anybody sells it."

"But you can find somebody. Please," Amber finally said, and in her eyes Leon saw her second-guessing the bullshit she'd started up with him. Was she to recognize the Leon she knew from before? Did the good times they'd shared ring a bell? They'd slogged through muddy waters holding hands in the lands of cranberries and midnight spirits and monkeys gone haywire, hadn't they? They'd sung together on the raspberry beret in the roll down of a dirt road in Tallahassee, Florida.

"Hey," Leon said, "what about them snails gone down to the mud? You 'member that? You put their shells back so they could find them come spring. I thought that was really cool of you. I thought you were telling me you'd be here for me like those shells, you know what I'm saying? Come to find out loyalty don't mean shit to you!"

The Queen did not now look confident nor scary. Her purpose and feel of pride and joy in power had done did the damn drain-down-to-nowhere-in-the-world thang, Mr. Yang. The power in the face of the childs too drained down to the nowhere place. At once they looked the group of ghost orphans to wander from the ward in the wish of not-dead, *Hey, why we got to be dead, Fred?* They wanted to be seen and loved like you and me, but *nothing doing!*

"Fuckin cocksucker." Leon slapped the money out the hand of the Winnie. The bills flew up and flipped around and the damn fool boy came to cry. That was Waterfall's son-ass motherfucker, yeah, Leon recognized him, and knew him by name. Damn Cedric. Leon had had fun with him on several occasions, and felt like apologizing. Instead he whipped his eye Amber's way with a fire that may well have blown her to the moon if not for the cooling powers of Leon's water arm. Damn arm had felt much heavier of late, ever since him and the Amb's arrival to the farm.

The kids in their black monster bullshit backed off, and Leon kick started the moped. Didn't have to run the bums over this time, of which he was glad. He drove Mouse to the Great House and they went in. She felt better, all splashing water on her face at the kitchen sink and shit, all got her zits under control, and thanked Leon for the save of her life. "I am eternally indebted to you, sir," she said, and offered to fry Leon the most killer omelet.

38.

MOUSE'S OMELET WAS awful delish. All on the spread of Dijon mustard it was, it smacked across its eggy moonlike surface, and she sprinkled it over with fresh ground black pepper. Each time Leon brought the fork to his face, he smelled her puss. He'd only run his fingers up its middle once, where it was slippery. That's all it took to pick up the smell of delish for hours to come. Leon wondered was the special delish of it aught to do with her hyena, like maybe Mouse was an extra virgin olive oil kind of girl, and her hyena, since it guarded the place where her eggs were kept, prevented the less delicious eggy flavor from seeping down into the picture.

Leon finished the damn good omelet, at which time Mouse had finished frying up her own awesome omelet. She set her plate on the table, climbed onto the stool beside where Leon was sitting, and began to eat, Leon still in the ponder of the faraway yonder. Of course, whether or not her hyena had been ripped had nothing to do with virginity, for he'd heard of women to rip theirs doing shit like skateboarding or falling out of trees. Hyenas were weird things. They didn't make much sense to Leon, so his inclination was to have nothing to do on them. His sister claimed to have ripped hers while running for the school bus.

Mouse ate. Leon smoked. He knocked ashes onto his plate, and he and the Mouse chatted on stuff like the weather, and the chickens-getting-ate-up-by-predators situation. The trick the dirt people did of peeing all around the coop seemed unsanitary, she said, but if it worked it worked. If she was a bobcat she wouldn't go near the place, she said, and Leon mentioned that before the bobcats came in it was the raccoons to eat the chickens, biting their heads off and ripping their bodies open so it was too gross to even look at. The dirt people shed many a tear over their dead chickens, but then they started sprinkling moth flakes out in the yard and the coons quit the restaurant business. Shit didn't work for the bobcats. That's when the communal pissing parties started up, everybody out there pissing together, the hunks running wieners side-to-side while walking, and the girls in squats holding hands, pissing for the chickens, to save their souls. Mouse said it didn't seem right, that to get to the eggs you had to walk through the nauseating pee smell. The dirt munchers were funny people, weren't they? She loved how they made houses for bats, and oh, by the way, when would they be back? The adults to a one had loaded up in the school bus. They'd done driven, drove, or druv to Asheville for the anarcho-syndicalist meeting that would not, Leon knew, be over 'til late of night, the Dirties all in the drink of things. In the drink they'd branch into parties in the hoods where bands played and poets read. Leon had been to a few such have-at-its. You'd wake up in somebody's basement alone and curled into yourself, or with somebody you barely recalled from the night before. The Dirties rarely returned to the farm before late the next day.

When Mouse was done with her omelet, she took their plates to the sink, ran a handful of dirt across their surfaces, and rinsed them, and Leon smelled his fingers more. In the smell of them he thought of Mr. Quigley, though, who'd all the time gone around sniffing his damn fingers like maybe he'd done dipped them into some hot chick's meat wallet. Back then the hot chick would've been his big sister, on the chubby side, or his mother of the long straight naturally blond hair. Though Leon did not remember ever feeling super duper close with his sister, they did build some nice memories together. These days, when he thought on Glindy, he felt queasy. He always had to stop his think short.

Mouse put their dishes in the strainer then sat with him.

Leon said, "I got some money in Alabama. You wanna drive down with me?"

"It sounds like a big adventure time, but you disrespected me, sir. Don't think I'm not grateful. I just think you didn't respect me enough."

"Beg pard?"

"I'm grateful that you saved me, don't get me wrong. I don't want you to think I'm an ingrate."

"Listen, it was an accident."

"But you shouldn't've done like that, sir."

"Hey, listen. I'm not trying to change the subject or anything, but I wanna ask you a question. You remember when we were in the mopáge and you were telling me all the stuff I needed to know about shit? Well, you said something on professionalizing the children. What did you mean? Would you mind explaining?"

"I'm not sure what you're talking about, sir."

"Stop calling me sir. My name is Leon. Don't you remember how you said professionals? You said Wolverina said you should stay at the farm to professionalize the children. Were you meaning like to build a office and have them make phone calls to try and sell the Dirt Control? I think that could be a great idea because the world has too many people in it. Would you mind telling me more about what you were talking about?"

"I never said anything about an office."

"Yes you did. That's why you stayed behind, remember?"

"No, that ain't it. I said proselytize."

"Proselytize?"

"It means make the kids into Christians."

"I know what it means, bitch. I just thought you said professionalize, so I wondered what you were talking about. Now that you pronounced yourself correctly you don't need to tell me nothing more on it, but you might should ought not to have done that. Did you ever hear about National No Means Yes Day?"

"For which nation would that be? I don't think we have it here in America. Are you talking about where the monkey came from?"

"No, I was just saying that the professle thing you were talking on was like National No Means Yes Day, how if you say don't do this, somebody's gonna do the opposite, and if you say do this, they gonna do the opposite of the do."

"That's called reverse psychology."

"I know what it's called, bitch. That's why I was telling you all about it. Why don't you listen for a second instead of running your mouth? Do you remember how Nancy Reagan said, Just Say No?"

"I don't remember that."

"Well, she said it about drugs, and then after she said it there were a million new drug addicts. It's the same shit, and I think you gave them rat-ass kids the don't of the do, and that's why they messed you up."

"No, I think they were possessed by devils, Leon."

"You wanna be my girl? Am I too old for you?"

"God don't recognize age, Leon, but I already told you about that other thing. I don't think you should talk to me in vulgar language. You seem to forget that I am a Child of God."

"Are you a virgin?"

"I'm not trying to be rude, Leon. I just don't answer vulgar questions."

"But have you heard of the proof's in the pudding? When you see a dog wag its tail you know it's gotta mean something. Same thing with a wet hair burger. When it gets wet, what does it mean?"

"Relief to the bladder," Mouse said, and tried to hide the smile coming on. Thought she was clever on that one, didn't she? Leon saw she liked him, like most hot chicks liked him, why, Leon could not say exactly for sure, just the proof was in the pudding of the smiles and hard nipples and such. In all truth Leon didn't understand how any chick could like any man. The females of the world were menahaulics, and sometimes they even tried to be like men. They loved the sonsofbitches, and in doing so it spoiled them sort of. A world of lesbos would be better, but that, Leon knew, was an unreasonable request to be making right here at the moment and everything, and then anyway where would Leon fit in?

QUIZZLEBOON

"Okay, have it your way," Leon said. "You want me to take you to the Cherokee Reservation? I heard you say that's where you lived, but I also heard that they didn't let no white people live there. I don't blame them. You know white men are the worst creatures on the planet, don't you? Everybody knows all what they did to the injuns, but did you know they did bad shit to black people, too?"

"Are we so bold as to question God's plan, Leon?"

"Forget I said anything."

"My family and Sarah's family are missionary families. We got a whole bunch of us and we came out from Oklahoma in a caravan of RVs and cars and stuff. We converted a bunch of Indians and stayed on after."

"Hey, I bet your daddy's worried sick about you right now."

"He'll kill me if I come back without Sarah—uhm, wait, I mean Wolverina. I mean, if I don't go back I won't have to worry about it, though."

"Fuck Wolverina," Leon said, but his mind flipped back to Ambrosia, that look of defeat. Her whole body had seemed to crumple when he'd said what he'd said to her. He didn't wanna remember it, would you? But he damn well knew what he'd said, and it wasn't just that he'd said it. It was that he'd sounded like he'd meant it. Was this not a pudding crawling over with tiny cockroaches with strings of turds falling out their behinds? It was disgraceful and gross. Was not Amber the brightest star in the skies? That would be a great big yesamoly, Bry. Leon had done popped her balloon, busted through her hyena in a figure of speech kind of way. Leon had watched the morale of the Black Monster Kids drain like so much hemoglobin out a circus parade—*goodbye joy, goodbye pride.* The lot of them had been mowed down by Leon's ugly. Here all they'd wanted was another bump was all. They were determined and hopeful. Leon knew the feeling. It was gonna get worse. *Crissssssssss* was the Devil's piss.

"Let's go, babydoll," Leon said.

So on their way they were, out, but Leon realized, holy crapamoly, he needed his jacket back. All he had on was a white Haines crewneck t-shirt, so he stopped before he reached the door. He cleared his throat. "Excuse me, but I need my jacket."

"Well, I'm not going out there bare-chested."

"Quit yer goddamn accusatory attitude before I get tired of it. I'm just saying that upstairs there's plenty. We got coats in the pantry. You'll need a belt."

"Well I don't feel comfortable rummaging through somebody else's stuff."

"I'll go with you," Leon said and they went upstairs to the penthouse room where there was a pile of clothes in the corner. Leon picked out a red and black flannel shirt and tossed it to her and Mouse unzipped his jacket. She peeled it away and held it out for him, and didn't seem abashed at all, maybe over this here philosophy to say once a man has seen a thing, no use to hide it no more, that what's been seen has been sawn, so pour the bleach down the drain hole, bitch, and hop your ass out the door. With her tits all out though, and the dark-ass nipples there to verge on purple, Leon took pause, and guessed her to know her pair was nice, cute more the word for it, them here dirty like from having been scrupped over wood floors—or scraped—and concrete like to throw on the scrap heap. Whereas Beacon's were pineapple-shaped, and whereas Deziray's were like rotted garlic cloves with fine blue veins you saw through the skin, Mouse's were like cut-in-two bananas, very unusual in term to the titties he'd been up close and personal with in his life. Not only that, but the top half of each banana looked nought but nipple. They were sorta swollen looking at the tips there, and midway of each bazonga, where the border took ring, some really big bumps were, kinda made you think of a coral reef. Kind Edward, Leon reckoned, would be damn happy to read their braille. When Leon took the jacket from her, he just shook his head.

"I got tuberous breast disease," she said.

"Huh?"

"Normally I'm very ashamed."

"What?"

"You are privy to my secrets."

"Hey, why don't you tell me your real fuckin name, bitch? Not no fuckin Church House Mouse shit, I'm talking about your *real* name."

"Laura."

"You got nothing to be ashamed of, Laura. Do me a favor and try and remember that, okay?"

Laura put the shirt on and, as she hadn't had time to get shoes when they'd been confronted by the monstrous children earlier, slipped her tiny foots into Potato's wheat-colored Timberland construction boots, which were way too big. Potato was sure to be sore on it, but screw the house down and chop off its head, Sid. They hopped down the stairs. Mouse grabbed a black coat from the pantry, the word SECURITY printed to its back.

39.

LEON DROVE MOUSE'S car down the mountain, Mouse shotgun to where she was like his girlfriend. Along the way a fine powdery snow started up. The force of gravity drew the flakes to the ground slow and soft. There was no wind. It was like a gigantic octopus turned a flour sifter up there in the clouds.

Leon parked a few blocks from the Center for Anarchist Healing, and he and Mouse walked the city sidewalks to the tall double doors. One door was cracked a little, and they pushed through it into the large meeting hall where the dirt people and their cohorts were gathered cross-legged on the floor before a man in black slacks and a suit jacket, also black. Standing on the stage constructed of strapped together plastic milk crates, the man strummed a mandolin while holding his head high singing, "Slave, I'm a slave, I'm a slave." The man's voice was pretty obnoxious, ask Leon, sounded too much like Peter or Paul from Peter Paul and Mary, all that puff on the magic dragon bullshit. Even more disturbing or weird or what have you, if you stopped to think on it more than five seconds, was everybody loved it, or seemed to. They swayed their heads back and forth and sung all along with the chorus.

Leon and Mouse watched on through the next song, and then that song ended. Everybody cheered. Everybody clapped. They stood. The man said a few things on congress and a local policy on panhandling. A donation cap was passed about. The guy was running for mayor.

At this point the Dirties and their fellow compatriots in the war against stupidity made for the table upon which the boxes of wine were set up for come get your refill, self-service style. It was about then that the Dirties noticed their king, Uncle L, he was in the house, and was that Mouse? Leon knew their thoughts. Mouse must be his new chick-adoodle-dandy, they were thinking, weren't they?

A dreadlocked dude with a guitar got up on stage to sing and play.

And the Dirties crowded in, Wolverina smiling her gums to the moon. Mouse pulled Wolverina over to the wall where she began filling her friend in on the weird shit to go down at the dirt farm. Leon watched the wolverine's jaw drop open in surprise, the two front teeth still missing, and the hug to follow, *Oh, poor poor Laura, what you have been through!*

The Center for Anarchist Healing was a cool place to gather. When you walked into it from the outside, it was like stepping into a Duff's Smorgasbord with everything removed from its interior. The many doors along the walls opened into rooms where self-defense classes were taught, and stuff like how to make tinctures. There was a room for weaving, a room in which they did the Macarena and other dance moves. There was a room for blocking out the world, what they called sensory deprivation workshops, and a bike room where anybody could get a bike, just you had to build the fucker yourself with the hundreds of parts strewn all over, tiny ball bearings rolling across the floor of their own accord. Come in and build your ass a bike, Dyke. Put on the handlebars and pump the tires up for an even glide, Clyde. Go ahead and pedal, Gretel.

Classes in yoga too were taught, and spirituality—a fine place for likeminded dropouts to gather. In a few minutes here the heavier drinking started up. Some folks busted out some coke, and Leon partook, as did Mouse. Even though she was a straight-laced extra virgin olive oil kinda gal, she wanted to try things, like in the way of the foodie. She had a bit of the Dez in her, Leon could see, and the dancing began. Leon balled his fists and brought them up in various positions while bumping his shoulders to the beat. Mouse was excited to see Leon dancing and she laughed and jumped in and danced with him in the way-too-big construction boots. It was a mix tape going on, songs Leon wasn't most familiar with, but he recognized the David Bowie in there. It was the song where the dude named Major Tom does shit in space. No shards of mirrored light moved across their bodies and faces like what happens at skate-inns, but there might as well have been for the clean coke high Leon had going on.

Even Wolverina snorted up, and she too was tearing up the dance floor. The coke had come in by favor of this tiny near-midget dude everybody called Godzilla. The missionary girls were totally rocked out on the wonder of it, just look at their faces. They looked as if gerbils had done took up residence in their titties and were licking them from the inside out.

Inside the *Women Rise Up Room* is where Leon

next was. Here he talked stuff up with Sparrow some, and Potato, and dropped his body into a green beanbag and got cozy. He took some heart-warming swigs off this here Wild Turkey bottle making the rounds, and soon was in the liquefied groove of the drunk. It always happened. You started feeling good and getting high and you kept getting high until you were holed up. Once the coke came out, which oft happened at these goddamned anarchist free-for-alls, you were snowed in for sure. That guy Godzilla had some good shit, about a dozen eight balls he was trying to unload in order to, as he said, buy the Echinacea seeds needed for the crop his collective up in Greenville hoped to plant come spring. A collection was took up and then it was snorty snorty in the *Women Rise Up Room* sporty, on the walls plaster boobs nailed and molds of vaginas and such, posters of Pippi Longstocking, Wonder Woman, Janis Joplin and Joan Jett and a few other women Leon vaguely recognized. They were heroes in the feminist movement. One black chick named Sojourner Truth caught his eye. She was old as a damn prune or some shit, but you could tell she was younger, physically, than Sally Field and Princess Leia and most of the other white ladies taped to the wall. The quote on the Sojourner Truth poster said: "It is the mind that makes the body." Leon thought on it, and looked around the room to see were there barbells and stuff a woman might use to build her body up with. He spotted some ten pounders, as well as a heap of lower weighters sorta pushed under the desk-table, which looked the good place, come to think of it, to bend a woman over to get with from behind. He spotted wrist-crunchers and back rollers. As a guy who'd lived on the dirt farm, he'd heard some things on feminism, and on being thin. If it was the mind to make the body, then what this Sojourner Truth character seemed to be saying was the overwhelming majority of women were deficient in brain health. As a result they needed to come together, unify their minds to where their brains became like one big brain. Then the collective body would get strong, and they'd be better positioned to beat down *the man*, which Leon was all for. Come on, ladies! *Rise up! Get thin! Rise up! Get strong! Rise up and beat down that sonofabitch with everything you got!*

Looking at the picture Leon saw, that if you took off Sojourner Truthy's clothes and pantyhose, you'd see an amazing body that, if you liked black chicks, you'd want to scrock from Lowe's to Home Depot's Landscape Supply, and go ahead and throw a Frisch's Big Boy into the middle along the way, as well as a Denny's and a Western Sizzlin'. The old lady was ripped. With a bod like that and last name like Truth he guessed she'd had no shortage of dudes beating down her door to try and get inside her panties.

The distractions here were many, though not so plentiful as to knock Leon's noggin back to the burner. Leon still felt shitty over how he'd left Amber, and thought, *You goddamned rascal varmint no-fer-good worm child!* After Leon had turned his back on her she'd even said "Please!" a second time, sort of shouted it as he'd hauled away with Mouse on the moped. If it wasn't the saddest sound he'd heard his whole life over, he didn't know what was. Maybe the what of Dezzie after her shot through the jugular, a sort of gurgle in surprise followed by the thud of her head on the rug and the splash of the blood. But

"Please!" the mischief-maker begged, and Leon didn't turn his head a tiny bit to the side to let her know he'd heard her and might give it a think later. That would've been the decent thing to do, but no. In Leon's steady unchanging movement away from her he'd condemned her.

Poor child had hard times ahead. Leon hated the think of it, so ejected her from his goddamned brain. Several snorts into the night, though, she wormed back in through his ear-hole. His conscience got to needling. "Please!" he kept hearing—her voice inside him bouncing off ribs—"Please!" and it was like Amber, right then, way over at the farm, still was saying it, "Please!" and each time she said it, her feeling was so terrible and strong that it traveled through the world to find the man to matter, Leon in his kick-back in the beanbag. He could smell her. Like a fart, her smell had followed him down the mountain. Whenever Leon looked to Butterfly over there, Amber's momma—*no, she wasn't no Amber no more, she was Ambrosia, that was her name, Ambrosia, the one who got named after a drink*—his blood bubbled and he wanted to tell of it, tell Butterfly he'd messed up her motherfucking pissant daughter, that the strange energy the brat returned from the road with was due more to *evil* than a feathery brush up with interesting people.

Oh, Butterfly was fine on the idea that her daughter may have had a few tantalizing experiences out there, some involving recreational drugs—*hey hey hey*—a corner cut from a blotter of LSD, say, or a mushroom bite, but what of this? It was the worst of the lot of what her daughter could do, and her daughter had done did it in plenty, had done did the sizzling *crissssss*. Thanks to Leon, Butterfly's dumb bunny had put the shit in by shot, by needle. What the dirty people had thought was that Ambrosia's enthusiasm was contagious. That's why their crotch fruits acted strange of late, and hyper. Truth was the Devil was pissing into their hearts.

Then it was morning. In the big room passed-out people slept in corners. Leon walked amongst the bodies that could've been dead, only his ears took in the sleeping sounds of snores and teeth. A blue-haired girl farted wetly, and Leon smelt barbeque sauce. He guessed if the others were up they'd criticize her meatly ways, put her in a piñata to smack with clubs and force to repent. Where was Mouse? Wolverina? Leon wondered ought he not to've kept a better eye on them? T'was their first time whopping up the booger sugar, but as night advanced he'd hooked into a long-ass conversation—more of a listen-to—with Potato, who said this here on the Wolf of the Ring: "Those missing teeth, man. Shit freaks me out. Think if you were to shove it in there. I can't talk to her without picturing it," and *the Tates* talked on onwardly into the night, on Bill Clinton, saying Bill fucked up big, that *Zippergate* was more important than anybody could know. If Bush was to beat out Gore in the upcoming presidential election, chances were it'd be over Monica Lewinsky stepping forward. Oh, just I gave knobjobs to Bill, the most powerful man in the world, the guy who plays the saxophone, *lookit'm go*, you really gonna care about that? *Bill* said the word "because" in a particular kind of rednecky way that made everybody love him and question his intelligence. The fuck-ass Democratic Party was screwed. From the selfish curling of Clinton's toes mountains of corpses rose. Clinton should've had the good sense to assassinate the bitch. "It's called one for the price of millions," Potato kept saying. He was so pissed off about it, and Leon remembered Potato going around asking people, "How many dead children can you fit on the tip of Bill Clinton's dick? Mark my words, that dickhole's gonna open up like a sinkhole and suck millions down into it. The blown-up buildings of the future, and the wars of the future, and the massacres. They all could stem from the mouth of Monica, man, don't you see it?"

Leon hoped the Mouse and Wolf—or Ring of the Vulva, *Wolverina*, and *Mouse*, a Linga of the Cheese-uh—stuck together through the night-uh, around no prowling yogurt slingers took shelter-uh. That's what dudes-uh were after-uh. Didn't matter did they love equality, or Mao the mayonnaise man from China-uh, could I get a order of fried plantains to go with my vagina? At bottom they wanted to break shit, so *Get yo ass in my Volvo, Slot!* That's why they loved the fire of bull, *Lot*, the slam of pick into ice, the drop of nail from a pneumatic gun, or whop you out the ballistic battering ram, Uncle Sam, punch a hole in a cow's ear, *mon frère*. Leon scanned the bodies to the big room. No Mousey padoodle-doo. So he stepped outside. The cold fresh city air popped him up a bit more peppy.

What Leon needed was to get to Kickback, get the goddamned Butt Money out the trunk before somebody came along to see the car in the hole. Whoever went down there could get rich quick. Leon was nervous on it, so walked through gently swishing snowflakes to hit a café where he sat a bit with pesticide-free Nicaraguan coffee, a blueberry muffin.

The people here said the muffin was organic, but the worlds of *or* and *not or—ganic*—were what Ray Oribison, bastard brother to singer Roy, talked on a lot. The *not or* and the *or* were the water and the fire, the Wing and the Wang—you needed a bit of each for good health.

Leon went back to the Center, saw Potato, said, "You wanna go with me to Kickback?" and filled him in on the details. Potato said it might could be interesting. They'd have to get to the dirt farm first, though. "I gotta feed my goldfish," he said, and said they could head out in his pickup afterwards.

Hours passed. People were getting up now, and they started partying, popping brewskis and smoking American Spirit cigarettes and rolling up blunts. Leon was happy to see the Mouse and Wolf emerge from the art room, though they looked disheveled and worn out. Leon nodded when he saw they could see him. He was standing with Potato at the time, and Potato saw this interaction of Mouse kinda waving back from across the room. Potato squinted his eyes at the two missionaries. "Holy fuck, Leon."

"Huh?"

"Those my waterproof boots?"

"Hey now, quit your shit."

"They are. Why didn't I notice this last night?"

"You were skrunked on Monica."

"Of all the . . . "

"Are you really gonna make a issue of it?"

"No, I'm not, I'm just saying, I mean, gee wiz, man, would I come along and take something of hers that she needed and then not even say shit? I got my name on those boots with a sharpie, right there on the inside part where anybody with a brain can see."

"Don't worry about yer fucking boots, man."

"I'm not, I'm just saying, it's so disrespectful, I feel violated."

"Fuck that shit. We need to load these bitches onto the bus." For the next hour Leon and Potato worked to round folks up. Took some effort, but by noon the Dirties stood by the yellow bus in the snow that fell, they were colorful, some fountain-like dreads over here, a Mexican blanket wrapped around a body. Handmade knitted scarves ran the gamut, and caps for cold, their eyes glinting colorfully. They said goodbye to each other, to the missionary gals. We family. Everybody hugged. That was a lot of hugs. The bible bitches promised to return, but before they left, Leon shared a private moment with Mouse, hugged her tight behind the bus, she thanking him for saving her from the children.

"I've thought about your kind proposal, Leon."

"Huh?" Leon backed away from her.

The gal looked as if she might could drip snot any second now.

"Forget it," Leon said, and kissed her zit-bespeckled forehead. "I know I was rude to you, Laura. I won't apologize, that's not me, but I—"

"You're a good man, Leon Hicks."

"Fuck that," Leon said, and told her to take off the fucking steel-toed construction boots. He hadn't planned to tell it, but Potato needed them for his part-time jobs. His boots. The extra cash went for smokes, and for farm projects like building hot air balloons. "Was up to me," Leon said, "I'd say take them, but you need to know that I am not a good man. You want me to black your eye to prove it? Right now both your eyes are half black from what the kids did, but I could make them full black. Would you like me to do that?"

Mouse pouted. Damn cute. Was tempting to claim her as his. Leon saw she'd go along with it, but how cruel. Look what happened when you hooked up with him. You got shot in the neck or hooked on drugs. Besides, Leon was too old. With Dezzie it was different over she was a thousand in spirit, but this here, no. Leon's sense of morality kicked in at the thought of them together, and he felt uncomfortable. As much as he'd like to partake of Laura's cuntly delights, and brainly delights, don't forget her brains, he was gonna stick to his guns. She leaned over. She pulled the laces. She got out of Potato's boots and handed them to Leon. Leon wished her luck in her missionary positions.

"Pursuits," she said.

"Huh?"

"We have pursuits, not positions, Leon."

"Whatever you say is fine by me," Leon said, and grabbed her by the pants. He pulled her close and did what he'd wanted to do in the mopáge, which was whisper something Fabio in her ear. "I can't believe you ain't butter, girl." He felt her melt into him, so pulled the pants material tight against her ass and smacked her, go eat some cheese. The smack was of perfect contact. He pushed her away then and she walked for the Datsun B210 where Wolverina waited behind the wheel, the engine warm of a steady idle, steam puffing from the exhaust pipe. The footprints Mouse left in the powdery snow could've been footprints on the beach in warmer weather in better times. Leon felt sad to see her go, but things were things. She got in the car. He waved one last time then drove the Dirties into the clouds.

QUIZZLEBOON

Leon had felt it, the Twizzleboon Quingle since the day before, this thing in his blood-filled stream that alerted him to Danger, and made him believe he might could be mighty special. The tingle of the pringle. The buzzy feeling of the arm both left and right said the man on the moon could be real. The counter-evidence was here counteracted in the green. The Lord ran a mysterious plan. If the Lord's things were true, so could this be. Leon wanted to believe.

But knew he'd done dug up some quack-ass bullshit on the Boon.

Either 1) Quizzleboon was fantasy, or 2) Leon was an idiot job.

Was the Quizzleboon jigamaloo a dumb punk trick he'd played on himself? An invention of the noodle? He wanted to believe. Too bad for his bouts of introspection that brought this out: Quizzleboon was the Quig, the S.O.B who'd exploited his good mommy, screwed his fat sister, and caused him to lose his eyeball on a goddamned foosball machine! The *quingle* had started up the day before, growing stronger, yet Leon ignored it. Now both arms prickled as if covered in dingleberries—talk of disconcerting—and the closer he got to the dirt farm—him driving the Dirties in the bus up there—the stronger the tingles of the dingles got.

Leon pulled onto the road to lead up to the Great House, the snow fast and thick in the air. The snow stuck to the ground good now, the wide world spread over with vanilla pound cake icing in the driving, and the people of the dirt here sung festive songs of love and contrition.

Leon killed the engine.

The singing stopped.

The snow fell.

It was not a nice lovely moment of quiet, for where were the children's voices? The thing of return was for kids to burst from buildings screaming. Where was the jump and shout and dumb-nosed joy and graceless dance? Where did the selves go? What of the happy reunite of small elf with big cheese?

Butterfly spoke first off: "Where are they?"

Leon pulled the lever of steel. The bus door folded back and he plunked down the steps to make for the Great House. He crossed through the snow, but the kitchen in there was empty and cold, so Leon stepped back. The Dirties followed him past the bell and across the field on over the black oak bridge. Arriving at the mopáge they heard sobbing sounds. In its midst a peal of laughter burst from the trees of the branches, or branches of the trees, take your pick. Leon looked up to see nothing. A few crows, as if irritated by his gaze, took flight. Had to be in his mind, a what brought on by last night's coke splunk. The growly laughter, though, had done electrified his arms. The dingleberries were blown off Leon's body by the Wing and Wang, and the shock sensation dropped down to his solar plexus, where it radiated like a sunburst. The quingle busted down to his groin. It sept, or seeped, or supt into his legs. Was like something coming together here. Was like Leon might soon could fly, maybe make things combust into flames through the focus down of some hate, or telecommunicate. Leon scanned the branches for wisecracks a number two time. He saw bark and snow and swatches of sky.

Leon slid the door free and stepped in where the kids sobbed and wept and some spoke in tongue as they'd done the day before, a bit of *biggety babba la dabba la doo,* though soft in the room where Amber and Barney hung from yellow rope. Damn girl was nekid, her club foot dripping in the stillness. Her big toe had swole up. It was bright red to its tip, like Rudolph the goddamn reindeer's shnaz. Thing seemed to be pointing at Leon.

40.

THE TWIZZLEBOON QUINGLE ejected Leon from the mopáge. He exploded over the snow-covered field on into the Pinto and seven hours later was passing through Virginia with a image: *Mr. Quigley*. Leon was gonna cut it, break it up, rip it, destroy it. He saw the nickel tube put to bone, the splash to follow of red and yellow smelling of burger grease and cumin and weird shit like Milk Duds and menstrual blood and tire sealant. In his drive Leon spoke some how he'd seen the children done: *Han dan dah ikida baku. Ban managa jigaboo beegeedi boo. Gigidi boogooda gagada goo!* and flashed on their jumps from the loft, the bottom out of Am*brosia* with her bowed-ass fucked up legs, and here came Barney to follow his *love*. See them twitch together then stop twitching. She'd removed the bands from her ankles and arms, but still wore the crown.

The QUEEN and her fucking monkey were dead! It was Mr. *Quigley* who'd did this. If not for *Quigley* none of it would've gone down. If not for Mr. *Dagobert* Quigley, who knew where Leon this very fucking instant in time might be?

At about come noon Leon rolled into the White Lady Motel parking lot. The long thin building stretched across the asphalt like a tapeworm. Damn thing'd crawled up brownly from the lake, what it looked like. The dead black trees out there festered like steaming fetuses in the cold. The room doors were red. The pole by the road clutched a plyboard cutout of a nekid lady in yellow heels, one leg stepping forward. Same as it was ten years ago. That's how it was now. The pole appeared to be reaming her up the ass.

Leon parked the Pinto. Quicklike he checked his butt buster, then stepped into the witch's titty of it all, the light falling around him like a waterfall of bright, all these glinted bits of sun filling shit up, shards to slash the eye damn ball. Was this fool caught in a light storm with no shades? He should'a bought a cheap pair in Suffolk when stopped for gas.

The glass door Leon opened of the check-in office, and stepped in, said to the girl behind the desk there, "Where's Quiz?"

Her expression got weird.

"Quizzle*boon,*" Leon said.

"You mean Mr. Quigley? I ain't never met you before."

"You gonna tell me?"

"What's it look like to you?"

The sassy one's blond hair was bunned up to the top of her head like the way Japanese women do, only a tassel squirted out sideways to give her a goofy-ass look. Her eyes were very close together. Had a kind of a rodent-like style of face going on, but she looked familiar.

"He pay you to work here?"

"Am I the Queen of the Nile?"

"Where's he at?"

"Who wants to know?"

Leon whipped the ass buster up. The days of fucking around with stinking little bitchass whore motherfuckers was over. He shoved it in her face.

"Hey," the girl said, hands out like to protect herself, what people did, as if hands stopped bullets. Ain't that what they'd said on Superman? That he stopped them? Or was it speeding lawnmowers? Leon couldn't remember, but bullets were dangerous. What a hand did on one was slow it down some, nothing more, and Superman was a fake sonofabitch, like Quizzleboon was a fake sonofabitch. Whatever Ambro thought she'd been up to, like to save the world by taking the plunge, taking the goddamn monkey along with her, yeah, it too was a buncha bullshit-ass fake reprobate swill.

"A hand ain't never protected a body from bull," Leon educated her.

She pulled her hands away. "You're not going to kill him, are you? I know he's a asshole, buuuut—"

"Where's he at?" Leon said, and she smirked. That was pretty badass. Leon respected it. A complete stranger points a gun in your face and you smirk? Well, the philly had a history.

"You gonna tell me or should I blow that apple off your head?" Leon raised his aim to the funny bun.

"I ain't hardly believing this shit," the girl said.

"I ain't playing now." Leon drew the hammer back.

"Okay, dude, shit, room fourteen, if you really got to know."

"That's the room I grew up in," Leon said, and backed out of the office and walked along the walkway to Room 14. Knocked. The door cracked and Leon pushed it hard, stepped in to see the fly of the Quig, how he'd flown halfway across the room to land on his back on the floor. Man still wore the beloved yellow suit jacket, but he started to rise, so Leon walked up and set his boot on the chest of him and pressed. Leon trained the barrel to the head bone above the eyes.

Mr. Quigley rubbed his fat white neck with thick dark curly hairs sprouting out of it here and there, checking to make sure nothing horrible had happened to him physical-wise. And the eyes Leon remembered damn for sure, all bulbous and blue in a kind of faded jeans way but that you could see through, and watery. And the dude had a brown mustache to plunge earthward either side to the mouth, only now, on his back, the things shot eastward.

Or maybe they shot westward or northward or southward. Leon could not have said which ward they shot for, and even if he could have, was it hardly a thing to think on?

That would be a big fat no from here to the Islamic Republic of Pakistan, Roseanne.

Once Mr. Quigley anyway felt reasonable to safe nothing bad had happened on his body, he focused in on Leon's face. Recognition registered in the forehead wrinkles, a smile in the making here, and Leon just now noticed how round the guy's face was. Mr. Quigley, since the last time Leon saw him all those many years ago, had done shaved off the wavy hair. The Quig had done gone ski-ball. The new style pronounced the round of the head. It was shaped like a fuckin moonball is what it fuckin was shaped like. Resembled one over the curdled yogurt make of skin, a thing to only look sexy on a woman's thighs—

cellulite, they called it. But the moon mouth opened, the Quig here to say, "Listen, Leon, your mother's been worried sick. Why haven't you called her? We've been so worried sick about—"

"Shut it!" Leon kicked the Quig a good one to the rib.

Man did not scream. He just said, "Worry is a killer, Leon, so say the sciences."

"Shut it!" Leon stomped the man's groin. "Don't think to spit your regular bullshit on me. I've thought on your ass."

The rib kick he'd done did felt good, but Leon sure ain't never had put a foot on another man's hairy wiener afore. The sock of Leon of course was there to prevent contact had the boot not abid, or abided by foot, and then there was the man's pants and underwear, but *damn*. Leon flashed on what it would be like had it been his bare foot to knock down on the man's bare thingamawhickey. The gross-ass thought of it started up the quingle in his arms again. It'd be worse than stepping on a roach barefoot. Something was happening here, as it had the day before as he'd stepped up to the mopáge, before he'd opened the door to see his "daughter" dead and the Cheeto-colored monkey hung up beside her. Felt like mystery things to come together. Leon kicked the mother's moonhead. He drew his foot back like to kick it again but changed his mind. "You know you're gonna die now, don't you, bitch?"

"That's not true," Quigley said.

"You stole my eye."

"That was a terrible terrible accident!"

"It was not no fucking accident."

"I was drunk, Leon, she attacked me!" Quizzleboon roared.

Leon kicked the man's moonhead. "You jumped off the bed and grabbed my head and slammed it into the foosball machine, didn't you?"

"That's not what happened!"

Leon felt dizzy. He sat on the bed.

"I called the ambulance. You were too little to understand what happened, Lumpkin. That's why we kept it from you."

"We?" Leon said, the fire in his voice gone out. The gun felt heavy.

"Your mother and I."

"My what?"

"Come on now, Lumpkin baby, that's a good boy, calm down. I know you don't mean to be cruel. Everybody gets down and wants to blame others. You're doing what's natural." Mr. Quigley was sitting up now, and backed against the wall to where he could look Leon over from a more respectable position. "I want you to know that your mother has been in agony ever since you lost your eye. That's a hard thing for a mother to accept, that she could have done something to prevent her son from turning into a freak. Things have become worse for her these past few years. She's very despondent, Lumpkin."

"She ain't never did nothing bad to me," Lumpkin—*no, he was Leon*—said.

"I think she needs to hear it from you. How do you think it's made her feel that you haven't—"

"Don't call me Lumpkin no more."

"You used to love that name. You were Lumpkin my Pumpkin, don't you remember?"

"If I was her I wouldn't wanna see me."

"Crazy bullshit sounds like," the Quig said, and Leon, dazed, saw that Mr. Quizzleboon—*no, he was*

Mr. Quigley—was gathering strength, curling up with his new ball of energy against the wall, maybe getting ready to spring on him? Seemed like it, but could a person trust his own brain to record stuff good? Could a monkey become a executive? That would be a great big negative. Needed was a body to see shit for us, a eye to play our lives back once they were over, like movies.

"I admit to fucking your sister, Lumpkin, but like I say, she was for it. She made me do it all the time. She called me her toy. Did you like to play with toys when you were little?"

"Yessir."

"So did Glinda," Mr. Quigley said. "Go ask her if you don't believe me, see what she says. Will you be able to see the truth when she lies?"

Leon's left arm was bloated, his fingers hoses out of which waters gushed onto the floor.

Mr. Quigley stood. Bloody-faced he sat on the bed beside Lumpkin—*no, he was Leon*—and draped his arm over Lumpkin's shoulder. "You are now the man I said you'd become. You are the one I delivered into the world, but stop worrying your mother, I say. Go visit her."

Leon tried to think. He tried real hard, but his mind felt blank. He tried harder to think, but he could not think.

"Okay, no pressure here, Lumpkin, but I see some shit's eating you."

Leon didn't move.

"I'll tell you what you wanna know, but I'm not comfortable with you holding that gun. You mind if I hold onto it? No, of course not. You're trying to make it in the world just like everybody else. Let's put this over there," Mr. Quigley said, and slipped Leon's ass buster from the fire fingers that weren't nothing much more than smoldering bullshit right here at this point. "That's a good boy." Mr. Quigley rubbed his hand in circles on Leon's back.

Leon mumbled something.

"What's that, my dear?"

"No."

"You want your mommy?"

"Where is she?"

"Across the river."

"Did you hurt her?"

"You know I would never."

Quigley's other hand was on Leon's thigh, ever so light.

Leon felt a tingle in his bratwurst. "I want my eye back, sir."

Quizzleboon chuckled. "Your eye went to a good cause, Lumpkin."

Leon imagined his eye up on the moon. He remembered entering the moon mountain where his eye was enslaved by the machine. He'd felt sorry for it, it dripping such as it was, as if overworked, and it had twitched Leon's way once as if its greatest wish was to be rescued from the torture it suffered all day and all night. What a thing, to look at every thing everybody in the world did. Was that not too much to ask of a man's eye? Thinking on it angered Leon. A rush of blood filled his head. His fire arm ignited and tore through his body.

"I told you what you needed," Quizzleboon said. "See how strong you are now?"

"I'm sorry, sir."

"You disrespectful child," Quizzleboon said, Leon

in the remember of the hold-down-on-the-floor shit the Quiz used to do to him. "What's that?" Quizzleboon said. "I didn't hear you. Say it again."

"I'm sorry, sir," Leon said, and meant it, all here while he'd thought he'd been playing along with shit. Turned out Leon didn't know a goddamned thing about any goddamned thing.

"Prove it," Quizzleboon said. "I want you to show me how sorry you are."

For some reason Lumpkin—*no, he was Leon*—got down on his knees on the floor.

"That's right, Lumpkin. Just like old times. You know what to do."

In the same way Leon had been possessed by Quizzleboon in the past, robbing banks and stealing off with funny monkeys and doing other crimes where a higher intelligence and strength was required, Leon was filled with something not his own, and it was of a meek and obedient variety. "You know what to do," Quizzleboon repeated, and Leon put his face in the man's crotch and sucked air through his nostrils. Quizzleboon ran fingers into Leon's hair and a few some moments later it turned out that the man's gozzler was in Leon's mouth. Leon sort of realized what he was doing suddenly out of nowhere and bit down and yanked at the damn thing, trying to rip it off but it wouldn't let go.

Leon ripped at it like a wild animal, but screaming Quigley had the piece. The Quig was to put it to Leon's head, so Leon let go of the mangled gozzler. He elbowed the dude's jaw, and the gun and the Quig dropped to the floor. Leon jumped to the quick to reclaim the piece, his thought being *Go, get out, don't think*. He would've done been gone quick but for the

Quizzy laugh that mocked him, as it had mocked him when he'd approached the mopáge, and opened the door on the dead slut to the end of the rope, the monkey beside her like a giant peach, and the drips and stuff all falling off her stupid feet.

Leon slapped into Quiggle's neck with his water hand. As if from a hovering eyeball he watched his fire arm rise. All was ready for the tooth-break slam, but the Quig said, "I named you, bitch."

"Peg pard?"

"I said I named you, bitch."

Looking into the man's face, Leon saw the similar. It was like what whenever he looked in the mirror he could see, and Leon didn't wanna think on it, would you wanna think on it? Would you wanna know you'd sucked your daddy's bladder extension thing? Don't even lie, bitch, so Leon slung his eye to the guy to say, "Where can I find her?"

"I ain't got to tell you."

"Oh yes you do," Leon said, and popped up his Buck 110.

41.

THE ROOM 14 door Leon left ajar, and into the bright assault of world stepped afresh and, *looky here, my brother*, it was the office clerk with a funny bun done up on the tippy top of her goofy varmint-ass-looking-like head—a blond. In her see of Leon in the lot on his way for the car she'd runt out, or maybe she'd ranned out, or did she runned? *Runt, rant, ront*, eat your heart out you goddamned three blind mice!

"I didn't call," the philly cried.

Leon stopped walking. "What?"

"The cops. I didn't call the cops."

"Is this my business?"

"In case you kilt him. I didn't hear no gun go off so I'm damn relieved."

"I ain't never killed nobody. I can say that without telling a lie."

"Hey, no need to get all touchy about it and shit. Where you going, honey?"

"To the moon."

"Can I go with, please? I wanna go there."

Now that her bottom half wasn't hid behind the check-in counter, Leon saw what a piece she was, not no big-assed nor wide side-to-side like what happened on chicks to fool you when you only saw the upper half. "What's your name, little girl?"

"Donna," she said. Seemed to be hyperventilating for some reason or other. Don't ask Leon why. He couldn't've told you to why.

Leon spoke her name. Tasted kinda nice. Girl hadn't a titty to stand on, but were titties all? Not by a long pile, according to the Gospel of Paul. Just everybody needed love, so drop on in, Slim. Leon dropped east for the beach, where who knew but that gulls pecked the sand for food scraps, and Sandra Hicks, or *Superscrub*, boiled grits ignorant on her son Leon coming to visit. "I just realized," Leon said to his new friend, "that all over the planet women are giving birth. I see their heads popping out, all at the same time. Each head is like a eye that sees, even though it's got two eyes."

"That's a pretty ridiculous thing to think," Donna said.

"Your boss is my dad," Leon educated her, his arms buzzing fuzzily, the intensity of each buzz fluctuating, a kind of seesaw streak of energy going on here and all right at the moment.

"Wow, talk some loop," Donna said.

Felt like a electric pulse dancing down his spine, all rays of light sent through his body in the pattern of a fish skeleton.

"He's my daddy too," Donna educated Leon.

The light, happy, buzz feeling entered Leon's face. His chest felt vandalized with seltzer, as if below the skin microscopic piranha fish swam whirly in tornado circles, their teeth to sling through the fields of fat.

"Pleased to meet you, sister," Leon said, and they shook hands. "Do you know my mother?"

"Yeah, sure, I know Sandra."

"Superscrub." Leon pulled their father's wiener from his jacket's front pocket. He tossed it onto the Pinto's iced-tea colored dashboard. It was bloody, but Leon didn't feel queasy on the sight of blood no more. He'd been cured of the weird curiosity. A light moon was visible in the sky as they cruised the country road beachward. The moon hovered over the penis like a watchful eyeball.

"That is *soooo* disgusting," Donna said.

Leon had a idea. He pulled out his prosthetic and dropped it into the pocket of his jacket. He grabbed Quigley's wiener off the dash and fiddled with it so the back part fitted into the socket with the right alignment. Leon was proud for accomplishing the task while driving, and felt rewarded in triple by the introduction of a new sensation.

"I wondered where all that blood on you was from," Donna said. "I suspected, you know, I mean I've heard about you. You're the son he talked on."

The wiener dangling out of Leon's eye socket twitched, and then twitched more, and the wiener got sucked about halfway down deeper into the eye hole. What it felt like was nerve endings being spliced together. It was extremely painful, yet Leon remembered the words of the wise man, Ray Orbison, bastard brother to singer Roy: "The power is in you, Leon, but you gotta find the trick to make it work. The responsibility is yours. You gotta brang them two bitches together, baby!"

Leon pictured the Wing in the stratosphere, flapping with just the one wing, and the head on it that had once been so beautiful in the eye of God flapping too, brownly as the men of Egypt all this way and that, listen to it flap, like the one-winged dove Stevie Nicks done sung on, and the blood and guts hung from the body's middle where it'd been cut in two. Damn thing was just all retarded all over and shit, and all it ever did was flap and flip, a pancake factory going on here, a flop party of the flapjacks, but what's this here? Oh, it's a drippy thing looking like another piece of wing or some shit with legs and toes swinging up to go throw the whole thing off balance, watch it drop twenty feet then zing up another thirty. Could it be? Was that the *Wang* in the mid-distance? What it looked like here and all was the Wang, finally, after so many thousands of years crawling along the bottom of the sea, dragging the wet wing behind like some kind of underwater sloth chained to a surfboard, had done swallowed a magic clam. That clam was Leon's water hand. It was Leon who'd done did this shit, reaching down to lift the Wang up out of the wet. He'd revived it. He'd brought it up into the sky! In his mind he had the Wing and the Wang collide. The bright explosion turned the whole sky a brilliant polarized pink color, and when the blue came back a beautiful gleaming man with shiny wings hovered. It was the man from Uruk!

"I ain't hardly believing this shit," Donna said.

"If you saw what I see," Leon said, staring dreamily out at the road. He watched the golden male glide away with perfect symmetry, and disappear, and in the place where the man just was Leon put *Superscrubs*, who also was a hero sort of person, just put a cape on her ass—a bed sheet for changing out rooms—and give her a TV show. Able to scrub toilets in five seconds flat! Able to fly room to room with a bottle of bleach, dump the shit into the bowl and *scrub* the shit clean. She was the hero that cleaned things!

That Superscrub still felt bad on Leon's eye was not good, but Leon saw she'd understood way back this thing on the Quig, that he was not one to claim for daddy-o. That's why she lied to him on who his daddy-o was, and whoever guv a fuck on daddy-os anyways?—or give or gave? It wasn't a thing to be brave by. It wasn't a thing to fill a bowl up with shit for. Let the past lie where it lay, Eula May, or live where it loved, Rita McCrae. Was not Leon made of blazes and rain? He could burn bad down and drown wrong from here to the Democratic Republic of the Kongo. So many Africas and Indias of the mind, ain't that right, Caroline? In his insides he felt strong and easy, but flipped his face Donna's way. The dangler looping down from his left eye socket slapped against his right cheek, then rolled sideways over his nose to dangle limp and snottily against his left cheek, all the way down to the side of his mouth.

Leon reached up and grabbed it and tried pulling it out, even as he drove, but it wouldn't give. In fact, it resisted, and hurt, so he let it go and wiggled his face back and forth to get a sense of what he was dealing with here. Thing flapped back and forth like a shrunk down elephant's trunk. It even lifted up some like maybe it had grabbed hold of a peanut. Would it feed it to himself? In this think of the trunk Leon saw his mistake. "I should've cut the eye out. I was supposed to put the eye in my eye to get my sight right, not no damn dong! Goddamnit, man, I can't believe how stupid I am! Why did I do that?"

"Hey, don't beat yourself up," Donna said. "What's done's done."

QUIZZLEBOON

Leon's dream of yore came back to him, the one where he cut Beacon's eye out and stuck it in his face to see in stereo. It'd been so real, and wonderful in a way. It'd been a message, but Leon was too stupid to make sense of it. He'd only had one chance. Now it was done got too late.

"Look on the bright side," Donna said.

"I ain't seeing no bright side here." Leon kept looking his face over in the rearview.

"You and I are brother and sister, Leon."

"Ain't my concern."

"We got different mothers, but we come from the same planet. A man's balls are like planets. You and I, we come from the same planet, I guarantee you me."

"Hey, would you do me a favor?"

"Of course, what is it, my brother?"

"Shut the fuck up, my sister."

Shit was so distressing, so Leon pulled over onto the road's shoulder.

"I recognize it," Donna said.

Leon grabbed the thing firmly with his right hand and yanked. He screamed out from the pain of it, his bad eye all alive again with a thing it had never been alive with before.

"Don't do that, is you crazy?" Donna shouted. "What're you trying to do? Kill youself?"

"Ray Orbison!" Leon screamed, and heard Ray laughing, as he'd sometimes done way back under the circus tents, hacking with a cough in the laughter of his laugh.

"You mean, Roy Orbison? The pretty woman guy? I love that song, it's *soooo* meaningful. I love when he says she's the one he'd like to meet."

"I ain't believing this shit."

"I've known on some strangeness," Donna said, "but on this there's not no category that I ever seen before. I mean."

"What should I do?" Leon asked his sis.

"I can see the me in you. I think we come from the exact same planet, not planets across from each other, but the same planet, the same ball, you feel me? You mind if I try something?"

"What're you talking?"

"I just wanna try something. You mind?"

Leon was so upset. He wanted to cry.

"The positive side is we found each other," Donna said, and touched Leon's new eye, the long eye, the eye that you couldn't know exactly what to call it in it was the first of its kind to exist in the world. As it did not see, it could not reasonably be called a eye, could it?

Leon flashed on something somebody might could say to him: "Hey, Dickface." As the thing would be true, Leon could only be ignorant if he got upset. Leon did not wanna be no ignorant sonofabitch from Virginia Beach.

Donna flicked it back and forth with her index finger. It filled with blood and got kinda harded up and she gave it a grab and let go. The thing pushed farther out of the eye socket. "Well goddamn," Donna said.

"Shit," Leon said.

Donna switched around in her seat so she could lean over and get it in her mouth.

"Holy fucking shit!" Leon screamed.

Donna had it going on, she was good at what she did, did not need no instruction or nothing, and in the thing of the lung of her Leon forgot all on his mommy, and forgot on Amber and the Dezzie and is not what happened next a thing of a billion bees a day? Our Lady of the Graces? When you went to your son to say, "Hey, baby, it's your mommy?" did not *the man* hit back with, *Depart from me, ye wicked woman?* Go check your bible, bitch! You'll see what *The Man* said was, *My mother is every woman*, or some such thing.

"Hell!" screameth many a preacher to Sunday.

And the people chime in with "Amen! *A*men! *A*men!" but they don't never say no "A*women*! A*women*! A*women*!"

Would that they did! Oh, would that they would!

The bruises Leon blew from his eye traveled down the esophagi of the sisters of him, and cut speedily through tiny pathways in the bodies of the hers to emerge through special cave walls and then, like in the way of the tides to suck, like in the whats of Salmons, the turns of the earth, or electric-shock shits in his arms, a child was conceived, and that child was named Leon Lumpkin Hicks.

They seemed to be stuck in a chasm of or, or was gas blowing into their masts as the cars passed by? Donna did the gasp and her mouth gaped in the gispage and she sunk sideways into her bucket seat to look Leon over and go into laughter, couldn't help it. It was a healthy laughter, Leon saw, it made her feel good, so Leon didn't say nothing over how offended he might could be. Was this a thing to get out of? Was prison any better?

"I don't know what to do," Leon admitted.

"Try sucking it in."

"Beg pard?"

"Try to suck it in, you know."

Leon tried to suck it in. The thing withdrew a tiny bit into Leon's head.

"Come on, now, my brother, you can do better than that!"

Leon tried again, and sure enough, the wiener slipped back into his head a tiny bit more. Leon kept trying and trying until only the head of Quigley's penis was sticking out from his eye socket. That was as far as Leon could suck it in. "I'm'a need me a patch before I can see my mother," he stated, but was also worried about the pee. What if pee came out both places when he peed? What then? Leon was filled with what-ifs, but started the Pinto and off they went, searching out that eye patch. Once they'd accomplished that chore, then they could seek out Leon's mother.

ABOUT THE AUTHOR

John Oliver Hodges lives in New Jersey. His other works of fiction are *The Love Box*, and *War of the Crazies*.

IF YOU ENJOYED
QUIZZLEBOON
DON'T PASS UP ON THESE OTHER
TITLES FROM PERPETUAL MOTION
MACHINE...

INVASION OF THE WEIRDOS
BY ANDREW HILBERT

ISBN: 978-1-943720-20-0
Page count: 242
$16.95

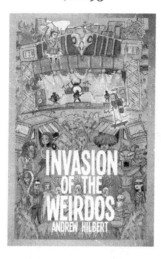

After getting kicked out of his anarchist art collective for defending McDonald's, Ephraim develops an idea to create a robot/vending machine with the ability to hug children. He is no roboticist, but through dumb luck manages to hook up with a genius—a like-minded individual who also happens to be the last living Neanderthal. Meanwhile, a former personal assassin for a former president is fired from the CIA for sexual misconduct with a couple of blow-up dolls. He becomes determined to return to the government's good graces by infiltrating Ephraim's anarchist art collective in the hopes that they are actually terrorists. What follows is a bizarre, psychedelic journey that could only take place in the heart of Austin, Texas

THE RUIN SEASON
BY KRISTOPHER TRIANA

ISBN: 978-1-943720-07-1
Page count: 324
$14.95

Jake Leonard has more than his share of trouble.

He's close to forty now and still suffers from bipolar disorder and the painful memories of the psychotic episodes that derailed his life and sent him behind bars as a youth. He lives in the rural south where he spends his days breaking horses and his nights training dogs in solitude. His nineteen-year-old girlfriend, Nikki, is the daughter of the sheriff, and she's just getting worse with drugs, alcohol and satanic metal, eventually leading into heroin and low-budget porn.

Soon chaos unfolds like a pocketknife.

The Ruin Season is a haunting, violent tale of a mentally ill man struggling in a violent and heartless world. It is the story of unrequited love, mad rage, and bloody revenge. It shows both the tender and horrible sides of insanity as well as the seedy underbelly of the American, backwoods suburbs.

GODS ON THE LAM
BY CHRISTOPHER DAVID ROSALES

ISBN: 978-1-943720-11-8
Page count: 322
$16.95

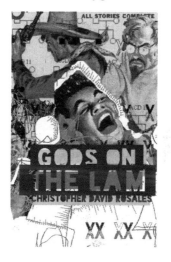

Wayne, a former forest service fire fighter, wakes up one day alongside the highway lacking a memory. Fate connects him with a woman named Ruby and together they continue her quest to locate her missing son. Their investigation will lead them to a rash of mysterious abductions haunting the small Northern Arizona mountain town of Show Low. *Gods on the Lam* is a jigsaw puzzle of surreal, violent hallucinatory madness recommended for those willing to leave their sanity at the door.

The Perpetual Motion Machine Catalog

Baby Powder and Other Terrifying Substances |
John C. Foster | Story Collection

Bleed | Various Authors | Anthology

Crabtown, USA:Essays & Observations |
Rafael Alvarez | Essays

Cruel | Eli Wilde | Novel

Dead Men | John Foster | Novel

*Destroying the Tangible Issue of Reality; or, Searching
for Andy Kaufmann* | T. Fox Dunham | Novel

Four Days | Eli Wilde & 'Anna DeVine | Novel

Gods on the Lam | Christopher David Rosales | Novel

Gory Hole | Craig Wallwork | Story Collection
(Full-Color Illustrations)

The Green Kangaroos | Jessica McHugh | Novel

Invasion of the Weirdos | Andrew Hilbert | Novel

Last Dance in Phoenix | Kurt Reichenbaugh | Novel

Like Jagged Teeth| Betty Rocksteady | Novella

Patreon:
www.patreon.com/PMMPublishing

Website:
www.PerpetualPublishing.com

Facebook:
www.facebook.com/PerpetualPublishing

Twitter:
@PMMPublishing

Instagram:
www.instagram.com/PMMPublishing

Newsletter:
www.PMMPNews.com

Email Us:
Contact@PerpetualPublishing.com

Made in the USA
San Bernardino, CA
27 December 2017